Jennie Dodd was raised in the picturesque market town of Shrewsbury, famous for its medieval castle, steep narrow streets, little alleyways, and timber framed buildings. Situated on the River Severn the town nestles in amongst the ancient Shropshire hills of the Stiperstones, the Long Mynd, Wenlock Edge and The Wrekin. Educated at the Wakeman Grammar School, Jennie developed a keen interest in art, history, and a love of English literature. Her novel reflects her appreciation of the works of J B Priestley and his socialist beliefs—that all men are born equal. *The Satin Moth*, as a result, explores themes connected to Britain's bloody colonial past.

Dedicated to all those whose lives have been blighted by slavery.

Jennie Dodd

THE SATIN MOTH

AUSTIN MACAULEY PUBLISHERS™

LONDON * CAMBRIDGE * NEW YORK * SHARJAH

A CIP catalogue record for this title is available from the British Library.

ISBN 9781035820016 (Paperback)
ISBN 9781035820023 (ePub e-book)

www.austinmacauley.com

First Published 2023
Austin Macauley Publishers Ltd®
1 Canada Square
Canary Wharf
London
E14 5AA

Table of Contents

Foreword

Our life is twofold; Sleep hath its own world,
A boundary between the things misnamed.
Death and existence

Lord Byron

The Dream

Chapter One
The Motherless Girl

The three-hundred-year-old ancestral home of the Montague family, Eastlyn Castle, was built to impress. Complete with its dungeons, ornate turrets, towers, reputed secret passageways and subterranean labyrinths it remained a place of awe and wonder. Set amid approximately six acres of gardens and terraces, the five-story granite castle featured seventeen bedrooms, a great hall with massive arched stone pillars, spiral stone stairways, library, drawing room, loggia, sunroom, wine cellar, huge kitchen and two equally grand dining rooms each with ornately decorated ceilings from which four massive crystal chandeliers were suspended and a total of no less than ten magnificent fireplaces.

The castle also boasted its own separate chapel complete with bell tower and a magnificent organ. This Gothic building, set on rising ground overlooking the estuary, displayed some of the finest stained-glass windows in the land. From the chapel a narrow gravel path led to a small, private, family cemetery. The cemetery, littered with granite crosses, marble lions, cherubs, angels, and a jumble of lichen covered tombstones, remained, however, hidden from view behind a thick yew hedge.

Maddie, daughter of the tenth Lord of Eastlyn, loved the castle with all her heart, even though she knew it was almost decadent in its grandeur. She adored the fireplaces most of all. She hated being away at boarding school during term time, even though she had the company of other girls. Maddie hated the cold and often, in the winter months, her dormitory could only be described as freezing. She suspected all the fireplaces had been boarded up to accommodate more beds and the unsightly, cumbersome radiators, more often than not draped with wet towels, were the only form of heating. As a result, her dorm not only felt cold but smelt damp too. She knew the cleaners fought a constant battle against black mould which grew in the wardrobes and around the window frames. Maddie was most definitely a home bird and therefore holidays were longed for and always brought her joy when they finally arrived.

The library fireplace in particular was said to be one of the grandest, with an inglenook boasting to be the largest in the country. On chilly days when the sun refused to shine, Maddie was often to be found seated within its giant alcove, warming her toes, and enjoying its welcome heat. She would stay there for hours reading her favourite books. She also loved the unusual firedog, with its sculptured limestone figures. The two front feet were embellished with large wolf hounds, placed either side as if to protect the fire. Two more, even bigger dogs sat on either side of the great iron fire guard, which ran the length of the hearth. The hound on the left held up a raised paw as if commanded to shake his master's hand. Maddie had given the dogs names; Drake and Nelson, the two smaller dogs guarding the firedog, whilst The General and Jasper stood guard on the front hearth. 'Good morning, General,' was Maddie's first greeting whenever she visited the library. She always said these words while lovingly stroking and patting The General's head.

In summertime, however, Maddie was rarely inside. She loved the outdoors and as the castle was surrounded by open parkland stretching right down to the mudflats and sandflats of the Menai Straits at its northerly and western borders and almost reaching the foothills of the Snowdonia Mountain range at its southern and eastern boundary, she never tired of its many walks. The estate in its entirety boasted over sixty acres of land, rich with beech, oak and small-leaved lime trees and fields of lush green grass, speckled with grazing livestock. The parkland also accommodated an abundance of wildlife, including badgers, foxes, squirrels, and rabbits. This wildlife, in turn, encouraged numerous birds of prey. Buzzards, red kites, tawny, and barn owls could often be seen.

Maddie's favourite animals were the seals and otters. She took great delight in watching the youngsters at play in the shallows of the estuary. Indeed, families of otters could be spotted on a daily basis. It was the ideal habitat for them thriving as they were, on the abundance of fish which inhabited the waters of the Menai Strait all year round.

Maddie also loved the British climate with its changing seasons and from an early age appreciated how the castle altered its appearance depending on the time of year. In autumn against the castle walls the Virginia Creeper was magnificent. Late winter and early spring would see the grounds carpeted with huge drifts of snowdrops, daffodils, and bluebells and, by May, the Rhododendron walk, above the estuary, was at its best. Extensive pathways ensured that every part of the garden, parkland, woodland, and formal gardens, could be explored and enjoyed.

The castle not only boasted wonderful, extensive formal gardens but also an exotic, magical bog garden. Here unusual plants from all over the world, chosen for their striking foliage created a strange, fabulous environment for Maddie to explore. There were magnificent Japanese maples and eucalyptus to be found, enclosed in an almost swamp-like area, containing giant tree ferns, taller than a man. Maddie particularly adored the rustling clumps of thick bamboo brought from China, clumps which made for great hiding places, as well as huge-leaved Gunnera (rhubarb). She never tired of visiting the bog garden and once there always felt as if she were in some weird and wonderful subtropical land, not in England at all.

Her particular joy was to follow the many different pathways criss-crossing the garden and she delighted especially in treading on the steppingstones. These followed the watercourses and as a result, were always wet and slippery. Many of the stones were covered in a green moss so thick that it was like walking on carpet when you trod on them. Walking on the stepping-stone pathways was the closest Maddie ever got to adventure and she delighted in it. With its beautiful design like a daisy-chain of lakes and ponds, the bog garden had one other advantage: it provided a rich habitat for wildlife. Maddie loved each and every kind of creature and here there were many to wonder at, including toads, newts, damselflies, dragonflies, water boatmen and freshwater eels.

Maddie also loved to wander around the Victorian walled garden, which unlike the bog garden was intimate in scale and yet contained just as many rare and unusual plants. Its top terrace had formal box-edged beds punctuated with groups of cordylines and Chusan palms and three ornamental ponds, teeming with beautifully coloured Koi carp. The second terrace consisted of four sloping lawns planted with specimen shrubs and trees, including a variety of striking summer-flowering eucryphias and all connected by geometrically designed pathways.

Whenever Maddie entertained guests at the castle, she would always take them into the formal garden through a stunning wrought iron archway, which at the height of summer would be draped in sweet smelling fuchsia blossom. Located near this archway was a magnificent tree, reputed to be one of the oldest Dawn Redwoods in Britain.

The castle was almost self-sufficient in terms of produce, growing as it did a vast variety of fruit and vegetables for all year-round consumption. Maddie loved to help the gardeners with their work. Gardening after all was one of the few things she was allowed to do. Hence, whenever her cousins went off sailing, hunting, riding, or climbing, activities Maddie was barred from doing, a miserable Maddie would head straight for the garden as consolation. Arthur Hawkins, the head gardener, and general all-round handyman was always delighted to see her and could lift her spirits in a matter of minutes.

Maddie was sitting in the library, reading. She was so engrossed in her book that she neither heard nor saw the door open. As a result, Bella's unexpected appearance gave Maddie the fright of her life. She jumped so much that the book she was holding flew high up into the air and would have landed in the fire had it not been for the old maid's deftness of hand. Stubby fingers, which always reminded Maddie of burnt sausages, snatched it away from the flames just in time. Maddie looked into the familiar face and smiled in recognition. A mop of silvery grey, curly hair sat like a crown upon an ancient, broad head of jet-black skin, deeply furrowed from forehead to chin and sagging loosely at the jowl. The distinctive eyes with their unusually large pupils at first glance appeared kind and gentle, but when given a second, direct glance a person might well feel that they were burning into their very soul. The deep, dark pupils were themselves surrounded by a huge iris of dark grey flecked throughout with streaks of red. The brilliant whites of those eyes, which were stained purple in the corners, opened widely as the book was restored to its owner. 'Your father wants you to join him in the great hall. He's sent me to fetch you,' Bella announced.

'Thanks for saving the book,' Maddie replied as she reluctantly left her fireside seat. Slipping her shoes back on, she raced to join her father.

'Ah, good,' said Lord Robert when Maddie arrived in the great hall. 'There you are. Your aunt Kate, uncle William and the boys will be arriving at any moment.'

'Great,' replied Maddie, when what she really wanted to say was, 'How horrid!' Almost immediately the sound of car wheels moving slowly across the gravel drive reached their ears.

'They're here,' observed her father. Maddie did her best to look pleased. Moments later her aunt and uncle were hastening towards her to receive the compulsory welcoming hugs and kisses. Her two elder cousins followed behind bearing gifts. Arms full of presents gave a good excuse to forgo the customary greeting.

'Merry Christmas Uncle,' and after a short pause, as an afterthought, 'Maddie,' said Frederick, the eldest of the three boys. 'We'll just deposit these presents under the tree, shall we?'

'Of course, dear boy, of course,' replied Maddie's father.

As Edmund and Frederick began to place packages of varied shape, colour, and size beneath the branches of a beautifully decorated tree; two large, boisterous grey and white puppies bounded into the room at full pelt. Muddy paws and polished floors do not make a good combination. Slipping and sliding totally out of control the two English Sheepdogs hurtled across the hall straight towards the tree. 'Bubble! Squeak! Stop!' shouted a flustered Tristan, as he rushed into the hall in pursuit of his runaway puppies.

Maddie noted with approval that due to the speed at which he was running the annoyingly long ginger fringe which always hid his eyes was flying upwards, as if it had a life of its own. She also noted the high, spotty forehead, reminiscent of his mother, and chuckled to herself as she remembered her Aunt Kate's favourite turn of phrase, 'High foreheads are a sign of intelligence.'

'You wish,' Maddie and her favourite cousins, Rowan, and Clarissa, would mutter under their breath.

Closely followed by, 'Queen Elizabeth I was a redhead too,' she would say, patting her own apricot French plait to make her point, 'highly intelligent and possibly the best monarch this country has ever seen.' Maddie and her cousins delighted in mimicking mother and son. Tristan was forever sweeping his hair out of his eyes with a very theatrical gesture. This habitual movement had become his signature mannerism and always inspired fits of giggles from his young relatives. Poor Tristan never quite understood the joke.

Just at that moment one of the dog chains Tristan was holding loosely in his hand decided to wrap itself around his ankles. He lost his balance instantly and appeared to swan dive into the air. Seconds later he landed on the floor with such a thud that even Maddie winced. 'That's clever,' she thought to herself, as Tristan's spread-eagled body did an excellent cleaning job. Muddy paw prints were swept away as he shot across the polished floorboards on an identical pathway to the puppies. The expensive cloth of his woollen suit gathered the mud and turned from a dark green to more of a dirty brown colour with every inch covered. Time seemed to stand still as Tristan hit the base of the tree just moments after the dogs.

Maddie, her father, Aunt Kate, Uncle William, Fred, and Edmund watched in horrified silence as the drama unfolded. The enormous tree, a good twenty feet high, began to lean and topple. It was like watching a monumental event take place in slow motion. Maddie raised two hands to her mouth to suppress a scream as the tree thundered to the floor. There was a sudden cacophony of sound as the glass baubles splintered and rolled out from under crushed branches in every direction. The dogs were howling and barking, Tristan groaning and shouting, 'Ouch!' as pine needles pierced every inch of exposed skin.

As if Fred and Edmund had been given a "get out of jail" card, at last they moved to aid their brother. The now less well decorated Christmas tree was slowly righted, and a red-faced, highly embarrassed Tristan released from its branches. The dogs, clearly delighted their master was on his feet again, leapt up and down on either side of him like two deranged, furry yoyos, yapping furiously in their excitement.

'I'm so sorry, Uncle! I'll get the maids to come and clean up the mess,' said Tristan, in a more than humiliated tone of voice, his shoes crunching on the broken glass under foot.

'Oh, no you won't,' replied Maddie's father. 'What you will do is to go and ask Mrs Reed for a dustpan and brush and then you can clean up the mess yourself.' Maddie couldn't stop herself from sniggering and received a withering look from Tristan as a result.

'Oh, and, from now on the dogs stay outside. Speak to Sam, he'll find somewhere warm and dry for them, I'm sure. The castle, however, is strictly out of bounds. Do I make myself clear?' Uncle Robert concluded in his firmest voice. Tristan nodded sadly and left to collect the necessary utensils from the kitchen. Fred and Edmund reattached the dogs' leads and escorted them to the stable block in search of Sam.

'Drama over,' thought Maddie.

The day was spent pleasantly enough, with Uncle Harry, Aunt Mary and their two boys, Finn and Harry arriving in plenty of time for Maddie to relinquish her role as hostess and accompany Aunt Frances on a walk through the forest. The trees were full of squirrels darting from branch to branch, quite unperturbed by two pairs of eyes watching and laughing at their antics. Pheasants in their dozens wandered across the path, oblivious as always to other company and changing their minds every thirty seconds as to the direction in which they wanted to go.

Great herds of red deer also provided wonderful entertainment. The enormous grounds at Eastlyn with their rich woodlands and dense forests provided the ideal habitat for breeding and raising these magnificent creatures. Whilst not getting too close Maddie and Aunt Frances observed the deer, browsers by nature, pulling off leaves from oak, birch, and rowan trees, nibbling ivy, lichen and twigs from rocks and bushes.

On leaving the forest they headed back towards the castle across open ground. To their delight they noticed vast numbers of deer were grazing, cropping grass, and browsing in amongst the wild heather. 'We've come at the right time,' Aunt Frances explained, 'feeding takes place during the early morning and evening. The deer tend to rest and ruminate (chew the cud) by day.'

'Gosh, look at him,' said Maddie, pointing to an enormous stag, clearly in his prime with fully developed antlers, a thick neck with a heavy mane and a stout, solid body. As if aware he had an audience the stag left his harem and strode majestically, head held high into a nearby peaty bog to wallow. They watched him covering his body with mud. At that moment, another stag arrived on the scene.

'Oh dear,' said Aunt Frances, 'I hope they won't start rutting.' The stags began to roar making a deep bellowing sound, the new arrival clearly wanting to make a challenge. They moved towards each other walking slowly side by side, a little apart.

'What are they doing?' Maddie asked nervously.

'Assessing each other's strength, I expect,' replied Aunt Frances. 'It's usual for the weaker one to walk away but if they seem to be evenly matched then they may begin to fight.'

'I hope they don't fight,' said Maddie sounding even more anxious. 'Why would they fight anyway?'

'They fight over who gets the females, of course, and the right to be the lord of the herd. We'll see them clashing their foreheads or sparring with their antlers if they do.' Aunt Frances noted Maddie's worried expression. 'Don't worry,' she said reassuringly, 'sometimes the stags can be injured during a fight, but they rarely kill each other. Mr Hawkins told me that on rare occasions the antlers of fighting stags can become so entangled that they are unable to unlock them. They end up both starving to death as a result.'

'How horrible,' commented Maddie. To her relief the smaller of the two stags trotted away, disappearing back into the forest.

Aunt Frances continued with her wildlife lesson. 'Did you know Maddie, successful stags, like our big boy here, manage to collect up to forty hinds in their harems. They spend most of their time endlessly patrolling a circle of ground around the hinds, chasing away any challengers, trying to prevent the hinds from straying. They mate with each one as she becomes receptive. Consequently, what with protecting and mating with their harem they hardly have any time to eat, and by the end of the rut, the stags are thin and exhausted.'

'Well, our stag looks in super shape,' said Maddie. 'He's not thin at all!'

'That's because the rutting season ends in late October, so this one's been feeding up for a good two months,' her aunt replied.

'I'm hungry,' Maddie blurted out. 'It's all this talk of feeding.' They returned to the castle, eagerly anticipating what Mrs Reed would put on the table for dinner that night. She served venison!

Chapter Two
Favourite Cousins

After a fitful night's sleep, Maddie was late getting up for breakfast. She was the last member of the family to enter the dining room. All her relatives were sitting at the table and tucking into a hearty breakfast. As she approached conversations ceased and every head turned to look at her. In the awkward silence which followed, she made eye contact with each one of them and found herself quickly reading the differing expressions posted on their faces.

Her father's face, for example, showed a mixture of relief that she had finally arrived combined with disappointment and annoyance that she had not been one of the first down. She ought to know her place and in the absence of a mother, she was the undoubted hostess of the castle. Sadly, for Maddie, as she had entered the world her mother had left it. Since her mother's tragic and sudden death, Maddie's father had chosen to remain a lonely widower, devoting all his time and energy into bringing up his only daughter. Maddie loved her father with all her heart, but sometimes felt almost stifled, suffocated by the constant, unremitting attention he showered on her on a daily, minute by minute basis.

Even more disconcerting was the unanimous expression in the eyes of all her uncles and aunts. If Maddie had been pressed to describe it, she could only have said it was a look of pity. Yet she couldn't for the life of her think why. Apart from the loss of her mother and that was such a long time ago, why ever should they feel sorry for her?

The expressions on the faces of her cousins, however, were altogether different. They looked positively resentful and the eldest, Frederick, was scowling at her. As she took her place at the table, Frederick turned to face his younger brother sitting next to him and whispered under his breath, 'Don't look now, Tristan, but her majesty the queen has just arrived.'

Tristan grunted a reply. Without even looking up he continued to butter his toast, deliberately avoiding making eye contact with his unwelcome cousin. As Maddie helped herself to a plate of kedgeree, she was aware that all adult eyes were watching her closely and her cousins, as usual, were ignoring her. 'How are we this morning, Maddie?' Aunt Kate enquired, smiling warmly at her niece.

'Yes, my dear,' echoed her husband, Maddie's much loved Uncle William, 'did you sleep well?'

'Yes, fine, thank you,' Maddie replied courteously.

'Good, Good, glad to hear it,' responded Uncle Harry. To a man they all watched her clear her plate of kedgeree.

'Anyone for more tea?' enquired Aunt Mary, picking up the milk jug.

'No thanks, mother,' replied Finn, her eldest son. 'We don't have time unfortunately. We've all arranged to go riding this morning and Sam has had the horses saddled and ready this past half hour. Come on, chaps,' he continued, 'we need to get going.'

'Just you be careful. We don't want a repeat of last year when Harry fell off Trojan!' warned Aunt Mary, looking decidedly anxious.

'Trojan bucked, mother. It wasn't my fault.' Harry replied indignantly. Heeding Finn's instructions, five cousins stood to attention and, making their apologies to their respective parents, left the room. As usual Maddie would spend the morning alone. Once her superior cousins had vacated the room, Maddie raised the usual debate.

'It's so unfair, father, why am I not allowed to ride? All the girls at school ride, their parents don't seem to have a problem with it. I just can't understand why you won't allow me. You know how gentle the grey mare is. Even Sam says she is the sweetest creature on the planet. Please father, please. You could give me Eclipse as a Christmas present and I'm sure Rowan and Clarissa would teach me all I need to know about riding and Sam would help of course.'

'Sam is a stable boy, Maddie, not a riding instructor or even an expert on the characters of horses. You know my feelings well enough. It is too risky. Your mother died bringing you into the world and it is my responsibility to keep you safe. I've made my promise. Once you turn fourteen, I will teach you myself. Until then you must be satisfied with being led around the paddock. If you like, I'll have Eclipse saddled and walk you myself.'

Maddie banged her fist down hard on the table. 'It's just not fair!' She shouted at the top of her voice, whilst at the same time giving her father the blackest of looks.

'Maddie,' interjected Aunt Mary in a stern tone of voice, 'I cannot believe you have such a short memory. Clearly you have forgotten Harry's accident last year! And in any case, you should not question your father's authority. He only has your best interests at heart.'

'Quite so,' reiterated Aunt Kate, 'Harry hadn't even left the yard when Trojan threw him. Your father is only trying to protect you Maddie, to keep you safe from harm.'

Maddie was not impressed by her aunts' interference. 'But that was just a freak accident! Nobody got hurt anyway, and I noticed you didn't stop any of the others riding even then. I'm sick of being treated like an imbecile,' she exclaimed angrily, 'of always being wrapped in cotton wool. It's no wonder all my cousins hate me when I'm never allowed to join in with any of their games. You won't let me climb any of the trees on the estate, not even the ancient oak with the steps going up to your old tree house, or sail on the estuary, or swim in the lake. I hate being a girl!' and with those parting words she left the room at top speed, slamming the door behind her.

Had Maddie stayed to see her father's expression, she would have felt guilty. Overcome with sadness, he slumped in his chair and resting his elbows on the table, he held his head in his hands. Aunt Kate and Aunt Mary both stood up instantly and moved to his side. They rested sympathetic hands on his shoulders. 'Oh, my dear sisters,' he said in a whisper, 'am I doing the right thing? Is it all in vain, I wonder? She is so like her mother in looks and temperament and such a comfort to me in my loneliness. How will I bear it if I lose her too?'

'Of course, you are doing the right thing, Robert,' replied Aunt Kate vehemently. 'Your only hope is to keep her out of danger. Do not let her outcry deter you from what must be done and anyway,' she continued in a more comforting tone of voice, 'Rowan and Clarissa will be here tomorrow, and they will lift her spirits in no time.'

Aunt Mary kissed the top of her brother's balding head. 'She's right, you know,' she said affectionately, 'I totally agree. No question about it.'

Maddie could barely eat breakfast. She was so excited. Rowan, Clarissa, and her Uncle Thomas were due to arrive at any minute. She simply adored them.

Rowan and Clarissa were twins and Maddie's favourite cousins by far. They were two years older than she, but kindred spirits from the start of their acquaintance. Clarissa was as fun-loving as Rowan was serious and as fair as he was dark. You would never guess by looking at them that they were siblings, never mind twins. They were not alike at all, either in terms of looks or disposition.

But they did have one thing in common; they both adored each other and more significantly, Maddie, whom they treated as if she was a baby sister, rather than a mere cousin. Their mother, like Maddie's, had died bringing them into the world and as a result there was a special connection and understanding between the three children, which the other cousins could not comprehend.

Indeed, and with good reason, Maddie was not at all sure what her feelings were for her other cousins. They were all boys and pretty spiteful to her most of the time. Only Rowan and Clarissa were kind and with them Maddie always felt loved and appreciated. She sat in the library, trying unsuccessfully to read a book. Strangely for her she was not by the fire, but seated on the window seat, high above the drive, with an unobstructed view out towards the main entrance to the castle grounds.

At last, she saw Uncle Thomas's grey Volvo, turning in through the wrought iron gate and making its way towards the castle. Maddie leapt to her feet and ran to greet her beloved cousins. Before the car had pulled up the back doors were opening, and two equally excited children stepped down onto the wide sweep of gravel which encircled the main house.

'Wait till you see how many presents we've brought this year,' shouted Clarissa joyfully. Maddie clapped her hands enthusiastically. Eyes full of love watched her cousins' approach, only her father's steadying hand on her shoulder kept her from running forward to hug them. Open displays of affection in front of the servants would be much frowned upon.

Rowan had pale skin, which looked almost white because of the dark curly hair that swept around his face framing his handsome features. Clarissa had long straight hair which reached down to the middle of her back. It wasn't quite light enough to be called blond but couldn't really be described as brown either. She wasn't as pale as her brother and her skin, in contrast, had a healthy pinkish glow. The only noticeable similarity between them were their unusual eyes the most amazing shade of emerald green and yet sparkling with pinpoints of gold light behind a fringe of long, thick black lashes. This striking feature would have made them both look feminine if not for Rowan's strong cheekbones and firm, chiselled jaw. Maddie always considered them the most beautiful, truly captivating eyes she had ever seen, a rich, deep green, which reminded her of the colour of moss in a rain-soaked forest.

Uncle Thomas handed the car keys to Sam who often doubled up not just as stable boy but as chauffeur too. He had the skills and expertise of a latter-day blacksmith combined with those of a modern car mechanic. Piles of suitcases were unloaded from the back of the car and then after a very formal handshake between Lord Robert and his younger brother the party entered the castle, where waiting serving maids chaperoned them to the great hall.

As always, a magnificent Christmas tree dominated the room and in the huge white marble fireplace a roaring fire was waiting to greet them. Holly, mistletoe, and fabulous decorations gave the whole of the hall a most wonderful festive feel. Hot mince pies freshly made tea and a decanter of the finest port were waiting on a large mahogany side table to revive the travel-weary guests.

Snatching a mince pie each but ignoring the tea and leaving a trail of sticky pastry crumbs behind them, the children left the adults to their own devices. They scampered up the main staircase like overexcited puppies, bounding along and sometimes clearing two or three steps at a time. Robert smiled at the sight of Maddie being dragged along by her older, bigger cousins, the three of them hand in hand and all laughing uncontrollably. 'This is how it should have been,' Robert thought to himself. 'Maddie happy in the company of her own brothers and sisters and the castle filled with the sound of children at play.'

Uncle Thomas too was watching his offspring. He caught Robert's eye and shook his head. 'Well, they seem happy at least!' he said warmly.

Rowan and Clarissa couldn't wait to unpack, and Clarissa in particular was desperate to visit the castle library. 'Soon as we're sorted, can we go and see the butterfly collection again?' Clarissa shouted excitedly.

The other two children laughed. 'Now how did we know she was going to say that?' asked Rowan with a wry grin on his face.

'I don't know,' replied Maddie with an equally wide smile on her face, 'but I've opened the cabinet for the annual inspection already and Clarissa's favourite tray is waiting on the hearth rug.'

'Hooray!' Clarissa called out as she disappeared into what was to be her room next door to Maddie's own bedroom. 'Meet you in the library in ten,' she shouted to Rowan, as Maddie followed her inside.

Back in the great hall it was time for the two brothers to catch up on their news. 'Well, Robert, are those mince pies and the port for consumption or decoration only?' asked Thomas in an amused tone of voice.

'My dear brother,' replied Robert, 'please sit down here by the fire and sample some of Mrs Reed's delights.' The two men hugged fondly, and port and pies were duly served. They ate hungrily and drank thirstily. Now, comfortably reclined in armchairs in front of the fire, the conversation continued. 'So,' Robert ventured, 'I'm disappointed to see that Veronica is not with you. After her visit in the summer, I had hoped she might be the one.'

'Alas, no,' replied Thomas, 'and in any case no one will ever replace Elizabeth. The children are a constant reminder of their mother, Rowan with his looks and Clarissa with her unbounded optimism and vivacious nature.'

'That might well be,' Robert returned, 'but the children seemed fond of Veronica, and she had clearly taken a liking to them too. I thought she would make the ideal stepmother. We all noticed how devoted she was to you. And, Thomas, if I am not mistaken, you also appeared very much in love with her.'

'Perhaps I was,' Thomas replied sadly, 'but we reached the point of no return, the ultimatum!'

'Ah, I see,' Robert nodded his head in agreement, as if he knew exactly what his brother was about to say.

'Veronica wanted marriage and children, like any normal woman I suppose. But I could never embark on that path again. How could I? No, Robert, I am resigned to my fate. I will remain a lonely widower for the rest of my days. Better that, than to place another innocent woman's life in jeopardy.'

'Those are exactly my feelings, Thomas, and the reason why I have remained single all these years.'

'Now to more serious matters,' Thomas continued, 'Clarissa. What has been put in place for her protection?'

Chapter Three
The White Moth Appears

The library at Eastlyn castle housed not only thousands of books but the biggest single collection of Lepidoptera in the whole of the United Kingdom. The collection was begun in 1807 by the third Lord Eastlyn, one Edward Charles Montague. Edward was an ardent lepidopterist. It was his great passion, and he took enormous pride in collecting specimens from around the world, most particularly Africa and America as well as his home country. That passion had skipped a few generations until Clarissa arrived.

Aunt Frances understood how people could become hooked on catching butterflies. It was a hobby she herself had enjoyed as a child. She often told Maddie, 'Nothing says summer more than barefoot children chasing butterflies across soft emerald grass. I love watching you children on your escapades, your eyes growing bigger at the wonder of these winged insects' zigzag flight and when you catch them your delight in the patterns and colours of their delicate wings. It is my considered opinion that collecting and preserving butterflies and moths is the perfect way to bring the magic of summer indoors, so I perfectly understand why Clarissa enjoys it so much.'

Clarissa was the only one who seemed able to read Lord Edward's hand-written instructions on how to perform this particular art. Rowan and Maddie could neither make head nor tail of the many detailed descriptions and the information, written carefully on separate sheets of old parchment paper, which were also to be found in the carefully constructed display trays.

Rowan, if truth be told had to feign interest. But loving Clarissa as he did, he deserved an Oscar in his pretence of equal fascination. To him a lepidopterist's display of butterflies was rather sad. After all, they were just dead winged creatures, pinned to a board, lifeless and still. Inert, with no hint of what flight and life really felt like. Now, catching them was another matter altogether, at least here he could join in with genuine enthusiasm. Net in hand running across summer meadows following the butterflies chaotic flight was great fun. Rowan prided himself on the fact that he had caught more and a greater variety than anyone else and it was he who had caught the White Satin moth last summer.

Clarissa had fallen in love with it straight away. She thought it the most beautiful thing she had ever seen. She cried real tears, when they added it to the collection and often, she could be found leaving the library red-eyed, after making a solitary visit by herself. Rowan suspected she had been sobbing her heart out again and all over the need to kill the moth in order to add it to the Eastlyn collection.

He remembered Clarissa's regimented organisation. Edward's instructions had to be followed to the letter and as she knew her brother and cousin found it impossible to read his handwriting, she had written her own list. That too remained with the specimen inside the display tray. Rowan picked it up and began to read it again. Instantly he was back in the past and reliving the memory of that day.

To be mounted

A female White Satin Moth with the thorax, or body segment, still attached.

Equipment/materials required.

A plastic airtight storage container

Four damp paper towels

A small cap full of antiseptic, suggest-Listerine. (Rowan to approach Arthur Hawkins for same)

Straight pins

Styrofoam

Wax paper

Tweezers

Strips of paper

Shadow box or frame (with mat) for display

Hot glue and super glue

Dried flowers (preferably red poppies) (Maddie I\C to seek advice from Aunt Frances if difficult.)

Rowan smiled to himself as he remembered Clarissa taking charge of the whole procedure.

'When you find a dead butterfly or moth, it is usually quite dry. You have to relax it in order to handle it without damaging its delicate wings. In this case, with our White Satin Moth alive just moments ago, we, I mean I, ought to find the process fairly easy.' Her voice stopped. The sudden realisation that they had brought about the moth's early demise caused an unexpected flood of tears. It took some time for Maddie and Rowan to console Clarissa and to stem the liquid flow of remorse. Once recovered, instructions continued anew, but this time it was Rowan who read whilst in the background Clarissa sniffed and dried her nose intermittently.

'Take the paper towels and moisten them, until they are damp but not dripping. Then line the bottom of an airtight container with the damp towels. Add a capful of antiseptic to prevent mould. Place the moth in the container and let it sit; two or three days for small specimens, up to a week for larger insects.'

'Oh, I think we need to leave this one for at least a week,' Maddie had commented trying to be helpful.

'I agree,' Clarissa had echoed. Rowan recalled that it was in fact five days later when they had returned to complete their task and Clarissa had taken over the reading once more. 'The wings should be limp, not brittle, if the moth is ready.'

'How do they feel?' Rowan remembered asking.

'Exactly right,' Clarissa replied.

'Now I need to cover this piece of Styrofoam with wax paper. Whilst I do that, Rowan could you very, very carefully take hold of the moth by its thorax and even more carefully insert this pin. Straight through the centre of the thorax mind. Take it steady! You must be sure to push it in a little more than halfway through.' With slightly shaky hands Rowan did what he was bid. He remembered clearly how tense he felt. The thought of letting Clarissa down had been intolerable. 'Good work,' she said as he successfully completed his part in the procedure, whilst Maddie watched on nervously.

'Now all I need to do is to pin our beautiful moth onto the Styrofoam. Oh no, wait a moment, I nearly forgot, I wanted to show you something. If I hold her up, you'll be able to get a good look at her delicate feathered antennae. The two cousins leant forward as instructed.'

'Oh yes,' Maddie said in amazement, 'I see what you mean.'

'Well, if you've seen enough, Maddie, please could you hand me the tweezers. Now the moth is in place, I need to spread her wings out really carefully. I've decided to open them all the way, before mounting her in the frame.' Clarissa had taken her time. Eventually the moth was pinned in place on the display tray. Maddie admired Clarissa's steady hand as she gently laid a piece of paper over the top of the wings to keep them flat. Then avoiding putting the pins through the actual wings, she placed eight pins at regular intervals around the wings, passing through the paper alone. 'There, job done,' she said with complete satisfaction. 'Now for the inscription,' she continued. Rowan could see it clearly in his mind's eye. Clarissa had taken her best fountain pen out of her pocket and with it she had written these words:

Leucoma Salicis:
The delicate and glistening White Satin Moth.
Female specimen noticeably larger than the male.
Please observe its beautiful, feathered antennae.

Rowan added two more logs to the fire and lay back on the hearth rug. 'The girls are taking their time,' he thought to himself. Closing his eyes, his mind wandered back to their last visit in the summer. Without warning a painful memory sprang to mind. They had all been out in the long meadow chasing butterflies most of the day. It was a day or two before the White Satin moth had been caught. Rowan could see it so clearly in his mind's eye that it might have happened only yesterday. Clarissa had suddenly gone very quiet. Rowan asked her if anything was the matter.

'No, not really,' she had answered. 'Did you know most butterflies only live for about two weeks? Of course, it depends upon the species. There's one in the display case from Costa Rica which only lives two days. Can you imagine that, just two days! Have you two seen the Mourning Cloak butterfly? Now that can live for up to a year. It's in tray ninety-three of the collection. Perhaps it will mourn for me,' she said sadly.

'No,' replied Maddie, 'I don't remember seeing that one. Will you show it to us when we get back?'

Before Clarissa had time to reply, Rowan remembered interrupting. 'Why should a butterfly mourn you, Clarissa? You're sounding very odd, almost melancholy.'

'Because I shall be like them you see. I shall have a short but scintillating life!' her reply was immediate and rather too convincing.

Maddie had begun to cry and with tears streaming down her face she had asked Clarissa for an explanation. 'Why are you talking of dying, Clarissa? It's not like you to be so morbid.'

Rowan could hear Clarissa's response as clearly as if she were speaking the words to him now.

'I'm sorry, little Maddie, but I'm not being morbid. I just know how it will be. I've seen my death so many times. You must both be prepared. It will not be long now. At least I will have had thirteen years as opposed to thirteen days!'

'Clarissa, you cannot seriously be saying that you are going to die at the age of thirteen?' Rowan asked trying not to sound distressed. He could see Maddie's tears all too clearly.

'That's exactly what I am saying,' she replied with conviction. 'It's what has to be. I have to prepare the way for Maddie, like John the Baptist did for Christ. Maddie will be the family saviour, you see, but I must go first.'

'Clarissa, stop! Stop this nonsense!' Rowan demanded angrily. 'You're frightening Maddie!'

'What I say is true. Both of you must know it and accept it. You will need to be ready to act when the time comes. Now, I've said all I'm going to on the matter. Let us at least try to enjoy the little time I have left.' Try as they might Clarissa resolutely refused to answer any more of their questions. It seemed to her that the more she tried to explain things the less they understood what needed to be done. Finally defeated, Rowan and Maddie had given up asking for explanations. With drooping shoulders, heads bowed and trailing feet, the walk back to the castle had been slow and silent. When they had finally arrived back, no one was interested in seeing the Mourning Cloak butterfly.

Just then, two giggling girls raced into the library and threw themselves onto the hearth rug next to Rowan. He was quickly and unceremoniously jolted from his reminiscing. 'Careful,' he warned, 'we wouldn't want to damage Leucoma Salicis, now would we!'

'Arthur Hawkins, come down from that ladder this instant! Good Lord, man, don't you know you're covered in whitewash and it's four o'clock already? You know full well we all need to be ready by 4.30 for me to serve up our tea. I've been slaving over a hot stove since early this morning, and I insist all the staff be in their places at the designated time. I simply can't abide food going cold.'

Mrs Reed loved December 22. It was a day designed to be a real treat for the staff, a truly special day on which the servants would hold their annual Christmas ball. The ball would be held in the great hall that very evening. All the servants had the night off. They would be wined and dined and then dance into the early hours. Everyone would have a wonderful time.

At Eastlyn castle it was traditional for the family to look after themselves on this particular night. Mrs Reed would prepare a self-service buffet dinner in the red dining room. Actually, it was also one of Maddie's favourite nights of the year, being very informal compared to normal dinners and, best of all, one could help oneself to whatever and as much of whatever, as one wanted.

Arthur slowly and reluctantly descended the ladder, bucket of whitewash and brush held securely in his right hand. 'All right, Mrs Reed, Arthur Hawkins reporting for duty as requested,' he replied in his good-natured way.

Mrs Reed, a wonderful cook, in her mid-forties smiled accordingly. 'Now off home with you,' she commanded, 'and get ready.' She turned on her heels and headed back to the kitchen.

'Fine figure of a woman that,' Arthur murmured to himself. Mrs Reed was of stocky build, average height, but with striking auburn hair, always neatly pinned up in a French plait. When cooking, she religiously tied a spotted scarf around her head. No one ever found a hair on any of the delicious dishes she served. She would have been mortified if they had.

Maddie was up in her bedroom admiring her newly bought dress in the long mirror. She was jumping up and down like a cat on a hot tin roof and flapping her arms in wild excitement. Bella, out of character, was smiling broadly. She was remembering another little girl who had once displayed identical mannerisms. It had taken ages to get Maddie dressed. The girl just wouldn't keep still long enough to get even the biggest button done up, never mind the intricate pearl ones. Bella's stubby fingers didn't help. Thoughts of her homeland, of long ago, filled her mind. Dressing her niece Adana had been equally as difficult. As a result, she had always allowed herself twice the time she thought necessary to prepare the little princess for some of her father's lavish celebrations. No one sensible would keep King Nazzor Eze waiting, not if you wanted to keep your head!

'Thank you, Bella,' said Maddie. 'You may go now and get ready yourself. See you downstairs. I hope you like my present.' It was customary for Lord Robert to present each of his staff with a Christmas bonus contained in a small brown envelope. Maddie too would then give each of them a little Christmas gift which she had wrapped and decorated herself with meticulous care. Indeed, sometimes the wrapping would be worth more than the gift itself. After their meal, the servants would line up in the great hall and the family would arrive to distribute the usual treats. Robert and his daughter made a wonderful team and genuinely enjoyed giving the staff their presents, well aware that in so doing, they were showing an appreciation for the devoted work of the servants over the year.

As Maddie left the room, she checked her appearance in the mirror once more. 'I do hope Rowan thinks me pretty in my new dress. Tonight, I'm going to be bold and ask him to partner me in the first dance.' It was tradition for the family to join with the servants for the opening dance and then depart, leaving the staff to let their hair down and enjoy a drink or two.

Chapter Four
Laughter Turns to Tears

Maddie hurried along the corridor outside her own room and up a flight of stairs. Aunt Frances had her accommodation on the fourth floor of the castle. She knocked on her aunt's door and waited to be invited in. 'Is that you, Maddie?' her aunt called from inside.

'Yes. Are you ready to come down?' was the reply.

'Yes, my dear. Please do come in. I'll only be a second.' Maddie didn't need to be asked twice. She was desperate to hear what her aunt thought of her party dress and burst through the door like a jack in the box. 'Oh. You look pretty,' said Aunt Frances, 'and what a beautiful dress. I do like the pearl buttons; they set the red velvet off perfectly.' In actual fact Aunt Frances was not Maddie's aunt at all. She was the daughter of the late Mr and Mrs Neale, butler, and housekeeper to Maddie's great grandfather. Frances was their only child, had never married and had entered into service herself at the tender age of fifteen. She began as a simple scullery maid, but like her parents, through hard work and devotion to duty had seen her status slowly rise eventually becoming the personal maid to Maddie's own mother.

Aunt Frances had helped to bring Maddie into the world, and it had seemed only right to Lord Robert at the time that Frances should have a key role in looking after his now motherless daughter. She had proved herself invaluable as a devoted nursemaid. Over time Maddie had come to consider her as much a part of the family as anyone.

'Right, I'm ready,' Aunt Frances announced, as she pinned her favourite brooch to her best silk blouse. 'Let's go, shall we?' Minutes later they were in the great hall. Aunt Frances watched proudly as the servants received their gifts. As the last presents were distributed the musicians began to arrive, making their way up the main staircase to the minstrel's galley above. At the same time, all Maddie's real relatives entered the hall. Tristan immediately ran over to Maddie and proceeded to whisper something in her ear. Before Maddie had time to answer Rowan too had asked a second question of her. Aunt Frances moved away, noting Maddie's happy smile as she did so.

'Well,' repeated Rowan, 'do I get the first dance or not?'

'Oh yes, Rowan, I would be delighted.' Maddie was overjoyed. Now she didn't need to ask him. He had beaten her to it and was clearly as eager to dance with her as she was with him.

Tristan interrupted her happy train of thought. 'I say, Maddie, I think it rather rude of you to ignore my question.'

'Oh, I do apologise,' Maddie replied, 'I'm sorry I did not hear you. What was it you asked me?'

'I asked you if you knew where Ms Reed keeps her chocolate brownies? She was baking some this afternoon and the other chaps, and I are famished. It'll be ages yet before we have supper. Be a dear and fetch some for us,' he instructed.

'Don't be long,' Rowan called after her as she raced from the room, 'I shall need my partner any minute.'

Maddie headed straight for the kitchen. She knew exactly where to find the brownies. They were always kept in the small pantry. She was in such a rush to get back to the great hall before the musicians started playing that she failed to notice the kitchen door had been left slightly ajar. Had she had the presence of mind to think about it, she would have realised this was very unusual. Mrs Reed was a stickler for keeping the door firmly closed. 'I don't want those perishing cats getting in here and spoiling my food,' was one of her pet sayings.

Maddie pushed the kitchen door hard and burst inside. A plastic bucket full to the brim with flour, which had been balanced precariously above the door frame, fell straight on top of her. She was covered from head to foot in thick white powder. Maddie was aghast. The red velvet dress was ruined. Her hair which had been so painstakingly plaited with ribbon to match was plastered with the horrid stuff. 'How would she ever get it out?' Realising what a mean and spiteful trick Tristan had played on her, Maddie ran to the servant's stairwell, sobbing her heart out. Racing back upstairs to her room, she passed Bella en route. The poor old Negro woman was given an almighty fright. Covered in white flour Maddie looked almost ghostlike. Bella followed Maddie into her room.

'Goodness child, you gave me a real fright. I thought for a moment I was being chased by a spirit of the dead and lord knows there be enough of them about me!' Maddie made no answer. She lay on her bed, sobbing into her pillow. Bella laid a comforting arm on Maddie's shoulder. 'How did you get in this state? You are a mess, child, a real mess!'

'It was Tristan! He did it. He laid a trap for me, and I was stupid enough to fall for it.' Maddie explained in full what had happened.

'Now listen to me, girl,' Bella advised, 'don't you go giving that naughty child satisfaction. If Bella can pretend, she is happy then so can you. No, you know nothing of Bella's woes. Bella don't show them see. Come, child, we must be quick. You are going to change that dress and get back down there. Quick now and maybe you can still have that dance with Rowan.' Bella helped Maddie change her dress and brushed out her hair. In hardly any time at all Maddie, wearing a brave face, was heading back to the great hall. 'Hurry child, run like the wind,' Bella called after her.

It was too late, however. The first dance was long since over. Maddie found Clarissa and Rowan in the library, while the other cousins had made themselves at home in the billiard room. 'What on earth happened to you?' Rowan enquired sadly. 'You missed our dance.' Maddie told them of the cruel joke Tristan had played on her.

'That was a mean and spiteful thing to do, Maddie. And I bet his brothers were in cahoots too. It was very courageous of you to come down again,' Clarissa remarked, sounding horrified and angry. 'I know what will cheer you up. Let's look at our beautiful Leucoma Salicis again.' She went to fetch the tray.

'Very apt,' replied Maddie with a giggle. 'I must have looked like a giant white moth myself a little while ago.'

Just then the dinner gong sounded. 'Great,' said Rowan, 'I'm starving.'

'Not a word to Tristan,' Maddie reminded them as they walked briskly to the dining room. 'Pretend that nothing has happened.' The children spent some time deciding on what to eat. Once again Mrs Reed had done them proud, with dishes of coronation chicken, baked gammon, cold roast beef, cocktail sausages, poached salmon, breast of turkey, sliced salami, and freshly baked bread still hot from the oven, as well as bowl after bowl of various salads all laid out beautifully to tempt them. Plates were piled high.

The table on which the desserts were displayed was equally impressive. Not only were all manner of cheese and fruit on offer but a delicious array of cakes too, including the infamous chocolate brownies. Tristan saw his opening to discover whether his trap had caught its intended prey and took it. 'Oh look,' he said pointedly, 'chocolate brownies. I take it you couldn't find them, Maddie?'

'No,' she replied nonchalantly, 'but I did look for you.'

'I see you've changed your dress,' he continued, 'any particular reason why?'

'I told her she looks best in blue,' interrupted Clarissa coming to her rescue. 'We girls know about things like that.'

'I agree,' added Rowan, 'Maddie looks stunning tonight.' Maddie's smile stretched from ear to ear. Tristan looked confused. The goading ended and all the family fell silent. Eating was far more important. Tristan however could not stop his curiosity. When he thought no one was looking he slunk from the room quietly to return to the scene of the crime.

Bella however had beaten him to it and by the time he arrived, the door, the floor and even the offending bucket had been thoroughly cleaned. Not a trace of flour remained. Satisfied she had removed all evidence of Tristan's foul play, Bella made ready to leave. She had just closed the kitchen door behind her when she heard light footsteps approaching down the servant's stairwell. Immediately she guessed who it was. So as not to be seen, she quickly hid herself to one side of a large Welsh dresser, positioned in the corridor just outside the kitchen. She stood flat against the wall holding her breath.

For a moment Tristan stood looking at the door. He rubbed his hand down the paintwork. There was no sign of any flour. All the kitchen staff were still at the servant's ball, and he couldn't imagine how Maddie would have had time to clear up the mess a whole bucket of flour would have made on her own. There could only be one explanation, she must have seen the bucket before opening the door! Had she escaped his trap? He had to know. Slowly he opened the door and entered in. He felt more than a little nervous. Only with Ms Reed's permission could you enter the kitchen. Switching on the light he took a good look around.

The kitchen like the corridor outside was spotlessly clean. 'Damn,' he said aloud, 'the bitch must have seen it.' He opened the door to return to the dining room and had the shock of his life. Bella's giant frame stood blocking his way, her large body completely filling the doorway. 'Aargh!' screamed Tristan, unable to help himself as he almost jumped out of his skin.

Bella gave him her look, the piercing stare that burnt into one's brain. 'What are you doing here, child?' she asked in her deep rasping voice.

Tristan, a quivering wreck by this time, tried to answer. He said the first thing that came into his head. 'Choc-ch-choc-ch-choc,' he stammered unable to complete the sentence. Bella, seeing his terror began to laugh. She stepped aside and Tristan tore past her and back to the relative safety of the dining room.

Much later that night, shortly before Tristan climbed into bed a knock came at his door. Once again curiosity killed the cat and to his horror, he opened it to find Bella standing outside, holding a mug of steaming cocoa. 'Here's your chocolate Master Tristan,' she said, 'just like you asked for.'

Tristan mechanically took it from her hand and closed the door, turning the key in the lock, before returning to his bed. His heart was pounding. Bella scared him to death. He was glad that she was Maddie's maid and not his. He sat sipping his cocoa and then slipped in between the sheets, pulling his covers tight around him. 'What a day,' he thought to himself as he lay back and tried to go to sleep.

The next morning Tristan woke late. Brother Edmund had been sent to summon him for breakfast. As he sat down at the table, his brothers took one look at him and started to laugh. 'What, what's so funny?' he asked, puzzled by their obvious amusement.

'Have you fallen under a lawn mower?' asked Frederick. Edmund enjoying the joke, slapped his elder brother on the back and guffawed with laughter even more.

'What on earth have you done to your hair?' It was his mother's turn to speak now. All heads turned to look at Tristan and everyone began to chuckle. His hair did indeed look very comical. A great chunk of his fringe was missing, as if he'd had a piece of chewing gum stuck to it which had had to be cut out. 'I hope you two haven't been playing silly jokes in the night on your brother. A typical and very stupid schoolboy prank,' said his mother frostily, glaring at her two eldest sons.

'We haven't touched his hair,' exclaimed Frederick indignantly.

'He had his door locked anyway when I went up to get him. So how could we have got into his room during the night? It's not us, mother I can assure you,' declared Edmund, looking at her with an expression of resentment clearly written on his face.

'He's right,' said Tristan, 'I did have my door locked.'

'Perhaps the pixies got in,' Rowan ventured unhelpfully. Maddie and Clarissa began to snigger.

'I'm going to walk the dogs,' Tristan snapped angrily and with that he strode from the room.

'Whilst you're at it, you should try teaching them some new tricks,' Rowan called out after him. 'Wiping the fur out of their eyes with their paws would be a good one, unless of course you just want to cut their fringes too?' Maddie and Clarissa burst into laughter and poor Clarissa ended up choking on her tea.

Later that morning, Maddie, Clarissa, and Rowan were helping Sam in the yard. Fresh bales of hay were needed for the stables. Mr Hawkins, Sam's father, was busy finishing the whitewashing. Tristan entered the yard from the field gate and immediately called his two sheepdogs to him. Once back in the yard he had been given strict orders to keep them on a lead. Choker chains attached he began to walk them to a small wooden shed next to the tallow room. Sam had suggested it would be a comfortable place for the dogs to be housed whilst Tristan's family were staying at the castle, warm and dry and much bigger than the kennels in which the foxhounds were kept.

Halfway across the yard Bubble and Squeak simultaneously spotted one of the farm cats. Barking loudly, they shot off in pursuit. Tristan was hauled off his feet and dragged along the ground, screaming at the top of his voice in a desperate effort to stop them. The puppies however were far too strong. His amused cousins watched him gathering speed and being hauled behind the two dogs working beautifully in unison. Shoulder to shoulder Bubble and Squeak looked more like two trained huskies than English sheepdogs as Tristan hurtled across the muddy cobbles like an Eskimo without a sledge.

Mr Hawkins, however, was less amused. Expecting the worst, a broken arm at least, he clutched on to the top rung as the dogs raced under his ladder pulling poor Tristan behind them. Unable to control his momentum the luckless dog owner accidentally crashed into one of the legs of the ladder. Fortunately, Rowan and Sam had seen the impending danger and the perilous position of the ageing Mr Hawkins. 'Quick,' Sam shouted, 'my dad!' They raced to his aid and just in time were able to grab the bottom of the ladder and prevent it from falling.

Maddie could scarce believe her eyes. The pot of whitewash began to swing ominously from side to side and then as if it had suddenly been given a life of its own, shot high into the air before tumbling earthward to land squarely on top of Tristan's head, covering him in white paint from head to foot. 'If I didn't know better,' Clarissa commented to Maddie as she stood at her side,' I'd say you orchestrated that.'

Maddie started to giggle, 'I know,' she said rolling her eyes, 'divine justice or what?' At that moment, a movement at an upstairs window caught her eye. Maddie stared up at it, trying to make out who or what was there. To her astonishment she could see Bella standing guardedly behind a curtain. She looked to be hiding, as if not wanting to be seen, but her face was showing a rare emotion. She was laughing.

Rowan and Sam helped a shaken Mr Hawkins climb down from his ladder. 'Thank you, boys. I'm right grateful you managed to keep that ladder upright. I could have had a nasty fall. Best help Master Tristan up,' suggested Arthur nodding at his son Sam.

Tristan refused the proffered hand and stood up of his own accord. Large droplets of whitewash dripped off him onto the cobbled floor. 'Come here,' he shouted angrily, running after the two puppies, who by now were cowering inside their shed. Bashing open the door Tristan went inside to punish his wayward sheepdogs. The cousins watched, feeling sorry for what they expected was about to happen to the dogs. Tristan slammed the door behind him, and moments later loud yelps could be heard from inside.

'Oh dear, I thought he might take his anger out on the dogs,' said Arthur looking distressed. 'I don't like to see animals mistreated. Dogs will be dogs after all. They just need the right training that's all.'

'Come on Dad. Let's get this ladder away,' said Sam, anxious to change the subject and noting that the children too looked sad. 'You won't be doing any more whitewashing today, that's for sure.'

The children said their goodbyes, and then Rowan led his sister and cousin back inside the castle. It was time for lunch. Sam helped his father to clean up the puddle of whitewash lying on the floor and then the two men made their way to one of the storage barns behind the stables in order to stow the ladder away. As they secured the ladder to the barn wall, they heard an almighty commotion going on in the hen house. The chickens were squawking, ba-kawing and clucking for all they were worth. Just then a loud warning cry sounded above the rest of the din. 'That's Esmeralda,' said Sam, 'sounds as if a fox has got into the hen house and is trying to murder them.'

'Come on, lad, best go see what's happening,' replied Arthur. 'Them pesky foxes never stop at one!' The two men raced out of the barn and headed to a field on the far side of the stables where the hens were kept. By the time they got there the commotion had stopped. Looking at the wet mud around the coop there appeared to be no obvious paw prints. 'Been no fox here, no tracks see,' Arthur commented knowledgably.

'No. But there are footprints here, Dad. Look, coming in off the lane,' Sam replied, 'and what's worst of all, is that I can't see head nor tail of Esmeralda.' I reckon someone's taken her!

Chapter Five
The Night Vigil

The two nurses arrived late in the afternoon on the 23rd. They looked as stiff and as starched as their uniforms. Miss Heath was tall and thin, had a large Roman nose with a wart on the end of it and oily, grey hair scraped back into a bun. She was so thin Maddie thought she might have been accidentally wrung through a mangle.

Ms Webb, in contrast, was just the opposite, a short, fat woman, as wide as she was high and without a neck it seemed. To all intents and purposes, it appeared to Maddie that her rather bulbous head had raised itself from straight out of her shoulders. Ms Webb also had a look about her which inspired sympathy. Her face was always very red, as if she'd just finished playing a full and very energetic game of netball and her skin was terribly pimply. If anyone needed a good cleansing lotion she did. The poor woman remained constantly flushed, perspired profusely, and spoke so rapidly it was difficult to understand a word she said. She also had an annoying habit of dabbing her face with a hanky every five seconds. Unlike Miss Heath, Ms Webb wore a nurse's cap. However, if there was a battle going on between hair and cap, hair was definitely winning. Despite obvious efforts to contain wild curls and bright ginger tresses, thin wisps of defiance projected out in all directions. Tiny metal hair grips, giving up the ghost in silent but total submission, continued to fall from shoulders speckled with dandruff onto the floor.

It was morning on Christmas Eve. Clarissa was summoned to the library. Rowan and Maddie stood outside waiting nervously, wondering what was afoot. When Clarissa reappeared, she looked pale and drawn. She glanced briefly at her two best friends but did not speak. Walking out into the garden she made her way to the stable block, where Sam was busy grooming Eclipse. 'Hi, Sam, would you mind if I see to her?' she said, taking the brush from his hand.

At that moment Rowan and Maddie arrived at the stable door. 'Well, I am honoured,' Sam remarked smiling, 'all three of you at once.'

'Can you leave us alone please, Sam,' requested Rowan. 'No offence, but we need to talk to Clarissa in private. You don't mind, do you?'

'No, of course not, Master Rowan.' Sam bowed humbly as if the children were royalty and promptly scurried away.

Rowan was the first to speak. 'Why did you have to speak with those two nurses? What are they doing here?'

'They are here to watch over me during the night,' replied Clarissa. 'The family are trying to save me you see, but it is all in vain. They cannot stop what will be, no matter how hard they try. I am going to die and that is all there is to it!'

Maddie burst into tears. 'Stop it, Clarissa. Stop saying those terrible things. Please, Clarissa, please, say you don't mean it. You cannot, must not die. Rowan and I could not bear it.'

'There are more things in heaven and earth, dearest Rowan, dearest Maddie, than are dreamt of in your philosophy,' she said quoting Shakespeare.

It was Rowan's turn now to plead through his tears. 'Clarissa, we do not understand. Why are you going to die? Don't be so silly, you're in perfect health!'

'Unfortunately, health has nothing to do with it. If I could stay with you, I would, of course I would.' She ran to embrace them and, holding them in her arms, she whispered, 'You must accept I will be gone and yet believe I will always be with you. Have faith,' she begged. 'Always know this. Years may pass but I will never leave you.' Kissing them on the cheek, she drew away. 'Remember,' she repeated earnestly, 'I will never, never leave you and I will be with you when the time comes to bring our family back into the light. Now, I must go. Time is short and I have farewell letters to write.' She handed the horse brush to an astonished and deeply distressed Rowan. Then walking very upright and with head held high she left the stable. Maddie clung to Rowan, sobbing uncontrollably.

A little while later and with at least some semblance of composure Rowan and Maddie approached their respective fathers and demanded to know what was going on. They were told only that there was reason to fear Clarissa might be in danger. They were doing all in their power to prevent a tragedy, hence the nurses had been hired to ensure Clarissa had a peaceful and uneventful night's sleep.

Neither father would be drawn any further, other than to say that there was something in the family history giving cause for concern, but that in their considered opinion, it was just misguided superstition and certainly nothing that children of their age should be burdened with.

Satisfied that he had done his best to alleviate Maddie's concerns, Robert went to see his brother. He knocked on the door. 'Come in,' answered Thomas. Robert opened the door and stepped hastily inside. Thomas was standing by the window, looking out towards the estuary. He looked pale and grim faced.

'I've just finished talking with Maddie. It was a difficult conversation,' Robert said closing the door behind him.

'Yes, I suspect it was,' replied Thomas. 'I've just been speaking to Rowan too.'

'Thomas, I've had something on my mind for a while. Something I should have mentioned to you months ago. Last summer when you visited, I found Clarissa in the gallery looking at the painting of *The Black Stag*. As a result, we had a most unfortunate conversation which bothered me.'

'Robert, why have you never mentioned this before? You must tell me,' Thomas demanded, looking anxious and almost angry at the same time.

'I was on my way downstairs. Walking along the upper corridor I saw her standing in front of the painting. For some reason I believed she had been staring at it for some. I asked her if she knew what the name of the ship was. 'Oh, yes,' she replied, '*The Black Stag.*' You can imagine my shock, Thomas. I've always kept my side of the bargain and have never mentioned that vessel or its history to Maddie, and I'm sure you will never have told your two.'

'Quite so,' Thomas concurred vehemently. 'I've not talked about it at all and neither do I intend to.'

'It was what Clarissa said next which shocked me to the core. "The painter has taken the wrong angle Uncle Robert. He should have painted the ship from the prow. Then we would have been able to see the great stag's antlers. There was a figurehead of a massive stag, you see, right here, high up on the prow", she explained and pointed to the exact spot on the canvas. "It was a massive beast and to the slaves it was terribly frightening. It had huge, long horns, like spears, pointing and spreading out in all directions".' 'Clarissa, how do you know all this?' I demanded, 'you, a mere child of thirteen!'

'To be honest, brother dear, I was a little outraged at the time and bellowed at her. She replied, "I may only be thirteen, uncle, but at thirteen, I know a great deal more than you think. *The Black Stag* was a slave ship of the worst kind. Our family has much to regret". Thomas, you can imagine my reaction. My heart nearly stopped at the mention of a slave ship!'

Thomas brought his hand to his mouth as if to stifle the horror which had suddenly engulfed him. 'She must know, Robert, she must surely know,' he said, when sufficiently recovered to be able to speak.

'She knows, all right, knows not everything, but I believe far more than you or I have ever suspected. I took her down to the library and asked Bella to bring us some tea.'

'Bella?' queried Thomas.

'Yes, Bella, she must have arrived just after us in the corridor. I should have questioned her as to why she was not using the servant's stairwell, but, anyway, it was convenient at the time. When the tea tray arrived, the conversation became even more worrying. "What, no biscuits, uncle? You know what a sweet tooth we have in this family".'

'Sweet tooth,' Thomas repeated. 'Can she know about the plantations too, do you think?' he asked in a faltering voice.

'I wasn't sure at the time, but in hindsight, I'm sure she does. Anyway, I beseeched her to keep this dreadful history from her cousins, and I must confess I used her fondness for Maddie to command her silence on these matters. She gave me her word she would say nothing to the other children. Forgive me brother. I now regret not mentioning this to you before.'

'Regret,' repeated Thomas. 'Please God let us hope we have no regrets at the end of this night!'

Chapter Six
Ashes to Ashes

Maddie sat in a chair almost hidden from view. She was wearing a plain black dress. Far from the fire she shivered with cold. From her position at the back of the great hall, she had witnessed the sad departure of the two failed nurses. Uncle Thomas and her father had shaken the women's hands and had gravely escorted them outside to the waiting car which had sped them away.

The small coffin, lid closed firmly down, lay on an ornately carved oak table, placed exactly in the centre of the room. Vases of Arum lilies filled the hall with a heady fragrance. Four church candles set on tall, wrought iron stands, positioned at each corner of the coffin burned brightly in the darkness. Curtains were drawn and the tall mirrors on the East wall were draped with black silk. The castle was in mourning.

Maddie could not cry, eat, sleep, or even speak. Clarissa's lifeless body lay enclosed in that most awful coffin. Maddie felt as if she wanted to rip it open, to tear off the lid, to reach inside and shake Clarissa by her shoulders, to scream at her and make her wake up.

The time came. The grandfather clock standing guard just to Maddie's left made her jump as it struck the hour. It was three o'clock and all Clarissa's relatives began to gather in the great hall. It was a short walk from the castle to the family chapel. Her father, Uncles William and Harry and cousin Frederick acted as the pall bearers, whilst Maddie and Rowan walked on either side of Uncle Thomas, following just a few feet behind the coffin itself. Aunt Kate and Aunt Mary, walking as a pair and dressed in thick black fur coats came next and behind them, also in twos, were Harry and Tristan with Edmund and Finn bringing up the rear. The whole family looked pale, drawn, with tearful, reddened eyes staring firmly straight ahead, their sense of loss, of grief almost palpable.

The weather suited the occasion. The sky was overcast. A grey tinge dominated the world, as if it had lost its colour in the wash and faded to tones of despairing monochrome. Dead maple leaves drifted down from an avenue of trees lining the driveway, trees struggling to stop the onslaught of winter, as if they too, were desperately clinging to life and resolutely refused to release their summer garb to the chill winds which blew relentlessly through their branches.

Maddie was conscious that as she walked beside her uncle, she could not stop her teeth from chattering. She found her eyes straying from the coffin to the green fields all around her. In her mind she saw visions of Clarissa, Clarissa running through summer meadows, chasing her precious butterflies; Clarissa skipping through fields blood red in colour such was the denseness of the scarlet poppies. Clarissa laughing with a rosary of ruby petals pinned in her hair. She could see Clarissa cartwheeling across carpets of bright purple clover and sitting in a sea of daisies making chain after chain, garlanding first Maddie and then Rowan with her handiwork.

Grief came flooding back and weighed so heavy on Maddie's young shoulders that she found it almost impossible to breathe. They had reached the gate to the family chapel and the graveyard. Two stone angels stood guarding the entrance. The funeral party passed through and continued on. In silence they followed a narrow path running between a jumble of tombstones which Maddie noticed were leaning over at a variety of angles and covered in lichen. The graveyard looked uncared for, almost abandoned, with not a single flower decorating any of the graves. Instead, huge granite crosses and a marble lion stood as testimony to the place where her ancestors lay buried. Her feet made a crunching sound on the gravel underfoot as she moved to read the tombstone nearest to her.

Remember me as you pass by,
As you are now, so once was I,
As I am now, so you will be,
Prepare for death and follow me.

Maddie's father did not like her visiting family graves. She wasn't even allowed to come to put flowers on her own mother's grave. She looked about her. It was a bleak, desolate place. The trees here had already surrendered to winter. They looked dead with their dark trunks and thin branches stripped of

44

their leaves by the advancing cold. Perhaps her father was right after all. 'Best concentrate on the living. No need to go visiting graves,' he would say, 'your mother is here with me, right here,' pressing his hand on his heart. 'Loving each other Maddie, that's how we honour her memory.'

A thick carpet of leaves, sodden, brown, and rotting, nature's own winter corpse, lay heavy underfoot as they walked those final steps to the chapel. Maddie looked up at Rowan's tear-stained face and as she gazed into those familiar eyes, so loneliness filled her, and sadness engulfed her. It was a sadness which hung tangibly in air rank with the scent of decay. In that awful moment, her grief knew no bounds. As the coffin was carried into the small chapel patches of blue were leaking through an overcast sky, spilling out through the clouds. A spirited wind followed them through into the lobby, ushering fallen leaves beneath their feet.

As Maddie took her seat, next to Rowan, she looked around her. The church was full, every servant, with one exception—every person from the village was present. She felt like a stranded ship, marooned in a sea of well-meaning faces etched with tension, as they too, tried to mask their real feelings. Almost unknowing she averted her eyes from their sad gaze. Aunt Frances came to sit beside her and rested a black gloved hand gently on her arm. 'Stay strong,' she whispered, 'stay strong for Rowan.' Once all the family were seated the service began.

A minister Maddie did not recognise regaled in his purple vestments, made the first address to the congregation. Instantly Maddie took a dislike to his voice. It sounded too rehearsed, too detached and she particularly resented the fact that he clearly could not have known Clarissa. 'Why couldn't their usual minister, Reverend Hatfield, take the service? Why had an outsider been brought in?'

'We have come together to worship God,

to thank him for his love,

and to remember the short life on earth of *Clarissa Elizabeth Montague,*

to share our grief,

and to commend her to the eternal care of God.

We meet in the faith that death is not the end,

and may be faced without fear,

bitterness or guilt.'

As the first hymn '*All Things Bright and Beautiful*' was sung, one of Clarissa's favourites, Maddie noticed wonderful rays of sunshine suddenly pouring in through the beautiful stained-glass windows. The magical streams of multi-coloured light almost lifted Maddie's low spirits. At first, they illuminated the whole church and then as if directed by an unseen hand they began to play upon the wreaths of white flowers decorating the coffin. Hues of red, green, and blue seemed to dance amongst the alabaster petals.

Just then, as they began to sing the second verse, another movement, high up in the Gothic arched windows caught Maddie's eye. The congregation sang on:

'He made their glowing colours,

He made their tiny wings.'

Something very small began to flutter down. Whatever it was flew on a zigzag pathway back and forth in the sunlight. Suddenly Maddie recognised a most beautiful, living specimen of Leucoma Salicis. A tiny white moth whirling round and round had joined the grieving congregation. It mirrored the dancing lights on top of the coffin. Maddie watched its chaotic movement fascinated. For a moment it was lost from sight as it settled amongst masses of alabaster petals. Then it began to flap its wings once more and was off and up again. The moth rose high into the air before landing on Rowan's wreath. Moments later it flew even higher, and this time it was Maddie's wreath it chose to settle on. The service continued but Maddie was oblivious to it all. Her attention, her entire focus was on the moth—the White Satin moth. It was only when Rowan stood up that Maddie's thoughts returned to the funeral. She knew he was to give a reading and that he had been dreading it.

'I'm all right Maddie, I can do this. I feel comforted,' he whispered as he squeezed past her in the narrow pew. He made his way to a lectern situated on the right-hand side of the coffin and with fumbling hand pulled a piece of neatly folded parchment from his pocket. The church was in total silence. All eyes were on the young man now about to read a poem dedicated to his dead sister, his twin, lying cold and lifeless in the wooden casket at his side. Rowan took a deep breath, cleared his throat, and began to read. His voice was loud, clear, and unfaltering. Maddie felt very proud of him, as she knew Clarissa would have been too.

'Tis only we who grieve

They do not leave

They are not gone

They look upon us still

They walk among the valleys now
They stride upon the hill
Their smile is in the summer sky
Their grace is in the breeze
Their memories whisper in the grass
Their calm is in the trees
Their light is in the winter snow
Their tears are in the rain
Their merriment runs in the brook
Their laughter in the lane
Their gentleness is in the flowers
They sigh in autumn leaves
They do not leave
They are not gone
Tis only we who grieve'

Rowan returned to his seat and, before Maddie knew what was happening, the funeral was over, and the bearers returned to carry the coffin outside to the church yard for burial. The white moth led the way, flying out through the now open church doors. Maddie followed. In her hand she held a small red rose. It had been decided that she, Rowan, and Uncle Thomas would all throw a flower onto the coffin as it was lowered into the grave. She stood outside blinking in the harsh sunlight. Rowan came to stand at her side and gently grasped her hand. 'Did you see the moth?' he asked quietly.

'Yes,' she said simply. 'But where is it now?' The coffin was lowered into the ground and the three roses gently cast down on top of it. Maddie kept looking for the moth but there was no sign of it. She had almost given up, when suddenly Rowan caught hold of her arm.

'Look, Maddie, look!' he exclaimed, pointing towards the sun. Maddie's gaze followed her cousin's outstretched arm up to the sky, to where chrome clouds had folded and blossomed into the shape of a great moth, hovering high above them, beating its wings at the red glow of the afternoon sun.

The cousins were transfixed, staring upwards, watching as the wind transformed the giant winged creature into a galleon. A great tall ship made from white cotton, with billowing ivory sails which now sped away, sailing towards the horizon across a rapidly darkening and threatening sky. The first drops of rain began to fall. Maddie and Rowan stood hand in hand oblivious to the impending downpour. They were both smiling. 'She's here with us,' said Rowan in a voice thick with emotion. 'She kept her promise you see. Clarissa will never leave us!'

'Come children,' said Aunt Frances, 'Clarissa wouldn't want you catching your death of cold. We need to get in the warm and dry.' Reluctantly the two children allowed themselves to be led away. Slowly as the torrential rain fell, the family—one by one—began to leave the graveside, until only Robert and Thomas remained. The torrential rain irritated Thomas as he watched a river of mud washing down onto the coffin and utterly obliterating sight of the red rose, he had lain in memory of his daughter. Neither man spoke and neither moved. They stood like stone statues, whilst a wet chill penetrated, invaded their thick black overcoats, causing them to shiver inadvertently. Frozen fingers sought the sanctuary of dry pockets or were raised to lips for warm breath to ease their painful iciness and then, as if taking pity, the rain eased.

The toll of dull, mournful bells continued to ring in an otherwise quiet churchyard, whilst a weak, almost dormant sun remained hidden behind dark, rain-filled clouds, depriving the land of all light and warmth. The brothers stood together at the graveside, oblivious to the shreds of fog which crept across the ground, encircling their legs like ghostly manacles. They were lost in memories of a child who, only days before had been the centre of both their worlds. Thoughts of her chained them to the coffin lying in the dark pit at their feet. Senses numbed by grief, their eyes saw only the casket and their ears were deaf to the call of kindly voices beckoning them away. Only the crunching sound of weary footsteps on gravel and a chill wind moaning through naked branches stripped of their leaves filled the otherwise eerie silence. The day lay quiet and time itself seemed suspended.

Robert wanted to comfort his brother but knew not how. He was haunted by so many painful memories that it made it difficult for him to speak. Would he ever forget his wife's passing. She had fought so hard, so bravely against a vile prophecy, an evil curse placed upon the family which showed no mercy.

Blood-stained towels had littered the floor of their bedroom on the night of Maddie's birth. He closed his eyes, trying to blot out the memory of her suffering, the ghostly-pale complexion, the dull eyes, and haggard expression, with specks of white saliva, dotted at the corners of a mouth trying to smile, trying to speak, trying to give him comfort.

'If only I could forget her suffering and remember the good times we shared,' he thought to himself.

Thomas too was remembering, and identical thoughts were racing through his mind. He was like a lost child, orphaned, abandoned, broken, and desolated by a sense of loss so deep, so intense, that it almost prevented him from breathing. How could he go on without her? Their daughter, Clarissa who had been such a comfort to him since the death of his wife. At that moment, a strong arm reached around his shoulders.

'She's at peace now,' said Robert standing beside him, 'and if you believe in an afterlife safe in her mother's arms. You must take comfort from that, Thomas.'

Thomas brushed his cheek as a solitary tear escaped from an eye sworn to remain resolute. Robert, noting his grief, attempted to pull him away.

'Come away, brother. You can do no more for her now,' he said softly.

'I'm alright,' he lied, as he allowed himself to be led away.

They walked in silence, deep in thought and neither heard the distant bark of a farm dog as it shivered down the afternoon half-light, locking the strange, unearthly stillness even tighter upon the land.

High up in a forgotten, unlit attic room, vulture-like eyes with unusually large pupils watched two lone men returning to the castle. The brilliant whites of those eyes, which were stained purple in the corners, opened widely as these melancholy souls dressed in black, with drooping shoulders and bowed heads, moved like slow-moving phantoms. They passed beneath her window and eyes with deep, dark pupils, surrounded by a huge iris of dark grey flecked throughout with streaks of red, filled with a look of sheer satisfaction. Stubby fingers which resembled burnt sausages, clutched at an ancient wooden doll, pulling it to pursed lips. 'You can be proud, Idema, you have worked your magic well,' a rasping voice whispered in the doll's ear 'We can console ourselves in the knowledge that we have achieved retribution for Adanna's suffering once again.'

Chapter Seven
The Power of the Witch Doctor

Three hundred years earlier, in the great continent of Africa, there had once been a vast area of land known as Dahomey. Situated in the Bight of Benin, it was a beautiful country determined by its geography into four main regions from the south to the north. The low-lying, sandy, coastal plain was at most, hardly ten kilometres wide, a marshy wilderness, though rich in wildlife, dotted with lakes and lagoons communicating with the ocean. The plateaus of southern Benin were split by valleys running north to south along the Couffo, Zou, and Oueme Rivers. Then came an area of flat lands dotted with rocky hills and finally, the Atacora mountain range extending along the northwest border and into Togo.

That was Benin, with fields of lying fallow, mangroves and the remnants of large sacred forests, some surviving trees of which lined the banks of the rivers, whilst in the rest of the country the savannah was covered with thorny scrubs and dotted with huge baobab trees. Inland to the north and the northwest of Benin huge herds of all manner of game roamed wild and free. It had been a good life for Nabila, although fraught with danger. She was a member of the Dahomey tribe and a highly trained warrior, skilled in the arts of war, but also of great prowess and repute as a hunter. Wild dog, antelope, wildebeest, lion, and tiger, Nabila had hunted them all. Often after a daring kill, she had brought the fresh carcass back in triumph to her village. The tribesmen always had crops aplenty to eat. Meat, however, was far scarcer and her gift therefore much appreciated.

The crocodile had been lazing in the shallows, partially submerged, and enjoying the feel of warm sunshine on its broad, scaly back. It was woken from its slumber by vibrations in the water which told it live game was close. The giant beast instinctively turned and effortlessly floated out across the river, allowing the current to propel it downstream towards the origin of sound now tempting its taste buds.

Princess Adana was laughing loudly as she and Entebbe grabbed the same vine simultaneously and, together, swung out high over the river. Screaming with delight, they let go at the peak of their swing and dropped like pebbles into the cool water below. Re-surfacing, they thrashed wildly with their arms and legs, racing each other back to the bank, both, desperate to be the winner.

Wangari, leader of King Nazzor Eze's Amazonian army and Nabila, Wangari's second in command, watched the children play from the shade of an ancient bushwillow. The latter was aunt and bodyguard to Adana and had hardly taken her eyes off her charge all afternoon. She watched her niece with pride and satisfaction as she reached the bank, well in advance of her playmate.

Entebbe, conceding defeat to her princess, stayed in the river, standing knee deep in the fast-flowing water, to watch four boys swing out high above her. Showing off, two of the boys performed flying somersaults as they catapulted back down to earth. There was an almighty splash as they hit the water. A huge cloud of spray soared into the air causing myriads of tiny droplets to sparkle brightly in the late afternoon sun. Adana, admiring the boys' skill, clapped enthusiastically, and called to Entebbe to join her.

'Come on,' she shouted, 'we can do better than that!'

Nabila stood up. She had noticed something floating downstream in the centre of the river. Shielding her eyes from the sun she stared at it intently and instantly recognised what it was. She relaxed. It was merely the branch of a fallen tree, barely moving in the water and in mid-stream. The children were in no danger.

'Nabila, watch me,' shouted Adana, leaping out from the very top of an enormous jackal berry tree and hurtling across the river on an even longer vine. In contrast, the crocodile remained motionless in the water, before taking a deep breath and sinking unnoticed below the surface. The royal princess showed great courage and physical prowess as she flew high above the river. At the height of her swing, she let go. Her muscular little body performed two perfect somersaults before she hit the water to rapturous applause from both her peers and minders.

Entebbe knew nothing of the crocodile's attack. Like everyone else, her eyes were focused exclusively on Adana's antics and just as the somersaulting princess hit the water, so sharp, conical teeth locked Entebbe in their powerful grasp. For a brief second, enormous jaws lifted the little girl clear of the water. She was swallowed whole, her body falling down into the dinosaur's cavernous gullet. The prehistoric head had disappeared completely, leaving only a small circle of ripples on the water, before Adana had even resurfaced.

Having made its kill, the crocodile, a full-grown male, over twenty-five feet long, moved silently along the riverbed and resumed a hunting position some yards from the bank. A child, barely six years old, was nought but a mere morsel to this killing machine and it was fully aware that other prey still remained in close proximity. It would lie in wait now, and for as long as necessary, until another opportunity to feed presented itself.

'Entebbe, did you see me?' shouted Adana, looking up and down the riverbank. Nabila came to stand at her side.

'Wait till I tell your father how clever you are,' said Nabila, gently stroking back wet hair from her charge's face.

'Nabila, where's Entebbe?'

'Wangari, did you see where Entebbe went?' Nabila called out to her captain.

Instantly, Wangari was on her feet and with narrowed eyes, the two elite warriors scanned the length and breadth of the river. Nabila noted immediately that there was no sign of a tree branch either up or downstream for as far as she could see. She raced to the edge of the riverbank, frantically looking for sight of it. There was none. A feeling of disbelief, quickly followed by total dismay engulfed her. 'We have a crocodile on our hands,' she warned her companion.

'Out, out of the water, everyone!' commanded Wangari. The children did as they were bid. Wangari was not a woman to be crossed.

The search began in earnest. The elder boys were kept behind to help, whilst Nabila escorted Adana and the younger children back to the village. Once Adana was safely inside the royal palace, Nabila and a squadron of spear warriors returned to the river. The hunt for Entebbe continued well into the night. It was dawn before a defeated group of disappointed, distressed, and disheartened searchers returned to the King and Entebbe's parents with the sad news.

Nabila's account of the large tree branch she had spotted just before Entebbe's disappearance, made them all suspect a crocodile attack. Adana was distraught at the loss of her friend and would not be consoled. Try as she might, Nabila could not stem the flow of tears.

The following day, a crocodile hunt was launched. By evening, five huge carcasses were returned to the village and opened up. The semi-digested remains of buffalo, gazelle and monkey spewed out onto the ground, but there was nothing that even remotely resembled human remains. Entebbe could not be found. No one could give precise explanations or an account as to her loss. Like Adana, Entebbe's relatives were inconsolable. Her parents, an elderly couple and childless until Entebbe's unexpected arrival needed constant supervision—they were so overwhelmed with grief that some of the elders feared they were in danger of taking their own lives.

Wangari and Nabila too were desolate. They blamed themselves for Entebbe's demise and begged the king to punish them for failing to keep her safe. He would not hear of it however, but he did summon, Adiamo, the village witch doctor. An announcement was made that a special ceremony would be held in the village that night, a voodoo ritual, in which the spirits of the dead would be called upon and Entebbe's ancestors would return to walk and talk with the living once more.

King Nazzor Eze knew what it was to grieve a loved one. He understood their pain. To lose a beloved wife or an only child, plucked from the world without rhyme or reason was the hardest thing for a man to bear. He also knew that to have a child taken away before that young life had barely begun was even more heart-breaking. When Queen Adana had died, he had held her in his arms, told her how much he loved her. But, for Entebbe's parents their loss was far worse. There had been no words of goodbye, no opportunity to express how much they had loved her. Indeed, they did not even have a body to mourn, or to hold, or kiss, or caress. There could be no burial. Hence, no way of mourning, of grieving in the normal way and no way either for them to speak to her spirit, to tell her how much they had loved her. Their grief was beyond measure. Worst of all was the uncertainty. Was she dead, or was she still alive and suffering?

The king had considerable faith in his witch doctor and the people enormous belief in their Gods. The voodoo ceremony would allow emotions to be expressed, sadness to be allayed and the healing process to begin. The entire village would be present and Adiamo would take his place centre stage. He was the master of his craft, and his supernatural powers were renowned throughout the land.

Adiamo left the king's chamber and made his solitary way out into the bush. It was a hot, humid day and the air about him was heavy and oppressive. In the intolerable heat, even the merest exercise felt like a punishment. He trudged on across the vast savannah, whilst a merciless sun scorched his drooping shoulders and burnt a now balding head red raw. A callous sun which continued to broil the land without pity, drying up streams and waterholes, baking the earth to a crisp and raising choking, suffocating dust swirls on rising spirals of stifling air.

An unexpected sudden gust of wind gave momentary respite from the heat. Adiamo stopped briefly and sniffed the air. He could smell it, a storm was coming and with it no doubt, a deluge of rain. Smiling to himself, in the knowledge that the rain dance he had performed yesterday, at the behest of several wealthy farmers, was certain of success, he continued on. For the present, however, there was no relief from the oppressive heat and sweat poured from his brow in rivulets as his ancient feet followed the well-trodden path leading to a particular place deep inside the mango grove.

As he walked, he listened with satisfaction to the drums giving out his clear message. Even miles from the village their sound echoed across the savannah. His high priests and priestesses were being summoned from every corner of Benin and Adiamo knew without doubt, that they would by now, be gathering at his lodge and awaiting his return.

On reaching the mango grove, he found the plant he wanted with ease and using a small machete he had carried with him, hacked out enough of its root to make the potion he required. The return journey with arms laden with this heavy material was even more difficult and he was relieved when finally, the village and his lodge appeared in view. As expected, his minions were waiting and had already prepared a large fire inside the voodoo temple. A giant cauldron of water steamed noisily upon it and hissed angrily as Adiamo pressed the roots of the plant he had harvested deep into the fiercely-bubbling liquid. The root would be left to boil for several hours.

On the central square outside the palace, normally used as a marketplace, members of the royal household were busy preparing a feast for the whole village. The feast would take place before the main ceremony. As the vast array of food was assembled with meats and fruits of every kind on display, a small group of woman created a pattern of cornmeal on a flat piece of ground measuring several yards across and positioned immediately outside Adiamo's impressive complex of lodges. It would be on this ground that the hooded dances would take place and where the ritual would be conducted.

Slowly, slowly an unrelenting, merciless sun sank below the mountain range marking the boundary of Benin to the east. Darkness fell and as it did so, so the sky changed from clear to cloudy. An anxious moon showed herself in brief glimpses only, as a rising wind blew storm clouds across her face. There was no lack of light however, as dozens of bonfires were lit all around the village. Bright flames would light the feast and the voodoo dances which would follow.

As Nabila watched the villagers assemble, with Princess Adana at her side, she was aware of the unnatural quiet. People moved like ghosts, silent, grey-faced with drawn, worried expressions. No one spoke, as one by one they took their places steadily, purposefully, as if guided by some unseen hand. Nabila felt anxious and passed her hand across her moist, furrowed brow several times as she stared into the flickering light created by the bonfires. Her heart was pounding as if she had already seen horrific spectres sent by an angry spirit world to punish her for the loss of Entebbe, for her failure to keep her charges safe and for the terrible, unforgiveable dereliction of her duties. Her right hand tightened its grip on the shoulders of her young niece.

Adana, on the other hand, appeared strangely calm and collected, like a young child about to spend a quiet, uneventful evening at home. Directly in front of her, Entebbe's parents were seated on the ground, but on a thick layer of animal furs and hides, which had been specially provided for them. Despite Adana's youth and immaturity, she was aware of their intense grief. It matched her own, the loss of her best friend, of Entebbe, filled her with dread and despondency and yet at this moment and for their sake, she knew she needed to show courage and so she fought to keep her true feelings in check. As the last families were seated, she looked up at Nabila with eyes full of love and sadness.

'Nabila, you may inform the King that all are assembled,' she said in a trembling voice she hardly recognised as her own.

Nabila walked briskly into the palace. Minutes later came the sound of rattles shaking and drums beating as the King and his entourage emerged from the palace. Behind them, dancing, and chanting, and following at a respectful distance, came Adiamo's priests and priestesses. As the King took his place on the high throne which had been prepared for him in the centre of the banqueting area and close to a huge bonfire, Adiamo and his minions became silent. The King stood to his feet and announced loudly, 'Let the feasting begin.'

It was unlike any other feast Adana had ever attended. There was an absence of laughter, voices were lowered, indeed, most people spoke only in whispers, and it was noticeable that Entebbe's parents ate nothing. Food which normally vanished in the blink of an eye disappeared slowly, and all the while, Adiamo and his followers walked about the people offering them a special drink from gourds which had been brought from Adiamo's lodge. Adana was no stranger to the effect's alcohol has on those who partake of it, and it was soon apparent to her, that whatever the liquor was that Adiamo had prepared, it must have been a potent concoction. Minutes after drinking it, several villagers acted as if they were completely inebriated, and some had even fallen into a swoon.

The king called the feast to an end. Sitting on his throne, he was carried by four strong palace guards to a raised wooden platform located at the back of the square. The throne was placed carefully upon it. From this high vantage point, the king would have an excellent view of proceedings; whilst at exactly the same time, Adiamo and the priests and priestesses re-entered the voodoo lodge. For a few brief minutes there was total silence. Then suddenly and with an increased intensity the drums began beating again.

Adana watched enthralled as six priests emerged from the temple dressed in animal skins and wearing ornate, fabulously carved wooden masks. They danced in a way which mirrored the natural movements of the animal they were mimicking. A gazelle leapt high into the air, twirling wildly, a snake slithered along the ground, but at times raising its head above the ground to strike at some unseen prey, a wild buffalo pawed at the soil, and charged chaotically in all directions. The dancers formed a semi-circle around the king's throne and, just then, Adiamo emerged from the temple carrying a small, live goat. He held it high in the air, before slitting its throat in full view of the villagers. A priestess fell at his knees and collected the dripping blood into a large, circular ceremonial bowl. Adana noted the distinct pattern with which it was decorated, a host of wild animals painted in vivid, eye-catching colours. Almost immediately, a second priestess arrived and poured in liquid from one the gourds Adana had seen earlier. The contents began to bubble and for several minutes, a thick grey vapour rose up from the bowl, spiralling skywards until finally disappearing from sight in the night air.

The priestess holding the bowl, walked to an altar situated inside four burning torches, staked into the ground, and positioned at the very centre of the marked area prepared earlier for the hooded dances. Placing the bowl upon it, she bowed low and then slowly retreated. Adiamo moved forwards and on reaching the altar, he circled his hand several times above the bowl, finally reaching into it and miraculously pulling out a large green mamba from inside. The snake hissed angrily, venom dropping from its exposed fangs, as he danced fearlessly, holding it high above his head for all to see.

He threw the snake to the floor, where to Adana's amazement it seemed to vanish. Adiamo now began to chant, and lifting the bowl up from the altar, he approached Entebbe's parents. They stood to their feet and taking the bowl from his outstretched hands, they drank until it was dry.

Adiamo's chanting became louder, his high priests and priestesses joined in and began directing the audience. Soon everyone was chanting, the villagers, Adana, Nabila, Wangari and even the King himself. Entebbe's parents as if overcome by emotion collapsed to the floor. It was Adana now who looked alarmed and frightened as it appeared to her that they were both fitting. She could see the whites of their eyes, grotesquely staring out from faces which appeared contorted with pain. There was froth too, gathering in their mouths and their bodies writhed on the ground as if convulsing uncontrollably. She made a move to step towards them, but Nabila caught her arm.

'Have no fear, Adana,' she said, 'the gods are with them.'

Before she had time to reply, there came a shocked gasp from all the villagers. Another priestess had stepped out from the voodoo lodge, but this time dressed in an enormous crocodile skin. Fascinated, Adana watched the giant head, its gaping mouth displaying the vile, cruel jaw with its sharp, conical teeth, as the prehistoric beast moved amongst them, twirling and dancing with ever increasing fervour. The drums too were beating louder and louder until a flash of lightning split the sky above them in two.

Instantly the dancing and the drumming stopped and as the priestess stood in front of Adiamo, Adana heard him call Entebbe's name. She listened, as if frozen to the spot, as he demanded Entebbe's spirit to leave the crocodile and return to the spirit world. Three times he called Entebbe to him, each time with an increasingly commanding tone and so loudly that his voice seemed to resonate through the entire village and out into the savannah beyond. In all her life, Adana had never heard so powerful a voice.

'She comes, Entebbe comes!' she heard him cry in triumph.

'Nabila, look,' she whispered, as she watched the priestess fall to the ground. Rising above the now clearly unconscious dancer was the body of her friend, of Entebbe. She saw her leave the crocodile and walk towards the prostrate bodies of her parents. For several minutes, Entebbe's ghost seemed to hover in the air above them and then, just as Adana had decided to run to her and to embrace her once more, the spectre slowly evaporated before her eyes, until nothing of it remained. A distant rumble of thunder echoed through the night air, causing Adana to shiver.

'It is done,' said Nabila. 'Entebbe is returned to us, she is with her ancestors.'

There was a hushed silence as awe-struck friends and family gathered around Entebbe's parents. To Adana's relief they were now clearly recovering from their ordeal and as Adiamo, helped them to their feet, they listened eagerly, whilst many spoke of seeing Entebbe's ghost and of hearing the voices of their long-lost loved ones speaking to them. Many arms embraced them, many hands stroked, patted their strained, wizened faces, which finally bore an expression which appeared less sad, as if now, they were better able to accept the terrible loss of their only daughter.

'My brother is a wonderful man, is he not, Adana? He speaks to the gods, and they answer him. Entebbe's soul has walked amongst us, and the gods have given us great comfort. We must be happy that she is at last free to join her ancestors in the spirit world.' Nabila's voice sounded thick with emotion.

Adana nodded sadly in agreement.

Just then, the weather, as if in sympathy, decided to reflect the melancholy mood of the village. A chill wind arrived from nowhere, blowing even darker storm clouds across the sky. The moon ceded complete defeat and a far-off horizon blackened deeply, whilst in stark contrast red and yellow bolts of lightning raked the savannah with increasing ferocity. As Adana leant against her aunt, Nabila could feel the little girl's body shuddering and as her niece's hand grasped hers securely, she remembered the young princess's lifelong fear of thunderstorms. Once again, lightning bolts shot across the starless sky and loud, deafening thunder rumbled, roared, and echoed through the vast mountain ranges surrounding them.

'Come, Adana, my precious little one,' she said kindly, 'it is time you were in bed.'

Chapter Eight
A Storm at Sea

Three hundred miles away and far out at sea, a majestic tall ship, boasting a superbly carved stags head graced with giant antlers as its figurehead, was being tossed about like a rabbit in the jaws of a wolf. As she tried to ride the enormous breakers pounding against her wooden hull, she would rise swiftly upon dark, angry, watery summits, only to plummet into even blacker, infinite craters without hope of ever surfacing again. The ship, *the Black Stag*, was taking on water at an alarming rate, as ice-cold, raging thirty-foot waves breached her deck and hurricane-force winds tore at her sails.

Mr Lawson shouted above the noise of the tumult. 'Fletcher, where's the captain?'

'Drunk in his cabin, I reckon,' came the reply.

The wind howled around them as another huge swell threatened to sweep them both overboard. Soaked to the skin and chilled to the bone, it was all they could do to remain at the wheel.

Lawson grabbed a thick rope from the base of it. 'Help me tie myself to the helm,' he shouted at the top of his voice. Struggling against the elements, Fletcher, the ship's bosun, assisted as best he could. It took several minutes before they had successfully completed the task.

'Get all hands up on deck,' continued Lawson, 'including the captain.'

'I wouldn't be rousing the captain, if I were you, sir. There'll be the devil to pay if you do, state he's in. Drunk a barrel by his self I shouldn't wonder,' replied Fletcher, with seawater pouring from his chin in torrents.

'Do as I say, man. Get the crew to batten down the hatches and then I want bare poles, fast as you can. Do you hear me, man? Bare poles and quick about it, our very lives depend upon it.'

'Aye, aye, I hear you.' Fletcher staggered away, clinging to the rails on the portside of the ship.

The crew was ordered on deck and several of the riggers told to climb aloft. 'Bare poles me brave boys, bare poles. Lash them sails in good mind, else we'll be dead in the water by morning… assuming of course we aren't dead already!' he added cynically.

One of the riggers, a young man on his first voyage, by the name of Samuel Thomas, clutched at Fletcher's coat. 'We can't climb the rigging in this storm, sir. We'll all fall to our deaths, taint possible, tis suicide is what it is,' he clamoured. The ship lurched violently to starboard, causing him to fall to his knees and so violently that he almost pulled his bosun down with him.

'Ripping the young man's hands from his lapel,' Fletcher thundered. 'You heard the order, now get aloft and do your duty.' Thomas, however, remained on his knees and resolutely refused to move. In the end, it was Fletcher himself who began to climb the rigging in an attempt to help stow the sails.

His feet had barely left the deck of the ship, when a huge gust of wind tore at the sails atop the Mizzenmast. The ominous sound of wood splintering and men screaming immediately followed and an array of cordage, metal pulleys, broken spars, and canvas rigging, crashed down onto the deck. Lawson only just managed to jump clear. Fletcher himself was thrown against the main mast, where he lay lifeless and crumpled, like a broken rag doll. Struggling against the waves, Lawson crawled towards him. As he did so, unseen, and unheard, two more riggers plunged into the raging swell on the portside of the ship. Just as Lawson reached the unconscious Fletcher, the body of another rigger, hit the deck right next to him.

There was a loud scream and the awful sound of bones breaking and flesh tearing. Blood spurted from the man's wounds into Lawson's face and a tide of red swept across his legs as great gushes of water continued to rush over the deck. For the first time, he realised how small the ship was in comparison to the vast, unpredictable, and oft times tumultuous sea into which they had ventured and feared for his life, his crew and that of his cargo.

Pushing those fears to the back of his mind, Lawson reached towards the man and attempted to turn him over. He did not succeed, the horrific sight of injuries suffered from the fall, stopped him in his tracks. The man's arms were half their normal length; limp, miss-shaped hands protruded from shattered elbow joints, and the bones of the lower arm now projected through jagged flesh wounds situated just below the shoulder. But it was the man's face which shocked him to the core. The lower jawbone had been forced upwards causing the face to concertina to a fraction of its normal size. Blood poured from the stricken man's mouth and nostrils, and the terrible sound of gargled breathing filled Lawson's ears. The man was dying and there was nothing he could do to help him or ease his suffering.

Struggling against the wind and cold, with fingers so frozen he could scarce move them, Lawson finally succeeded in lashing the injured rigger, Fletcher, and himself to the toe rail. All he could do now was to wait for the storm to abate. For hour after painful hour, somehow the ship remained afloat, riding the waves and wind like a reckless cowboy on the back of a bucking bronco. Lawson would remember the sounds of that night all his life. From down below he could hear the pitiful wailing of petrified slaves, haplessly chained in their reeking prison, now awash with vomit, whilst from the upper galley the noise of pewter plates and tankards clattering to the floor and stowed cargo now loose from its bindings crashing about like an enraged bull, as it was thrown from one side of the ship to the other. A cacophony of noise bombarded his ears. He would often recall that strangest of all, even above the relentless howling of the wind and the hullabaloo which surrounded him, he was aware of the grown men on deck with him, praying, groaning, and crying like small children who had lost their parents. Worst of all, was the sound and sight of the fatally injured rigger lying next to him.

Repeatedly, angry waves crashed down upon them, as the ship plunged down vertical troughs thirty feet deep as *the Black Stag* was pushed, shoved, kicked, lifted, and dropped by a relentless sea. Cold, dark waves which hit them with such malevolence and force that the ship's wooden hull creaked and moaned under the strain, like a hapless boxer in the ring, battered and bleeding from the punches of a far tougher opponent and with no referee to stop the fight. Without remit, giant, thundering waves of saltwater cascaded down upon the three exhausted men, tied together, and surviving only because of the rope which bound them. It seemed to Lawson that the deck itself was moving, as a violent tide endlessly ebbed and flowed beneath his body.

So, the ship lurched on, out of control. There were moments when it was particularly unbearable for Lawson, the sheer power of the sea left him helpless, oft times he felt as if he could only look on and watch his comrades drowning, minutes would pass before their heads were clear of the freezing water. He could do nothing to help the rigger, only watch the whites of his eyes writhing in a grotesquely disfigured face and listen to the awful guttering, choking, rasping noise he made, as each painful breath was taken.

In that part of the world, severe gales often dissipate as quickly as they come and, as if God had finally decided to answer his prayers, Lawson noted with a huge sense of relief that the wind had begun to ease. The howling tempest no longer deafened his ears. Soon the waves too began to subside and the sky to lighten. Dazed and bruised from the night's events and the violent motion of the ship, Lawson hauled himself to his feet, untied the rope from around his waist and began to rally his crew.

Soon sailors were shouting and running across the decks. Following Lawson's instructions, the injured were carried below, the captain roused from his cabin and the ship's surgeon ordered to do whatever he could for the unfortunate rigger. A fully recovered Fletcher, ignoring a deep gash down his right cheek, dressed in his foul weather gear and with a rigger's knife in his hand, gallantly climbed aloft. While he clung to the mast, he quickly cut the remaining rigging lines that held the damaged, flapping sail aloft. Shouting a clear warning to the men below him and much to Lawson's appreciative eyes, he saved the mast with that one quick cut.

Whilst the sea remained calm, and, content that the ship was once again fully crewed, Lawson left Fletcher in charge and went below. He immediately called on the doctor and watched him tend to the wounds the sailors had suffered whilst fighting the storm. Many had slashed arms and legs and a great many more had cuts/lacerations to their heads and hands. Lawson himself was called upon to use a mending needle to sew up one sailor's leg—a large piece of a mast had cut through it.

That done, he excused himself from the doctor's presence, and without seeking the captain's consent, returned on deck to Fletcher and ordered that rum be given to all hands to help them forget the pain they were suffering and the horrors of the night.

It seemed to Lawson that it was a miracle the ship had survived the storm. He wondered if his wife's prayers had stopped God from judging them—why else would they have been spared? Whatever the cause, he was grateful that the wind had dropped to nothing more than a light breeze and that the ship and crew were safe. He thanked Fletcher for his bravery during the storm and in cutting the damaged rigging free that morning. A surprised bosun, unused to such high praise, handed over the helm to an experienced mariner, and went eagerly to fetch a well-earned barrel of rum for his men.

'And while your down below, get that cut seen to,' Lawson called after him.

Lawson looked about him. All was in order. 'The mizzen can wait for now,' he thought wearily to himself. He left the deck and retired to his cabin for a late breakfast. Having eaten, it was not long before he was fast asleep and dreaming of home, his wife, and his children. He was unceremoniously awoken from his slumber by the captain.

'Do you not know your duty, Mr Lawson? Must I advise you, on what is expected o' a first mate?'

'Begging your pardon, Captain, but it was a long night.'

'I need none of your excuses, Lawson. We got a matter of discipline to sort. I want you up on deck and in full uniform this instant.' At that, the obese, red-faced, heavily perspiring captain, Lord George Montague, turned on his heel and strode out of the cabin.

By the time Lawson stepped on deck, the whole crew had been assembled. Standing on his own, stripped to the waist and in irons, was Samuel Thomas. Lawson listened as the charge was read out—disobeying orders, which had resulted in the ship and crew being put at peril. He knew what was to follow. Depending on how bad Montague's hangover was, Thomas would be sentenced to up to a hundred lashes. Montague always administered the first twenty lashes himself and then handed the cat-o'-nine-tails over to Lawson. It was a duty he reluctantly performed with unwelcome regularity.

Despite being deep in thought, unexpected, and to him incomprehensible words reached his ears, shocking him to the core. Incredulously, he listened as his captain announced a keel hauling as punishment!

Lawson immediately approached his captain and stood at his side. 'Might I have a word, your Lordship?' he enquired. He spoke quietly, deliberately, so that no one else could hear. 'Sir, the young man is not yet fifteen years of age and, he be one of the many of this crew, new to sailing. This is his first voyage. The storm last night—well, it was worst I've ever seen, it frightened the best of us. There's some that stayed below deck, despite orders,' he stated pointedly and with feeling.

'If you've come to plead for leniency, you're wasting your breath, Lawson. Carry on, Fletcher,' Montague commanded.

'You'll as like kill him,' warned Lawson, 'and you know as well as I that we're short of men as it is. Even now, we have a rigger who will not see another sunrise, and two more also were lost overboard last night, when the mizzen mast was split asunder!'

'Perhaps he should have thought about that before refusing orders,' replied the captain. 'You are as mindful as I, that many of the men who man this ship, were snatched against their will. As a result, they are resentful towards me regarding their circumstances, not least, that they are here at all and prevented from returning home. One sign of weakness, Lawson, and I, you, and the other officers on board this ship, are all dead men. A show of strength, of strict, unfaltering discipline, whatever the circumstances is a necessary precaution to prevent any mutiny. Be silent now or you'll find yourself kissing the gunner's daughter. I'll hear no more of it.'

Lawson watched, helpless as Samuel Thomas was tied to a line that had been looped beneath the vessel. Begging for mercy and struggling with all his might, the young man was thrown overboard. Fletcher and two other men dragged him under the ship's keel, from the port to starboard side. Although the gale had subsided, the waves were still strong, and it took some time to haul the boy's body through its lengthy underwater passage.

'What the fuck!' exclaimed Fletcher, just as the body became visible a little way below the surface, the line seemed to snag. Try and try as they might the rope could not be moved. 'Pull it back the other way,' Fletcher screamed at the top of his voice. 'It's caught on something—damnation!' Eventually the rope was freed and Lawson himself joined the exhausted trio, anxious to raise the boy in time to save him from a certain drowning.

Indeed, to Lawson in particular it seemed an age before they began to pull Samuel Thomas's body from the foaming water. 'No one could hold their breath for that length of time,' he thought to himself. He was not wrong, and it was a lifeless body that was pulled up onto the deck. The hull too, had done its worst. Blood poured from gaping wounds all over the young man's back. Sharp barnacles, encrusted on the ship's timbers had cut deep into his flesh. Worse still, he had also lost an arm! Lawson's grief was tempered by that fact. Mercifully, Samuel Thomas had already drowned. There was no denying that there was little use in the world for a man with only one arm, let alone on a boat. Minutes later the boy was pronounced dead by the ship's doctor, and without so much as an 'Amen,' his body was committed to the deep.

And so it was that *the Black Stag*, a purpose-built slave ship, of massive proportions, just one of the Montague fleet sailed on. Lawson stared miserably at the horizon. He should have been able to see the beautiful coastline of Africa, but on all sides a now calm sea stretched out in every direction. The gale had blown them way off course. It would be hours before they reached their intended destination, another fortified Portuguese port containing a garrison and a holding prison for slaves.

The ship's lower decks were barely half-full of the cargo Montague was seeking—more slaves for his Jamaican plantations. Montague would not be happy until he had his full quota. Lawson had been astonished at just how many slaves he had seen transported in his three years of service. He had quickly realised that life expectancy (never mind in the slave ships) but on the actual plantations themselves was horrifyingly brief. He had heard rumours that once a slave became too ill or too weak to work, they were deprived of food and water to hasten their demise. It was a sickening business.

His hands gripped the wheel more tightly and as the hours passed, he tried to clear his mind of all thoughts of the ship's mission. He tried to remember his wife, his home, his children and to visualise what his life would be once he had completed his contract with Montague. How he would celebrate never having to see that man again.

'Land ahoy,' the man in the crow's nest called out.

Lawson steered the ship inland, they would hug the coastline now until reaching port. There would be nothing to celebrate on arrival today, however, only regret on his part for yet more human suffering to come. He tried to close his mind to memories of previous voyages, but they would not be stayed. He had witnessed suffering of the acutest kind and once the ship had anchored at her destination, he knew that wanton cruelty and abject misery would be unleashed all over again. Lawson hated the wicked trade in which he was involved. He longed to be free of it. A chill wind blew against him causing him to shudder. Silent now, he returned to the quiet solitude of his cabin, anxious to remove himself from the task of weighing anchor. He would leave that to Fletcher.

He sat on his narrow bunk bed and remembered his first voyage and how shocking it had been. He had certainly not been prepared for the lavishness of the captain's quarters, which were strictly his domain alone. The opulence of the cabin seemed deplorable, considering the living conditions of the crew never mind the slaves. Polished oak floorboards, ornately carved woodwork on every wall, plus fine furniture, drapes, silver table ware, crystal glasses and a never-ending supply of the finest brandy, port, and rum to be found in the western world. Unlike his cabin, light poured in through row upon row of wide, lattice paned windows all with panoramic views out to sea and he particularly recalled the captain's hanging cot with its delicately hand-embroidered drapes. At least the Captain slept well.

Lord Montague used the area as his day cabin, his office, and his meeting room. It was a space that no one entered without his permission. A marine guard posted at the door twenty-four hours a day saw that this rule was enforced. It was common for Lord Montague to invite his officers to dine with him, though he was under no obligation to do so. Although the food was always excellent, Lawson hated the man so much he would have preferred to dine with the rest of the crew, albeit on very meagre rations by comparison. To refuse to attend, however, would have given monumental offence and one did not wisely make an enemy of Lord Montague, not if you valued your life and liberty. Most shocking of all had been his discovery that the captain's sleeping quarters, which consisted of a small cabin on the starboard side of the ship connected to the main cabin, also opened up directly into the women's chamber.

On his very first voyage, Lawson had noted with disgust that between twenty and thirty girls and young women were selected from the cargo brought on board and consigned to chains in that particular quarter. He was well aware of the captain's voracious appetite for female flesh and these poor, helpless, unknowing victims would satisfy his perverse sexual needs throughout the ship's long passage.

It disgusted him even more that Montague preferred his personal harem to be as young as possible. The younger the better, or so it appeared to Lawson from his own shocked and appalled viewpoint, as he witnessed girls, no older than his own eldest daughter, as young as eight or nine years of age consigned to this section of the ship's hold. Many did not survive their ordeal, damaged and bleeding from Montague's drunken ravishes, they would often be thrown overboard immediately he had finished with them or die later of a resultant infection.

Lawson's introduction to this foul practice of his captain was in the form of a detailed narrative from the ship's bosun. Whilst at the wheel one night, he listened to Fletcher boasting to another crew member how he had earlier served his precious master and helped to take a female slave to Montague's quarters.

'The younger of two sisters, bout nine or ten I'd wager from the looks of her,' Fletcher explained, 'He likes them young he does. Anyways, he doesn't know it, but we watch him like, got a little spy hole right above the door. See everything we do.'

Lawson listened in silence.

'He asks for a bathtub of sea water first—always knows from that just what he's planning. Well, sitting in shite aren't they, so he likes to clean them up a bit. Bring me a young girl and be quick about it, Fletcher,' he says. 'We do as we are told. Dragged her up from the hold, screaming and kicking she were, so much so I had to give her a right slap—shut her up see—he doesn't like them making a racket. Christ, he'd been drinking heavy tonight, must a' been six, seven empty bottles on his table, when we brought her in. We sat her in the tub like, fastened her chains to the metal handles on each side and left him to it.

'Never get tired of watching though. He has a procedure like, always does it the same way, starts by forcing them to drink see. Waste of good rum if you ask me. Makes them open their mouths and pours it down their throat. Oft times they'll choke good and proper. I've seen him empty a whole bottle many a time. Anyways, that done he starts by washing their backs first, then their face, if they'll let him. This one wouldn't, kept turning her head away and shaking like a leaf she was, I could see her body trembling.

'Then he puts his hands on her breasts, well call them breasts if you will, just little soft mounds if you ask me, but with nipples right enough. Keeps fingering them he does. Then he drops his hands lower like, rubbing her stomach, real soft. She starts kicking her legs, tries to pull her hands free. It's no use though. He grabs her neck with one hand and pushes her back, almost throttles her if truth be known. You can guess where the other hand goes. Must have been a good ten minutes he was feeling his way round there. Hurt her too I reckon from the cries she was making.

'The best bit is him trying to undo his trousers. His paunch is that big, can't find his buttons can he—it takes him ages, it does. It's a wonder to me his purple-headed soldier was still standing to attention, by the time he hauls her out of the tub and forces her to the floor. Anyways, gets it where he wants it and bangs away. Rough bastard he is too and bloody long winded—don't know where he gets the energy at his age, must be the drink.

'It's always the same, soon as he's finished, the sweaty old lech calls us back in. We take them back down below and more often than not, we'll take it in turns to give them one too, but not tonight. This one left a trail of blood. Bleeding bad she was, damaged her insides I shouldn't wonder. She'll be dead afore the weeks out, and I'll be throwing her stinking carcass overboard. Still, he's got plenty more to choose from.'

The vivid account of Montague's rape of the girl came as no surprise to Lawson, he had suspected as much. What did shock him was Fletcher's disinterest in the girl herself and a total lack of conscience for the brutal way in which she had been treated, with not a thought given to her suffering. Indeed, all the captives were treated in the same vile way, even worse than the beasts of the field, like human cattle, but sub-human and undeserving of any kindness or pity.

Chapter Nine
Shanghai Tricks

The Black Stag lay at anchor in Bristol dock. Layers of dirt, grime and human excrement had been wiped clean from its lower decks and yet still the stench of death and suffering hung in the air. Lawson added the last items of clothing to his trunk, smiled, and shrugged his shoulders. 'Free at last,' he murmured to himself.

At that moment, Lord Montague entered his cabin unannounced.

'Will you not reconsider your decision, Mr Lawson? I venture another voyage in the current economic climate could prove most advantageous for you. Indeed, the price of sugar has more than trebled in the last quarter and is certain set to rise again.'

'I thank you, no, your Lordship. After three long years away, I am most anxious now to return to my family,' he replied, whilst at the same time trying to hide his disgust for the man addressing him.

Lord Montague, however, was not going to give up without a fight. 'Come, man, three years is nothing in the scheme of things. And, think of it, another profitable trip as a trusted member of the crew and you could go home in a twelve month a wealthy man. My offer remains and I shall be as good as my word. One more voyage, Mr Lawson, as first mate at twice your normal pay and a three percent share of the profit to boot?'

'That is most generous, Lord Montague, but I fear I must abide by my original plan. It is home for me and the joy and comfort of being with my wife and family once more. And, besides, I have more than enough put by to set myself up in an honest trade. The title of shopkeeper will suit me admirably.'

Once more he struggled to hide the look of contempt rising in his eyes as he thought back in time to the voyages he had already completed under this barbaric, ungodly man. 'Man'—the word stuck in his craw, more monster than man. A monster intent on pursuing his despicable, dishonest, and inhuman trade, a feeling of guilt pricked Lawson's own conscience, for he had been a party to it all and was well aware that every coin in his coffer had been purchased with human suffering of the acutest kind.

'Well, if you are sure, I cannot persuade you, I'll say goodbye and good fortune to you. I thank you for your three years of service.' Mr Lawson watched in silent relief as Lord Montague left the cabin. Once alone he continued with his packing. Lord Montague, however, returned to his very different quarters and immediately sent for Mr Fletcher. Mr Fletcher, bosun's mate and a long serving member of the crew arrived in a matter of minutes. He knocked at the door. 'Is that you, Fletcher? Come in if you please.'

A sailor of swarthy complexion, with a vicious looking scar stretching the entire length of his right cheek, from just below the eye to his unshaven, square-shaped chin entered the master's cabin. He seemed edgy. Narrow eyes with a distinct appearance of cunning about them, shifted uneasily, glancing at his Captain and then back at the door through which he had just entered, as if he expected an intruder to burst in on them at any minute. 'Well,' demanded the captain, 'speak up man. Is everything set?'

'Aye, Captain, 'tis all set, just as you instructed,' was the reply.

The captain nodded his approval. 'Good. See to it. I want no mistakes, Mr Fletcher, or you will pay the consequences!'

Bags in hand Mr Lawson stepped out on deck. Squinting in the strong sunshine, he stood for a moment, collecting his thoughts, enjoying the feel of warmth on his back as the heat of the summer sun's rays penetrated his jacket. It was a minute to savour, leaving the ship at last, never to return again. He felt elated and allowed himself to smile.

Boarding the ship was a bevy of bawdy-looking women, rouge-cheeked, with tousled hair and dressed in dirty, crumpled, revealing dresses. Lawson could guess their occupation. They were accompanied by several of the crew, some of whom were carrying large barrels of beer over their shoulders. The smile vanished. The men would enjoy their shore leave to the full. Most would remain on board ship and tragically, families, loved ones at home would be forgotten as their men folk sank into a haze of alcohol and a pit of depravity. But at least the captain would keep his crew. They would wake with sore heads and find themselves at sea again, whatever their intentions had been on arriving in port.

Mr Lawson waited for the gang plank to clear and then made his way down to the quayside. Several groups of people were stood around, including some of the crew. He recognised Fletcher—bosun's mate, a man for whom he had little time. Fletcher and his cronies were standing to one side of the quay, a little way off from everyone else and Fletcher was whispering in their ear, clearly wanting to avoid anyone eavesdropping on their conversation. Lawson moved through the crowds of people and made his way to the wide stone steps which led up to the main harbour and the town. At the top, he turned back for one last glimpse of *The Black Stag*. 'Sorry to be leaving her, I expect?' It was Fletcher. He had left his earlier comrades and had followed Mr Lawson along the quayside.

'Quite the contrary, Mr Fletcher, I am glad to be at liberty again and most eager to be reunited with my family.'

'Never had a family, me. Grew up in the poor house and been at sea since the age of seven. Are you going into town?' Fletcher enquired innocently.

'Yes, the coach to Bath leaves the market square at three this afternoon. I cannot wait to board. My family will meet me at the other end. I may sound a sentimental wretch to you Fletcher, but I long to see them. My youngest son was born in my absence. He celebrates his third birthday next month,' Lawson replied happily.

'Nice place Bath, is it? Never been me.'

They walked along together side by side exchanging idle chit-chat parting company only when they reached the market square. Lawson strode to the coaching office to purchase his ticket. Fletcher meanwhile ambled aimlessly up and down. To anyone watching, he had a preoccupied look about him, and did not even bother glancing into the many brightly decorated shop windows which lined the cobbled street. His earlier comrades passed by without acknowledging him and entered a narrow side-street situated at the far end of the market square. Lawson was surprised to find Fletcher waiting for him when he returned with his ticket.

'Well now,' Fletcher remarked, sounding more hospitable and friendly than Lawson had ever known him, 'seems to me a third birthday should be celebrated'—wet the baby's head like. 'It will be my pleasure to buy you a pint of the finest ale Bristol has to offer. I'm told the Landlord of *The Moon and Sixpence* makes his own brew and that it is a rare treat.'

'I thank you, but no thank you. I have presents to buy and it is now near noon.' Mr Lawson replied firmly.

'Nonsense, tis only the one drink I'm offering, us bosuns don't earn anything like a first mate. A quick pint for old sea comrades to say goodbye, and I won't take no for an answer. Come now, the inn is just there across the road from us. You'll be five minutes at most.' Reluctantly, Lawson allowed himself to be led away. The entrance to the inn was up a cobbled alleyway off one corner of the market square. Lawson shivered slightly as they stepped from bright sunlight into shade. The alley felt cold and smelt dank. They pushed passed a number of men gathered outside and entered in.

The tavern was dimly lit, a single bare candle pressed into the centre of each table and a very few more in simple iron holders attached to the walls flickered reluctantly in an atmosphere almost devoid of oxygen. Lawson found himself coughing as his lungs adjusted to air so thick with tobacco smoke it felt as if he were breathing in treacle. There was a great deal of noise, men talking in raised, animated voices set against a backdrop of raucous laughter. All that, together with the constant commotion caused by dozens of inebriated sailors crammed in like sardines in a tin, inevitably falling and stumbling over each other. Lawson kept a firm hold of his bags as they pressed through the crowd to the bar.

Fletcher directed Lawson to a solitary table situated in an alcove at the far end of the room. The table was placed directly under dark mahogany stairs which led to the upper rooms of the inn, rooms normally used for accommodating overnight guests. Due to the cramped space Lawson chose a chair at the front of the table and sat with his back to the room. Living on a ship for a prolonged period of time made one appreciate space and, in any case, he did not intend to stay long. Sitting where he was, he could make an easy escape. Fletcher returned with two tankards. 'Your very good health,' he said as Lawson took his first sip.

Mr Lawson awoke with a sore, swimming head. He tried to look about him and immediately felt sick. The room and ceiling were spinning! 'If I didn't know better, I'd say I was in the throes of an almighty hangover. I feel as if I've consumed a barrel of brandy all to myself.' Memories began to flood back, Fletcher, the pint of ale, the inn! He did not, however, remember being hit over the head with a cudgel or the Landlord of *The Moon and Sixpence* directing his assailants and Mr Fletcher to an upstairs room where he was held captive for a full two days and forcibly plied with drink at every sign of regaining consciousness.

On the very day that *The Black Stag* was due to set sail, the Landlord of *The Moon and Sixpence* called a constable to his inn. Accusing a semi-conscious and very drunk Mr Lawson of non-payment for drinks he demanded that Lawson be taken to Bristol's debtors' prison until such time as payment for the amount owed was met. Fletcher had immediately summoned his master. Lord Montague arrived in a sedan chair and spoke at length with both the Landlord and the Constable. The bill was settled, with an agreement that Lawson should serve a further voyage in order to repay his debt to Lord Montague. Fletcher and his cronies half-dragged, half-carried Lawson back to the ship where he was thrown into his cabin and the door locked.

He knew at once that he was at sea. He could feel the movement of the ship with its accustomed rise and fall on gentle swells. Lawson also knew that he had been tricked and as that bitter realisation dawned, he swore vehemently under his breath. He was back in his quarters all right and he could guess who's doing this had been. The familiar ship's cabin was dark and airless. Reluctantly his nostrils picked up its usual, unpleasant odour; thick, musty, and stinking of rot as well as something new, the smell of his own vomit.

He pulled himself up in his bed and, rubbing his right temple, immediately winced with pain. A lump resembling a large, boiled egg was sore to the touch of even tender fingers. Looking around he noted with dismay that his bags had been thrown into one corner. Instinctively he moved his hand to feel the inside pocket of his jacket. It was empty. No doubt his bags would have been rifled too. Lawson was only glad that he had already sent money home to his wife and family. 'At least I have that consolation,' he said aloud. Then another thought crossed his mind, and his heart sank. 'Were they still waiting, waiting in vain for his return?'

He could guess what had happened. Next time he would be more careful and make sure of his escape. 'That is if I survive another voyage,' he thought to himself. What a fool he had been! He should have known the captain would have laid plans to bring him back. He knew he was the only one Montague trusted and that without him on board, to watch his back, the Master of *The Black Stag* feared for his life and with good reason.

'Why ever did I go for that drink? I must have been mad.' He could remember taking only one sip from the pint of beer that Fletcher had bought him. The cosh which had struck him must have landed instantly afterwards. He touched the lump again. 'I'm lucky to be alive, damn near fractured my skull.'

Lawson had joined the crew three years before. In hindsight it always amazed him that he had actually applied to join the ship as first mate. The advertisement had been posted in the Bristol Gazette and he had gone in person to seek an audience with the ship's Master, one Lord George Montague, first Lord of Eastlyn Castle, who also happened to be the owner, not just of that particular vessel, *The Black Stag,* but also the entire Montague fleet, four great tall ships in total, all harboured at Bristol dock. His application was accepted immediately. He was thrilled and had written to his wife:

My dearest heart,

You must not be jealous, but I cannot help the tremendous romance I have with this tall ship. The sheer size of The Black Stag is amazing. The length of its decks must be twice that of most other vessels. Indeed, it was only when I stood on the quayside her true size became apparent.

She is a beautiful thing, majestic, magnificent. I cannot begin to describe the great height and breadth of her masts and rigging—they dominate the sky. As for the incredible figurehead—a huge male deer, with gigantic antlers—the sight of it takes one's breath away. This massive structure projects proudly from the prow of the ship. My sweetest girl I can only say that so immense was the impact of this great ship upon me I had to wipe the tears from my eyes. I can honestly say I have never been so awed by a tall ship in my life.

Within days, however, he had realised his mistake. Most of the crew had been recruited from the many rough drinking taverns in Bristol. They were always taken by the trickery of Lord Montague himself. Montague may well have been one of the richest men in England, but he was also one of the most miserly, preferring to take on the role of captain aboard his ship rather than have to pay someone else to do it. He was desperately looking for crew to man his slaving ship and would go to any lengths to get the men he needed, cut throats and vagabonds alike.

Manning a slave ship was a dangerous business. In terms of health alone there were serious risks. This was because illness, dysentery in particular, the terrible heat and the threat of slave rebellions made the trip to Africa arduous if not fatal. Sailors tried to avoid joining a slaving voyage and of those that did, many did not return and were buried at sea.

Consequently, foul play was one of the few ways that captains could get sailors. They would pay pub landlords to help them trick men into joining the slaving voyages. Pub landlords would lend money to sailors so that they could afford to buy drinks. Once the sailor was drunk and not minding his "p's and q's", in other words making sure he could pay for his pints and quarts of ale, he would run up a bill he would be unable to meet. The corrupt landlord would then give him a choice. Either the sailor would go to jail, or, to repay the debt, could join the crew of a slaving ship bound for Africa. Most sailors would choose the second option rather than go to jail. The landlords would be paid for their help and so recover their money that way and the sailors would be forced to pay the debt from their wages for the voyage. Often, they worked for nothing!

Lawson hated the inhumanity he witnessed on these voyages. Most sailors on their first slaving voyage might not have liked the job of taking slaves, but by the second or third voyage they were used to it. As a result, there were times when he found himself sickened by their cruelty and hard-heartedness. He often wondered why it was that he had not become hardened to such suffering and was grateful that he remained compassionate to the plight of the slaves. It also surprised him that he had not at first realised that *The Black Stag* had been purpose built as a slave ship. He knew all there was to know about boat design, for his own father had been a master ship builder.

In a later letter to his wife, he had written:

The lower deck should have given the game away immediately and especially the airports just above the waterline! You know if you are carrying sugar or timber or manufactured goods you don't need to ventilate that lower deck, but if you are carrying a human cargo you do. So, you will understand how sad I am that this beautiful tall ship hides a malevolent purpose beneath. I must be a part of this for three years. That is the contract I have signed. I cannot wait to be free of it.

He did not write to his wife of the disgust he felt at the considerable number of slaves who died along the way; their bodies thrown over the side of the ship to the sharks that would follow all the way across, from Africa to the Caribbean Islands for which they were bound.

Chapter Ten
Treachery Unveiled

There was a knock on the cabin door and Lawson was abruptly pulled back into the present. Without waiting to be invited in, Lord Montague entered the room. 'Ah, I see you are recovered, Mr Lawson. I had hoped as much. I trust you will be joining me for dinner this evening.' Mr Lawson remained silent and nodded his head very briefly, just once. 'I hope finding yourself back on board is not too disconcerting?'

'I am only curious as to how that came about, your Lordship. My contract of employment being over, it was my intention to return to my family.'

'There was a skirmish at the inn where you were drinking. I understand from Mr Fletcher that you were struck by some rascal or other. Quite a blow I believe. It rendered you unconscious. Once I had been informed of your predicament, I had no choice but to have you brought back here.'

'Forgive me, your Lordship, but as you know well, I had money about me. Could you not have left me with the landlord? He would have been well paid for his services.'

There was a slight pause before the reply came. 'It would have been impossible to have left you at the mercy of the mob, my dear boy, with riot and mayhem all about. You might have been killed. Not knowing who to send word to of your circumstances posed another grievous problem. Had I known your wife's address I could have considered leaving you at the inn, but as it was, I had no option but to bring you back here. And in any case, you had been robbed, the Landlord could find no money about you. I myself was called to settle the bill.'

Now it was Mr Lawson's turn to remain silent. The two men stood unmoving, staring at one another like two bare-knuckle fighters eyeing each other up, looking for a weakness. It was Lawson who broke the silence. 'I did not think unconscious men could drink, your Lordship, and am at a loss as to how I therefore came to build up any kind of a bill.'

'Well, there it is,' Montague replied in a steely tone of voice. 'I was not in a position to argue with the landlord or the constable and had no option but to take their account of events.'

Once again there was an awkward silence. Finally, with his mind racing and thoughts of the long voyage ahead Lawson took stock of his situation and decided upon the most sensible course of action. As a result, his reply sounded almost grateful. 'I thank you for your concern and as things have turned out it is just as well that I am come back to the ship. My money does appear to be gone, stolen, I fear. As a result, I will undoubtedly need this voyage to recoup my losses.'

'Capital, capital! I am glad you see it that way,' replied his Lordship.

'My main concern is my wife and my children. They will have been awaiting my return with great anticipation and by now I suspect will be most anxious and concerned as to my safety and my whereabouts.'

'Have no fear on that score Mr Lawson. I sent word immediately you were back on board. Knowing that we had to sail with the tide, I felt it only right and proper to inform your family of your situation.' Lawson registered the contradiction and the lie immediately but made no comment. 'Well, well,' continued his Lordship, 'I'll leave you to unpack your belongings. Dinner at eight sharp, as always,' and with that he left the squalor of his first mate's cabin to return to the luxury of his own.

With a sense of outrage and relief Lawson watched him go. For the life of him he couldn't decide whether the captain was a buffoon or an intellectual. His grotesque bodily features, his enormous girth, his bloated overhanging paunch, his sagging, cumbersome folds of fat, the swollen red face, with its bright puce, mottled, constantly perspiring skin made him obnoxious to the eye. This combined with his contemptible qualities as a man, made him in Lawson's opinion the most hateful of men. Lord Montague was old, lecherous, dissolute; corpulent beyond measure; constantly drunk and absolutely unscrupulous in his choice of means for procuring money. Lawson suspected the captain was not above stealing even from him. But it was his cruelty and vindictiveness which he despised the most.

'How does his wife stand to be with him,' he thought to himself. He had noted the mouth sore had still not healed and the rash on his hands looked even more pronounced. He also wondered if any hair remained underneath the wig. Indeed, he had seen him de-wigged on the last voyage when he had collapsed in a drunken stupor, and he had almost been completely bald then.

In fact, Lord Montague's wife was as disgusted by her husband as any woman could be. She had been forced to marry him at the tender age of fifteen and was a good thirty years younger than her revolting husband. But being one of the wealthiest men in the land, he was viewed by her family as an excellent catch. Her father's estate had been in debt, for heavy gambling on his part had brought it to its knees. Lady Ellen Forsythe had no choice in the matter; the wedding was arranged even without her knowledge. Her parents simply expected her to do her duty whilst they themselves were overjoyed at the prospect of the two great houses joining. Indeed, not only was Montague prepared to pay a handsome dowry, but he would also settle their debts, proving the ideal son-in-law and the answer to all their financial prayers.

Sacrificing Ellen therefore to a loveless marriage, a marriage to her made in hell seemed of little importance if the family name, reputation and, most importantly, the solvency of the Forsythe estate could be saved. So it was that a timid, pretty girl, with long blond hair and radiant blue eyes became mistress of Eastlyn Castle and the miserable wife of Lord Montague.

Indeed, Ellen had only seen Montague on two occasions before her wedding day. Their first meeting had taken place one summer's afternoon when she and her two younger sisters had been down by the lake, attempting to draw charcoal sketches a pair of black swans with their seven cygnets. Ellen was assisting her sisters in securing their sheets of paper to their easels. 'When you start a charcoal drawing, it's best to work vertically on your easel,' she advised, trying to remember all the tips the art teacher had given her before his departure. 'This allows the charcoal dust to fall away, and lets you see the whole drawing without any distortion or foreshortening like you might see if working on a flat surface.'

'She's such a clever girl and so talented,' she heard her mother say behind her. Turning around she had watched the approach of a fat, old man, dressed in the finest clothes she had ever seen and wearing a ridiculously small tricorne hat on top of an elaborate powdered wig. Her initial reaction was a desire to laugh. 'One sharp gust of wind,' she thought to herself, 'and that'll be in the lake, or one of the swans will be wearing it.'

The man, Lord George Montague, was accompanied by both her parents. Lady Sybil Forsythe, walking to his left, seemed to feel the need to keep curtsying as she struggled to maintain his brisk pace. Lord Algernon Forsythe, in contrast, and to the man's right, matched the man's pace with ease, but for reasons as yet unclear to Ellen, kept bowing and waving his right hand as if he were greeting royalty.

'These are my daughters, Lord Montague,' her father announced proudly. 'Ellen, my eldest, has just turned fifteen, Harriet, the middle one is eleven, and Catherine, the baby of the family, turned eight last month. Well, step forward, Ellen, let his lordship get a good look at you.'

Puzzled and confused, Ellen did as she was bid. Montague's eyes surveyed her physique from head to foot and as he did so, Ellen felt herself strangely anxious. At close quarters, she noticed he was perspiring heavily and that his skin had an odd, red, mottled tinge to it. He did not look healthy at all. But it was the expression in the narrow, pig-like eyes which disturbed her most. A more mature, experienced woman would have described it as lustful, but even to Ellen, who was not worldly wise at all, it was as if he were undressing her in his mind. She felt naked, exposed, and humiliated. Inadvertently she crossed her arms across her chest, covering, hiding her breasts from his penetrating stare.

Much to her relief, Montague now switched his attention to her two younger sisters. As he admired their sketches, she watched him place his right hand, first on Harriet's back and then on Catherine's. The unwelcome hand seemed to linger here, as if her younger sister were some kind of family pet. She watched the hand gently stroking, rubbing, and patting, and felt her own skin crawl.

'He's horrid,' said Catherine, as soon as the party of adults had gone. 'I didn't like him touching me at all.'

'He was horribly sweaty too,' Harriet added in a derogatory tone of voice, 'and did you notice he stank of brandy?'

The second meeting happened ten weeks later. Ellen had finally succumbed to parental pressure and had reluctantly agreed to the marriage. The agreement had been reached after weeks of confinement to her room, starvation, scolding and even a number of beatings from her father. Had she been privy to the joys of a happy marriage, she might never have consented to Lord George's proposal. Sadly, this was not the case. Her father had quickly captivated her mother, with his dashing looks, elegant manners, and clever way of talking. Despite the fact that it was common knowledge he had lost his own fortune through obsessive gambling, and that his estate was heavily mortgaged and owing a mountain of debts, Sybil accepted his proposal of marriage immediately it was made.

Unlike her future husband, Sybil was plain, stupid, and dull. But she was however the heiress to a large fortune. They all but raced down the aisle and within a fortnight, Algernon had settled his debts and put his estate in order. Less than a month after their wedding, his true colours were already being displayed. He could no longer be at the trouble of showing his new bride any attention. Indeed, he made it quite clear that her company and conversation were irksome to him. It pained Ellen to see the way he treated her, and she often wondered how they had come to have any children at all.

On the morning of Ellen's second meeting with Montague, she had been dressed by not one, but two ladies' maids, her own and her mother's. To her surprise and for the first time in a long time, she had been bought a new dress. The dress was low cut at the bodice and tight fitting at the waist. It took the women over an hour to lace up the under bust corset to achieve its twenty-inch fitting. As they pulled hard on the stays it was sheer agony for Ellen. When they had finished, she felt she could scarcely breathe, let alone walk. Another noticeable effect of the corset was to enhance an already ripe bosom and had the neckline been just one centimetre lower, her nipples would undoubtedly have been exposed.

She was summoned to the library to meet her fiancé. Struggling to breathe and taking the tiniest of steps, she almost glided across the carpet, her voluptuous breasts and deep, dark cleavage leading the way. Montague was talking to her sisters as she arrived, his hands once again touching their shoulders, their backs, and his face, she observed, was much too close to theirs for comfort. 'He has no social decorum at all,' spoke a warning voice in her head.

It was a distinctly odd meeting. Even with the sight of that painful but provocative dress displaying her nubile breasts, he seemed almost disinterested in her. His attention was markedly more focused on her younger sisters, Catherine in particular. Ellen found herself strangely pleased, relieved that he had not latched himself onto her, or, more importantly, that she had been spared having to make conversation with a man she despised, albeit that she was to marry. She hoped against hope he would show an equal lack of interest after they were married. Several hours later, she happily waved his coach and four a more than merry goodbye.

The Montague family owed their huge wealth initially to the mining of slate. Their lands were rich in this particular resource, and they could well be described as one of the founding families of this lucrative industry. Already having more money than he knew what to do with, it was not long before the first Lord Eastlyn was informed by close acquaintances that he was missing a most profitable enterprise. Sugar had become the most sought-after commodity in the Western world and was worth its weight in gold. It was a sound investment and brought a return not even George could have guessed at.

He congratulated himself on his success and commissioned the building of several tall ships, the Montague fleet, the prize of which was *The Black Stag*. These ships carried many cargoes between Africa, the Caribbean and England, cargo which included tobacco, cotton, rum, molasses, and sugar. *The Black Stag's* main cargo, however, from Africa to the Caribbean were the slaves needed to work the Montague plantations. Indeed, the main source of labour on all the sugar plantations were Black slaves, kidnapped from their homelands in Africa and forced into a life of cruel, brutal, and unrelenting bondage.

On this voyage *The Black Stag* had sailed her normal route to one of the many slave ports along the African coast to collect her cargo. For Lawson, the days and weeks had dragged by. He had kept busy, doing his job to the best of his ability, and taking command whenever the captain was the worse for drink. The tedium of life on board ship was broken only by the occasional flogging or keelhauling, punishments meted out to any sailor refusing orders or falling asleep on watch. Lawson was not the only sore head to wake up on ship having been shanghaied from a waterside tavern, hence resentment was rife and rebellion waiting to surface at every opportunity.

An elderly man, suffering from the effects of too much rum, following a well-deserved order to, 'splice the main brace' had fallen asleep on his night watch. Fletcher had him thrown in the booby hatch until the weather set fair, at which point Captain Montague was called to decide the man's fate. Depending on the Captain's level of inebriation no one ever received less than ten lashes, some poor souls had ten times that number. On this occasion the unfortunate wretch was sentenced to fifty.

The order 'All hands on deck' was always given for these punishments. It was an opportunity to make an example of the offending sailor, leaving shipmates under no illusion as to what would happen if rules were broken, or orders disobeyed. Thus, the rest of the crew would assemble to bear witness to the plight of the man to be whipped. On ships with a full quota of men, the space on deck could be very limited. Often the cat 'o' nine tails would cause injury to onlookers as well as the person being punished, hence the expression, 'not enough room to swing a cat!'

Lawson could never decide which was more painful, the actual flogging or the treatment given to the prisoner afterwards. Cut down from the whipping mast, they would be taken back to the booby hatch. The fortunate few would be forced to drink a goodly portion of rum before being tied face down on a bunk. Mouths would be prised open to insert a wooden stick between the teeth to prevent them from biting through their tongue and then salt would be applied to the wounds. Lawson always thought that their screaming at this time was even worse than when they were being whipped. Due to the intensity of the pain, some lucky souls would fall into unconsciousness.

It was early December when *The Black Stag* reached her destination, a wide horseshoe shaped bay of golden sand edged by a crystal clear, blue sea. Had it not been for the large Portuguese fortress which dominated the landscape one might have been forgiven for describing the scene as picturesque. However, the huge stone castle built high on the cliff top, cast long dark shadows from its base, stretching out like creeping, ominous black fingers not only across the beach but out into the sea. In these shallow waters the shadows here resembled the tentacles of some monstrous, obsidian-like octopus lying in wait for its prey.

On arrival the ship had been anchored a little way offshore. Lawson himself had remained on board, whilst Lord Montague, the ship's Doctor and a number of armed guards were rowed to the prison jetty. Lawson watched them disappear from view as they were escorted by the slave traders into the interior of the slave fort, where the merchandise, Negro slaves, men, women, and children were to be put on display.

What Lawson did not know was that at the slave forts the captive Africans were placed in holding cells, where they sometimes waited for prolonged periods for the slave ships to collect them. As a result of the suffocating and unhealthy conditions in which they were imprisoned, many Africans died while waiting to be collected. There were also gender differences in the experiences of the enslaved, for example the women were targets for rape and physical abuse. Conditions were made worse by the long waiting period, which could vary from days to weeks to months. By the time the tall ships arrived many were already dying. Disease was rife amongst the slaves, diseases which might put the whole crew at risk, not least the ship's captain.

It was the job of *The Black Stag's* Surgeon to examine them and eliminate those who were either sick or not fit for purpose. On this occasion, having selected over two hundred slaves in total a deal was struck between Lord Montague and the traders. Lawson was sent word what cargo was to be brought up from the ship's hold and sent ashore. He was well aware therefore what items had been offered. In this case, the purchase of the "human merchandise" had depended on guns, ammunition, and beads.

He watched, sick at heart as this new cargo of Negroes were brought on board. It took three hours to fill the ship and was not an easy job. He noted that the refractory ones were clapped in irons or forced to drink rum. Many were carried aboard in a stupefied condition. Once on board they were stowed in a sitting position, with the knees drawn up so closely that they could scarcely breathe, much less move.

Had Lawson not seen with his own eyes the suffering those poor wretches endured he would not have believed it. What he witnessed on those dreadful voyages would live with him forever. The wailing, the pitiful cries, children homesick, men and women horribly seasick, half starved, naked, crying for air, for water, the strong killing the weak for one more mouthful of bread or for another foot of space. He would watch the hold become a perfect charnel house of death and misery.

Montague, like Lawson, also wrote home to his wife. However, his was a different letter which contained the following information.

Our black cattle are intolerably noisy, and I'm almost melted in the midst of the two hundred or more of them. However, I am satisfied that we have fulfilled our objective. The Black Stag is full. It was my intention that she should take as many as possible. The cargo of a vessel such as she of a hundred tons, or little more, is calculated to purchase from two hundred and twenty to two hundred and fifty slaves. We have the latter number, and most seem in reasonable condition. I anticipate we shall deliver a goodly two hundred at least to our plantations in the Caribbean.

Chapter Eleven
The Dawn Raid

For as long as Nabila could remember, her people had been at war with many tribes whose lands bordered Dahomey, not least the Yoruba tribe. Tribal hostilities had existed for centuries. There were ancient feuds, old grievances such as disputes over land, hunting rights or water, and in the case of the Yoruba—adding fuel to the fire—they had embarked on a campaign of surprise attacks, creating hatred, animosity, and fear. Deep divisions persisted between the tribes, setting one against the other and making them bitter, sworn enemies. Yoruba raiding parties would come in the night to plunder and pillage Dahomey villages. Men, women, and children would perish at the hands of merciless Yoruba warriors, warriors wielding vicious blades intent on killing, maiming, or mutilating their victims. Survivors would often be kidnapped and sold into slavery by their evil captors.

But Nabila herself had never been just a defenceless villager. As a skilled Amazonian warrior, she had been trained in the use of the javelin, the bow and arrow, and a deadly adversary in close combat fighting, armed with her twin daggers which she wielded with lethal, almost brutal efficiency. In those days, Nabila had commanded profound respect and had earned a well-deserved reputation as a formidable fighter.

Nabila sat watching the sun slowly rise above the jagged peaks of the western escarpment, its light reflected in the rose-pink waters of the lake which stretched along the entire length of those rugged foothills. A huge flurry of flamingos, taking advantage of a brisk morning wind, soared high into the air, the sound of their loud nasal honking breaking in on Nabila's daydream. They swooped noisily towards her, and then as one body, veered sharply away, slowly disappearing, like some vast peach-coloured cloud over the mountaintops. To Nabila it looked as if part of the lake itself was flying off into the distance.

She stood, drinking in the cool air, and admiring the dawn's new colours, as low sunlight stained the familiar acacia trees bright orange. Something moved in the shadows behind her and sent her heart into her mouth. 'I am glad to see you are awake.' With relief Nabila recognised the voice of Wangari, leader of the Amazonian army to which she belonged. 'We are needed,' Wangari continued. 'The King has sent me to fetch you. He has received disturbing news of an attack on a Dahomey village by a wild elephant. We are ordered to slay the beast. A man has been killed, gored to death. Come, we must leave immediately!'

Arming herself with her weapons, Nabila followed Wangari out into the bush. As they ran side by side, Wangari continued with her account. 'It is thought that the red cloak the man had been wearing had incited the elephant to chase him. The creature is terrorising his village, destroying all their crops, and trampling many huts into the ground.'

The two women ran tirelessly covering mile after mile until at last the village concerned was before them. Almost hidden in long grass they made their first discovery, the body of the red cloaked native, completely crushed and with his limbs torn off. There was no sign of the creature itself, only the damage and mayhem it had left behind. Moments later a runner from the palace arrived breathless, saying that the bull elephant was even now attacking the royal quarters. Other warriors had rallied to protect the royal household, but the animal appeared unstoppable, and the men were in desperate need of help. 'Hurry,' he had begged, 'you must hurry!'

Fearing for the King's safety Wangari and Nabila raced to the palace. They arrived to find the crazed bull was killing man after man. Warriors were bravely trying to fend the enraged creature off with their raised spears only to have them broken like mere twigs. Now unarmed, the defenceless men would be tossed in the air like rag dolls, gouged by the mighty tusks or trampled underfoot.

Nabila watched in horror as arrow after arrow failed to penetrate the elephant's thick hide. There was nothing else she could do but to attack at close quarters. Drawing her short knives, "Giver of Night and Taker of Life" from their sheaths she sprinted towards the monstrous, towering beast, crying her war cry, as if fear was a stranger to her. In truth Nabila's heart was pounding furiously, she had never seen a bull so large before.

The maddened beast turned to face her, rocking back and forth on its enormous feet, ears flapping wildly shaking its head from side to side whilst it continued to trumpet and rumble loudly. Just then the elephant stopped dead in its tracks and directly eyeballed Nabila as she sprinted across the ground towards it. Tossing its head back to roar noisily at the many warriors surrounding it, the rogue bull began to charge towards her. As it approached, she waited her moment and at the last minute jumped fearlessly onto its massive head, unawares that at the same time Wangari had hurled her javelin at its underbelly. Both warriors hit their mark. Nabila plunged her two short knives deep into the great bull's eyes. The wild staring eyes were no more only a mess of torn, sightless sinew and deep wells of blood remained.

A new sound ripped through the air, an ear-splitting shriek, followed by a strange, gurgling noise which seemed to last but briefly. Then the oddest thing: no sound at all only a deathly, uncanny silence. As Nabila realised the elephant was falling, keeling over, she tried to jump clear, but in so doing had been caught on one of the rogue bull's enormous ivory tusks. It had pierced her side. With hands pressed firmly against the wound, she landed on the ground some feet away from the fallen beast. Looking back at it she instantly spotted Wangari's javelin sticking out of its chest. Then, had come the overwhelming feeling of relief, the creature was dead, and the village made safe once more.

In minutes she was surrounded by people wanting to congratulate her, to thank her for her bravery. Wangari took hold of her arm and led her away from the gathering crowd and into the palace. As she entered through a doorway, she turned to look at the rogue elephant for one last time and was amazed to see children already swinging from its tusks and clambering over its now lifeless body. Minutes later, Wangari was dressing and treating her wound. It was then, and much to Nabila's surprise, that the King himself arrived to praise her courage.

Nabila lived in a mighty town lying at the heart of the Bight of Benin. Its King, Nazzor Eze, dominated the political landscape at the time. His word was law, and his vast armies did their best to preserve the King's power and protect the Dahomey people over whom he ruled. The town was surrounded by a mud wall with a circumference estimated at six miles. The wall was pierced by four gates and protected by an outer ditch five feet deep, filled with a dense thicket of prickly acacia. Within the wall's small clusters of earthen structures, in the shape of round huts with thatched roofs, were separated by fields.

At its northern end and on higher ground was the Royal Palace, consisting of terraced rows of larger structures with wooden walkways built above ground level connecting each dwelling to the next. In front of the palace was a wide grassed square and beyond that the marketplace. The southern border was dominated by the stockade. Here, contained within an inner mud and stone wall were the living quarters of the garrison, housing over one thousand fighting men.

Nabila's wound had healed quickly. She was now fully fit and back on guard duty. 'Let us hope the rest of the night passes peacefully. A few hours more and we can return to the village. Your turn to cook breakfast,' said Wangari cheerfully, coming to sit at her side. Nabila nodded and forced a smile. There had been rumours that the Yoruba were planning another raid and hence, despite Wangari's comforting words, she felt her body still tense and alert, her ears pricked for any warning sound. The two women were guarding the northern gate and it had been a long and difficult night, made worse by the sudden arrival of Princess Adana in search of Nabila. The latter had been furious with Adana's maid for allowing the little girl into undertaking such a mission. Harsh words had been spoken as a result. The maid would not repeat the exercise, that was certain!

A solitary pelican, its white wings dyed apricot by the rising sun, soared low over Nabila's head. The sound of its sudden arrival, like cloth tearing, sent Nabila's heart into her throat. Wangari too was on her feet and staring out across the bush land. As the shadow of the bird flashed across them, Nabila felt her mouth dry and an increasing sense of panic. Wangari had only just a minute ago dismissed both Faiza and Tisha to escort Adana back to the palace. Adana's unexpected arrival had caused considerable consternation. It was far too dangerous for the little princess to remain with them, guarding as they were, the gateway into the village which was furthest from the stockade. Reinforcements if needed, would take some time to arrive and Nabila knew only too well that they would not be relieved of their duty for at least another two hours. Should there be an attack, she and Wangari would have to fight alone.

Her eyes strained across the landscape, looking for any sign of movement. The wild beauty of the rift valley in which they lived was lost upon them. They did not see the red stone craters, the magnificent lava falls or the lily-strewn lakes, their eyes saw only a savage and treacherous country full of danger and brooding menace. Wangari stepped back and without speaking gestured to Nabila to close the gate. The two women worked quickly, the heavy wooden gate was securely fastened in place and the giant holding beam rapidly lowered into position. As Nabila pushed the first of the ten spiked poles used for additional defence through the gate and attempted to lodge it securely in the ground, the attack began. Without warning, four Yoruba warriors suddenly leapt onto the heavy timbered doorway and began to climb over.

Nabila scrambled back, clutching at the bow resting on her shoulder with one hand whilst trying to retrieve an arrow from her quiver with the other. Wangari had prepared with more haste and her arrow hit its mark with accuracy, penetrating clean through the throat of one of the invaders. Now it was Nabila's turn, a second arrow pierced the eye of another soldier, although in truth Nabila had been aiming for his torso. Wangari shot again, the arrow splitting bone and flesh as it lodged in the shoulder of the attacker.

Wave after wave of Yoruba warriors stormed the gateway and still the two women fought on undeterred, though they were hugely outnumbered. Bows were thrown aside as their short twin blades were drawn for close hand to hand fighting. Calling on her God for protection, Nabila fought like a woman possessed, believing she could not die, not even be injured, such was the strength of her faith. Time and again blade after blade struck her body, but Nabila fought on as if unaware of her injuries.

Nabila felt no fear, no pain, only blind anger. She did not hear the reinforcements arriving; she did not hear the screams of the injured or dying, neither did she see the vicious descent of the cudgel which finally brought her to the ground. Two days later Nabila regained consciousness. She was lying on a bed of animal furs, in the safety of her own thatched hut. Her eyes slowly focused to see Zina standing in the open doorway, as if on guard duty. Adana was kneeling at her side and holding her hand. 'The little princess has not left your side for a single moment, and she has had hold of your hand the whole time. She believes the spirits cannot take you if she holds you here in this life,' said Zina, Adana's old wet-nurse smiling warmly. 'Now you are awake I will fetch the King.'

'You're not going to die are you, Nabila? Father said you might!' the little princess enquired, with tears brimming in her brown eyes.

'No little one, Nabila is magic, she will never die,' was the reply. 'I have prayed to the Gods, and they protect me. Nabila will never leave you, I promise.' Nabila enjoyed a short convalescence. Except for the village witch doctor, who believed that Nabila had been given great spiritual, almost supernatural powers, she amazed everyone, in how quickly her body healed. Deep, vicious wounds inflicted by Yoruba blades during the raid and evil-looking scars had become barely visible in little more than a week, whilst Wangari with fewer and less serious injuries remained bedridden for some time.

Nabila visited Bello, the village craftsman. He was a bald, bent, toothless old man, rumoured to be over a hundred years old, but with a reputation for his special craft which circulated the whole of the Bight of Benin, not just Dahomey land. Knowing of his exceptional skills, people came from far and wide to see him. Nabila had a particular request to ask. Bello was a skilled carver of wood, and he made all the talismans that were used in the many voodoo rites practised at the time.

Talismans were bought and sold as fetishes. These could be statues representing voodoo gods, dried animal heads, or other body parts. They were often sold with good intention, a need for medicine perhaps or for the spiritual powers that the fetishes were believed to hold. There was also a dark side, however, and it was equally as common for voodoo to be used by participants to summon evil spirits enabling them to cast hexing spells or curses upon adversaries.

The Voodoo religion with its countless deities could be terrifying at times, causing demonic possessions, and requiring animal sacrifices. Many of the voodoo rituals conducted by Nabila's people were incredibly elaborate, steeped in secret languages and involving spirit possessed dances. Often special diets had to be eaten by the voodoo priests and priestesses to prepare them for the scared ritual to be carried out. The ancestral dead were thought to walk among the living during the hooded dances. Touching the dancer during this spirit possessed trance was believed to be dangerous enough to kill the offender. A belief in the power of the spirit world was deeply entrenched in Nabila and all her tribespeople. So it was that shortly after leaving Bello, Nabila paid a visit to her brother, Adiamo, to arrange for a very special voodoo rite to take place.

Adiamo was the village witch doctor. The people relied on him to conduct many functions. If a member of your family was ill, it was Adiamo you turned to. But it was not just healing for which he was required. He would often perform ancient rituals or undertake religious ceremonies to call or pacify the spirits and it was he who held the initiation ceremonies for new priests and priestesses. Adiamo also excelled in telling fortunes, reading dreams, casting spells, invoking protections, and creating potions for various purposes. These potions were for anything from love spells to death spells; all for a hefty fee of course. Adiamo was a very wealthy man.

A price was agreed and Adiamo whole heartedly consented to Nabila's request, informing her that she would need to bring a full-grown cockerel for sacrifice to the Gods in order to perform the required rite. She was also told to bring a sample of Adana's hair and fingernails and instructed that fresh blood would be taken from Nabila herself during the final part of the ceremony. Nabila assured Adiamo that everything would be provided and so it was that the ritual of embodiment, known as Caligri, spirit possession, was arranged. All Nabila needed now, was the doll.

Bello, true to his word made a wonderful, lifelike talisman for Nabila. He had in fact carved a beautiful wooden doll with the face of an angel, but an angel nevertheless which could easily have been mistaken for Adana. Bello delivered his gift in secrecy and a delighted Nabila could barely wait to give it to her little, royal princess.

Nabila went missing for a whole night. She returned next morning, black lipped, fatigued and with eyes swollen and reddened as if from crying. But she was anything but sad. Quite the reverse in fact, she was ecstatically happy. Adiamo had done his work and the doll was ready. Adiamo himself, however, had not seemed quite so content at the night's events. He wondered whether Nabila had fully understood the power of the doll and the inherent dangers which it now possessed. 'I must warn you Nabila, you will need to be careful how you use the doll. It has power beyond your comprehension.'

Nabila pretended to listen, but not even Adiamo's warning could lesson her joy. She took no notice of his words, choosing to ignore them. In any case, as she had told him herself, she did not dream so there was no danger of Adana being frightened by something Nabila did not intend her to see. As for immortality, that did not concern her either. If the doll now contained part of her spirit, her soul, so that she could not die unless the doll was destroyed, so much the better. She could fight in battle fearlessly, secure in the knowledge that she could come to no harm. 'I will be the greatest warrior of all time,' she had boasted to Adiamo.

'Be careful what you crave,' he had replied. 'Immortality may become a burden. Life is sweet when we are young and virile. You will not die Nabila, but you will age. There may come a time when all those you loved are dead and gone and you are left alone, suspended in time, without purpose, joy, or human comfort. Remember my words and remember too that this doll is the key. For death to take you, she must be destroyed.'

As usual Adana had taken supper with Nabila. Every night after they had eaten Nabila would tell Adana a story, always with a happy conclusion and then put her to bed. Nabila would stay by the bedside of her young charge until she fell asleep, just as she had done on the night before the raid. As Nabila helped Adana into bed, she asked a question. 'Do you think you have room for one more in that bed?'

'Oh, are you going to sleep in my bed?' was the excited reply.

'No,' said Nabila, 'but your new friend would like to.' Nabila pulled the doll from under the blankets, where she had hidden it earlier. Adana's face lit up in an instant. She squealed with delight and taking hold of the doll, pulled it to her, kissing its face several times over.

'Oh, Nabila, she is the most beautiful doll in the world. Is she really for me?'

'Yes,' replied Nabila laughing, 'and she needs a name. What will you call her?'

'I'm going to call her Idema. Yes. Idema. Do you like it?'

'I think it a lovely name,' answered Nabila. 'I have given you that doll for a reason and you must now make me a promise.'

'What promise?' asked Adana looking intrigued.

Nabila took hold of Adana's shoulders and staring directly into the child's eyes, she spoke in a most serious tone. 'If ever you wake in the night and find yourself alone or afraid, you will find comfort in Idema. You must promise you will never again come looking for me or anyone else for that matter. You will stay here in your room and cuddle Idema to you in the safety of your own bed. Idema is a magic doll, and she will protect you in my absence. Now listen carefully to what I say. Idema's powers are many, Adana. If I am not here to tell you your bedtime story Idema will bring you a wonderful dream whilst you sleep. Now do you promise never to leave the palace alone again?' Nabila gave her charge a piercing look, but it was clear Adana was only half-listening.

'Will she be able to tell stories about you, and if you have been fighting, how many enemies you have killed in battle?' Adana asked as she jumped up and down in her excitement, whilst at the same time flapping her arms like a wild goose taking off the water.

'Of course,' was Nabila's immediate and amused reply. 'Now, keep still for goodness's sake before you start flying round the room, and give me that promise I asked for.'

'I promise,' was the solemn reply as lips opened in a wide smile and wings stopped beating.

Chapter Twelve
King Nazzor Eze

It is midday on a humid, hot, and blustery day in Nabila's village. For many weeks now there has been a drought and the parched ground in front of the royal palace is covered in dry, red dirt. People have gathered from miles around. There is to be a display by the Dahomean troops, and the square is packed with spectators, eager to watch their troops perform. Crammed so tightly together, they are an easy target for a mischievous wind, which seems to delight in sending red dust clouds spinning and swirling across the open square, blasting grit into unsuspecting eyes. Gust after gust torments the waiting crowd, lifting the loose sand from beneath rows of assembled feet and hurling it into unprotected faces. Many hands are raised to shield them from this onslaught, as eyes close sharply to avoid the entry of unwanted dirt.

The drought is about to end. On the horizon huge cumulonimbus clouds can be seen approaching. Like giant white mushrooms and extending several miles across, these dense, towering, vertical clouds move ever nearer, their anvil-like tops dominating the skyline.

On one side of a huge, open square right in front of the royal enclosure, with its terraced rows of earthen huts, Nassor Eze, the King, is seated on a large throne, draped in animal skins. Two slaves stand either side of him, holding and continuously waving giant fans made of ostrich feathers in an attempt to cool him. Their efforts are in vain. In the sticky, oppressive atmosphere, sweat pours in rivulets from his brow, collecting in salty pools between the deep furrows of his expansive flesh.

He is a proud, clever man, much feared throughout the land. His country, Dahomey is renowned as a "Black Sparta", a fiercely militaristic society bent on conquest, whose soldiers strike fear into their enemies all along what is still known as the Slave Coast. The whole tribe has gathered to watch a display by his two armies. Manoeuvres begin despite the threat of an impending rainstorm. The tall, lean, and muscular Wangari is eager to show off the finest Amazonian unit in her army. These warriors are not only skilled with the bow and arrow but reputed to be the best close quarter fighters in the kingdom, armed as they are with two short, razor sharp daggers. Wangari wishes to impress her King and outdo her male rivals, the Spear warriors led by Waitimu.

To the left of his King, Waitimu stands proudly. Behind him are his army, kneeling on the red dirt in silent ranks. These three hundred heavily armed soldiers have already performed for their King. Nabila had watched with special interest as Waitimu marched them into the square. Once assembled, they had begun a mock assault on a series of defences designed to represent an enemy capital. The Dahomean troops are a terrifying sight, barefoot and brandishing heavy, spiked wooden clubs and fearsome looking spears. A few, known as Reapers, are armed with gleaming three-foot-long straight razors, each wielded two-handed and capable of slicing a man clean in two.

Now it is Wangari's turn. There is a distant, low rumble of thunder as she commands her female warriors into action. They advance in silence, reconnoitring. Their first obstacle is a wall of huge piles of acacia branches bristling with needle-sharp thorns, forming a barricade that stretches the length of the square. The troops rush it furiously, as if impervious to the wounds that the two-inch-long thorns inflict. After scrambling to the top, they mime hand-to-hand combat with an imaginary foe, fall back and scale the thorn wall a second time. Standing on top of the thorn covered branches they signal to their left. Another squadron of soldiers storm a line of huts and drag a group of cowering prisoners, bound, and trussed, captured during that Yoruba early dawn raid to where Nassor Eze sits assessing the performance.

Meanwhile, two more of Wangari's fighters haul a dead leopard to the far right of the square. Its paws are tied to a wooden frame tall enough to ensure that its body is raised to its full height. The head hangs limply. The women lift up the head making sure the mouth is open and that the vicious teeth are on full view. They remain where they are, unflinching. Twelve of Wangari's finest archers, including Nabila herself, line up on the left of the square, some forty yards from the leopard. They each take an arrow and at a signal from Wangari, the bows are drawn, and the arrows released. Twelve arrows simultaneously enter the leopard's mouth with a loud thud.

Nabila steps into the centre of the square for it is time for her to demonstrate yet another skill for which she is well known, an attacking move for close quarter fighting she has developed herself. She runs at the leopard at full speed, jumping high into the air as she reaches it. Her two short knives in hand, one above the other and held at shoulder height, the right knife, Giver of Night, slashes from left to right across the animal's eyes. The left knife, Taker of Life, makes a deep cut from right to left across its throat, severing the jugular vein. A great cheer goes up from the watching crowd as Nabila lands deftly on the ground and holds her bloodstained knives aloft. The two warriors holding the leopard's head untie it from the frame and drag it towards the King. Its carcass is laid at his feet.

The watching crowd cheer, whilst the King nods his head in approval. Wangari is instructed to line her troops up before him. The bravest are presented with belts made from acacia thorns. Proud to show they are indifferent to pain, the warriors strap these trophies around their waists. The sound of their jubilant ululation is almost drowned by another loud clap of thunder.

Now it is the King's turn to receive a gift. The leopard is presented to him and Wangari proudly announces that its teeth will be used to make a royal necklace and that its fur, undamaged, untouched by the arrows will carpet the floor of his personal royal residence. In the distance on the horizon there is a huge flash of lightning. The sound of thunder quickly follows. The King looks up. The sky above him is darkening by the minute. His gaze switches to the cringing prisoners, grovelling in the red dirt in front of his throne. He speaks loudly, so that all can hear him.

'Go back to your villages with this message from the great Nassor Eze, King of Dahomey. My people will tolerate Yoruba raids no longer. If you send your warriors to capture but one man, woman or child, my armies will descend on your homes and not one life will be spared. We will take no longer take prisoners to toil as our slaves. All will perish on the blades of my warriors. Can your foolish kings not see that Benin bleeds, weeps, is weakened, whilst the Yoruba continue to trade with the Arab or the white traders. Our men are taken in droves to work in bondage and your foolish kings aid them. Soon, ours will be a barren country, bled dry of her menfolk. I will see to it that this does not happen to the Dahomey people, my people. My armies will make sure of it. Now go and give my warning to your kings. Release them,' he orders.

As the first drops of rain began to fall, the prisoners were set free, running from the village as fast as their feet would carry them. Petrified men released from their captivity fled past the women warriors guarding the gates of the Dahomean town. Hardly able to believe that their lives had been spared they looked back in dread, half expecting that the King had changed his mind and that his soldiers were now following them. It was then that their eyes caught sight of the severed heads of their own defeated soldiers adorning the walls. The King's message would be delivered and soon every tribe across the length and breadth of that great land would know that the Dahomey people would tolerate raids no longer.

The King turned now to speak to his captains. 'Wangari, return your troops to the palace. The storm comes, we will feast inside. Waitimu, you will take your men back to the stockade. Food and drink, enough for all will be sent directly. My soldiers have performed well today. Your King is proud, very proud.' His tone of voice altered dramatically as he asked, 'Has the guard been set?'

'There are four of my soldiers at every gate already,' replied Wangari. 'Waitimu's men will relieve them at sunset. If there should be a surprise attack by the Yoruba, we will be ready this time.'

'Good,' replied the King. 'The Yoruba outnumber us greatly and remain our chief enemies. They would see all our men taken into bondage if they could. We must not let that happen. Let us pray my message reaches ears that will listen.'

'Yes, we must hope they heed your wise words my King,' replied Wangari as she gave the signal for her soldiers to return to the palace. The women warriors had come into existence as palace guards from the moment King Nazzor Eze had taken the throne. As a result, the women had the advantage of being permitted in the palace precincts after dark (Dahomean men were not), and a royal bodyguard had been formed from among the King's "third-class" wives—those considered insufficiently beautiful to share his bed and who had not borne children. Dahomey's female soldiers were formally married to the King and since he never actually had relations with any of them, marriage rendered them celibate. So devoted and dedicated were they to their role as fighters that it was common for their right breast to be cut off or burned out in order that they could throw their javelins with greater accuracy.

The deluge began. Lightning crashed and thunder rumbled loudly all around. Soon the square was empty, as servants and soldiers quickly worked together to carry all the food and drink prepared for the feast indoors. Within minutes a virtual torrent of water gushed through the town like a river of blood as the red dirt was washed away. Nabila stood alone in the torrential rain, chanting, dancing, and calling to the gods for their protection. In her mind's eye she could see her enemy, the Yoruba. She would keep Adana safe, so that she would never be at risk again. Taking her knife from the amulet around her waist she began raking its sharp point across her arm, blood poured from her wounds as she looked up at the dark clouds overhead. Believing she now had the attention of her Gods, she sang loudly:

'The blood flows,
You are dead.
The blood flows,
We have won.
The blood flows, it flows, it flows.
The blood flows,
The enemy is no more.'

An air of excitement enveloped the thatched mud huts of the King's residence. Runners had arrived with wonderful news. The latest band of Yoruba raiders had been caught and executed, their prisoners released without injury, or even the loss of a single Dahomean life. Every warrior would return home triumphant.

Word spread quickly and many of the tribe's people left the safety of the fortress town to go out into the bush in order to give their soldiers a rapturous welcome. There would be a great celebration in the main square outside the royal palace tonight. Adana pleaded with Zina to take her outside too. She wanted to cheer Nabila as she arrived home, victorious and proud. Reluctantly, Zina agreed and the two of them joined a large crowd, who obviously had the same idea.

They walked through a gateway close to the royal quarter and stood in the early morning sunshine, straining their eyes to see far into the distance. They heard the army before they saw them. Waitimu's warriors, fifty of them, bedecked with ostrich feathers and hammering on the taut hides of their war shields jogged along behind Wangari's battalion. Then, mixed in with the sound of their fierce drumming, the ululation of the women soldiers could be heard too. Adana jumped up and down excitedly as the high-pitched sound grew ever nearer. 'Child, will you keep still,' Zina advised. 'Save your energy for Nabila, she's bound to want the biggest of hugs, when she sees you.'

Adana, however continued to bounce up and down even more wildly and as a result, Idema inadvertently slipped from her hand. The precious doll fell to the ground and remained hidden in the long grass at their feet. Now Adana could see sunlight glinting on the gleaming, broad blades of the warrior's spears, and at once the great army was in full view. She ran forward, arms flaying wildly in the air, howling with delight as Nabila too broke rank and raced to meet her.

As the sun sank below the summit of the jagged range of mountains to the west of the town, taut monkey-skin drums began to beat out from the great square in front of the royal palace. Others took up the rhythm eagerly. Soon the sound of a hundred drums echoed back and forth between the rocky crags encircling the town of Dahomey. In the centre of the square many fires sprang up and random men, women and children began to dance. As the dancers shuffled and swayed together in the flickering light the rapidly growing crowds about them sang and clapped in time to the music.

Adana entered the square with her father. She looked magnificent, dressed as she was in her finest leopard skin robe. The robe had been a special gift from Nabila and was only ever worn on important ceremonial occasions. Head held high, adorned with a beautiful headdress made out of ostrich feathers, richly decorated with strips of gold and huge emeralds which glittered and sparkled in the firelight, she made a striking figure. The drums instantly stopped. People dropped to their knees, bowing down in homage to the great King. Nassor Eze spoke loudly. 'Rise my people, rise. Tonight, we celebrate a great victory. Let the festivities begin.' Loved and respected by his people as he was, his words provoked a huge cheer. People stood to their feet and the drums, and the dancing began again.

Chapter Thirteen
Taken into Bondage

Adana gazed up at her father admiringly. About forty years of age, he looked to her older. The King was tall, even when judged by the standards of his own tribe and he had the massive chest of his father, but he was hugely overweight. Years of excessive eating and drinking, of being waited on hand and foot had taken its toll. A once proud hunter, revered for his prowess and skill in the field, he was now largely inactive, and the lean muscle of his youth had turned to folds of flabby middle-aged flesh.

But he was a wise ruler, a man of exceptional intelligence and presence. He walked amongst his people, addressing everyone by name and encouraging them to make the most of their night of celebration. Soon the square was noisy with the sounds of people enjoying themselves to the full. Adana watched beer gourd after beer gourd being rapidly emptied and noted to her amusement that joining in with this task, and clearly relishing it, were both Nabila and Wangari.

By now, the victory celebrations were well underway, huge fires burning furiously. The area surrounding the town had long since been denuded of trees and the wood had been brought specially from the river valley a good two miles distant from Dahomey. The King wanted no expense or effort spared to make this a night his subjects would remember for many years to come. Around the fires the beer gourds were passing from hand to hand and mouth to mouth, the drinking accompanied by shouted bawdy jokes and loud uninhibited giggling.

In the cleared space between the fires, Wangari assembled her warriors. The women danced in long, linked lines, stamping their feet, bodies newly anointed with animal fat and glistening in the firelight. Nabila was wearing her finest beads around her neck and on her head a beautiful handmade wooden headdress, elaborately decorated with strands of coral and intricately painted with henna, charcoal and white chalk. Adana thought she looked magnificent, even if she lost her balance at times and her sense of rhythm, as she occasionally stumbled over her own feet. Wangari would come to her aid at such times and holding on to each other they would both guffaw with laughter.

A highly amused King watched their antics, whilst drinking vast quantities of beer himself. His throne had been placed far too near the fire for comfort. Adana found herself having to move away, the heat from the flames burning her young and pretty face. Her father however, remained where he was and seemed not to mind that glistening rivulets of perspiration were forming salt pools in the deep creases of his elephantine body. With a gesture of his hand, he signalled for more beer. A royal hand maiden immediately rose to her feet to obey his command, rushing to his side with a refill. The beer brewed and drunk by the Dahomey had the consistency of a well-watered porridge. It smelled sour but the taste was pleasant. The King drank deep, licking the froth from his lips with relish.

It was many hours later when Adana finally lay down on her bed. She closed tired eyes as she instinctively felt under her pillow for her beloved Idema. Tonight, as always, she wanted to dream about Nabila. She would ask Idema to show her a dream of Nabila in battle. She sat up abruptly and lifted the pillow. Idema was missing! Panic clutched at her heart. Where was she? Surely, she could not have been lost, or worse still stolen. As she searched every corner of her room, she consoled herself with the thought that no one would have reason to take her. Why would they? Idema was special only to herself and Nabila. They alone knew the secret voodoo power the doll had been given.

Adana shuddered, as if someone was walking over her grave. She wrapped a blanket around her and ventured outside. Peering through the window of the hut next door, she could just make out Nabila and Wangari lying huddled together on a raised wooden bed spread with the soft furs of a number of dead leopards. They were both snoring loudly and the air about them was thick with the smell of beer. There was a sudden flash of lightning, followed by the crash of thunder overhead, but neither of the women so much as stirred.

Rain began to fall heavily, dousing the now dying embers of the fires outside in the square as Adana made her solitary way to the north gate. The gate was shockingly wide open. She shook her head in disapproval and told herself that she would close it securely on her return. The little princess stepped through easily, tiptoeing past the deepening puddle now growing at the feet of the two sleeping guards.

Trying to remember exactly the point where she and Zina had stood as they'd waited for the army and Nabila to return that morning, she scoured the ground all around her. Idema must have been dropped in the grass. 'She just has to be here somewhere,' Adana thought to herself. It was a challenging task with the night sky hidden, enveloped in a thick grey rain cloud which completely blotted out the stars and moon. Then, to make matters worse the torrent of rain began again, even heavier than before. Water washed over Adanna's skin so strongly that she felt as if she were in the flow of a river. Huge raindrops fell painfully into eyes desperately seeking her beloved prize. Driving, blinding rain which reduced visibility to a few yards. After several minutes of frantic searching her endeavour was rewarded. She found Idema lying in the long grass and raised her to her lips. She lovingly kissed the wet, mud-spattered doll and clutching it to her breast, turned happily, anxious now to run back to the safety of the town.

Her eyes met a fearful sight. Three strange, vicious looking men barred her way. She screamed loudly, but her screams were lost in another loud clap of thunder. Desperately clinging on to Idema, she found herself being dragged away. Rough hands gripped her and smothered her mouth. She tried to cry out but could not. A little over an hour later she was bound and trussed and thrown onto the back of an ox drawn cart. Adana knew she been captured by Arab slave traders. Her only consolation was the fact that she was still holding Idema tightly in her hands and that its magic powers, powers she believed in wholeheartedly, would summon Nabila and bring her to their aid. 'Don't worry little Idema,' she whispered, 'Nabila will rescue us.'

In just one night of celebration, Nabila had drunk more beer than she had ever consumed in her life. Still, she did not sleep well. Unpleasant memories haunted her dreams. She was a young girl again, trying to give comfort to her sister, a sister in agony, vainly struggling to give birth to the breeched child in her womb. She had helped her brother, Adiamo, the village witch doctor, deliver the child, but even with his magic and skill he had not been able to save the mother. It had been a terrible night, the darkness had come. Inside the delivery room, they could hear men, women and children wailing with fear as the moon had slowly moved across the sun completely blocking out its light, plunging their world into total blackness.

King Nazzor Eze had come to hold his wife in her final minutes of life. Tears streaming down his face he had carried her outside to see the night sky. 'You are a mighty Queen, Adana. See how the Gods honour you,' he said in a voice thick with grief. Nabila had followed. Above them a long, bright line shot across the heavens, like an arrowhead moving very fast, leaving a glorious trail of gold against a backdrop of the deepest blue. 'They burn a path for you. Look it moves from west to east, to where the sun sets. They come to guide you to your eternal resting place. I too will join you there, one day.' King Nazzor whispered as he buried his face gently into that of his wife. Adana had died in his arms at that moment.

Nabila held the tiny baby girl close to her, weeping bitter tears of anguish and regret that the child's mother, her own sister, whom she had loved dearly, had been taken from the world at the very moment the infant had entered it. It seemed too cruel a fate, unjust, and without mercy. 'Do not worry little one, I am your mother now and I will give you all the love I can,' Nabila promised with all her heart.

She had woken crying a river of tears. Sitting up slowly, holding her sore head she realised she had just been dreaming. Still under the influence of far too much alcohol she closed her eyes again and was asleep as soon as her head touched the pillow. In her dark dream this time she found herself standing a short distance away from a funeral pyre with the baby in her arms. It was the pyre she had helped to build for her sister. She could feel the heat from the flames as she watched King Nazzor Eze struggling to control his emotions. She knew the enormous grief he was feeling, her sister had been his first wife, his favourite and he was inconsolable in his loss.

Little remained of the fire, a few glowing embers only before the King finally returned to his royal quarters. Nabila followed slowly behind him. On entering his throne room, she prostrated herself at his feet. 'I am come to ask my King to name the child. My sister would wish it.'

'I'm sorry Nabila,' he replied, 'sorrow has prevented me. It shall be as you wish. Let it be known the child will be called Adana, after her mother and she will bear this name with pride.'

Sprawled on her bed of furs, oblivious to the storm outside, the Amazonian warrior slept on and still the dreams flowed, like rivers from the past, full of torment, a torrent of unwelcome emotions and a deluge of bad memories in which to drown. Nabila awoke from her dreams with a start, clutching her side. She had fought with the rogue elephant again and relived the intense pain she had felt as its tusk penetrated her abdomen.

She lay back in bed and elbowed Wangari, who was still snoring loudly. 'I can do without these dreams,' she thought to herself. It immediately occurred to her that Adana could well be having the same dreams. Nabila shot out of bed. 'The child will be terrified!' It was then that another thought crossed her mind. She gasped, scarce able to gather her wits, with fear clutching at her very heart and soul. The dreadful dreams that had come to her in the night were all of Adana in moments of crisis. Something was very wrong. Was Idema reaching out to her and her beloved princess in danger?

Feeling a little nauseous and dizzy, she staggered outside and as quickly as possible made her way to Adana's room. Zina was still asleep in one corner, but Adana's bed was empty. Heart pounding, she began the search, calling louder and louder for Adana to answer her. She closed her eyes and allowed her mind to wander, praying for Idema to bring her a vision of where the little girl was. Idema did not fail her. Within seconds of asking the horrifying vision had come. She saw the slave caravan; she saw Adana in chains; she saw the child's terror and heard her desperate cries for help. Nabila wasted no time and raced to Nazzor Eze with her shocking news.

Shortly before daybreak, Nabila and Wangari took their leave of the King. 'I have sent a runner to the stockade with orders that Waitimu send his best tracker and a squadron of twenty of his finest Spearmen. They will be hot on your heels,' King Nazzor Eze assured them in an anxious voice. 'May the Gods speed you in your task. Bring her back, Nabila. Please bring my daughter back.'

'We will not return without her,' Nabila promised.

It was easy enough to pick up the trail left by the caravan. They followed the deep tracks of the carts left in the rain-soaked earth, leading them through a series of steep sided valleys, tucked between well-wooded hills. Eventually after half a day of trailing they came out into another valley that must have been three miles wide and extending into the distance for as far as the eye could see. But there was no sign of the caravan. Without speaking they both picked up the pace, running now rather than jogging.

After a demanding, gruelling afternoon, not dropping the pace at all, they began to ascend rising ground. Mountains loomed from the earth all around them and finally, reaching the top of a low peak, they had the view they wanted. The caravan with its ox drawn carts and its long lines of people in chains could be seen in the distance. They were moving slowly away from a wide, swollen river, having crossed by a treacherous looking ford. A mighty torrent now lay before, separating them from Adana. The two warriors raced to its muddy banks and plunged into the deep, cold, swirling water.

The hippopotamus came with a suddenness that took both Nabila and Wangari by surprise. They were halfway to reaching the far bank when there was a great commotion in mid-river. The slave caravan stopped. All eyes turned back to the raging torrent they had only minutes before escaped. Eyes widened and jaws dropped as they watched the glistening dark grey bulk of a fully grown three-ton male charge towards the two women desperately trying to swim through the fast-flowing water. The great animal had been making its way down river, below the surface. Reaching the ford, it surfaced and immediately spotted the two women rashly invading its territory.

'Swim, Nabila, swim for your life,' Wangari cried loudly, thrashing the water with her arms in a desperate effort to save her friend and draw the angry beasts attention to herself. Nabila wasted no time, using all the strength she had left to pull herself towards the shore. Even with her head under water, Nabila heard the ground-rumbling charge, as the hippo bellowing loudly and swinging its head like a giant sledgehammer, charged at Wangari.

Despite her efforts, Nabila was making slow progress through the water—a great athlete on land; the finest runner ever seen in the Amazonian army—she was not a good swimmer. Lean, hard muscle which normally served her so well on dry land could do little to aid her movement through the brown swirling river that now engulfed her. She managed to raise her head above the turbulent water hoping to see her friend escape. It was not to be, and she watched in horror as the massive gaping mouth with slashing teeth closed in on Wangari.

Wangari did not call out again. The great jaws opened and closed upon the brave woman, the huge yellow teeth almost cutting her in half. Nabila's screams lingered in the air as she watched the hippopotamus disappearing back into deep water, the dead Wangari dangling from its cavernous mouth. Bloody bubbles raced to the surface of the raging river, as the creature now turned its attention to her. Fighting the current, dragged down by huge whirlpools, Nabila fought in vain to reach the bank. She was being swept downstream by the sheer force of the flood water, whilst the hippo seemed impervious to the power of the mighty torrent and hurtled towards her like a great black torpedo.

Then, her feet touched solid ground. She could feel the muddy riverbed beneath her tread. She tried to stand, to move her feet, but the pitiless mud held her back, refusing to allow her to move. It clung to her, like a starving child clings to its mother's breast.

From the caravan train, riders armed with rifles pulled their horses to a halt. They looked down at Nabila from their position high up on the riverbank. The weapons were aimed and fired simultaneously. Loud cracks ripped through the air. A bullet glanced off the side of Nabila's head, detaching her left earlobe. Instantly, Nabila dropped back into the raging water. Ignoring her injury, she flailed her arms wildly, desperately trying to stop the vicious current from sweeping her away. The enraged beast was upon her, as a second volley of bullets hit their mark. The hippo was stopped dead in its tracks. The riders cheered, as the beast rolled over onto its side, finally succumbing to the power of the water. Now floating belly-up, with the torso of Wangari still trapped in its great jaws, it was swept away downstream.

Intent on her capture, many cruel, vulture-like men with rough, calloused hands descended on the exhausted warrior. A net was thrown over Nabila and she was dragged semi-conscious from the water. She tried to draw her short knives to cut herself free, but helpless against her brutal captors she was beaten into total unconsciousness as heavy wooden cudgels rained down upon her head. Within minutes she was unarmed and at the mercy of the slavers. Adana watched in terror as Nabila, now also in chains and with blood gushing from a nasty head wound, was thrown unceremoniously onto the back of an ox cart.

The caravan set off again moving slowly, cart by cart, slave by slave, along an endless, waterlogged, and rutted dirt road, dirt which the heavy rains had turned to sludge. As the hours, days passed, bodies bent with exhaustion and eyes too tired now to survey the changing landscape failed to notice the stretches of gorgeous tropical coastline through which they passed. The convoy of pain snaked its silent, winding way through acres of farmland, whilst goats and pigs scrambled out of their way, seeking safety on the shoulder of the road. Then, without warning, the long thin ribbon of reddish dirt ended, and a cluster of mud homes topped with straw roofs appeared.

Beyond these primitive houses the road widened, passing between two huge dark grey, jagged rocky outcrops. It then dropped steeply, descending to the sea and to a thriving, bustling town which hugged the coastline. Men in the uniforms of the Portuguese army marched through those hot, sun-baked streets, streets dominated by an enormous stone-built castle, overlooking a large port. Out at sea the masts of several tall ships at anchor swayed back and forth as the vessels were gently rocked by the calm waters of the Atlantic Ocean.

The caravan trudged its way past the mud huts and on towards the waiting castle. Shackled bodies, shuffled painfully along a blood-spattered road. Nabila also left her mark on that well-trodden path, her ankles now oozing a thick stain of red as the heavy manacles around them chafed raw skin away to the bone. Eyes invaded by flies, and into which beads of perspiration continuously dripped were oblivious to the beauty of the scenery about them. Long golden beaches stretched for miles, onto which a blue and sparkling sea ebbed and flowed. Gentle rolling hills surrounded them enclosing well-irrigated green pastures, punctuated here and there between the growing crops by coconut palms, baobab trees and umbrella thorns.

They entered the town. Soldiers stood each side of them now, guarding the road leading up to the castle. They passed huge black cannons housed in their casings on high walls above the sea, pointing like fingers of doom out to the horizon. Suddenly Adana stopped dead in her tracks, the chain about her wrists and attached to Nabila's neck collar yanking unexpectedly, causing the older woman to cry out as a neck rubbed red raw and bleeding felt the sudden, painful tug. They were no longer in bright sunlight but standing in dark shadow created by the high walls of the castle which loomed ominously above them. Adana began to whimper and tremble visibly.

Cape Coast Castle, under Portuguese control, opened her expansive mouth. A wide, wrought iron portcullis was lifted and the hapless slaves were marched inside and swallowed. Prodded and pushed by soldiers carrying bayonets, they were taken, still in their chains down steep steps into the waiting dungeons.

Chapter Fourteen
Leaving African Soil Forever

Nabila and Adana were destined to be amongst the black cattle in the stinking hold of Montague's ship. On arrival at the slave fortress, they found themselves locked in a dungeon with over a thousand men and five hundred other women, all kept captive waiting for the slave ships to dock. As Nabila's eyes became accustomed to the darkness, she had taken stock of their situation. They were manacled to heavy iron rings set into the floor. The walls of the dungeon were dripping with rank, evil smelling water, green mould and fungus entirely covering the rough, red brick of which they were made. There was no sanitation. Slaves were standing in their own excrement, hence the vile smell which had hit them as soon as the prison doors had been opened. High above her, barred windows did little to afford any light and what fresh breeze they let in gave small comfort to the slaves held captive below. In the middle of the floor Nabila noted a narrow channel had been gouged out of the rock. It ran the length of the cell. Down this channel, a thick slick of urine and faeces continuously drained away, moving slowly towards an open well at the seaward end of the dungeon.

Since their incarceration they had endured these heinous conditions without abatement, foul air filling their lungs day and night. What little food they received was rotten and the scant water available was filthy and brackish. It was seven weeks later when *The Black Stag* anchored in the bay. During those long weeks and in those awful conditions Adana had become ill. She was hardly recognisable. The sight of her emaciated body, her swollen belly, her protruding rib cage tore at Nabila's heart. She could scarce bear to look at her without tears welling up in her eyes. Even Nazzor Eze her father would not have known her. Adana had lost more than half her body weight, both through lack of food, water, and illness, diarrhoea and sickness weakening her so much that she could barely stand. Nabila was at a loss as to what she could do to help her.

Then, one day, unexpectedly, the guards had come. All the slaves were driven out of the dungeon like cattle to the slaughter and lined up outside in one long line. Baked under a hot sun, they had waited their turn. Nabila watched as a fat, white skinned man inspected each slave and was puzzled by something he wore on his face. She had never seen spectacles before. She recognised another man for what he was, a king. Sitting under a canopy of white canvas, sheltered from the heat of the sun, fanned by two naked Black boys armed with giant ostrich feathers, the Master of *The Black Stag* watched proceedings with interest.

The slaves were forced to open their mouths, to cough, their ears were examined and whilst their bodies were inspected from head to toe, including their genitalia, they were made to hold a heavy iron weight in their hands. It was the same weight for adults and children alike. The sick, the infirm, the injured, the ones with infected wounds caused by their cruel fetters were often aided by a rifle butt to march back to the dungeons. In contrast the slaves who received a nod of approval from the man examining them were marched away, down steep stone steps to the shore. Down on the beach Nabila watched them being doused with water, two men ready with buckets of sea water to throw over them. Washed clean of prison grime they would then be taken to waiting row boats which would ferry them across the bay to the great tall ships waiting at anchor.

Nabila began to panic. Adana was very sick; she could not pass the inspection. Her worst fear was separation for without Nabila to protect her Adana would surely die. Closer and closer the white man came. Nabila could see him perspiring, she watched him mopping his brow with a piece of cloth. The midday sun continued to beat down remorselessly. Nabila could feel its burning heat on her bare shoulders. Just then and to her great surprise, the man suddenly stopped in his tracks. He appeared to look along the line and simply count the number of slaves remaining. There were eight including Adana and herself. Nabila heaved a huge sigh of relief as the man, wiping the sweat from his brow with one hand waved at the slaver with the other and nodded his approval. He had clearly had enough.

'Clean bill of health, your Lordship,' he called out loudly to the large, fat, heavily perspiring man who had been watching the process with close attention. The consignment was complete, he had met Lord Montague's target. The two hundred and fifty he had examined and authorised could be loaded onto the boat. His job was done. All he wanted now was water and shade.

If the imprisoned slaves had thought conditions in the castle dungeons were bad, they would seem as nothing compared to what awaited them on board the slave ship. Nabila limped across the beach, the heavy leg chains had cut into her ankles and the rope collar around her neck had chaffed the skin red-raw. Trying to ignore her pain and discomfort, desperate to allay Adana's fears, she encouraged the little girl to follow her. In no way did she comprehend as they stepped into the small row boats which would carry them to the great ship with it tall masts that she was stepping on African soil for the last time.

Had fate not taken a turn for the worse, they might have fared better than many of the others who had been boarded earlier. Nabila and Adana were in the final twenty of the two hundred and fifty taken on board. As they clambered, struggled, still in chains, to make their sorry way up the netting draped over the side of the ship and onto the deck, a sailor spotted Adana's doll and snatched it from her hand. Nabila heard the instant scream from the little princess and immediately turned on the evil perpetrator, attempting to grab him with her manacled hands. So shocked was the sailor concerned by Nabila's rebellious attack that the doll was instantly dropped, landing in a thick coil of rope which was lying to one side.

'Lash that woman to the mizzen mast, Mr Lawson, and fetch me my cat o' nine tails. Keep that last batch of cargo on deck. They can see what happens to one of their kind when they turn on their masters. I want no rebellion on my ship.' The fat puce-faced, and heavily perspiring Captain began to remove his jacket and waited for the whip to be placed in his hand. Nabila was seized by three other sailors and pulled towards the mast. A rope was secured to the manacles at her wrist, and she was hauled off her feet, dangling like a puppet doll several inches off the floor. There would be no mercy. Her ankles were tied to the mast and her body positioned so that her bare back was completely exposed. The flogging began.

Even hardened sailors were to feel their stomachs turn at what they would witness. Captain Montague had decided on one hundred and fifty lashes as a suitable punishment. 'I want every piece of skin stripped from that black devil's back, and then some,' he announced to Lawson as he was handed his whip. 'It is my intention to make an example of this rebellious wretch and in so doing, frighten the remaining slaves into abject submission. Word will soon pass amongst them as to what happens to any bitch or bastard who turns on his master, they'll not trouble us again.' The woman would die of course, but the loss of one insignificant slave, a female at that, would not affect his profit margin.

He struck the first lash with all his might. There was a gasp from everyone on deck, but Nabila was silent. No scream left her lips. Indeed, she made no sound at all. 'You bitch, you filthy bitch! Scream, why don't you?' The cat struck again and still there was silence. 'I'll make you scream if it's the last thing I do.' Nabila did not scream, but, after twenty lashes, Captain Montague was exhausted and handed the whip over to his first mate. 'No letting up now, Mr Lawson, or I'll have you tied to the mizzen and whipped.'

Mr Lawson knew the captain well enough by now to know that he would keep his word. Hence every stroke was struck with full force. It was a vicious, callous assault on a defenceless woman. Adana sobbed, eyes tight shut, unable to watch such cruelty. The other slaves cowered, shivering, trembling, whimpering, terrified and wide eyed, whilst blood flowed like a tide of red down Nabila's back. Strips of lacerated flesh flapped in the wind and a river of blood dripped to the floor. It washed across the deck and onto a coil of rope, staining it bright scarlet and a wooden doll, trapped in those coils opened and closed its mouth as if drinking Nabila's pain.

One hundred and fifty lashes had been delivered, the last thirty, by Fletcher. The remaining slaves were taken down below and chained into their fetters whilst Nabila's lifeless body was left where it was. Mr Lawson attempted to cut it down but was prevented from so doing by the captain. 'No. Leave it be. It will serve as a useful warning. The body can rot where it is,' he ordered.

The anchor was weighed, the sails hoisted, and the Black Stag's voyage began. Lawson tried to close his ears to the cries of terrified prisoners, chained in the purpose-built hold below, many of whom had never seen the sea, let alone been on board a ship before. Within hours, the stench of vomit filled his nostrils, as most of the ship's cargo, unused to the motion of a ship at sea, suffered wretchedly from seasickness. Unable to move in their close confinement, they, and the prisoner on either side of them were quickly covered in vomit as well as foul smelling excrcment. The helpless captives had no choice but to urinate or defecate where they were. There was no sanitation, no fresh water or clean food to be had, and as Lawson knew extremely well, many would die before the ship had even neared her destination.

Adana too, was slowly dying. Conditions aboard the ship were wretched. She lay in virtual darkness manacled to a narrow wooden ledge, denied fresh water, starved of food and all human comfort. Imprisoned with her in the darkness full-grown men, women and children were crammed into every available space in that dreadful, stinking hold. So tightly packed in, that they were like human bricks in a wall and Adana found she was unable to move, even to sit up. All she could do was to turn her head and even then, the vomit and excrement of the person on the ledge above, still dripped relentlessly into her face. In the stifling heat below deck the mere task of breathing became a struggle and the awful stench of human filth was overpowering.

Worse still were the vivid, awful memories of Nabila's flogging. Adana truly believed that Nabila had perished in that savage beating, and she was heartbroken. She had been forcibly wrenched away from her homeland, her family and now to make matters worse both Nabila and Idema had been taken from her. Nabila, the woman she had loved more than anyone else in the world, more even than her own doting father. Adana longed for death to take her too. Death would reunite her with Nabila and in the spirit world which awaited her she could once again walk hand in hand, side by side with her brave Amazonian warrior. Death would free her and so she refused the little food or water she was offered.

Two weeks after the ship had set sail the slaves in her section of the hold were taken up on deck. Adana was now so weak one of the other slaves was made to carry her. To those around her, she seemed a little creature, indifferent as to life or death and as she tried to stand her legs failed her. She collapsed to the floor, sick and helpless. Managing to raise her eyes in the unaccustomed, blinding sunlight she saw Nabila's pitiful body still tied to the mizzen mast.

Had her eyes been able to focus clearly, she might have been amazed by the changes to Nabila's body. Changes which not even the crew or Captain had noticed. Far from rotting, the flesh on Nabila's back was healing. But sadly, Adana did not see, she had no reason to hope and instead she cried out, calling to Nabila, calling to the Gods for mercy, for death to take her and the Gods answered. 'Throw that wretch overboard,' commanded the captain, 'she's neither use to man nor beast.' Adana's body, heavily weighted by iron manacles quickly sank below the waves.

Chapter Fifteen
Shipwreck

As soon as Adana's fragile body vanished from sight, a fierce wind began to blow, and the sky quickly darkened. Mr Lawson watched the storm clouds gather, drawing sharp breaths every time the blackening sky was lit with giant forks of lightning. The captain turned to look at the slaves who had been brought up on deck to be fed. 'Get those men below,' he commanded. 'I want them back in the hold. See to it, Mr Lawson, thank you. And once they're back in chains, board up the shutters. I don't want any of them escaping.'

The storm gathered in intensity, a ferocious wind swirled about them, thick black clouds blotted out the sun and freezing, driving rain chilled every man to the bone. 'If the ship were to sink, all the African slaves chained below deck are doomed,' Lawson thought to himself. He waited for the call, 'All hands on deck,' but it did not come. Instead, he listened incredulously to sounds the like of which he had never heard before. The wind howled about him, whilst wave after wave crashed over his head. *The Black Stag* careered from side to side, like a feather in a whirlwind, whilst at the same time, rising up vertical swells forty feet above her and then crashing down on the other side as if diving into a deep, dark chasm from which there would be no escape.

He could scarce believe the captain had not given the order for bare poles. It was suicidal to try to continue under sail. The rain and wind lashed his face as he staggered slowly towards the stern. Time and again he lost his footing, so much so that he could barely move. Holding on to the side rail he gradually edged his way towards the quarter deck and the brutal, incompetent Captain, whom he had come to hate.

At last, he reached the mizzenmast to which the Black woman's body still remained tied. Only a few more steps now and he could advise the captain. But it was all too late. Fork lightning struck the ship, and above the roar of thunder which quickly followed, came the familiar sound of timbers splitting, as this time, every mast was torn asunder! Rigging crashed to the deck, pinning numerous sailors beneath its heavy ropes and poles and its battered and shredded sails.

It was then that the final blow to seal the ship's fate was struck. Driven off course and at the mercy of the sea, *The Black Stag* smashed into a huge outcrop of jagged rock. Monstrous, angry waves slammed the ship against a vengeful, wicked, solid mass of granite, rising eighty feet up out of the sea. Battered and buffeted to such a degree and causing every timber to creak and groan, the ship surrendered to the onslaught and split in two. Finally, the Captain gave an order. 'Abandon ship. Man, the lifeboat.'

Miraculously Lawson, aided by the ship's bosun, managed to launch the single rowboat *The Black Stag* possessed and six of the thirty or so crew members scrambled aboard, including the captain. As they pulled away from the stricken ship, they could hear the desperate cries of the slaves above the noise of the tumult. Slowly, slowly, first *The Black Stag's* prow and then her stern sank beneath the raging sea. The men stopped rowing and watched in silence as the great ship disappeared from view.

Suddenly there was a sound. The survivors looked down into the water. Something had bumped against the side of the boat. It was a woman's body, floating in the water, a Black woman, still alive. As Lawson hauled her shivering frame into the boat, he noticed she was clutching a small wooden doll in her hand.

Captain Montague said nothing as the woman was pulled from the rapidly diminishing waves. His mind was elsewhere. He had lost his ship, his cargo, his profit and had nearly lost his life. It occurred to him that he might still lose his life. They were after all dependent now on being rescued. All they could do was to hope another ship sailing the slave route would find them and quickly. He didn't like the idea of cannibalism, especially when it might mean eating black meat. Inadvertently, his right hand strayed to feel inside his jacket pocket. Much to his satisfaction, the ships log, although wet, was still intact. He congratulated himself on having had the presence of mind to retrieve it from his cabin, before climbing into the lifeboat. Despite the desperate situation, his mood improved. Afterall, the logbook was proof of the Black Stag's cargo, and he was in no doubt that his insurance company would have to reimburse his losses to the full, including his black cattle and the ship itself. Added to that was the thought that his pretty, young, nubile wife would be waiting to pleasure him.

They were fortunate. As if the gods had decided to change sides a ship called *The Phoenix* picked them up just in time. They had been without water for eight days and were lucky to survive. Conditions in the long boat did not favour survival, without shade from the sun, which beat down mercilessly during the hours of daylight, sweat poured from their bodies. When their water supplies ran out, they were forced to drink their own urine. Twice two crew members had to be forcibly restrained by Lawson and the ship's doctor from drinking sea water.

It was Lawson who had first spotted the ship. He could not believe his luck and quickly roused his shipmates from their sleep. They had rowed hard towards the great tall ship, their dry throats struggling to call out, to alert the longed-for rescuers to their desperate plight, Lawson and three others had stood up, waving their arms wildly, trying to attract attention. The sudden movement had almost caused the lifeboat to capsize. A sharp-eyed lookout in the crow's nest saved the day and *The Phoenix* was duly directed to their position.

Lawson was ecstatic. It was of little consequence to him that he would return home penniless or that he might not now have sufficient funds to set himself up in trade, to purchase his shop. He was simply overjoyed at the prospect of being reunited with his beloved wife and family. That was all that mattered. He made himself a promise that day, a promise he would keep, that on his return he would never again be separated from them.

The Phoenix had set sail from Jamaica and was on her way back to England. Loaded with a cargo of sugar and molasses she arrived in Liverpool ahead of schedule. A jealous, arrogant Lord Montague did not even thank her captain for the rescue of himself and his crew. Lawson, embarrassed by this display of ingratitude, took it upon himself to express the crew's heartfelt appreciation for their timely rescue and safe passage to England.

It was early evening when *The Phoenix* finally docked. Not wanting to stay another minute longer in the uncomfortable quarters he had been given, Lord Montague ordered Mr Lawson on shore with strict instructions to find suitable accommodation in a reputable lodging house. Mr Lawson had the presence of mind to enquire of the ship's captain if he knew of any nearby location which would satisfy Lord Montague. The captain, a Liverpudlian himself, immediately suggested *The Old Bell*, a well-established coaching inn and only a five-minute walk from the harbour.

'You'll not find a cleaner or a better place if you were to search for a month,' he advised with confidence. 'I'll wager not even his Lordship will be able to find much to complain about.' Mr Lawson, however, doubted that could be true, he knew his master too well. Nonetheless he made his way directly to the inn and, pleased with what he saw, booked the necessary rooms. He returned to *The Phoenix* with his news.

Less than two hours later they were all comfortably settled at their new-found hostelry and enjoying a hearty meal. All that is except for Nabila, Black slaves were not permitted even to enter *The Old Bell*. Lawson had to persuade the landlord to agree to a compromise and thus it was arranged that Nabila would sleep in the stables under an armed guard. The surviving crew members would take it in turns to watch over her just in case she tried to escape.

The innkeeper was also horrified by Nabila's attire, or lack of it. She was a huge woman well over six feet tall. The scant rags she was wearing did little to hide her muscular physique or the mutilation she had endured to become an Amazonian warrior. The missing breast and earlobe, the clearly visible scars of battle did little to enhance her femininity, indeed she could hardly be called feminine at all, her large square head, her towering frame, her long limbs with enormous hands and feet at the end of them giving her much more of a man-like appearance. It was the landlord himself who supplied new clothing. Rummaging through garments which by accident had been left behind at the inn, he managed to find a shirt and a pair of trousers to fit. Although slightly on the small side they did the job. Nabila was made to wear them and duly marched off to the stable block.

However, things did not go exactly to plan. As soon as she entered the stables all hell broke loose. It was as if the devil himself had arrived. Every horse tethered inside began to panic. There was such a rearing and a bucking of which no one had ever seen the like. Lawson had never heard a horse scream before and the chaotic din of twenty or more horses either snorting loudly or making high pitched whinnies, plus the sound of hooves clattering against stable doors and walls only added to the hubbub which was almost ear-splitting. Owners descended from every direction trying to secure reins in a desperate effort to stop their horses from bolting. It was only when Nabila had been taken well away that the animals began to calm down.

A narrow passageway ran down one side of the inn leading to a small, enclosed yard where empty bottles and various utensils were stored. The yard had a cobbled floor and a lean to just big enough to house a man. The guard slept in the lean to, Nabila on the hard stone floor. It was a chilly night. The guards hardly slept at all, even though there was no risk of their prisoner escaping, bound as she was hand and foot and chained to an iron ring in the floor. Nabila, in contrast slept like a baby.

The next day the party set off by horse-drawn carriage to Bristol. Nabila's iron neck collar was attached to a thick rope, a good twenty yards in length, which was then tied to the back of the coach. She was kept well out of view of the horses and much to the amusement of the crew would have to run all the way. Lord Montague and Mr Lawson sat inside, the crew on top, exposed to the elements and enjoying typical British weather at its worst. Heavy rain fell all day, turning the road into a mud track loaded with treacherous deep puddles, perfect for damaging wooden wheels or getting them stuck.

In between stops to get the coach out of waterlogged ruts the rain-soaked crew entertained themselves by taking bets as to how long it would be before Nabila was being dragged along. Training with Wangari, Nabila had often run for days at a time without stopping, so no money exchanged hands. Many hours later the coach reached its destination, Montague House in Bristol.

Mr Lawson left the next day for Bath, overjoyed at the prospect of returning to his family. He would be true to his word, his sailing days were over, his future as a respectable shopkeeper assured. As his carriage pulled away from Montague House, he heaved a huge sigh of relief. He would never again be in the company of the first Lord of Eastlyn. That was a blessing in itself!

Lord Montague took up residence in his grand town house and waited for the return of his other ships. Nabila was put to work below stairs. Somehow Nabila had made herself useful on the voyage, in particular tending to his needs where his gout was concerned. The ship's Doctor had been unable to help, but Nabila with her strange potions had managed to alleviate some of the pain. Montague as a result took the unexpected decision not to sell her at the well-established slave market in Bristol town. A surprisingly grateful Nabila thanked him instead, when she was informed, she would be taken to Eastlyn Castle, Montague's lavish newly built residence where she could serve as a scullery maid.

Her first job on her arrival at Eastlyn Castle, however, was to unload contraband. Lord Montague did his best to avoid paying excise duty. When the tall ships arrived back in England as much as a third of their cargo would be unloaded before the ship officially docked in port. In the dead of night, rowing boats would go out to meet the great ships anchored a little way out to sea, near the mouth of the estuary. Loaded with goods the boats would return to the castle. Nabila was an asset, her strength enabling her to carry as heavy a load as any of the men Montague employed.

Nabila quickly learnt to speak English. Over time she became a trusted servant, often tending to the needs of his young wife and she was now known and answered to the name of Bella. She never complained, did as she was told, tried hard to please, and worked tirelessly. In truth, secretly, patiently, Nabila waited her chance to seek justice for Adana and the other slaves who had perished so cruelly at Montague's hands. She believed wholeheartedly in the power of her Gods, Gods who would ensure her vengeance.

Time passed quickly and all too soon that chance came. Nabila was struck with the ease of it all, how fitting was the opportunity which now arose. Ellen, George's wife of just two years was pregnant.

Chapter Sixteen
Nabila's Curse

A dinner of six courses fit for royalty had been served and cleared away. Ellen, however, had eaten very little. She looked pale and wore a slightly nervous expression on her face. Sitting some distance from the fire, she held her swollen belly in her small white hands.

His Lordship had helped himself to a hefty glass of port and standing in front of the roaring fire he had turned to face his pretty wife. 'You do not eat enough, my dear. You leave too much food upon your plate. Waste, pure waste,' he commented once the servants had left the room. 'And you are eating for two, you know. I want you delivered of a strong, strapping son, to carry on the family name.'

For several minutes, Ellen made no comment. 'I am tired, George. I am going to bed. I will see you in the morning.'

'You'll see me before then,' he replied, uncharacteristically opening the door of the dining room for her to leave. As Ellen struggled to her feet, so the butler returned.

'Will there be anything else, your lordship?' he enquired.

'Yes,' replied George immediately. 'Get her ladyship's maid to run a bath for her and bring me another decanter of port.'

'No, no, not tonight, George, thank you. I'm too tired. I'll bathe in the morning.'

Ignoring his wife's words, George repeated his request. 'You heard me,' he said in an irritated tone of voice to the butler, 'my wife requires a bath, now. See to it!' He commanded.

The decanter was empty. Lord Montague made his way upstairs to his wife's bedroom. He closed the door behind him and turned to stare at her. She made a tragic figure, sitting up in bed in her fine woollen nightdress, ashen-faced, sky-blue eyes full of fear and loathing. Her delicate fingers were gripping the starched, white sheets, her long blond hair hanging in soft swirls about her shoulders.

For many weeks now, she had begged him to leave her alone. It annoyed him that she had clearly defied him and had refused to bathe. Did she dare also to deprive him of his conjugal rights, to deny him access to her tender young body? Did she think he could happily content himself with those disgusting Black wenches below stairs? Pregnant she might well be, but it was the duty of every wife to meet the needs of her husband. She was being grossly unfair. He licked his lips, his tongue clearing away the bright, yellow pus oozing from the sore at the corner of his mouth. He moved towards the bed.

'Please, George, please, for pity's sake, no. No. God help me! No!' Her plea was ignored.

At the request of Lady Ellen, Doctor Armitage, the family's longstanding physician had been called to Eastlyn Castle. Lord Montague was vexed and annoyed. 'How dare she send for the Doctor without his permission? The woman needed a good thrashing and to know her place.'

The Doctor spent some considerable time examining his patient and then had the audacity to demand a private audience with him. 'Well, Doctor, what is it you wish to say to me,' Montague enquired in an irritated tone of voice.

The good Doctor took some time before answering, choosing his words carefully. 'After examination, I am not at all satisfied with the health of your wife. It is clear to me that she will need extra bed rest and care at this time. I must insist therefore that until she is safely delivered of the child, you refrain from all marital relations.'

Lord Montague replied angrily, 'Doctor Armitage, what goes on between my wife and I in the privacy of our bedroom is sacred to us and has nothing whatever to do with you!'

Unknown to Lord Montague, the Doctor had made his distraught patient a promise and he would be true to his word. He began again. 'Forgive me, your Lordship, but, if I may say, you are a heavy man. Every time you lie with your wife, you risk crushing the child and, in her condition, cause her considerable discomfort. Indeed, there has been some bleeding which fortunately I have managed to stem. But if you continue to ignore my advice in this matter, I cannot be held responsible for the outcome. You risk losing both your wife and the child she carries.'

Only three weeks later, Lady Ellen had gone into labour. Doctor Armitage was summoned immediately. He remained with his charge all day. Lord Montague was eating supper in the library when an anxious doctor disturbed his victuals with some unwelcome news. 'I have serious concerns regarding the health of your wife, your Lordship. I believe you should send for her parents immediately. There are complications, alarming complications. The delivery is likely to be most difficult. The child is unfortunately breeched.'

'Stuff and nonsense, man,' was the reply, 'it's always the same with the aristocracy. Why, we're known for it, don't you know, our women always struggle giving birth? These bloody peasant women produce their bastards at the drop of a hat.'

'Lord Montague, I repeat. I shall do my best to bring your wife and the child safely through, but I must warn you even with my skill and experience it may not be enough. Lady Ellen is already much weakened.'

'Damnation, man, are you deliberately trying to spoil my dinner? Deliver my son is all I say. Name your price. Whatever the cost I'll pay it.'

'May I suggest you pray to your God, your Lordship. It is he, not I, nor any amount of money which will decide the fate of your wife and child.' Lord and Lady Forsythe were duly summoned to Eastlyn Castle. They arrived early the next day.

Ellen's labour continued for two whole days and nights. Her screams of pain echoed through the long castle corridors. Everyone spoke in a whisper, hardly daring to breathe. All thoughts were with Lady Ellen and her baby. The staff gathered in small groups, trying to get on with their normal jobs whilst at the same time fearing for the wellbeing of their beloved mistress. Only Nabila was missing, but no one noticed her absence.

Nabila sat motionless in almost total darkness as if somehow paralysed. She had been in her special, secret room for some time, trapped in memories which still tormented her. In her mind's eye she could see Adana running through long grass to meet her. She could hear her laughing, see the happy, bright smile, and almost feel the warmth of a soft loving embrace as a child's arms encircled around her. But now, suddenly, other recollections invaded her thoughts.

She closed her eyes as she remembered a child's body thrown overboard and sinking beneath the waves. She remembered the terrifying sounds of an angry sea, the groaning and moaning of a sinking ship and the desperate cries of hundreds of helpless, drowning souls, dragged mercilessly to the bottom of the ocean. Bodies in chains, taken to a watery grave, imprisoned for eternity in a forgotten cemetery miles from their homeland. Nabila shivered violently. The stone floor on which she was sitting was cold and damp, the room itself dank and rank with air thick with the smell of decay. The chill breeze which whistled eerily through the labyrinth of passages Nabila had come to know so well, plucked at her flesh, stealing what little body heat she had left. A match was struck, the waiting fire at Nabila's feet lit. Soon, very soon, the room would be full of the aroma of melted wax, the spirits of her ancestors would gather, and the ritual could begin.

Nabila rose to her feet and began to dance around the fire, turning, whirling, and chanting incessantly in an eerie high-pitched voice. Her strange singing intensified, and her dancing became even wilder. Her deep-set eyes had an odd, glazed look about them and sweat poured from her brow. Now in a state of trance, of spirit possession, the flames could not harm her. She plunged her hand into the boiling wax, lifting out the red-hot mould of Idema which now contained the first of many voodoo dolls Nabila would create. She called to her gods and evoked the ancient curse, the power of belief consummating her vow of revenge.

The sound of a baby crying penetrated the darkness of the library, the fire had almost gone out and there was little other light to be had. Numerous candles had been allowed to burn down indeed more than half in the room had already been extinguished. Eyes opened, sleep drifted away, and ears listened expectantly to that long-awaited sound. It was a pitiful wail, barely audible but it woke the family gathered in their vigil. The servants too were instantly alert and back on duty flying in all directions to get everything in order once more. Maids rushed hither and thither carrying trays, whilst fires were stoked, and curtains drawn to let in the rays of the early morning sun.

One could have compared Eastlyn to Sleeping Beauty's castle, being brought back to life and waking up to a new dawn. Celebration, however, was short-lived. As Eleanor Montague had taken her first breath on entering the world, so her mother, Lady Ellen Montague, had breathed her last on leaving it. Doctor Armitage entered the library to give the family the tragic news.

Montague sat motionless in his chair, whilst Sybil and Algernon were escorted upstairs to say their mournful goodbyes to their daughter and get a first glimpse of the baby. When Algernon re-joined Lord George in the library, Sybil remained at Ellen's bedside, holding a now cold, limp hand, and crying uncontrollably.

'If there's anything you need, George, you have only to ask,' said Algernon stonily, 'anything, anything at all.'

'Anything?' repeated his lordship.

'Yes, anything we can do to help, we'll do,' replied Ellen's father.

'Perhaps, Ellen's younger sisters would like to visit for a while? Indeed, they would be such a comfort to me and afford an old man such solace in his hour of need,' he suggested in a slightly trembling voice.

'I see,' Algernon responded, stroking his chin, and looking directly into George's eyes. 'Mayhap we have a little more business to attend to though before we can finalise the details. What say you to that, George?'

George did not answer but rose from his chair and walked over to a large mahogany bureau situated near a window. Pulling back the curtains, he then opened one of the drawers and took out a banker's draft. 'Shall we say the same amount again?' he asked.

Only Nabila rejoiced in Ellen's passing. In her secret place, alone and unobserved she praised and thanked her Gods that revenge had been granted. She cried out to Adana with tears streaming down her face, invoking her spirit to come to her. 'Vengeance, vengeance is ours, my little princess, Idema has worked her magic.'

It seemed to Nabila as if fate had shown her what to do. The retribution she required, its precise form, how to punish Montague for his wickedness appeared to have been delivered into her lap. Adana's mother had died in childbirth and the child herself had had her life cut short, taken away without kindness or mercy. Lord Montague, his wife, and his seed would suffer the same destiny. So it was that Nabila plotted her terrible revenge and in so doing was able to set in motion a curse on the Montague family which she intended would last for eternity.

The final transaction agreed upon between Algernon Forsythe and George Montague benefitted only one person. Fortunately for two young girls, his Lordship did not long outlive his wife, but his demise was not due to any sense of grief or remorse on Ellen's behalf. In addition, he neither showed interest nor cared about his daughter; not being a boy and unable to carry on the family name and, more importantly, inherit Eastlyn, she meant less than nothing to him. Eleanor was left entirely to the care of her wet nurse and not once did Montague visit her cot to see her or make enquiries as to her progress.

As if divine retribution itself now stepped in to punish him for the crimes he had committed, the illness he had contracted over many years called time.

Hidden for a decade or more it began to ravage his body. Try as his doctor might he could not control its onslaught. Within a few weeks' paralysis had set in and Montague could barely move. His great bulk made it incredibly difficult for the servants to cope with his infirmity. Too heavy to carry and unable to move of his own accord he was now bedridden. He had become a virtual prisoner in his own body and dependent on others for all his needs. Shortly afterwards this situation was made even worse when he also lost his sight. His blindness was too much for his servants to cope with and trying to give him either food or water became nigh on impossible.

The great castle echoed now with his screams, more distressing even than those heard during the ordeal of his wife throughout her long and tragic confinement. At the end Lord Montague was little more than a mindless vegetable, without speech or reason he hastened to his grave, much to the annoyance of Nabila. The last days of his life passed slowly, and Montague suffered great pain. During those final hours Nabila did all she could to prolong his life. She did not desire his death. Quite the contrary, the longer he suffered the more she felt avenged.

So it was that less than two months after the birth of his only child and the death of his young wife that Montague joined Ellen in the grave. Once more he would lie atop her, but this time for eternity. For Nabila life would go on unchanged. She kept herself to herself and performed her duties to the full. Nabila was not liked by the other servants but her devotion to Lord Montague in those final, dreadful weeks had not gone unnoticed.

George's brother, Henry, a very different kind of man to the first Lord Eastlyn, arrived with his own family not only to make all the funeral arrangements, but also to take possession of the Castle. The castle could only pass to a male heir. Hence as the second of four brothers he was next in line.

Henry felt fortunate. He had never much liked his elder brother and had always disapproved of his unchristian way of life. As the second son he had certainly not expected to inherit the Montague fortune and on leaving university, due to his religious calling had decided he would make his career serving the Church. An intelligent man and gifted orator he had done well, procuring the post of Bishop of Bristol, a position in which he had happily busied himself in ecclesiastical affairs.

The prize of Eastlyn Castle, however, would tempt even the most devout of souls. Henry happily resigned from the church and gladly accepted the title of the second Lord Eastlyn. He and his wife, Verity, had been blessed with three sons, but no daughters and so they were thrilled at the prospect of taking over the guardianship of their niece. Eleanor would be loved, cherished, and raised as if she were their daughter.

On the day of the funeral, Doctor Armitage talked at length to Henry of Nabila's extraordinary dedication as nurse to his dying brother. 'She refused to leave his side, stayed with him, twenty-four hours a day during those final weeks. The other servants were most grateful.' Her reputation was thus established as a trustworthy and diligent employee. She was still not liked amongst the other staff, but her situation was now made secure. The second Lord Eastlyn duly promoted her to the position of housemaid, much to the annoyance of many.

In stark contrast to his late brother, Henry sat completely on the opposite side of the debate on slavery and was a staunch abolitionist. *The Black Stag* would not be rebuilt and although the remaining three tall ships would continue to transport goods between the America's and Europe, the Montague fleet would take no part in any enterprise which involved a human cargo.

Moreover, Henry was also aware that contraband had been brought into the castle through the purpose-built secret passages. That too was going to stop. He was an honourable man after all and valued his honesty and good name far more than simple profit. At his order, the labyrinth of passages, were duly sealed off.

Of the household staff, only Nabila knew of their existence; everything to do with them had been kept secret for fear of word reaching the excise men. Servants with a grudge tend to have loose mouths; a slip of the tongue or a deliberate accusation by someone with an axe to grind could have had serious repercussions for Lord Montague. Evasion of tax would mean a prison sentence, wealthy or not. Henry wanted that era put behind him as soon as possible.

Rowboats no longer entered the estuary with their barrels of rum, brandy, or Madeira. Boxes, barrels, and crates were not carried into the castle by way of those narrow, steep stairs cut by hand into the rock face. The labyrinth of tunnels with rooms branching off them were no longer filled with rolls of silk, fine wines, rich fur pelts or sacks of sugar. Those days were over.

Only Nabila worked the tunnels now and she made them her own. The labyrinth of passages was not a maze to her, she knew them inside out. She watched unseen the goings on within the castle, able to overhear conversations between masters and servants alike. No part of Eastlyn was closed to her. Locked doors did not prevent Nabila from entering any room she chose.

Chapter Seventeen
A Glimpse of the Future

It would be a day never to be forgotten and for two reasons. Firstly, people would remember Abigail's quite exceptional funeral, for if a person's laying to rest could ever be an event described as beautiful, then this was such a one. Secondly it was the unprecedented fog which descended upon the land-a dank embrace, cocooning the world from all light, heat, and colour. Indeed, the first thing that Robert had noticed on the morning of the funeral was the grey gloom beginning to surround the castle. Drawing back the curtains in the room which now served as his bedchamber he watched wistfully, as a bleak mist invaded the castle grounds, slowly obliterating and obscuring his vision of the gardens and the courtyard.

By the time Reverend Hatfield arrived to lead the funeral party to the chapel, the fog could be likened to a thick, amorphous, lingering blanket—a malicious, flowing dark pall—in Robert's imagination like the Angel of Death would have appeared as it engulfed and smothered Egypt. As he walked behind the coffin, he noticed there was something about the fog which meant that its movement was most visible at the periphery of his vision, just as ghosts are said to be discernible only out of the corner of the eye. Abigail's ghost, how he would have loved that to appear before him!

Instead, only the tall trees which lined the walkway with their bent and twisted branches seemed to emerge out of nowhere, their dark shapes looming upon him like mythological demons waiting to pounce out of the mists which swirled about them. The fog was now so dense, he could scarce see his hand in front of his face, let alone the coffin on its horse-drawn carriage. He followed just a few feet behind, resolute, and steadfast in his desire to accompany Abigail as she made her final journey.

There was no daylight to speak of, the sun and sky had been completely blotted out. All sound too had been muted. The carriage wheels appeared to move silently across the stony causeway and even the slow, mournful toll of church bells was hushed and stifled. Surprisingly, as he listened to the muffled sound of his own footsteps on gravel all the anxiety that had been an ever-present symptom of his distress and grief since the loss of his wife left him. For the first time in a while, he felt rested, calm. As he took his seat in the front pew, he let out a breath he didn't know he was holding. It mattered not that all eyes were on him, he would listen to the service, knowing that she had planned everything, each minute detail carefully selected and with purpose. Every hymn used, every reading, every sentence, indeed every word, would be for him, to give comfort and sustain him.

All too quickly the service and the burial were over. The day now lay quiet, and time seemed suspended, as Robert stared down at his wife's mahogany coffin and gently dropped a single red rose upon it. He spoke to no one. In this bleak hour he had abandoned his fellow man. There was nothing anyone could say or do that would bring his beloved Abigail back. Like a lost ship he was marooned in a sea of well-meaning faces etched with tension, as they too, tried to mask an overwhelming sense of loss. Some struggled to speak but could not. Unable to find the words of consolation and solace needed to raise Robert from his state of deep despondency, they remained silent. So it was, that one by one the mourners began to slowly drift away. Respectfully, Robert was left alone to his own thoughts. He, however, was too lost in his grief, blind and deaf to all about him, even to notice their departure or hear the sound of Thomas's kindly voice trying in vain to beckon him away.

'Go home, Robert, go home. Our daughter needs you.' A familiar voice spoke softly in his ear. He shrugged his shoulders, realising that grief and desolation was playing tricks on his mind. How he wished he could hear the voice of his beloved wife once more. But that would never be, death had torn her from him, and his life had lost all its joy and colour.

Nonetheless, as if responding to her request, 'I don't like to leave you,' he replied thickly.

The grey mist swirled about him. He watched its silvery strands slowly seep into the grave at his feet, cascading down onto the coffin and encircling the solitary red flower head with its soft, silk-like petals. And suddenly, without warning his mind reluctantly returned to the night of Maddie's birth. He had held

Abigail in his arms, desperately praying for a miracle, for God to save her. He remembered her dying words and how they had confused him. Even now, he had no idea, what it was that she had tried to tell him, but he had heard the desperation in her voice and to comfort her, had feigned an understanding of her words. Once again, it was as if he could hear her voice speaking to him.

'I will always be with you, Robert. Remember that Maddie's destiny has been foretold and you must have faith. I will not be alone. There are many here waiting for me to join them. I, they, all rely on you. Believe me. You have a task now and you must not fail. Keep our precious daughter safe, protect her at all costs and one day, you will see, Maddie will lead us out of the darkness and back into the light.'

'Robert, we must return to the castle, the wake.' Thomas, Robert's younger brother laid a comforting hand on his shoulder. 'Time to go,' he said.

'Yes, you go on, I'll follow in a moment.' Tears pricked anew in Robert's eyes as he finally turned and made his way back to the castle. A trembling hand wiped them away as he prepared to re-join his guests for the wake.

On reaching the main entrance, an iron-bound door of hard oak, was slowly drawn open and an old, Black woman, with a mass of silvery-grey afro textured hair framing a heavily wrinkled face, greeted him unsmiling. Standing on the top step, she loomed above him, her piercing eyes staring into his as if trying to read his innermost thoughts.

Robert shivered unwittingly and looking up into the large vacuous eyes he knew so well, yet understood so little, he was reminded of her unusual stature. Big-boned, brawny, tall even by a man's standard and still incredibly muscular in spite of her advanced age, he felt almost threatened by her presence.

'They are all waiting for you,' she said in a low, rasping voice devoid of emotion.

Robert watched her shrivelled, lizard-like lips moving, stretching the deep furrows which lined her face and chin. He noted again the withered, pitted skin, the cold eyes, and wondered not for the first time, why his wife had ever engaged her as her personal maid. 'Bella, the unfathomable, the stranger in our midst,' he thought to himself as he strode past her and re-joined the living world once more.

Maddie was less than two weeks old when her mother was buried in the small, private cemetery which belonged to the Montague family. Robert, her father, and the tenth Lord of Eastlyn Castle was heartbroken at the loss of his wife and yet somehow it appeared to certain close relatives, he seemed resigned to the cruel fate which had been thrust upon him.

'I'm amazed you carried yourself so well today,' said Thomas when the wake was finally over. 'I know how much Abigail meant to you. She would have been proud and not least of the service itself.'

'Oh, don't credit me with any of that,' Robert replied. 'Abigail had the funeral planned out months ago, well before Maddie was born. All I had to do was to follow her instructions to the letter. She'd studied our family history you see and was under no illusion as to what might happen to her in childbirth, especially if the baby was a girl!'

'I'm glad Elizabeth and I, were unaware of the danger. She was so happy you know. We knew she was having twins and we were so excited. It's been hard bringing them up alone. I still miss her terribly.' Thomas instantly noticed the flicker of pain which flashed across Robert's eyes. 'Sorry old man,' he continued, 'I don't mean to make things worse for you on this awful day of all days. It does get easier in time, or at least I grieve less often than I used to. I even have days when an hour or two can pass and I haven't thought about Elizabeth once. The children have helped. They've been such a comfort, just as Maddie will be for you.'

Robert nodded, trying to maintain his composure. A shaking hand lifted a decanter of port from a side table and poured a goodly measure into the glass his brother was holding.

Thomas raised it to his mouth and drank deeply. 'If there is anything I can ever do to help, you only have to ask. It's no consolation I know, but at least you only have the one to raise and Aunt Frances will give you all the support she can. She loved Abigail like a daughter. Maddie will be her joy, her treasure.'

The two men moved closer to the fire. Drinks in hand they gazed silently down at the red coals, both drowning in a river of unhappy memories which now invaded their thoughts. There came a knock at the library door, and Bella, a servant of long-standing at the castle, appeared once more. 'Will you be wanting anything else, master?' she enquired.

'No, Bella, if you could just check on little Maddie for me, you can retire for the night.'

'I've done that already, master. Miss Frances is sitting with her, and the baby is fast asleep.'

'Nevertheless, check again on your way to bed,' he replied, turning away, and pouring yet another drink into his now empty wine glass.

Unseen, Bella's mouth twisted irritably. She left the room, carefully concealing the black anger in danger of darkening her already ebony face. The door closed quietly behind her.

'Top up?' Robert asked his brother, proffering the half-empty decanter.

'No, not for me thanks, I've had more than enough. I think I'll follow Bella's example and head off to bed.' Thomas approached his older brother and embraced him fondly. 'Don't stay up too late,' he advised, 'and don't drink too much. Believe me, it doesn't help.'

Left alone, Robert pulled a chair close to the fire. He stared vacantly at the flames, hardly even noticing the warmth they provided. His mind was full of Abigail, the only woman he had ever loved, his helpmate in life, his best friend, his very soul mate. How would he live without her?

'You must live, Robert,' he imagined her voice saying, as if she was speaking to him from the grave. 'You have our daughter to care for now and I'm relying on you to be father and mother to her. Do not forget the prophecy. Stay strong.'

The decanter was empty by the time Robert finally went to bed. En route he called into the nursery. Aunt Frances was fast asleep in an armchair placed right next to the cot. The baby too was sleeping peacefully. She looked beautiful, the perfect likeness to her mother and so angelic. 'How could God do this to us?' he thought to himself with bitterness. Tiptoeing out of the room, he made his way along the corridor to his own bedchamber. Since the loss of his beloved Abigail, he had taken into sleeping in a room, adjacent to the marital suite he had once happily shared with his wife.

He made to open the door and then stopped in his tracks. His eyes focused on a large oil painting hanging on the wall above him. It was a portrait of one of his ancestors, the first Lord of Eastlyn to be precise, one Lord George Montague.

'You may be of my line, George, but there is something about you I do not like,' Robert whispered to the face in the painting. It was a fat face, swollen, bloated and with a sagging jowl, 'and you certainly liked to dress to impress didn't you.' Robert looked closely at the canvass and observed with interest the elaborate uniform worn by his ancestor.

The first Lord of Eastlyn was attired in a sumptuous suit of scarlet. He wore a double-breasted dress jacket, embellished with two parallel columns of gold buttons and with lavish shoulder epaulcttes made of gold facing. The epaulette on the right, in particular, with its additional ornate aiguillettes attached, left one in no doubt that here was a man of considerable wealth. Further gold stitching and decorative panels could also be seen on the jacket's distinctive raised collar, peaked lapels, and generous cuff bands. Underneath the jacket, he wore a white ruffled shirt, with a black cravat tied around his very thick and expansive neck. A gold, silk waistcoat, intricately embroidered with silver thread and worn over the shirt did little to hide his vast paunch. Below the waistcoat, bulging hips and thighs were covered with matching scarlet breeches buttoned just above the knee with yet more gold buttons. From the knee down, white leggings were fastened and held in place with garters decorated with golden tassels, whilst contrasting black shoes endowed with enormous gold buckles adorned his feet. The white powdered wig he wore was the fashion of his day. A black tricorne hat trimmed with gold lace, completed the ensemble.

Robert read the inscription at the bottom of the painting.

Lord George Montague 1st Lord of Eastlyn Castle and Captain of The Black Stag, Merchant Vessel of the Montague Fleet. The painting was dated December 19, 1752 and signed, Thomas Gainsborough.

'1752, about the time this all started,' Robert murmured to himself. 'If only you could talk, George, give us an explanation as to how this curse came about. Three hundred years of misery, George, that's what you have bequeathed our family. But would you even care, I wonder.' Robert could not help but notice the expression depicted by the artist in Lord George's eyes. They were heartless, cold, clinical, and devoid of all human kindness. 'No, George, I certainly do not like the look of you,' he repeated, 'and looking at all the gold on display, I've no doubt that everyone around you, knew exactly what a fat, rich bastard you were.

If only someone who had survived the shipwreck had written a detailed account of the events which took place prior to the ship sinking,' he thought to himself, 'someone who could have given information on the 1st Lord's character and with knowledge of his business dealings.' Robert knew the extent to which the Montague family had been involved slavery. It was something of which he was not proud. He also knew that *The Black Stag* had been shipwrecked in 1753 and that she had been a purpose-built slave ship of the worst kind. Sinking at sea in a violent storm she had taken her entire cargo of Black prisoners with her. All had perished, or so Robert thought.

He sighed and opening the bedroom door made his way slowly to the unfamiliar bed. Too tired even to bother undressing, he lay on top of the duvet and tried to blot out memories of Maddie's traumatic birth and of his wife dying in his arms.

Deep in the castle vaults, Bella, the Black maid, was also lost in memories from the past. Voices called to her from long, long ago. Cries for help, she could not heed. She clasped her hands about her ears, but she could not stop the pitiful pleas which tortured her day and night. Awake, asleep, it made no difference. Ghosts walked about her, demanding vengeance and they gave her no peace.

She closed her eyes and allowed her mind to wander. No longer lying on a cold stone floor, she was resting in long grass, with a brilliant sun high in the sky above her. No longer old and tired, she was young again, muscular, powerful, and back in her beloved homeland, Africa.

Bella's mouth curved into a satisfied smile. How good life had been once upon a time. She remembered her youth with pride, her warrior status, how she had been valued and admired by all her people. Servants had waited on her in those bygone days, and she had been a loved and cherished member of the royal household.

Eastlyn Castle and its pompous lords were nothing in comparison to the Dahomey palace in which she had lived and the mighty kings who had honoured her.

Chapter Eighteen
The Loneliest Christmas

A year had passed since Clarissa's funeral. Maddie was home from school. She had been at the castle but two days when the news she had been dreading arrived. Uncle Thomas had written to say that he and Rowan would not be coming for Christmas this year and Christmas without Rowan was like champagne without bubbles. Maddie's father explained that the memories were for the present too painful. The loss of Clarissa had been a terrible shock for all the family but that for her father and brother the wound was still too raw. They needed more time to grieve, to recover. By next Christmas they would feel better.

However, there was one consolation. To celebrate Maddie's thirteenth birthday on January 6, the family would be driving down to Bristol to stay at Uncle Thomas's house for a week. Aunt Frances would accompany Maddie on the journey down on January 4. Maddie's father would arrive just in time for her birthday. Maddie contemplated what their trip to Bristol would be like. 'When we visit,' she thought to herself, 'I must be careful what I say to Rowan. I don't want to rekindle painful memories. I ought not to mention Clarissa at all. I think I'll speak to Aunt Frances about it. She'll know what to do for the best. I'm on my own so often nowadays, the last thing I want to do is to alienate Rowan by making a thoughtless remark. I'd hate him to be like my other cousins. But I would like him to know how much I miss Clarissa. I could suggest we light a candle in the cathedral for her. Oh no, that would never do. It would be bound to upset him.'

There were just two days to go to Christmas Day. Maddie was in her room, putting the finishing touches to a parcel she had been wrapping for her father. After adding the final blue bow and ribbon, she wrote out a loving message on the label, carefully trying to make her handwriting the best she could. Her school report had made mention of her much-improved penmanship, it read:

'Magdalene's beautiful cursive script is hardly recognisable to the illegible scrawl it was at the beginning of the year. She is to be congratulated on the hard work she has put in to improve.'

Her father had been very impressed with the report in general and delighted with the comments from her piano and vocal tutors in particular. Both had been rapturous in their praise of her significant talents. The beaming smile and the pat on the head had said it all. Maddie as a result was thrilled by this unfamiliar response. She usually felt she had somehow disappointed him with her lack of progress. Her dearest wish in the world was to make him happy, at Christmas time especially, when she knew he missed her mother most.

She skipped downstairs to the great hall to place her father's final present under the giant tree. Around its base lay dozens and dozens of parcels almost hidden from view under fragrant pine scented branches. Package after package, all beautifully wrapped in brightly coloured Christmas paper was just waiting to be opened. As Maddie surveyed the scene with eager anticipation an unexpected, unwelcome thought crossed her mind. 'Yes, there are lots of presents, but there'll be none here this year for Clarissa, Rowan and Uncle Thomas.' Her mood changed immediately as she realised that just like her father, she was terribly lonely too, even unhappy. She walked over to the window with heavy heart and gazed absentmindedly through the small lattice glass panes and out across the castle grounds.

Her eyes immediately spotted her cousins. They were out riding together. She could see Finn on Warrior leading the way. Judging by the route they were taking she guessed they were heading for the forest. How she wished she could ride with them. 'Not that they'd want me, of course,' she thought sadly to herself. Maddie returned to her room to collect her winter coat. A necessary decision had been made. She really didn't feel like being on her own and with her father and Aunt Frances gone into town to do some last-minute shopping, the only option to find pleasant company to amuse herself with, was to seek out either Arthur or Sam.

As expected, they were working in the yard. She could hear the sound of wood being chopped as soon as she stepped outside. They were each standing beside a large block of wood, 'The individual sections that must have been hewn from a massive tree trunk,' Maddie thought to herself. For safety reasons Maddie guessed the tree trunks had been placed several yards apart, and both men were wearing protective goggles. She watched in silence for a minute or two admiring their skill. The axes struck with great force and time and again a small log placed on the chopping block was cleaved with absolute precision and split perfectly in two. 'Sam, Arthur, can I help?' Maddie called out loudly as she ran towards them.

'Oh, my Lor, careful child,' shouted Arthur. 'These here sticks have a nasty tendency to fly off at all angles. We wouldn't want you getting one in the eye now would we. Stand back, Miss Maddie, there's a good girl. Don't get too close.' A disappointed Maddie stopped dead in her tracks.

'You all right, Miss Maddie?' asked Sam, noting her sad expression.

'Yes,' she lied. 'I'm just a bit bored, that's all.'

'I tell you what, soon as I've finished these logs, how's about we saddle Eclipse up and I'll take you for a ride in the paddock?'

'Oh, would you, Sam. That would be great,' Maddie replied happily. 'Dad's gone into town, you know, so I could get her ready myself, if you agree, of course?'

Sam looked anxiously at Arthur. 'Yes, go on lad, it is Eclipse. You do know how much that old grey mare loves Miss Maddie. And in all my life I've never known a horse so placid—steady as a rock she is. She'll be safe enough, I guarantee.' Arthur advised with conviction.

'Go on then,' Sam agreed, giving Maddie a smile and a nod of consent. Maddie didn't need telling a second time. She shot off immediately for Eclipse's stable and lovingly saddled her up. Sam's timing was perfect. He arrived just as the last buckle was being fastened. Maddie was given a leg up onto the saddle and after checking the straps were tight enough and that Maddie's feet were correctly placed in her stirrups, Sam led Eclipse and her rider out of the stable and into the paddock.

'We'll do some long reining today, Maddie. You'll feel more in charge of Eclipse that way, but I'll have her on this lunge line to reinforce your commands.' Sam attached the rope to the bit in Eclipse's mouth and then moved away, standing a good nine feet back from the horse and rider. 'Okay,' he said, 'start by telling her to walk on.'

The lesson continued with Maddie loving every minute. It really did feel as if she were in complete control. She asked Eclipse to walk on and halt, steering her right and left as required with consummate ease. 'I'm going into a jog trot now, Sam,' Maddie called out happily, as she and Eclipse began a full circuit of the paddock.

'Well done,' shouted Sam after two full laps had been completed. 'Try taking her on a diagonal now. Do a full length plus the bottom side and then turn her on a diagonal and come through these two cones I've placed here in the centre.' To Maddie's great delight, just as Sam had finished speaking, the sound of horses' hooves approaching told her that her cousins were arriving back. Sure enough, the boys and their mounts were soon entering the yard. She desperately wanted them to see how well she was doing.

Fred, the eldest, had observed Maddie on Eclipse. 'Listen lads, best if we put the horses back in the stables ourselves today. Looks like Sam's got his hands full with her ladyship at the moment,' he shouted, pointing to the paddock. A little while later all but two of the cousins had returned to the castle in search of Mrs Reed and refreshment. Fred and Finn, however, curious to see how Maddie was getting on had come to stand by the wooden fence which surrounded the paddock and were watching her efforts with interest.

She now had Eclipse working in a slow trot and looked very comfortable in the saddle. Just at that moment Bella entered the yard carrying two enormous Norfolk Black turkeys, one in each hand. She and Eclipse reached the far-left hand corner of the paddock at the same time and although on opposite sides of the fence, the horse reacted immediately.

Maddie felt Eclipse's body tense, Sam saw it happen. In seconds, the startled horse had bolted across the paddock. Sam did well to keep hold of the lunge line. For several minutes' chaos reigned as Eclipse bucked and reared, whinnying noisily. Somehow Maddie managed not to fall off, clinging to the saddle for all she was worth. Finally, Sam had hold of Eclipse's bridle. He turned the horse round and whispering to her gently, calmly led her to the far side of the paddock and as far away from Bella as possible. Eclipse soon began to settle.

'Pity that, I had hoped her ladyship might fall and break her neck,' Finn said cruelly to his older cousin.

'Why don't you come with me then, Master Finn,' suggested Bella who was standing right behind him. 'You can break these two necks instead, if you've a mind to?' Two large turkeys were held high in the air, their long necks dangling in front of his eyes. Bella watched the colour drain from Finn's face. 'Best to kill them in the old way though,' she continued, her eyes piercing his with a fixed stare of pure evil. 'I hang them up by their feet see.'

Finn felt a rope being tied around his ankles. He saw himself being strung up from a metal hook projecting from a rafter in the roof of the hay barn. 'Then I feel for the jugular in the neck.' Finn felt strong fingers pressing into his throat. 'Then with me sharp knife I cut right through the vein. The bird's alive see, the heart's still pumping, so all the blood gushes out.' Finn could hear his blood dripping onto the floor. 'Yes, the blood flow is strong if you make sure you cut deep enough,' Bella continued. 'During the bird's last gasp, they flap their wings see, mighty powerful their wings are, you might get hurt.'

'Was that a veiled threat?' he wondered.

'You got to watch out for these claws too. See how sharp they are? Well,' she concluded, 'you coming to help me or not?'

It was Fred who answered in a nervous tone of voice, 'Thanks for the offer, Bella, but we'll decline on this occasion, if you don't mind.'

'Suit yourselves,' she replied, and releasing Finn from her stare she turned and headed off towards the kitchen, carrying the two turkeys to their imminent death.

'You idiot,' said Fred when she had gone. 'Wanting Maddie to break her neck is going a bit far, don't you think?'

'Fred you can't seriously think I meant it. I was just joking, of course.'

'Trouble is, Finn, I'm sure Bella thought you meant it. You've made an enemy there for life!'

Finn shrugged his shoulders as if he didn't care. 'Come on,' he replied, 'best help Sam getting Maddie and Eclipse back to the stable.'

Chapter Nineteen
Out of the Saddle

On Christmas Day one of the Norfolk Black turkeys made the centrepiece for dinner. 'Hawkins tells me we've prepared over two thousand birds this year, which by all accounts should make a tidy profit for the estate.' Lord Robert announced to the family as the bird was carved.

'He's a good man, Arthur Hawkins. I've got a lot of time for him,' commented Uncle William, 'and he's very proud of his Norfolk Blacks, spent some while the other day telling me all about them. He reckons that they are a quality product which explains why they sell so well. All free range and allowed to roam on Eastlyn's herb-rich pastures as well as being fed the finest corn and windfall apples on the farm.'

'Well, I must say,' said Aunt Kate agreeing with her husband, 'this is a most delicious meat with a lovely texture and flavour. I think I can manage another helping.' Only Finn and Frederick seemed less enamoured with the turkey served on their plates. Each in his mind's eye had a clear vision of Bella cutting through a jugular vein and blood spurting out of a long dangling neck.

As Finn buttoned his polka dot pyjama jacket that night there was a knock at his bedroom door. He wondered who it could be. He wasn't expecting anyone and had already said goodnight to all the family. Wrapping his dressing gown around him he made his way to the door. On opening it he was most surprised to see a particular visitor. It was none other than Bella.

Indeed, it took a few moments for Finn to realise exactly who it was. The person was holding a bright candle in one hand and a mug at his shoulder level in the other. At first the brightness of the flame caused him to squint a little. Gradually Finn's eyes adjusted to the flickering light, revealing Maddie's Negro maid standing just a step back from the centre of the doorway. She towered above him, her huge, expressionless face looking almost inhuman.

Finn could not help thinking that Bella's face was like a Halloween mask made up of thick, black, wrinkled skin not too dissimilar to rhinoceros hide. But it was her eyes which startled him most. Their odd colour and piercing whiteness made her look ghoulish and infinitely frightening like some infernal phantom. 'A cold night, master,' she said in a low-pitched, gravelly tone. Despite his best efforts to look calm, Finn felt his body flinch at the sound of her voice. The mask slipped for a brief second and an expression flashed across the staring red-flecked eyes. Finn struggled to read it.

'Old Bella has brought you this, master. You must drink it whilst it's hot, 'twill warm you. Ready the young master for his bed. You need a good night's sleep. It will be a big day for you tomorrow, what with you leading the hunt.' With that Bella thrust the mug of hot cocoa she had prepared into his now waiting grasp. Finn closed the door and listened. He stood where he was for several minutes. He could hear the sound of shuffling slippers slowly moving away down the corridor until only a heavy, ominous silence remained. Finn locked the door, turned the knob, and pulled. The door did not budge, it was safely locked. He returned to his bed, drank the now lukewarm cocoa, and placed an empty mug on his bedside cabinet.

'Hmm, the cocoa's not half bad,' he thought to himself, 'but how bizarre that she should have bothered.' Finn had always had the distinct impression that Bella herself, or whatever her name was, didn't like him. In fact, he would have gone as far as to stake his life on the supposition that she positively disliked him. And after the other day, when he had joked about wanting Maddie, her precious little charge, to break her neck and in Bella's earshot, it made the gesture even more surprising.

'God, she's weird. I hope she hasn't poisoned this,' and picking up the mug again he looked at the residue in the bottom. 'Come to think of it, it does have an odd aftertaste and what is it about her and candles? Just switch the ruddy lights on, woman. Electricity has been at the castle since it was first invented. Goodness only knows why Uncle Robert keeps the tallow room going.'

Finn slept soundly that night and had it not been for the great kerfuffle down in the yard, he would have slept late. He woke with a jolt to the sound of hounds barking and horses' hooves clattering on cobbles right below his window as the hunt gathered.

'Oh, my Lord!' he exclaimed, leaping out of bed, and racing to the wardrobe where his riding gear had been carefully stowed, ready, and waiting. Moving so quickly he suddenly felt a little light-headed, almost dizzy and grasped a nearby chair to stop himself from falling. His mouth too felt dreadful, dry, and sticky, and the schoolboy expression 'tastes like the bottom of a birdcage' sprang into his mind.

He reached for the pitcher of water on his dresser and returned to his bedside cabinet to make good use of the mug Bella had brought him the night before. It was missing. He knelt down and examined under the bed; perhaps he had knocked it off during the night. There was no sign of it. The only thing he did spy was a small lock of what appeared to be his own hair lying on the carpet. 'Odd,' he thought to himself and looking in the mirror he noted that some of the hair above his right temple had been cut away.

A stone rapped sharply against the windowpane, breaking his train of thought if not the glass. Angry and irritable now he strode across the room and undid the latch. Tristan was standing below in the yard. 'You're missing the jugs,' he shouted, raising a half-full silver tankard high in the air above his head. 'Come on, slowcoach. Sam's had Warrior ready and saddled ages ago. The great beast needs its master! What on earth is keeping you?' Finn needed no other encouragement, he was dressed in seconds. The door was unlocked and drinking from the pitcher itself he raced down the main staircase and into the great hall. Cheers went up from some of the riders already gathered inside.

Finn slammed the now empty pitcher down on top of a chest of drawers, before rushing outside into the bright sunshine. The day might not have started well but he was determined the rest of it would be glorious. After all this was to be his big day, his moment to show everyone his riding skill, his courage, his chance to be at the front with the pack.

Since the ban in England and Wales in 2004, when fox hunting was outlawed, the Eastlyn hunt had turned to drag hunting for its sport. This involved an object being dragged over the ground to lay a scent for the hounds to follow. Some considered it a beneficial change, it was quicker, with followers not having to wait for the hounds to pick up a scent, and often covering an area far larger than a traditional hunt. Aunt Frances in particular definitely agreed with the ban and had always considered foxhunting as being, in the words of Oscar Wilde, 'the unspeakable in full pursuit of the uneatable.'

Uncle William had the task today of laying the trail. He would be riding on Trojan, a magnificent field hunter, renowned for his endurance, level-head, and bravery. As a draft-cross, Trojan was well suited to rocky terrain, steep climbs, plunging descents and would jump any and all obstacles put in front of him. The route Uncle William had planned was going to test the skills and abilities of every horse and rider in the field, however experienced, and had been carefully planned to cover a diverse and challenging landscape. Quite by chance he had come across a fox lying dead in the road just days before. The fox, which had clearly been hit by car had been wrapped in a cloth soaked in fox urine and would leave a clear and easily recognisable scent for the hounds to follow. As soon as he saw Finn emerge from the house, he was off.

Leaving the yard and the sound of barks and yelps from a forty strong pack of hounds, all with tails wagging furiously and eager for the hunt to begin, he rode Trojan towards the forest. The lure, attached to his saddle by a length of rope, dragging on the ground behind him. Riding to the highest point in the forest, he would turn left and take a well-known bridle path which dropped steeply into plummeting dips and at times clung to the side of distracting, sheer drops which illuminated this section of the forest. Then he would begin a gradual descent though dense woods, crossing rivers and streams on route and all the while, with a backdrop of spectacular pine forests and rugged mountains to admire.

The concluding sections of the route would traverse rich farmland consisting of a patchwork of arable fields and lush water meadows, all dissected by shoulder height hawthorn hedgerows needing to be jumped, or, for the fainter hearted, wooden crossbar gates needing to be opened. The trail would eventually lead down into a green valley beneath the Snowdonia Mountain range. The actual destination for the hunt was a giant oak tree on a hillside slope above the *Old Man in the Moon* pub. High up in the branches, Uncle William intended to suspend the roadkill well above ground level. He would attach the yellow victory flag to a lower branch for the first rider to grasp in triumph and with which to lay claim to the much-prized annual trophy.

The pub was an old coaching inn, equipped with stables and a paddock in which the horses could be tethered, fed, and watered after their long ride. Even now, in pride of place on the bar inside the main lounge, the silver Boxing Day trophy was sitting awaiting the victorious rider. For the remaining, and disappointed participants of the hunt, a superb buffet was laid out ready and waiting to be served. Add to that the huge variety of homemade ales, for which the pub was famous, there was more than enough sustenance to cheer and revive every rider, quench any thirst, and satisfy even the hungriest of appetites.

Finn watched his uncle depart and began to time the customary twenty minutes before he would lead the hunt out after him. It was a proud moment, and he was determined to be the first to catch up with the lure, and best of all he would be riding on the finest horse in the county, his very own, mighty Warrior. Since Finn's eighteenth birthday in the spring when he had been given the colt by his Uncle Robert, he had spent every possible hour riding him, preparing him for today.

At last, everything was ready. Twenty minutes had passed, and the horn sounded for the hunt to be off. But, in that moment of great excitement and anticipation disaster struck. Even before the first hound or horse had cleared the yard, Finn was out of his saddle and on his back on the cobblestones.

Warrior could easily have been mistaken for a wild, unbroken stallion being ridden for the first time, he bucked and reared like a thing possessed. The huge horse crashed into rider after rider, its massive hooves creating damage and havoc everywhere. Stable doors were kicked off their hinges, fallen riders trampled underfoot and Finn himself badly injured. Madness and mayhem reigned as Sam desperately tried to grasp Warrior's now loose and trailing reins.

Finally, bravely, with no thought for his own safety, Sam managed to bring the horse under control. 'Steady boy, whoa. Good boy, yes, there's a good boy,' he spoke soothingly, calmly, gently coaxing the majestic horse into silent submission. The snorting and loud, high-pitched roaring slowly stopped as Warrior began to settle. Finally, Sam was able to lead him away from the carnage of the yard and keeping tight hold of his rein he walked him out into the paddock.

'Fetch Dr Golding at once!' shouted Uncle Harry. 'Finn's badly hurt.' Sometime later, word reached Maddie's ears that Finn had suffered a broken leg. Aunt Mary had been in a terrible state, indeed the whole household was in complete uproar. Maddie had excused herself from her distressed relatives and had sought sanctuary in the kitchen.

'Poor lad, his injury must have hurt something terrible,' said Mrs Reed as she poured yet another cup of tea for Sam and Maddie. 'I saw the horse stamp on his leg myself, with my own eyes. It was a terrible sight, truly terrible. I doubt I'll be able to sleep for a week, never mind tonight. That memory will haunt me for a very long time. Shocking it was, quite shocking.'

'It'll be something I'll never forget,' echoed Sam sadly. He began to cry again. Maddie put her arm around him but try as she might she could give no comfort.

'I had to do it, see,' he sobbed. 'If anyone had to do it, it had to be me. He trusted me, he knew me inside and out, just like I knew him. Reared him from a foal I did, and I never known him like that afore. Big horse he was, the biggest ever, but no harm in him. I only called him Warrior as a joke. Gentle giant he was really, obedient to a fault.' Sam could talk no longer; the sobs took over again, tear after tear splashing onto the old oak table.

'Don't take on so, Sam, my dearest boy. You had your orders to do what you did. There was nothing you could do about it,' Mrs Reed said kindly. 'She cupped Sam's bent head in her hands and kissed the back of it, allowing her lips to rest against the softness of his hair. You need to take comfort in Warrior's foal when it comes. By the looks of that roan mare, she's due any day.'

Maddie's ears pricked up immediately. 'Warrior's foal?' she repeated.

'Yes,' replied Sam. 'Warrior took a fancy to the roan when she arrived last year. I'll know soon as the foal is born if it's Warrior's or not.' He tried to smile, but then his grief over having to put Warrior down flooded back. He covered his eyes with his hands and began to sob again.

'You best get back to the family, Maddie, and see if there is any news from the hospital as to how your cousin is. I'll stay here with Sam, don't you worry.' Mrs Reed concluded.

Maddie gave Sam one final hug and did as she was bid, leaving the kitchen with heavy heart.

'I'm beginning to hate Christmas,' she said to herself as she slowly made her way back to the library in order to re-join her family. The news on Finn was not good. The patella in his right knee had been broken and dislocated. He would be kept in hospital overnight and would not return until next day.

'He's had a plaster cast fitted the entire length of his leg, from hip to ankle. It'll be a while before he's back in action,' Uncle Harry announced sadly. 'Let's just hope there's no permanent damage. Broken-hearted over that horse he is too and blaming me for having it put down. But, Robert, surely you agree with me, what else was I supposed to do? The animal seemed to go berserk for no good reason.'

'I don't think you had any option but to do what you did,' Robert replied. 'Let me pour you a brandy, you look like you could use one.'

It was later than normal when Maddie finally said her goodnights and slowly made her way back up to her bedroom. Aunt Frances accompanied her. 'Would you like me to read you a bedtime story,' she asked, with a worried expression on her face. 'You're never too old, you know.'

'You don't need to worry, aunt. I'll be all right and anyway I'm really tired, I'm sure as soon as my head hits the pillow, I'll be asleep,' she lied.

Aunt Frances kissed her forehead. 'In that case I'd better go and check on your Aunt Mary. I think both she and your Uncle Harry are still in shock,' and with that she returned downstairs.

Maddie opened the door to her bedroom to see Bella kneeling on the hearth rug, stoking up the fire with fresh logs. 'It's been a horrid day,' Maddie heard herself say. Bella made no reply at first. She stood up clutching the now empty log basket in her left hand. The basket hung at her side like a dead animal. Maddie looked into the large, round, furrowed black face. It had no expression, a blank canvas devoid of human kindness and warmth.

'The eyes are pitiless,' she thought to herself, swiftly averting her gaze from Bella's stare. She often wondered if Bella could read her mind, and on this occasion, she knew her old maid would have had good reason to be offended. 'Did you hear about Finn?' she asked, wondering what Bella's reply would be.

'I heard as he won't be riding again for some time. One good thing about it, the next time Sam takes you out on Eclipse, you're not likely to have him making fun of you.'

'Oh, Bella, that's a dreadful thing to say. He may have upset me on the odd occasion, said or done unkind things, but I would never have wished him harm.' Bella responded to Maddie's comment with a withering look and left the room in silence.

Chapter Twenty
Warrior's Foal

Finn was brought home in an ambulance the next morning. Maddie watched him being carried in, along with a wheelchair. He looked pale and drawn, as if he hadn't had a wink of sleep. There were dark circles around his red and swollen eyes. 'He's cried a river over Warrior,' she thought to herself. At three o'clock Maddie paid Mrs Reed a visit in the kitchen. 'I don't suppose you've got any chocolate brownies, have you?' she asked.

'When have you ever known me not to have?' replied Mrs Reed with a wry smile.

'I'd like to take a tray up to Finn if I may? Aunt Mary said he'd hardly eaten a thing at lunchtime,' Maddie explained in a worried tone of voice.

'What a clever idea. I'll make a pot of tea for two and help you carry it up. It's bound to lift his spirits,' she continued kindly. Minutes later Maddie was performing the role of concerned hostess with as much loving attention as she could muster. She served Finn with a plate on which sat a delicious, moist, freshly baked brownie. A cup of piping hot tea, into which two heaped spoons of sugar had been added, was then placed on a little card table positioned at his side and within easy reach.

'I'm so sorry about what happened yesterday. If there is anything I can do to help, you only have to ask,' she offered, whilst looking directly into the now sad eyes.

'That's very kind of you, especially considering how mean I and the other guys have been to you at times.' Finn replied, surprised by her real concern.

'Oh, don't fret about that,' she returned happily. 'I understand why you do it. I'm a girl, aren't I, so I don't quite fit in with all you boys. I try not to take it personally. I know you don't really mean to be cruel, you all just see it as a bit of harmless fun.'

'I've never really thought about it until now, but I expect what you've said is probably right,' he remarked, relieved that Maddie did not hold a grudge.

'I listen to my mother,' Maddie continued. 'She helps to explain things all the time, especially when I'm upset.'

Finn looked concerned, confused and if anything, slightly embarrassed. 'Maddie, your mother is dead,' he pointed out in a gentle tone of voice.

Maddie was going to add that Clarissa spoke to her too, but correctly reading the look of disbelief in Finn's face, she altered what she was going to say to; 'Well, sometimes I think I can hear her, it's as if she can speak to me from the grave. Whenever I'm unhappy or troubled, I hear her voice comforting me. When father's sad too, she advises me on how to lift his spirits, what to say, to help him. Of course, most of the time he puts on a brave face but at certain times of the year, like the anniversary of their wedding, or the day of mother's birthday and Christmas time especially, he changes, becomes very distant, withdrawn. I know he still misses mother terribly, even after all these years. He always says how much mother loved Christmas and that even in her twenties she was as excited on Christmas morning as she had been as a little girl. Her happiness and enthusiasm were infectious. Father says it was as if she could light up the whole castle. She made sure each of the servants had a lovely Christmas gift, and of course they adored her. She's been helping me with that task for years. She always knows exactly what to get everyone. It was at this point that Maddie noticed Finn's anxious, open-mouthed expression and he was clearly struggling to find the right words to reply. 'I expect it's just wishful thinking on my part. I hear what I want to hear, I suppose,' she concluded helpfully.

Finn looked relieved. For the first time in his life, he felt sorry for her. She was lonely for sure and clearly missing having a mother. He had also been impressed by her acumen and perception. 'I've underestimated you, little Maddie,' he thought to himself. 'Would you like to sign my cast?' he asked. 'Everyone else has.'

'Oh, yes,' came the reply. Indecipherable scrawls rather than the signatures of her cousins traversed up and down the entire plaster cast. Maddie chose an empty spot and began to write in her best cursive handwriting. At the end of it, Finn was laughing. 'What's so funny?' Maddie asked starting to laugh too. Finn had an infectious giggle.

'The lads signed in less than ten seconds. You've just taken the best part of ten minutes!'

'Girls for you,' Maddie suggested as if endowed with some kind of superior knowledge. Clearing up the now empty plates and teacups, Maddie left the room saying; 'I'll come and see you again tomorrow. I might have a little surprise for you, just the thing to cheer you up!' She smiled at him and left the room before Finn had the time or presence of mind to question what she meant.

Returning to the kitchen, Maddie was pleased to find a much happier looking Sam enjoying a glass of beer with Mrs Reed. 'To wet the baby's head,' he explained. 'And it's Warrior's foal all right, I'd stake my life on it.' Maddie gave him a huge congratulatory hug before rushing off to see her father. She found him in his office. He was sitting at his computer checking through his e-mails.

'Hallo,' he said warmly. 'What brings you here?'

'Why must I always have a reason for coming to see you?' Maddie asked in an aggrieved tone of voice.

'Well, in that case I apologise,' responded her father, sensing that he had inadvertently given offence.

'Father, did you know the roan mare had her foal today?'

'Yes,' he replied. 'Sam called me to see it about an hour ago. He reckons the mare's going to be an excellent dam and much to his special delight the foal is definitely of Warrior's lineage. Chip off the old block.'

'I was with Finn earlier today,' Maddie continued. 'He's that upset about Warrior being put down. I wondered if there was anything we could do to cheer him up?'

'If you have any good ideas, I'm open to suggestion,' her father chirped happily. From the distinct twinkle in his eye, Maddie wondered if her father had second guessed the purpose of her visit.

'Finn doesn't know anything about Warrior's foal,' she continued. 'I think he'll be so pleased when he does, especially, father, if you were to offer to give him the foal as a gift just like you did with Warrior. He could see him whenever he likes and then take possession of him when he's full grown.'

'Ah, I see,' her father replied. 'Sounds like an excellent plan to me. Do you want to give him the good news or shall I?'

'Why don't we tell him together in the morning? We could take him down to the stables in his wheelchair.' Maddie suggested, her face beaming with happiness.

'I'll mention our idea to your Aunt Mary and Uncle Harry at dinner tonight—in the strictest secrecy of course. I'll suggest Finn leave the sick room and join the family for breakfast tomorrow. We can take him to the stable directly afterwards.'

'Thank you, father, thank you so much,' Maddie replied ecstatically. 'Finn will be over the moon I know.'

'You're a good girl, Maddie, a very good girl. I'm proud of you. Your mother would be too. It's lovely to see you have such feeling for others,' her father concluded, hugging her to him and brushing her hair back from her forehead gently with his hand. Maddie smiled up at eyes she loved dearly.

Finn shed tears of joy when he saw his little foal. It was a time for healing, not just of broken bones, but of relationships too. Finn would never forget his cousin's kindness and finally there was a real bond between them.

It was Maddie's last day at home. She would be leaving for Bristol in the morning. Since Finn's earlier departure she had taken it upon herself to visit the little foal every day, taking with her apples and carrot pieces with which to spoil the dam. On reaching the stable block she found Arthur hard at work, filling an old wheelbarrow with horse manure. 'For the rose garden,' he explained. 'Care to help?'

'Well, I would normally,' she replied, 'but after I've given the dam these little treats, I've promised Aunt Frances I'd help Bella pack my trunk for school. The term will already have started you see so I'm to go straight there after our visit to Uncle Thomas. Aunt Frances doesn't trust Bella to do it by herself, so she's told her to wait for me and you know Bella, she hates to be kept waiting.'

'Don't go talking to me about that there Bella. Sorry Maddie, but I can't stand the woman, frightens me she does. Our Sam, he thinks the same too and he's young and open minded, not old, and cynical like me. Even Sam hasn't got a good word to say about her, excepting that she seems to look after you right enough. But how long for, that's what I want to know?'

'Whatever do you mean?' asked Maddie, eyes wide with curiosity.

'Well, for one thing, that Bella never goes to church not even Easter or Christmas. Our Ethel and me, we brought our Sam up God fearing. He knows his scriptures and that to live in the ways of Jesus is the right way.'

'Perhaps she likes to pray on her own or goes to a different church,' Maddie answered, hoping to resolve Arthur's obvious concerns.

'No, Miss Maddie, I'm not telling no lies, that woman isn't God fearing. Not even last Christmas when poor Miss Clarissa died. All the servants went to the funeral.' We all loved her, see. Church was full to bursting at the seams. Only one person was missing, that Bella! 'Taint right, 'taint proper.'

'Perhaps she was too upset to go,' said Maddie, remembering her own grief at the time and struggling to find a plausible excuse.

'No. You're wrong little miss. She hasn't got feelings for any of us. I reckon her hearts turned to stone. She never talks see and eats alone whenever she can. We hardly ever see her in the kitchen at mealtimes. All the other staff gather around the table, like we've always done. Mrs Reed is a grand cook, does us proud she does. I love a good old chin wag: we gossip, tell jokes, have a mighty fine time in general, we all know each other so well, see. Ah, make a fair old team we do.

But not that Bella! Keeps herself to herself, she does. Sam says as much, and he do say that she proper scares the horses. They go all skittish, crazy like when she's around. Sam prefers it if she stays well clear of the yard and the stables.'

'Yes, I noticed how Eclipse reacted when she passed us in the paddock the other day!' Maddie replied.

'Our Sam told me about that,' Arthur continued, 'said he was proper afeared for your safety. Had to hold the reins real tight he did, least wise until the horse calmed down again. And that's not all Miss Maddie. Sam and I reckon she's one of them there shapeshifters.'

'What on earth is a shapeshifter?' exclaimed Maggie, by now sounding alarmed.

'You know,' replied Arthur, 'one of them devil creatures. They can move through walls and the like, appear in one place one minute and then somewhere else the next! You ask our Sam, he'll tell you same as me. A few months back we were out fishing on the estuary. Walking back to the castle with our catch we spotted Bella by the old boat sheds. Right down at the water's edge she was, washing some kind of metal bowl. Big bowl it was too. Our Sam made a joke about it, said it was her witch's cauldron. Anyway, we passed right by her on the path see, close as I am to you now. She never even acknowledged us, just kept on doing what she was doing. Must have been something not very nice in that bowl, water was dark brown where she was working, looked filthy.

So, Sam and me we just kept going and carried on up the path back to the castle. It was a long walk, you know how steep the climb is coming back from the estuary. And there be only one route, the sheer sides of the valley don't allow for no other way. Well, as true as I stand here before you, Miss Maddie, as we were walking across the yard to the kitchen, who did we see coming out of the tallow room carrying a ruck of candles?' He paused for a brief moment and then continued, 'It was her, see, that Bella. Now you tell me, how could she have gotten from the river back to the castle afore us. She sure as heck didn't pass us on the way. Shapeshifter see, least ways that's what Sam and I think!'

Maddie was too dumbfounded to speak. Arthur continued with his warning. 'Now you listen to old Arthur here. You got to watch yourself. Don't want anything bad happening to you, like it did Miss Clarissa, God rest her soul.'

'Why, why should I watch myself?' Maddie asked in a frightened tone of voice.

Arthur saw the sudden look of fear in Maddie's eyes and realised he had said more than he had originally intended. 'Oh, take no notice of old Arthur, expect I'm just being silly and superstitious. Don't you pay me no mind, little miss?' But then, as if he had a sudden change of heart, he caught Maddie's soft, slender hand in his large, grimy, rough one. 'Just do me a favour,' he said with genuine tears in his eyes, 'don't go trusting that Bella with all your heart. I know she's your servant and you think she looks after you well.'

'And cares for me,' interrupted Maddie.

'Well, even so, just keep your wits about you. I dread to think,' he continued, 'another year will fly by, and Christmas will be here again before we know it.'

'What's Christmas got to do with it?' Maddie asked in all innocence.

Once again Arthur feared he'd said too much. 'Well just that it's that time of year. Anyway, here's me prattling on about nothing. Best get back to work. I need to get them roses seen to, and Mrs Reed wanted some Bramley apples picking an hour ago. I'll be getting shot at this rate,' and with that he released Maddie's hand and strode off briskly towards the orchard.

Maddie watched him go. Her mind was in turmoil. 'What could it all mean?'

Chapter Twenty-One
The Birthday Girl

Where her birthday was concerned Maddie always felt a bit hard done by. Being so close after Christmas she always suspected she didn't get as many presents as she might otherwise have done. In fact, the reverse was true and had she realised, it explained why her cousins were so resentful of her. They thought she was spoilt and that year after year she received preferential treatment even from their parents, let alone her own father.

However, legitimate grievance or not, Maddie could at least lay claim to one particular source of consolation, Aunt Frances. The adopted aunt doted on her. Accommodated in a suite of rooms on the fourth floor of the castle, it was Maddie's favourite port of call. The rooms provided a virtual treasure trove of memorabilia. Hence a visit to Aunt Frances was guaranteed to raise Maddie's spirits in a matter of minutes.

Aunt Frances's living room had a particular smell Maddie adored of old silk and old books and a happy atmosphere too. It was decorated with pretty floral wallpaper and matching chintz curtains. A rich red carpet lined the floor and a beautiful black slate fireplace above which hung the most enormous mirror with an intricate gold surround, provided a focal point for the room which never disappointed. A blazing fire would be waiting to greet you on chilly winter days.

Dotted about the room were small, beautifully engraved tables festooned with vases of fresh cut flowers filling the air with wonderful scent and affording the eye glorious colour. Aunt Frances loved roses, lavender, lily of the valley and anemones in particular and flower arranging was one of her much-cherished skills. There were also deliciously soft chairs and sofas you could sink into, book in hand and velvet covered footstools on which to rest weary legs. Best of all was the green and white china biscuit tin with a silver lid which sat on the top of the dresser. The tin was never empty you could bet your life on finding a custard cream or a chocolate digestive on any day of the week.

There was one other thing Maddie truly adored, all the old photographs. The room was full of them. There were dozens and dozens of pictures of the castle and the staff who worked there, taken long before Maddie was born. More importantly there were photos of her mother. Maddie never tired of hearing stories about the servants of long ago and she especially liked to hear about her mother. Aunt Frances was ready and waiting for the first request. 'Tell me about my—' Maddie began.

'Mother's wedding day,' Aunt Frances interjected immediately.

Maddie laughed. 'Yes, please do,' she continued, 'you know I love that story.' She listened in raptures and for the umpteenth time to the story of her mother's wedding day, how beautiful she had looked, how she had surprised all the family and guests at the wedding breakfast by playing the grand piano and singing a romantic love song to Robert. Aunt Frances had a wonderful way with words and as she described the wedding dances Maddie could almost see herself on the dance floor too, dressed in a fabulous ball gown.

'Your mother and father danced the first dance as is usual, but they completely broke with tradition by dancing the American smooth and not the customary waltz. Oh, Maddie, I can remember it as if it were only yesterday. They were wonderful, gliding and turning about the great hall like Fred Astaire and Ginger Rogers. Professional dancers could not have given a better performance. It was amazing, simply amazing, and your father lifted her as if she were as light as a feather.'

'I wish I could have known her,' Maddie said sadly. 'It would be wonderful if she was still alive, then I could wake up on my birthday and find her here.'

'Speaking of your birthday,' replied her aunt, glad to be able to change the subject, 'there is a trunk of mine up on top of that wardrobe over there,' she said, pointing to a large mahogany wardrobe next to her bed. 'It's not too heavy, I'm sure if I help you, we can lift it down. Inside are all my favourite books, toys, and jewellery from when I was a girl. I'd like you to choose a gift for yourself, something to celebrate you becoming a teenager.' Minutes later a small wooden chest was placed on the floor. Maddie tried unsuccessfully to open the unusual, silver clasp in the shape of a dragonfly. Aunt Frances went to her writing bureau and returned with a key. 'Here, Maddie,' she said, handing it over. 'You'll need this to unlock it. Take your time choosing your special present. I'll get myself another cup of tea whilst you decide.'

It hardly seemed any time at all before Maddie was back at her aunt's side. She had a gold locket in her hand attached to a fine filigree chain. 'Can I have this?' she asked excitedly. 'It's beautiful.'

'Of course,' replied her aunt, smiling warmly. 'I used to keep a picture of my mother in it, many years ago. You could do the same and one of yourself too. You could have great fun getting people to guess which one is who. You are so like her.'

'What a clever idea. It's just a pity about the clothes. The clothes will give the game away as to who is who,' replied Maddie. Aunt Frances began to laugh hysterically.

'What's so funny?' asked Maddie in an indignant tone of voice.

'Oh, Maddie, you can be so comical at times,' replied her aunt. 'Look at the size of the locket, see how small it is. One only ever puts a head shot in, never the photo of someone's whole body. If you were to do that, the person would resemble a tiny ant!'

'I see what you mean,' Maddie said opening the locket and realising how small the space inside was for photos. Now it was her turn to laugh.

'If you go over to my bureau, you'll find a box in the bottom drawer full of old photographs. I'm sure they'll be something there suitable for you. Then all you need to do is to cut it down to size,' suggested her aunt.

'Thank you, aunt that is exactly what I'll do. Thank you so much,' repeated Maddie, 'it's lovely, really lovely.'

The long-awaited day had finally arrived. They were to leave for Bristol straight after breakfast. Bags packed and loaded, Aunt Frances and Maddie sat side by side in the limo. Sam was driving and as usual listening to music from his own iPod. Maddie tried to ask him a question about the length of the journey and what time they were likely to arrive. After several attempts, almost shouting, she gave up and turned instead to Aunt Frances for conversation.

'I'm so glad to be getting away, Aunt Frances. This has been a horrible Christmas!' Maddie said in an injured tone of voice as she watched the castle disappear from view. 'Nowhere near as bad as last year of course, losing Clarissa,' Maddie stopped mid-sentence, overcome with emotion she was unable to continue on.

'Maddie, you must not dwell on the past and for Rowan's sake do not mention Clarissa's death unless of course he raises the subject. He may want to talk about it, often talking about things helps us to get over terrible events that have happened. You will need to be very mature and very strong if he does.' Maddie nodded her head and grasped her aunt's hand in hers for comfort.

'I blame those nurses,' Maddie blurted out suddenly, 'if they had done their job as they should, Clarissa might still be alive. Father should have taken them to court for dereliction of duty!'

'I'm sorry, Maddie, but I cannot agree with you there. I for one felt very sorry for those two poor women. They were very upset you know,' her aunt returned, 'and both so ill that morning, your father felt he had to send for me to look after them. I shall never forget the conversation I had with them, couldn't stop thinking about it for weeks afterwards.'

'Why what did they say?' Maddie asked curious to know how they could account for falling asleep whilst on duty.

'You may not like this Maddie, but it involves Bella.'

'Bella,' echoed Maddie, 'what has she got to do with it?'

'Apparently Bella knocked on Clarissa's bedroom door just before midnight. She had made two cups of cocoa claiming that she had put a little brandy in to help Ms Webb and Mrs Heath stay awake. Ms Webb told me she had thought the cocoa tasted funny but assumed it was just the alcohol. Mrs Heath said there was something about Bella which made her feel uncomfortable, nervous, and even a little threatened, although she couldn't quite put her finger on what it was. Anyway, they claimed to have locked the door for safety's sake when Bella left. They both remembered drinking the cocoa but nothing afterwards.'

'What are you saying, Aunt Frances? That somehow Bella had drugged them? Why would she do that? It just doesn't make any sense.'

'But did you see how very ill they looked that morning? I noticed their complexion straight away. They both looked so pale. Their skin had a strange tinge, yellow, almost jaundiced. There was something wrong in their manner of expression too, a slight slurring of their words. I tell you Maddie, they really were not well at all.' Maddie listened in silence, not knowing what to think.

Her aunt continued with her account, 'The strangest thing was that when they awoke the next morning to find poor Clarissa dead in her bed, they remembered racing to the door and having to unlock it to raise the alarm. They stayed sitting by Clarissa's side until the doctor arrived and during that time only your father, your Uncle Thomas and myself, of course, gained admittance to the room.

At one point they both begged me to get them some water. They were feeling incredibly nauseous—the shock I expect. Anyway, when I said I'd fetch a couple of glasses, they said not to bother, just to use the mugs Bella had brought the night before. Trouble was, Maddie, there were no mugs in the room. We hunted high and low!'

'That's strange,' Maddie repeated, 'especially if the door had been locked all night.'

'I find it all very disturbing,' continued Aunt Frances, 'not least the fact that they have been doing this kind of work for years and have never fallen asleep during a night vigil before. And, Maddie, I'm telling you too much now, but the doctor's diagnosis was even stranger.'

'Why, what did he say?' Maddie asked in consternation.

'That to all intents and purposes Clarissa appeared to have drowned in her sleep!' replied her aunt.

'How can that be possible, Aunt Frances, how can anyone drown in their sleep?'

'Well, of course, both your father and your uncle scoffed at the doctor's supposition. Robert was adamant that Clarissa must have caught some terrible kind of virus, a rare illness which attacks the lungs and about which medical science to date has no knowledge. But, Maddie, when they lifted her poor little body from the bed, I couldn't help noticing her nightgown. It was soaking wet and clinging to her slender frame, small droplets of water falling from it onto the floor! I remember thinking it was like a trail of tears.'

Chapter Twenty-Two
Visit to the Museum

Uncle Thomas and Rowan were waiting to greet them when the car finally pulled onto the drive. Maddie noticed immediately that her uncle had lost weight and that his hair had turned completely grey. Much to her relief, she observed little change in Rowan, and he was clearly as delighted to see her as she was to see him. He helped her carry her bags inside and showed her to her room.

They spent a pleasant evening. After dinner had been served the monopoly board was brought to the table and as always Rowan won. Maddie was bankrupted when her token—a tiny model of an old tall ship—landed on his Park Lane with its three hotels. 'I'm glad we're only playing with pretend money,' Maddie exclaimed as she handed over her final ten-pound note.

'Well, we won't be playing with pretend money tomorrow,' Rowan replied. 'After breakfast I'm taking you into the city to do some birthday shopping. I've been saving my pocket money for weeks so I can buy you a really special present for your thirteenth.'

'I prefer surprises myself,' commented Aunt Frances. 'But if you will allow me to join you, I'll treat you both to lunch. I have some shopping of my own I need to do.'

'Better and better,' said Maddie excitedly.

The next day Sam drove the party of three into the city centre. Uncle Thomas had hoped to join them, but in the end, he had to work. It was arranged that Rowan would ring Sam's mobile when they were ready to return home and that they would be picked up from the same place where they had been dropped off, on Anchor Road not far from the cathedral. Aunt Frances walked the two cousins to *The Glass Boat* restaurant where she had booked a table for lunch. It was a beautiful place and really did look like an actual boat. Situated right on the River Avon its wide panoramic windows afforded the diner wonderful views both up and downstream. 'We'll meet here at one o'clock sharp,' she instructed. 'Don't be late now.'

'Oh, we won't be late,' Maddie cried out excitedly, 'I can't wait, the restaurant looks fabulous!' Aunt Frances threw her a grin and departed.

'Follow me,' said Rowan, 'we'll head to some of the best arcades and have a shop around.' They window shopped for some time. Maddie was spoilt for choice. Rowan had given her so many options she just couldn't decide what she wanted. 'Let's go and have a coffee, while you try to make up your mind!' he said looking around for a suitable place.

'Would there be a coffee shop in there?' asked Maddie, 'pointing to a massive building which dominated the street.'

'Bound to be,' answered Rowan. 'That's the City Museum and Art Gallery. I've always wanted to have a look inside. Come on,' he continued, 'there's no time like the present.' They headed first for the cafeteria where Rowan purchased two large cappuccinos and sat down to enjoy their drinks. For several minutes they chatted happily and then Rowan fell strangely silent. Maddie noticed he was staring at his cup and stirring the froth at the top round and round with his spoon. 'Maddie,' he said breaking the silence, 'have you seen that white moth again, since the funeral?'

'No, I've often looked,' she replied and before she could stop herself added, 'I do miss Clarissa terribly.' A single tear escaped and slowly trickled down her face. She wiped it away quickly, hoping he hadn't seen it. The sound of a chair leg scraping the floor made them both look up. The bright sunlight which had been streaming in through the teashop windows seemed to have vanished, as if the sky outside had clouded over. The room looked darker and much less inviting than it had when they arrived.

'It's chilly in here,' said Rowan, wrapping his coat around him. 'They ought to put more heating on.' Maddie nodded in agreement and wrapped icy fingers around her coffee cup for warmth. She shivered in the chill atmosphere. They saw it at exactly the same moment. A moth, a white moth fluttering in the air just yards away from where they were sitting. The tiny, winged creature began to fly away. Leaving cups, still with more than half their contents inside the two cousins stood to attention and instinctively began to follow. Neither one of them spoke.

The moth flew up a wide flight of stairs, journeying on along an equally wide corridor. It seemed to pass through closed, wooden double doors straight ahead of them. Above the doors a large sign was fixed to the wall, it read: The Slavery Museum. Rowan pushed the doors open and waited for Maddie to enter inside. Fearfully they looked around for the moth. They need not have worried. It was waiting for them and remained hovering in the air just above their heads.

It was off once more on its zigzag journey, finally coming to settle on a large painting hanging on the far-left wall of the museum. Hand in hand Rowan and Maddie approached the dark canvas, the moth's white body, clearly visible against the black background of the painting. The moth vanished as the children found themselves gazing at a familiar picture. It was a copy of the painting hanging in the minstrel's gallery at Eastlyn, a huge oil painting of a tall ship, *The Black Stag.*

Positioned on the floor below the painting was a large lectern with a glass top, inside which numerous sheets of paper were displayed. The sheets contained detailed information about the ship which Rowan began to read aloud. There was also a diagram of the slave quarters, showing how the ship had been designed to accommodate as many slaves as possible and a piece of parchment taken from the ships log, water damaged but still clearly legible. It read, ship sank December 24, 1753.

The cargo two hundred Negro males and fifty Negro females all perished, drowned at sea. *The Black Stag's* owner was Lord George Montague, 1st Lord of Eastlyn Castle, who survived the shipwreck along with six other crew members. There was other disturbing information to be had, drawings of the sugar plantations in the Caribbean, sketches of slaves working in gruelling conditions or receiving horrific punishments. Maddie felt physically sick as she comprehended some of the wicked practices which had gone on.

The whole room was devoted to information on slavery. After their initial shock at seeing the painting, they were curious to visit all the items on exhibition. They now felt drawn to learn as much as they could and together, taking it in turns to read aloud, closely studied all the literature, pictures, and diagrams on offer. They discovered that slave owners had been free to punish their slaves on the slightest provocation, such as incorrectly sweeping the floor or spilling water. Punishments ranged from whipping, branding, getting put in the stocks or the ducking stool, slapping and kicking, to being tarred and feathered.

There were several posters in the exhibition about runaway slaves. Masters had clearly done their utmost to have escaped slaves recaptured. Rewards were offered and the treatment meted out to any slave unfortunate enough to be discovered was often cruel beyond comprehension. Hunting dogs were used to chase the runaways and when caught the slaves were often mauled by the animals or hit senseless with wooden staves by the handlers. Once returned to the plantation owner, worse was likely to follow. To make an example of the runaway in front of the other slaves, men were often castrated or had a body part such as an ear cut off, or their tongue cut out. There were even instances of limbs being amputated. Many slaves died from these brutal and inhuman punishments.

Maddie had returned to look at the painting of *The Black Stag.* Rowan, conscious that time was passing, called to her from the other side of the museum. 'Maddie, we ought to think about leaving. We don't want to be late for Aunt Frances.'

'Rowan, look at this. I didn't see it before. It's a copy of a speech by someone called Thomas Lawson. He was the first mate on *The Black Stag* and one of the survivors.' Rowan came to stand at her side.

Maddie pointed to a framed document pinned on the wall adjacent to the painting. It was a copy of a newspaper article, dated May 19, 1777. 'Mr Thomas Lawson of the city of Bath, a respected Draper and elected to the post of Mayor, formerly first mate aboard *The Black Stag,* has for many years now been a prominent voice in the anti-slavery movement. Today at the Guild Hall, Bath, he delivered an impassioned speech denouncing this wicked trade in which he himself confesses to have once been an unwilling party.'

Gentlemen

I thank you very sincerely for the opportunity you have now afforded me of expressing to you the sentiments which I entertain on the subject of Colonial Slavery. I know that subject is so near the heart of every man who claims a philanthropic or Christian character, that not merely in regard to the circumstances in which I now stand, but for my fair fame among those whose good opinion I am most anxious to cherish and deserve, I am extremely desirous that my sentiments upon it should be distinctly understood. It is, I assure you, a great satisfaction to my own mind, that I can appear before you this day, and can state in all sincerity of heart, that the opinions which I profess now are the same as I have always professed. No man can charge me, therefore, with having assumed these opinions for the promotion of any selfish or personal object. From the moment I joined the crew of The Black Stag to the hour I now stand before you, I have been, (and hundreds can bear testimony to the fact) the zealous and ardent promoter of the Abolition of Slavery.

'Pity he's not still alive. He could have told us everything we need to know about that ship.' Maddie said sadly. Rowan put a comforting arm around her shoulder.

Thanks to Rowan, they left just in time to meet Aunt Frances at the designated hour, although both children had by now completely lost their appetite. The restaurant which had appeared so beautifully designed in the shape of a boat earlier in the day now simply reminded Maddie of *The Black Stag*. As she stepped aboard, she could almost hear the cries of desperate slaves chained and fettered in the most squalid of conditions in the hold below.

Aunt Frances could sense something was terribly wrong and assumed they had been remembering Clarissa. She tried her best to lift their spirits but to no avail. Sam was summoned immediately they left the restaurant. Perhaps because they had been so shocked by what they had seen in the museum neither Rowan nor Maddie felt able to talk either to Uncle Thomas or Aunt Frances. They spoke at length in private.

'I think our fathers know a lot more about all of this family history than they are letting on,' said Rowan. Maddie nodded in agreement. The more they discussed their visit to the museum the more convinced they became that slavery, the slave trade was in some way connected with Clarissa's death. 'December 24, Maddie, did you see the date? The day *The Black Stag* sank to the bottom of the ocean! December 24, the very same day that Clarissa died. There must surely be some kind of connection, but what I wonder?' Rowan added, sounding even more confused than ever.

'Rowan, what are we going to do?' Maddie asked on the day of her birthday.

'For today we just pretend everything is okay. The adults will expect us to be happy and cheerful, you especially, it's your birthday. Can you do that Maddie, can you put a brave face on? Dad's been so unhappy since Clarissa died, I don't want to make things any worse for him, not just at the moment.'

'I agree,' Maddie concurred trying to sound convincing, 'I think we should wait a while, think things through carefully and then decide the best course of action to follow.' The children did their level best over the next few days to act as if everything was normal. They both deserved an Oscar for their performances. They parted company promising to ring each other every day and agreed that each of them would try to come up with a plan.

'I've asked Dad to let us spend the Easter holiday with you at Eastlyn. I'm sure the castle holds the key Maddie. Wait for my visit. We'll try to sort everything then. In the meantime, do as much research as you can. The more we know about what went on the better. And try not to worry. Easter, Maddie. We'll decide what to do at Easter,' said Rowan as he kissed her goodbye.

'Miss Maddie, are you sitting in the back or up front with me?' asked Sam.

'With you please, Sam,' was the reply.

Aunt Frances and Lord Robert stood with Thomas and Rowan until the limousine with Sam driving had disappeared from view. 'Have a good term Rowan,' said Robert before departing with Frances in a separate car.

It was not long before they arrived back at the castle. They entered the great hall to see Bella descending the main staircase. Robert was immediately irritated. 'Bella should know her place and use the servant's stairwell. The main stairs ought to be the domain of family members and invited guests!' he thought to himself. Bella, unaware of his displeasure, or not caring, made her way slowly towards them. 'Is Miss Maddie with you, Sir?' she asked in her gravelly voice.

Her reference to him as 'Sir' grated even more than her use of the staircase. 'I think you mean, Your Lordship,' replied Aunt Frances. There was a moment's silence, Bella did not respond.

In an exasperated tone of voice Lord Robert answered the initial question. 'No, Bella, since the school term has already started, we thought it best she goes back there direct from Bristol. Maddie will not be home now until Easter.'

'Oh,' replied Bella, 'I had hoped to see her before she went back to school, but she'll be back for half term, won't she?'

'Don't you remember Bella? Maddie will spend her half term in Rome, with me as a special treat to celebrate her turning thirteen.' Again, there was a brief, awkward silence.

'As you will,' Bella said gruffly, 'Easter will just have to do!'

'Was this an unusual display of fondness for his daughter?' Robert wondered to himself. He looked into the old Negro woman's eyes, normally devoid of expression expecting to see some kind of emotion. There was a flicker of something, but was it sadness, disappointment, or annoyance? Whatever it was he found it impossible to read. As always, he could never fathom out what Bella was thinking. Chastised, criticised, reprimanded or even praised the black face stayed the same, impenetrable as a blank canvas.

Bella was a complete mystery to Robert and in his heart of hearts he knew he didn't much care for her. But as Maddie seemed happy enough to have her as her personal maid and because of the countless years of loyal service she had given to the family he felt his hands were tied. Other than his dislike of the woman there were no real grounds for dismissal.

Perhaps the thing which infuriated him the most about Bella was that whilst she remained a closed book, he felt that in complete contrast he was an open one. Those piercing eyes of hers disturbed him. He made a point of not looking directly at her, avoiding eye contact at all costs. The rare times he was forced to, he felt she was searching/reading his mind and exploring deep into his soul. It was very unnerving! He was certain however, that if our eyes are the window to our souls, then Bella was soulless.

A little while later Frances and Robert were enjoying afternoon tea in the library. Sitting close to a blazing fire they were relaxing in warm, familiar surroundings and discussing the events of the day as well as their stay in Bristol. 'It a true saying, there's no place like home,' Robert remarked, as he reached for his third cream scone.

'Well, I must say I did like Thomas's town house. It has every modern convenience. you could think of. But you're right. Eastlyn is very special, even with its troubles. Speaking of troubles, Robert, did you notice any change in the children towards the end of our visit?'

'Actually, Frances, I did. But you know how Maddie is. She hates school at the best of times and combining that with having to say goodbye to Rowan, I'm not surprised she was a little low in spirit.'

'I'm not sure you've judged it right,' Aunt Frances warned. 'The day I took them out for lunch I'm convinced something untoward happened. Put it this way, the two happy children who left me to go shopping, were by no means the same children when they returned.'

'What do you mean?' Robert enquired, putting his cup down and edging forward in his chair as if afraid of missing a piece of vital information.

'I can't exactly put my finger on it,' Frances replied, sounding anxious. 'They both seemed very out of sorts and neither of them had any appetite. Maddie especially was as silent as the grave and you know how bubbly and chirpy, she is normally.'

'They could have been talking about Clarissa, opening up old wounds,' Robert suggested. 'In which case its little wonder they appeared distressed?'

'No, Robert, there is more to it than that. Maddie and Rowan were clearly in cahoots over some issue or other and were trying their hardest to appear normal and keep whatever it was from me. I truly believe they had discovered something which had shocked and upset them. I know them too well to be wrong. I'm certain, Robert. Maddie is greatly troubled, burdened by whatever it is. I shall have to wait until our trip to Rome to find out the truth of the matter.'

'Speaking of Rome,' Robert concluded, 'whilst you are away, I'm giving most of the staff a bonus week's holiday. I'm going to have the castle exorcised, even the outbuildings this time, leaving no stone unturned as it were. I've made all the necessary arrangements with the Bishop of Bangor already.'

'Sensible to send the staff away, we don't want that old superstition about the castle resurfacing. There were rumours starting up again last year, after Clarissa's death. Let's hope the exorcism works, this time!' Aunt Frances whispered in a voice filled with fear and trepidation. 'But, Robert, I must say I'm surprised by this decision,' she continued with a very worried expression on her face. 'I thought you'd given up on God and religion.'

'Oh, don't get me wrong, nothing has changed in that respect, I still feel exactly the same as I did when Abigail died. How can a caring God allow such things to happen? There is no God, Frances, he does not exist. No, it is not for myself I do this but for her. I don't think I've ever told you how incredibly brave Abigail was at the end. She was sure she was going to die giving birth to our child. I found her one day in the library reading the old family bibles. It's all there, the Montague wives, destined to the same terrible fate. Verity, Eleanor and Constance, they all died giving birth to a daughter.'

'But in those days, Robert, childbirth was a risky business. Most women viewed pregnancy with dread.' Aunt Frances interjected.

'And what of Elizabeth, Thomas's wife, strong and healthy with the best medical help money could buy. No problems, all going well as Rowan was delivered and then, without rhyme or reason, the sudden, fatal haemorrhaging as Clarissa was born? No, Frances, it is all too much. And how are you going to explain the daughters, Agatha, Harriet, and Margaret all dying on Christmas Eve at the tender age of just thirteen and sweet little Clarissa suffering the same, cruel fate? No, Frances, I do not believe in God. I lost my faith long ago.'

'But, Robert, can you not see, none of this is God's doing. This is the work of the devil. Think of Abigail, I was with her at the end,' Aunt Frances urged. 'Her faith never waned.'

'I know,' he replied, 'do you not see it is precisely for that reason—for Abigail—that I have organised the exorcism. She would have wanted it. She tried her best to persuade me that she had accepted her fate and that I should accept it too. That somehow her death was her destiny and out of it would come good. She told me so many times that if you believe in God and the bible then you must also believe in the existence of the devil and that the castle was in the clutches of an evil spirit. It was a spirit full of hatred, seeking vengeance of some kind and that it would not release its grip easily.'

'Why have you never told me this before?' Frances asked, her voice trembling.

'Blind terror, awful dread, has kept me silent,' he answered. 'I felt that if I spoke about these things, to anyone, that somehow it would make them real. It was easier to bury my head in the sand like the proverbial ostrich rather than confront my fears. I've been so afraid of losing Maddie. However, shall I bear it if she follows Clarissa to the grave?'

Aunt Frances stood to her feet and hurried to his side. Putting her arms around him she said, 'Poor Robert, I cannot believe you have carried this burden alone and for so long.'

'There is more, Frances, I ought to tell you.' He paused for a moment before continuing. 'Just before she died, she spoke these words.'

"When our daughter is born, promise me you will carry her to the window and let her see the night sky. Out of the darkness there will come a great light. She must see it and know it for what it is; a portent of things to come. She must know it from the crib, from the moment of her birth that she is the chosen one. Call her Magdalene, Robert, like she who walked with Jesus. I have seen it and I know our little girl will be our salvation".

'How strange!' replied Aunt Frances. 'What can she have meant? How is Maddie to be our salvation? But I do remember the darkness and that awful eclipse. It seemed to last forever. All the servants were convinced it was a bad omen. They had feared the worst even before it was confirmed.'

'I did her bidding you know,' Robert continued. 'I carried little Maddie to the window and, just as Abigail had said, a bright light appeared in the sky as soon as the eclipse was over. It was like a blazing streak of gold and red, a shooting star I think, moving west to east, to where the sun rises. As I watched, it was as if I could hear Abigail speaking to me, "Our child will bring new light, new hope", she said.'

Chapter Twenty-Three
The Roman Holiday

Although only three days into their Roman holiday they had already visited the Vatican City, the Trevi Fountain, a giant fortress called Castel Sant'Angelo built on the River Tiber and the Villa Medici with its grand gardens. Aunt Frances had been more than satisfied with Maddie's response to everything that had met her eyes. She had wondered at the fine marble sculptures contained within the Vatican City. So convincing were the robes carved by the hands of those ancient sculptors, Maddie had found herself having to touch the statues with her own inquisitive fingers to check that they were actually made from stone and not real silk.

Keeping up with tradition and encouraged by Aunt Frances she had thrown the customary coin into the Trevi Fountain and made her wish. No amount of probing from her aunt, and there was plenty of it lasting all through their lunch, would make her divulge her secret request. The fortress too had brought its special rewards. Now a museum it housed drawings by Leonardo da Vinci, a wealth of Renaissance paintings and pottery, as well as a unique display of various terrifying medieval weapons of war, most particularly a huge antique cannon. Maddie was flabbergasted at the size of it. They had discovered that the best photographs of the Castel Sant'Angelo were to be taken from a viewpoint on the Ponte San't Angelo, a bridge which spans the Tiber River. As they walked across, taking snapshot after snapshot, Aunt Frances pointed out its ten very famous angel sculptures, all of which were created by the artist Bernini.

Having time on their hands after the visit and without any plans of where they wanted to go, they had decided to visit The Villa Medici. They walked along narrow, cobbled lanes, bought cheese and bread from pretty little shops, laughing at their often-pathetic attempts to speak Italian to the locals.

Finding their courage, they had finally hired a taxicab to take them to the Villa. It had been a terrifying ride, but the most exciting experience Maddie had ever had in her life, which incidentally flashed before her three times on the journey. Lewis Hamilton himself would not have driven that vehicle with more daring or verve. One blink and you missed at least an entire street such was the speed at which the driver was intent on going. It was like being on a dodgem ride at a fairground except on real roads and pitched against real cars. Aunt Frances had to sit down for a good half hour on arrival to recover from the experience.

They found a nearby coffee shop and sat down to enjoy yet more light refreshment. Maddie watched people going by and enjoyed some quiet time. She could see into the gardens of the villa from where they were sitting and spotted some marble lions by the stairs leading into what looked like a courtyard. The lions reminded her of the family cemetery back at Eastlyn castle and immediately the bubble burst. Yes, she was enjoying her holiday, yes, she was with her favourite aunt, but in her heart of hearts she was unhappy. She knew an enormous challenge lay ahead and that there were terrible secrets at the castle needing to be discovered.

Aunt Frances now fully recovered began to read from a guidebook. 'The Villa Medici became at once the first among Medici properties in Rome, intended to give concrete expression to the ascendancy of the Medici among Italian princes and assert their permanent presence in Rome. It has become a virtual open-air museum. A series of grand gardens recall the botanical gardens created at Pisa and at Florence and provide lovely walks sheltering in plantations of pines, cypresses, and oaks.'

'A bit like Eastlyn being built to show off Montague wealth. I can't imagine that the gardens here will be as beautiful as those back home though,' was Maddie's only reply. Her thoughts now were of the castle. She listened to barely one word in ten as her aunt continued reading.

Today, however, Maddie's spirits had revived. She'd had a dream about her mother. 'Your father brought me to Rome on our honeymoon and, Maddie, I think it the most beautiful city in the world. You must allow yourself to enjoy this holiday with your aunt. There is no need for you to feel guilty about having a little pleasure now and again. Make the most of it, my darling, and of course for your aunt's sake too.' Maddie woke up feeling cheerful and comforted. 'Where are we off this morning then Aunt?' she enquired enthusiastically at breakfast.

'You seem very happy,' her aunt had replied, 'and ready to explore the Coliseum I hope?'

'I wonder if my father took my mother to see the Coliseum when they were here on honeymoon.' Maddie said looking at her aunt quizzically.

'Oh yes. I'm sure he did. I remember your mother talking about it on their return to Eastlyn. She loved Rome to bits. I expect your father has told you all about their visit,' her aunt continued.

'No, actually, he's never once mentioned it,' answered Maddie. Her aunt looked slightly puzzled.

'Well, this is going to be a most exciting day and if visiting the Coliseum doesn't give you an idea of what ancient Rome was like then nothing will,' she concluded. Maddie was not disappointed. They arrived at the elliptical amphitheatre shortly before midday. The hotel they were staying at was situated right in the heart of the city thus the walk to the Coliseum took less than twenty minutes. They had strolled hand in hand in the bright sunshine Aunt Frances telling Maddie how the purpose and use of the great arena had reflected the Roman way of life.

'Did you know this is the biggest amphitheatre ever built in the whole of the Roman Empire,' Aunt Frances instructed. 'It's made of concrete and stone and is considered one of the greatest works of Roman architecture and Roman engineering.'

'When was it built?' Maddie asked.

'I believe it was started in 72 AD. In its heyday it was capable of seating fifty thousand spectators.'

'Fifty thousand spectators?' Maddie repeated in an astonished tone of voice.

'Yes,' replied her aunt. 'People would come from miles around to watch the gladiatorial contests. Brutal battles they were too! Often men would be pitched against wild beasts of every kind imaginable: lions, tigers, bears, wild boars, you name it. But, worst of all, were the man-to-man fights, deliberately made as vicious and as blood thirsty as possible in order to entertain the crowd.

Rich, wealthy Romans trained their slaves to fight. To own a winning gladiator in the arena was seen as a status symbol. Those poor slaves spent their entire lives either training or fighting. You lasted for as long as you could survive. To lose inevitably meant your death and in those days medical help was non-existent. The injuries they suffered in combat were often horrendous and not forgetting of course the infamous thumb up or down from the emperor! The crowd would bray for their death or life as the case might be and he would make the decision, to kill or not to kill. A vanquished gladiator was rarely shown mercy!'

Maddie listened in awed silence to her aunt's account of the amphitheatre's bloody past, not just to tales of gladiators but of mock sea-battles and brutal executions. 'Sometimes extraordinary gladiators could earn their freedom because of their victories in the arena. Many strove to do so, desperate to escape from the vile bondage of slavery. To be sure the life of a slave was a miserable one, totally at the mercy of your master, good or bad,' her aunt explained.

Suddenly the word "slave" triggered Maddie's memory. She was back in the museum in Bristol with Rowan, gazing in disbelief at the painting of *The Black Stag*. It was exactly the opening she had been waiting for, but when and how to broach the subject? That was the question! Maddie waited until her aunt was sitting down, knowing that what she was about to say might well come as an unfortunate shock to her elderly companion.

Satisfied Maddie had seen all there was to see Aunt Frances decided it was time to leave the Coliseum and grab a late lunch. They made their way down a number of busy, noisy streets, staying well in on the pavement so as to put as much distance as possible between them and the traffic. On the road itself vehicle after vehicle sped past at ridiculously high speeds, their horns tooting furiously.

Even the pavement was fraught with hazards as they found themselves bumped and jostled by passers-by in more of a hurry, or so it appeared to Maddie, even than the cars. Then, to get out of the crowd, they turned into a narrow, deserted, cobbled alleyway. In a matter of minutes and much to their delight, they found themselves entering an endearing little piazza with a fountain at its centre.

They were spoilt for choice with numerous bars and cafes dotted about on all four sides of the square. Aunt Frances selected a small, quaint looking pizzeria with whitewashed walls decorated with black ceramic pots containing bright red geraniums. A large wooden pergola built above the doorway was festooned with stems of the most beautiful deep purple bougainvillea, flush with petal and climbing wildly in and out of the open rafters. 'We'll eat here,' said Aunt Frances sitting down at a vacant table in the shade. 'Look, Maddie, this place is full of local people dining out, so the food is bound to be good. There's hardly a tourist in sight.' She commented happily.

It felt good to be out of the sun. Maddie fanned her face with the menu to help her cool down. She noticed her aunt was perspiring too. 'Can we order drinks first?' she requested. 'I'm gasping.' They ordered lunch, deciding jointly on a delicious sounding pasta dish containing breast of chicken, cheese, cream, and basil. A few minutes later the waitress returned with their drinks. Aunt Frances was pushing the boat out requesting a large white wine spritzer, whilst Maddie had her usual diet coke with lots of ice and served in a very tall glass. They drank thirstily.

It was time to strike. Aunt Frances looked relaxed and comfortable as she sipped her drink contentedly. 'Now or never,' Maddie thought to herself. She was keen to interrogate her aunt as to how much she knew about the family history. Had she known about *The Black Stag* for one thing and, if she did, why had she kept it secret from her? This would be her practice run and then she would tackle her father.

'Aunt,' Maddie began, 'I've been meaning to ask you something important for some time now. Do you remember that day in Bristol when Rowan and I were at the city museum?'

'Oh yes, I remember, you're referring to the day I took you both for lunch.'

'Well,' continued Maddie, 'we saw a painting at the museum which surprised us very much. It was an exact copy of one we have at Eastlyn castle.'

'How interesting,' replied her unsuspecting aunt, 'which painting is that?'

'The one hanging in the minstrel's gallery of the ship, the tall ship called *The Black Stag*. You must know the one I mean?'

The ice cubes in Aunt Frances's wine glass began to rattle slightly. She hurriedly placed the drink back down on the table. 'Oh yes, dear, I know the one you mean.'

'Did you know it was a slave ship and that the first Lord Montague, who built Eastlyn castle owned huge sugar plantations in the Caribbean?' There was a moment's pause, as if her aunt was considering what her answer should be.

'Yes, Maddie, I did know. But I really think it is your father you ought to be speaking to. Neither he nor any of your uncles are proud of the connection the family has to those matters. I believe he has not wanted to broach the subject with you, for fear of upsetting you. No doubt now that you are the age you are he may feel more inclined to discuss these issues with you. My silence and his has been for your protection only, to spare your feelings. I hope you can understand that. We have waited until we felt the time was right and as I can clearly see from your concerned expression that time has now most definitely come.'

'Rowan and I were shocked at what we discovered at the museum. They even had a page of the ship's log. It sank, you know, on December 24, 1753, with over two hundred slaves on board. They all perished, went down with the ship, drowned! It's horrible, isn't it?'

So, this was the reason Maddie had been out of sorts that day. Aunt Frances felt vindicated. She now knew she had been right all along. It had been finding out about the family's involvement in slavery, the sinking of *The Black Stag* and the subsequent terrible loss of life that had provoked the look of mortification she had seen etched on Maddie's face. 'Every family has a skeleton in the closet,' she replied.

'Not a skeleton like this one,' Maddie exclaimed ruefully.

'Maddie, you really need to talk to your father about your concerns. I'm not sure we should be discussing these matters at all. But I will tell you this, the first Lord Eastlyn was a singular and I may say rather unpleasant man. After his death, his brother Henry inherited the castle and immediately put a stop to any involvement the family had with slavery. In fact, he was one of the chief protagonists for the abolitionists and in his day gave a great many speeches to further their cause. We none of us are proud of what Lord George did, nor can we excuse it. Unfortunately, we cannot choose our relatives or our ancestors. We can only live our own lives and try to make the best of what we are given.'

Maddie nodded in agreement. 'Yes, aunt, I can see the sense in that. I'll speak to father the next time I'm home. Thank you for being so honest with me. Rowan and I just want the truth that's all.'

Seeing the distress, she had clearly caused her aunt, Maddie did not divulge anything to do with Clarissa. She wanted to ask for advice, to confess her fear for what lay ahead. Clarissa had told her that she had a special date with destiny, a task to perform, something preordained which would somehow help the family. Maddie was currently at a loss to understand what on earth that might be. 'You'll know when the time comes,' a reassuring voice said in her ear. Maddie looked across at her aunt. She was sipping her drink and gazing silently at the fountain, clearly deep in thought.

Bowls of pasta arrived at that very moment and conversation ended. Maddie began to devour her meal, relishing every mouthful, Aunt Frances ate more slowly. Her stomach was in knots. 'I'll telephone Robert tonight,' she thought to herself. 'Warn him that Maddie knows more than we thought. She'll have to be told the truth and the sooner the better.'

Chapter Twenty-Four
The Minister of Deliverance

At the same time, back at Eastlyn castle, Lord Robert was talking on the telephone. The Bishop of Bangor had called to say that he and his colleague would be arriving that evening at around 6.30 pm. Robert had congratulated him on his timing, saying that dinner would be served at seven o'clock exactly. Mrs Reed, aided by Sam, had served them their meal. They were the only two staff to be kept on at the castle, everyone else had taken their extra week of holiday with good grace, all except Bella that is.

Bella had point blank refused the offer of a lift from Sam. The poor lad had been sent by Lord Robert to make sure she was transported into the village and comfortably installed at one of the local inns. Bella had been adamant there was nowhere she wanted to go and no one she wanted to visit. She would much prefer to stay at the castle. It had been quite a battle to get her to accept that she had to go.

The staff had received instruction they were to be out of the castle by twelve noon on Monday and not to return until Friday afternoon at the earliest. Once again Sam was sent on a mission, to spy on Bella and make sure she did actually leave. He was washing his Lordship's limo, when Bella stepped out over the threshold, carrying a very small leather case. Pretending not to notice, Sam continued on with his chore.

Out of the corner of his eye, he watched her make her way down the lane towards the estuary. He couldn't help thinking that it was an odd route for her to take to get to the village. The footpath followed the course of the river and winding round and round as it did was a good five miles longer in distance than simply taking the main road. The road should have been the obvious choice as it led directly to the village.

Sam waited for her to round a bend in the lane and then, once out of sight, gave chase. He ran to a section of rising ground which overlooked the estuary. It had an unobstructed view of the footpath, and he ought therefore to be able to see her progress towards the village with ease. He was not disappointed, within minutes he could see Bella's large frame trudging along, still carrying her rather lightweight-looking overnight bag. 'Perhaps she intends to wear the same clothes all week,' he thought to himself with a wry chuckle.

No sooner had he had that thought than Bella stopped walking and slowly turned round. Sam quickly darted behind a tree conveniently growing in the ground just to his left. Bella stood where she was for several minutes looking up exactly in his direction. Sam was convinced she somehow knew he was there and could feel his heart pounding. To his relief, she began to walk on. Rounding a sharp corner which lay adjacent to the old boatsheds, she disappeared from view again. Sam heaved a sigh of relief and duly went to seek out Lord Robert to tell him that Bella had indeed left the castle. Where she was actually going to stay, he didn't know and, frankly, didn't care.

Had Sam taken the time to go down to the estuary path, he would have discovered Bella's large footprints in its muddy track, at least as far as the boatsheds. From that point on, the footpath was clear, except for the imprint of horseshoes. It was a popular bridleway. Bella had no intention of leaving the castle. She knew from overheard conversations with Aunt Frances what Lord Robert had planned for that week and was determined to stop him.

She entered the castle via her usual route, a secret doorway right at the back of the smallest boatshed. After twisting the second of five ancient iron rings embedded in the rear wall, a narrow passageway opened up, making its usual grating, groaning sound as enormous giant stone slabs separated. Inside the tunnel, a small table had been laid and a box of candles and matches were waiting ready to be used. Lighting a candle, she began to make her way up the familiar steep steps with a look of purpose and determination in her cold, grey eyes. Bella's dark shadow moved slowly, steadily upwards, back into the interior of the castle. To anyone watching she would have appeared phantom-like, her giant frame reflected in the flickering light of the candle against a backdrop of black, barren rock.

It was no challenging task for Bella to hide in the castle. Indeed, she was in her element. Not only did she have the labyrinth of tunnels at her disposal, but she was also easily able to use both her and Aunt Frances' rooms, coming and going through secret doors about which only she knew. Bella didn't like Aunt Frances and resented the fact that her accommodation was vastly superior to her own. So it was that ample provisions for the week had been systematically stowed in the tunnels. Of course, she could have helped herself to anything she wanted, but thought it best not to arouse suspicion by taking food or drink from the kitchen. Things mysteriously disappearing would be bound to cause concern. Bella needed to remain hidden inside the castle if she was to achieve her aim, to stop the exorcism.

Suitably wined and dined the three men retired to the lounge with a full decanter of port. As they sat comfortably in armchairs stationed near a roaring fire the conversation turned to matters in hand. 'You were right to call us, Lord Robert. There is an undoubted presence within the castle,' said the Priest in a sombre tone of voice.

'What exactly are you sensing?' asked the bishop.

'A battle,' replied the Priest. His comment was met with two pairs of raised eyebrows.

'Please be so kind as to explain,' Lord Robert requested, before taking a large gulp of his port.

'There is an evil spirit here. I felt it as soon as we arrived. It is soulless, unmerciful, consumed with hatred and enmity, seeking revenge. But it wishes to remain hidden and anonymous and will do all in its power to protect its secret. Unless it is forced, this demon is unlikely to reveal itself to us. But there are other beings within the castle. They are gathering, gaining in strength. These spirits are opposed to the dark force which keeps the castle and the Montague family in its wicked grasp. They ready themselves. They plot and plan. Their aim is to outwit this devil and remove it from the castle once and for all.'

'Do you truly believe in what you do?' Lord Robert asked looking directly at the Priest.

It was the bishop who answered, however. 'Lord Robert exorcism has been an accepted and valued procedure within the Roman Catholic Church for hundreds of years. The bible itself tells us of Christ casting out demons. It became impossible for us not to act such was the demand from our own followers. Hence in 1974, the Church of England set up the deliverance ministry. As part of its creation, every diocese in the country was equipped with a team trained in both exorcism and psychiatry. According to its representatives, most cases brought before it have conventional explanations, and actual exorcisms are quite rare; although, blessings are sometimes given to people for psychological reasons. We normally deal with individuals who believe they are possessed, rather than, as in this case, a building.'

'Does your colleague have a wide experience in these procedures?' Lord Robert continued with a look of disdain on his face.

'He is the most experienced of our Anglican priests, hence my reasoning in bringing him here. You ought to know that Anglican priests may not perform an exorcism without permission from the diocesan bishop. An exorcism is not usually performed unless the bishop and his team of specialists—including a psychiatrist and physician—have approved it. As we are not dealing with an individual and you wished this affair done in secrecy, I have omitted the psychiatrist and physician from our team.'

It was now the Priest's turn to speak. 'Lord Robert, I have considerable experience in these matters, but I feel I must warn you. Exorcisms do not always go to plan. Only last year I was called to exorcise a young man in his early twenties. He was a patient in a mental hospital at the time, suffering from severe depression. The poor fellow blamed himself for the death of his parents. They had been killed in a car accident. He was the driver. Certain disturbing events had taken place on his ward and his doctors had deemed it necessary to call for my services as a result.

During the exorcism, the young man's chest became covered in arcane lettering carved into his flesh and claw marks appeared on his arms and legs. Far from removing the demon, it took complete possession of him. To this day, he remains in hospital, in an isolation ward, a danger to himself and those who try to help him. Insanity is never a pretty sight.'

There was a deathly hush and for several minutes no one spoke. Lord Robert refilled three empty glasses with a generous measure of port. It was the bishop who eventually broke the lengthy silence. As if deciding on a lighter topic of conversation he began: 'The Reverend Hatfield tells me you no longer attend his Sunday service,' the bishop remarked. 'Is there any reason?'

'When Maddie is away at school, I go but rarely,' Lord Robert replied.

'I am sorry to hear it, and the reason?' he continued.

'I see no advantage to be gained. My beliefs are not what they were.' Robert answered.

It was the Priest who spoke next. 'Lord Robert what we are about to attempt is a dangerous procedure. To conduct an exorcism without faith would be foolhardy to say the least. I have witnessed a great many over the years, some of which as I have already explained, have had drastic consequences for those taking part.' Robert remained silent, forlornly peering into his glass.

'Lord Bishop, I must have assurance,' continued the Priest, 'if I am to carry out this exorcism, I need to know that Lord Robert has a firm belief in the power of the Almighty, a steadfast belief which will not be shaken should the Demon decide to put us to the test.'

'Lord Robert, my colleague is quite correct. Are you telling us that you are no longer a believer? In which case what are you, agnostic or atheist?'

'I do not want to give offence, but since the death of my wife, I believe I would describe myself as an atheist.' The two men of the cloth looked shocked. Robert tried to explain:

'If you're an atheist, you know, you believe, this is the only life you're going to get. It's a precious life. It should be a beautiful life. It's something we should live to the full, to the end of our days. From the moment of our birth atheism makes us answerable for our actions. There is no divine forgiveness from some unknown god. Being an atheist makes you responsible for the decisions and choices you make in life. When death comes, however cruel, we do not need to seek for explanations, we simply accept that a life is over.'

'You surprise me,' continued the bishop. 'Do you not think that God must have had some purpose when Maddie lost her mother? Would it not be better to be able to take comfort in that?'

'Forgive me, Bishop, but to me there is something infantile in using religion as a crutch or believing in the vain hope, the presumption, that somebody else has a responsibility to give your life meaning or that God has brought suffering and death to a member of his flock for some higher purpose.'

The Priest stood to his feet. 'This is impossible,' he said. 'I cannot understand why we have been called here. If you do not believe in God, why ask for an exorcism? Either you believe in supernatural powers, or you do not.'

'My wife was a believer,' Robert replied, 'and I know she would want me to do all I can to save our daughter.'

'If you believe Maddie to be at risk, I urge you to bring her up as a Christian child, with the Almighty's protection,' the bishop advised.

'There is no such thing as a Christian child: only a child of Christian parents,' Robert responded wearily. 'I ask you here because my wife cannot. She is dead, lost to me. Her religion, her devout faith could do nothing to save her. How can

I believe in such a callous God? Turn on your television and consider the news for ten minutes and in that time, you will see the total amount of suffering on that day in the natural world is beyond all decent comprehension.'

'I will certainly give a blessing,' the Priest responded kindly, 'in memory of your wife. That is the least I can do. We will meet in the chapel tomorrow morning at 8 am after breakfast. But with your views, an exorcism is out of the question. Now if you'll excuse me, I have some reading to do, so I'll say goodnight.'

'I too have letters to read and write,' said the bishop looking more than a little displeased. 'If you don't mind, I will also retire to my bedchamber,' and with that he finished his glass of port and left the room.

At the same time, Bella was adding another log to the fire in Aunt Frances's living room. She was warm and comfortable. Relaxing back in an armchair, she reached for the mug of tea she had made herself and another biscuit from the green and white porcelain pot she had placed on the small table at her side. She began to sing to herself an ancient Dahomey song of victory, one she had sung to Adana many years ago. Every so often she would stop her singing and glance at the clock, as if she were waiting for something to happen at a particular time.

Robert too was remembering, thinking back to happy memories from the past, his marriage to Abigail. How delighted he had been when she had accepted his proposal. Deep in thought he remained where he was for some time. His mood began to change. The night had not gone well. He regretted expressing his feelings, in particular acknowledging his loss of faith. Abigail would have been disappointed in him. He finished the entire decanter before retiring for the night.

Robert walked to the chapel alone. To add insult to injury he knew he was late. The conversation of the previous night still echoed in his ears. He had much to regret. Abigail would have wanted the exorcism carried out. She would have done all in her power to protect Maddie and that included lying. He knew he should have kept his mouth shut and his opinions to himself. Had he done so, the exorcism would still be taking place.

For the time of year, it was an exceptionally chilly morning. He was glad to enter through the church door and get out of the ravages of a freezing wind, which had buffeted him mercilessly throughout his walk. Once inside he could see the priest already standing in front of the high altar, turning the pages of an old bible he was holding in his hands. The Bishop of Bangor was also busy as he proceeded to light numerous candles on every wall of the chapel. Robert sat in his usual pew and waited in silence. Eventually the Bishop came to sit beside him.

Laying the open bible on the lectern in front of him, the Priest turned to face them and opened his mouth as if about to speak. He uttered not a sound for at that moment the wide, oak-panelled doors flew open and a sudden blast of ice-cold air tore through the chapel, extinguishing every candle and almost blowing the Priest off his feet. Robert watched in horror as the Priest struggled to remain upright battling against the force of the wind. Then, as if grasped by some unseen entity, the arms of the Priest were violently stretched out to their full extent on either side of him. Slowly he rose into the air, several feet above the ground, his body now in the shape of a crucifix. Shocked to the core, Robert listened to the sound of four loud thuds, instantly echoed by deafening screams, as huge nails appearing from nowhere were driven into the Priest's hands and feet.

Robert gasped as the invisible cross on which the Priest's body was nailed, slowly began to turn. He could hear the sound of a whip. Lash after lash ripped through the darkness, striking the rotating target in a merciless attack. 'God help me, God help me, save me,' the Priest cried as the flagellation continued unabated. Robert tried to move, to run to the Priest's aid, but his body would not respond to his will. He felt paralysed, as if he had lost all the use of his limbs. He wanted to close his eyes to blot out the horror of the scene before him, but even his own eyelids refused to obey his command. He sat helpless, powerless to stop the terrible onslaught he was witnessing.

As he watched as if frozen to the spot, he could see the Priests clothing being torn from his back, his vestments in tatters, flesh ripped away to the bone. Unexpectedly the whipping stopped, the crucifix slowing turning until the Priest's body faced its appalled audience. For a moment there was silence, then invisible spears seemed to penetrate and gouge out both eyes. Blood poured from the wounds whilst anguished screams rent the air all around them. To his even greater horror, Robert realised that, just like the young man the ministry of deliverance had tried to exorcise a few months before, arcane lettering was being carved deep across the Priest's chest and bloody claw marks were appearing on both his arms and legs.

Deep within the bowels of the castle in her secret chamber, Bella dropped the cockerel claw she was holding and plunged a small wax doll into the fire burning at her feet. At the same moment, the Priest was engulfed in flames.

Robert sat bolt upright in bed. He was in a cold sweat and his heart was racing. He leapt out of bed and was dressed in seconds. 'I must have been dreaming. Please God let it just be a dream!' He raced down the stairs, across the great hall and into the breakfast room. The Bishop and Priest were just beginning to eat the eggs and bacon Mrs Reed had served them. Robert collapsed in a chair, head in hands. When he had recovered and composed himself sufficiently to be able to speak, he stood up and said: 'I wish you to leave immediately after breakfast. I thank you for your time, but there'll be no blessing at the chapel today. Forgive me. I have my reasons,' and with that he left the room leaving behind a very surprised Mrs Reed and two equally confused men of the cloth.

The trip to Rome had been exactly the tonic Maddie needed. All through that first half term at school she had scarcely been able to concentrate on any of her subjects. Thoughts of the museum when the moth had miraculously reappeared and their subsequent discovery of her family's involvement in slavery together with the history of *The Black Stag* had constantly been on her mind. Even in lessons she would normally have enjoyed, her concentration would be lost in minutes as memories of that day came flooding back.

Talking to Aunt Frances had been such a help. It had given her a different perspective, for whatever terrible things the first Lord Eastlyn had done, neither she nor her father nor any of her ancestors were to blame. The guilt lay purely and entirely with him. 'It is the past,' Aunt Frances had said, 'best leave it in the past and look to the future. Use your talents, Maddie. Use them well and wisely. That's how to make amends, not that you need to make amends anyway. You've done nothing wrong. We can none of us be held responsible for the sins or wrong doings of our ancestors. It's how we live our lives that matters.'

Returning to school for the second half-term it had been business as usual, except for one thing, Clarissa's prophecy! It troubled Maddie greatly. When the time came, what was it that she was supposed to do? It was the not knowing which was the worst. If only she had at least some idea of the task which lay before her. She felt powerless, helpless, and dreaded that somehow, she would fail in her mission. To make matters worse, other than Rowan, there was no one else she could turn to for advice, for although Maddie loved her aunt dearly, she felt unable to talk to her about Clarissa. Consequently, Clarissa's warning and her mysterious death, played on Maddie's mind whether awake or asleep. She would often hear Clarissa's voice as if calling to her from the grave. 'The time is coming Maddie, soon, very soon. You must be ready.'

Maddie could not wait for Easter to come. Rowan and Uncle Thomas were to arrive on the same day she was due home. There was important work to be done. She couldn't wait to begin. True to their promise to each other they had been in constant contact over the phone. They had come to a joint decision, a mutual agreement that at whatever cost, however upsetting it was, they would find the underlying cause of this mystery. They would find out why Clarissa had been so convinced she was going to die and why she clearly believed Maddie was the next in line.

Chapter Twenty-Five
Family History

Easter had arrived and with it a blaze of colour. The castle gardens had come back to life after a cold, bleak winter. Green lawns swept around the castle bedecked with the bright golden heads of swathes of daffodils dancing in the breeze, whilst red, white, deep purple and orange tulips swayed to and fro in wonderful synchronicity.

Maddie was in her element; four weeks off school, all of which would be spent with Rowan. It was not going to be like a normal holiday, however. For one thing there would be no Clarissa and for another they faced the unenviable task of finding out as much about her death as possible. It would mean considerable research into the family's history, requiring hour upon hour of dedicated reading. They were also well aware they would need to know all there was to know about the castle's past and the sinking of *the Black Stag* in particular. Nevertheless, Maddie was overjoyed at the prospect of spending quality time with her beloved cousin.

She arrived home on Friday evening. Her father had driven down to the school to collect her. He was supposed to watch her play in the inter house netball tournament, which had started at 1.30 pm on that final afternoon of term. He was late, much to Maddie's annoyance and disappointment, watching only the last ten minutes of play as a result. She had played well, but in the final quarter an elbow in the eye from her opposing goal defence had affected her vision. Determined not to be substituted she had made light of the injury. In truth, her eye felt very sore and just would not stop watering. She missed a number of easy goals costing her house dear. They should have won, but instead, finished as runners-up.

To make matters worse, her father was horrified at the sight of her eye. Embarrassingly he accosted her P.E. teacher, demanding an explanation as to how the injury had occurred. The unsuspecting woman didn't know what to say, other than accidents happen and in sport, injuries are to be expected from time to time. Maddie wanted the ground to swallow her up, as her father made mention of poor umpiring being to blame, at which point she grabbed his arm and dragged him away. There was one consolation, however. Due to the black eye Robert decided not to stay for the parent/teacher meeting. Maddie was relieved she knew she'd had a term of two halves, the first bad, the second only slightly better. So it was that by mid-afternoon they were well on their way home.

An apologetic Mrs Reed greeted them on their arrival back at Eastlyn. Dinner would not be ready until eight o'clock that evening, but a tray of sandwiches and cakes would take minutes to prepare if father and daughter so wished. 'No need,' replied his Lordship, 'we stopped on route back for some light refreshment. Dinner at eight will be fine.'

'Would Miss Maddie like a piece of steak for that black eye?' Mrs Reed asked looking at her with concern. 'The old remedies are the best,' she advised.

'Oh, no, I'm okay really,' Maddie replied happily. She was home and nothing could cloud her joy.

Unlike his cousin, Rowan was to be late arriving at Eastlyn. As arranged, Uncle William was to collect all the boys from school. Rowan and his cousins, Fred, Edmund, and Tristan were all at school together. Indeed Edmund, being the identical age to Rowan, was even in the same class.

Their term also ended with a sporting competition, the eagerly awaited inter-house rugby tournament. Uncle William, a rugby fanatic, arrived well before the first match. The Montague boys were all in the same house, Disraeli. Their first game was against Churchill.

Standing on the side-line, wrapped up warm against the elements in his thick winter coat, scarf, fur gloves and ushanka (Russian hat) Uncle William looked the epitome of a seasoned rugby parent. His sons and nephew could not have asked for a more enthusiastic supporter, despite being too vocal at times. He had yet to agree with a refereeing decision, even though he had been watching Fred play for over ten years. As senior house captain, it was Fred who led all the Disraeli boys onto the field of play. They began a complicated, intricate warm-up of which even the England team would have been proud.

Warm-up completed, they waited for the referees to arrive. Rowan was captain of the intermediate team. Edmund was his vice-captain, whilst Tristan would be playing for the juniors. It had been agreed that Uncle William would watch parts of all three games, starting with the youngest team. He followed Tristan to the smallest of the three pitches. Much to his annoyance the whistle sounding the start of play for the intermediate and senior matches had sounded even before the junior referee had arrived. Finally, ten minutes into the game, a stout, little man, five feet tall and equally as wide, panting heavily and wearing a bright yellow shirt which reached all the way down to his knees, jogged into the centre of the field. Uncle William commented to the person standing at his side that the referee looked like a tennis ball wearing rugby boots. He turned to grin at his companion; the headmaster did not look impressed.

The junior game began. It was all going swimmingly well. Disraeli were leading 7-0 after a deserved converted try in which Tristan had more than played his part, firstly by winning the ball in the line-out and then kicking accurately between the posts. Disaster struck. In the middle of a ruck, Tristan was kicked unconscious by one of his own players. The nursing sister attending the game launched into action. Using her mobile phone, she attempted to summon an ambulance. 'What's going on? What's the hold-up for?' Uncle William demanded, stopping her in the process.

'Your son's been kicked unconscious,' replied the nurse, 'he could have concussion. I never take risks where head injuries are concerned.'

Uncle William knelt at Tristan's side. Awake now, the dazed young player was rubbing his head and trying to sit up. 'Tristan, sit up, there's a good chap. Now then, no pain no gain. Look at my hand. How many fingers am I holding up?' he demanded, whilst showing the proverbial victory sign.

'Ugh, ugh, I think I can see four,' Tristan replied.

'Close enough,' said his father, 'good lad, play on.' Nurse Jenkins was not amused. Only last week she had witnessed an example of gross stupidity on the part of a visiting games teacher. One of his players had gone down injured. The boy's ankle had been so badly damaged to the extent that his foot was facing the wrong way!

She arrived on the scene to hear the teacher saying, 'Just get up, lad. You'll soon run it off.'

'But, Sir,' the boy had replied, 'I think it's broken!'

'Nonsense, utter nonsense,' the teacher had insisted. 'You just need the magic sponge.' Before Nurse Jenkins had been able to stop him, the sponge had been duly applied with vigorous pressure to the offending limb. The stricken player had fallen into an immediate swoon. Ten minutes later he had been stretchered off the field to the waiting ambulance.

At the end of the afternoon, a delighted Fred led his players back to the changing rooms. Disraeli house had won all three age groups. They would shower, change back into uniform, and then assemble in the dining room for the traditional hot team tea. At such times it was absolutely taboo to sit in partisan groups. Players were expected to mingle with their opponents. They may well have wanted to kill each other on the field of play, but the final whistle was the signal for the end of hostilities, and everyone was expected to kiss and make up, although not literally of course!

As winning captain, Fred especially did his duty, sitting with members of opposing senior teams, Rowan and Edmund followed his example. Nobody spotted that Tristan was missing. Uncle William along with all the other parents, staff and visitors went for high tea in the school's Old Hall. He was in his element, listening to compliments about the special rugby talent of all the Montague boys whilst remembering his own playing days as a schoolboy. He and his elder brother, Robert had both made first team captain.

His reaction to Tristan's injury had been very different to that of Robert in regard to Maddie's black eye. There was good reason for the contrast. William had been little affected by the curse which plagued the Montague family. His wife was alive and well, and he was the father of three healthy, strapping boys. It was, however, true to say that the death of Clarissa had brought unexpected heartbreak; it had also come as an unwelcome shock. Old myths and superstitions had most certainly been unearthed again. Yet, somehow, he remained distant from those concerns, untouched by the circumstances which had so traumatised his other brothers. Unlike them he did not live his life in constant fear.

Robert's situation was very different. He had lost his wife in childbirth and his niece had died at the age of thirteen. Maddie was that age now and Robert was burdened by the weight of fear he felt for her safety. He did not want to believe in the curse, he did not want to believe in a spirit world that could affect the lives of his loved ones. But the history of the family haunted him. He too had read the family bibles and often times the inscriptions on the gravestones in the family cemetery. It was there in black and white, engraved in stone and recorded, written indelibly on old parchment paper, Montague women died giving birth to daughters. Daughters died at the age of thirteen on December 24. Try as he might he could not ignore those facts or come up with a satisfactory, reasonable explanation to explain those awful events.

The meal was over. The boys assembled with their trunks by Uncle William's Land Rover. It was then that Tristan's absence was noted. No one seemed to know where he was. Nobody could remember seeing him after the game. A search party was organised. It was Rowan who found him wandering around the rugby pitches still in his games kit. In minutes Rowan had used his mobile phone to ring for Nurse Jenkins and alert his uncle that Tristan had been found. Tristan was not in a good way. He had difficulty in walking and speaking and appeared not to understand what Rowan was trying to say to him. He couldn't remember what he was doing down on the rugby field, or how to get back to school.

An embarrassed and now very concerned Uncle William drove Tristan to the local hospital. He was diagnosed with concussion and kept in overnight for observation. His father booked the rest of the party rooms at a nearby hotel and Rowan rang Maddie to give her the unwelcome news.

Fortunately, Tristan recovered quickly. By late afternoon the next day, the doctors were satisfied no serious damage had been done and were happy to discharge him. The Land Rover arrived at Eastlyn shortly before 6 pm. Aunt Kate had arrived earlier, having made revised plans with Robert. Due to Tristan's injury, they would now also stay at the castle for the first week of the holiday. Robert, though concerned about Tristan's injury, was secretly delighted. He loved it when the castle was full of guests, the more the merrier.

At Eastlyn Castle it was traditional for the Easter service of light to take place at the family chapel on the last Sunday in March. By that time, Rowan and Maddie had spent exactly one week together. During those seven days they had hardly stirred from the library, except for a visit to Reverend Hatfield's home and a second, on his advice to the town library.

They had begun the week by discussing their findings regarding the first Lord Eastlyn, his connection with slavery in particular as well as his involvement in the production of sugar. Rowan was the first to speak. 'I discovered that by 1700 the Montague family were already incredibly wealthy. They owned a vast amount of land which was rich in slate and employed many men to extract and process it,' he explained. 'The slate was then used most commonly as a roofing material, a flooring material or for making gravestones and memorial tablets. Montague slate came from two sources. It was either quarried from a slate quarry or reached by tunnelling in a slate mine, dangerous work in the 1700s, but with spectacular financial rewards for the owners. Lord George was definitely born with a silver spoon in his mouth.'

'I did some research into the production of sugar,' Maddie responded eagerly. 'After 1625 the Dutch carried sugarcane from South America to the Caribbean islands, where it was grown from Barbados to the Virgin Islands. The years 1625 to 1750 saw the price of sugar skyrocket and the Montague fortune must have been ripe for investment. From all accounts George wanted a piece of the action and so he invested large sums of money allowing him to buy the land he needed in the Caribbean. In both Jamaica and Barbados, he owned some of the largest sugar plantations of the time.'

'And he needed the workforce to man them,' Rowan interjected.

'Exactly,' Maddie replied. 'Men like George Montague played a major part in the European colonisation of the Caribbean which became the world's largest source of sugar. These islands could supply sugarcane using slave labour and produce sugar at prices vastly lower than those of cane sugar imported from the East. He wasn't alone Rowan, there were a great many other plantation owners just like him. At least we can take some comfort in that, although I'm not excusing what he did. It was a hateful trade, cruel, barbaric, and done purely for mercenary reasons.'

'Well at least we know now exactly what we are dealing with,' said Rowan, 'but how do we discover the connection between Lord George and Clarissa's death? There has to be a link. It is too great a coincidence for *The Black Stag* to sink on December 24 and my poor sister to die on the very same day.'

'Aunt Frances suggested we read through the family bibles. She says all our ancestors kept detailed records in them so there'll be lots of information about births, deaths, marriages etc. If we can locate the bibles, they might well give us a clue, or even tell us something important, if we're lucky,' Maddie proffered hopefully.

'Right you are,' agreed Rowan. 'Let's set about finding those bibles.' They began their search in the library. It was not an easy task. Systematically they scoured every shelf and every book. It took days. Much to their disappointment they had no success in their hunt and so decided to visit Reverend Hatfield to see if he could throw any light on the matter.

'Well,' he said in response to their question, 'at one time the bibles were kept at the chapel. There used to be a large bookcase especially for them in the baptistery. I believe it was your mother, Maddie, who requested they were sent up to the castle for safe keeping. Have you looked in your own library?'

'Oh yes,' replied Maddie. 'We've spent hours searching every shelf. They're definitely not there.'

'In which case,' he continued, 'have you asked your father if he knows where they are?'

'Father says they ought to be in the library, but we know they're not there.'

'Maddie is right,' said Rowan, 'we've hunted high and low for them. They are most definitely not in the castle library.'

'And you say you've already made a thorough search of the chapel?'

'Yes,' replied the cousins simultaneously.

'There's just one other place they might be,' continued Reverend Hatfield. 'But I must say it's a long shot. Do you think it possible that your mother donated the bibles to the town library? Local people have always had a fascination for Eastlyn, so you may find them there. Ask Mr Phillips, the librarian. He's been at the library for donkey's years, so if anyone knows of their whereabouts it will be he.' The visit to the library and the interview with Mr Phillips had been fruitless. Maddie and Rowan were beginning to feel slightly despondent. Hence the special Sunday service could not have come at a better time. Designed to raise spirits, it did exactly that.

Chapter Twenty-Six
The Lichen Stones

As always, the chapel was packed full for the Easter service of light. True to tradition it began with the village choir walking in procession down the aisle. Each person carried a small palm branch in one hand and a candle in the other. Reverend Hatfield followed behind carrying the lighted Paschal candle decorated with red studs to celebrate Christ's wounds. The palm branches were laid on the floor in front of the altar and then the choir turned to face the congregation. One by one the Reverend lit their candles as everyone joined in the first hymn, '*There is a green hill.*'

At the end of the hymn the choir placed their candles into the beautifully carved candle holder which Arthur Hawkins had made for the chapel only that month. It was a wonderful piece of furniture made out of solid oak. Arthur, who was also a member of the choir, took his seat with the rest of them, as Reverend Hatfield prepared to give his first sermon.

He was a wonderful orator and had a way of making even the smallest child understand the import of his sermons. Maddie listened to the central theme and understood his message, that Easter is a celebration to be joyous about the triumphant resurrection of Jesus Christ. A message that shouts loud and clear.

'God's not dead! He's alive.'

The service continued until it was time for the penultimate hymn. This was a duet which Maddie and Sam Hawkins were to sing together. They gave a beautiful rendition of the first and third verse of, '*Jesus lives and so shall I,*' the choir joined in with the second verse and the whole congregation sang the fourth and final verse. Lord Robert felt very proud of his daughter, and everyone remarked on the fact that she had clearly inherited not just her mother's good looks but her wonderful singing voice too.

After the service everyone congregated in the chapel's Easter Garden. A large stone had been set against the mouth of an old tomb. Reverend Hatfield rolled the stone away and then handed out all the chocolate eggs which had been placed inside. Every child in the village lined up to receive one.

The traditional Easter Bonnet Parade followed. Chairs had been set up in the church garden for the judges to sit on. One by one the contestants paraded in front of them with Arthur doing his usual excellent job as the show compere, introducing everyone, and describing each hat in rich detail. Hats of every description were on view, although there was a clear and popular theme consisting either of baby ducks or chickens as well an equally strong field of entries to do with lambs. Ethel Hawkins, Arthur's comely wife was the winner. Her hat was enormous, at least three feet across in diameter and depicting a spring meadow full of flowers. The judges, including Lord Robert and Aunt Frances, had been particularly impressed with the fine detail which had gone into it.

Finally, it was Rowan's favourite part of the day. Everyone made their way to the castle where tea would be served in the great hall. It was the one day in the year when the whole village were invited to Eastlyn. Rowan began by selecting a giant slice of Simnel cake. He was soon munching away on the deliciously rich fruit cake, covered with a thick layer of marzipan and with another layer baked through its centre. Each individual Simnel cake he noted was decorated with eleven balls of marzipan, representing the eleven true disciples (excluding Judas). Mrs Reed had explained that particular detail to him last year.

No sooner had Rowan finished his slice of cake, than he was up again and helping himself to a plate of custard tarts and spicy Easter biscuits smelling sweetly and tasting of cinnamon. Maddie tried her best but failed to keep up with him. 'I don't know where you put it!' she exclaimed in hoots of laughter as Rowan started on his seventh biscuit.

'Maddie,' said Rowan, with his mouth half full, 'I've had an idea. As we were walking past the cemetery today, I noticed all the gravestones. They all have a different inscription you know. I think it would be worth our while to take a closer look at them.'

'Father won't like that,' replied Maddie in a worried tone of voice. 'You know how he hates me visiting the cemetery.'

'Well, don't tell him then. We'll go in secret and if anyone should ask, we'll simply say we're going to put flowers on Clarissa's grave. No one could argue with that.' Rowan insisted emphatically. It was decided. They would visit the cemetery the very next day.

After breakfast, the children went straight out into the garden. It was a glorious day, the sun already high in a bright blue sky. A gentle breeze caressed Maddie's fingers and face as she stooped to cut the fragrant spring flowers. They were so engrossed in collecting their much-needed array of tulips and daffodils that they did not see Fred approaching with the two dogs on lead.

'Woof,' barked Bubble. 'Woof, woof,' agreed Squeak as if in greeting.

'Sit,' commanded Fred and the dogs immediately sat, the only movement now being their wagging tails brushing across soft, green grass.

'Gosh,' Rowan remarked grinning widely at his eldest cousin, 'the dogs are making good progress aren't they with their obedience training.'

'Whilst Tristan's been at school Mum's been taking them to special classes. It's cost a fortune, but worth every penny by the look of it. Watch this,' he said proudly.

Maddie and Rowan watched in admiration as Fred demonstrated a number of basic commands which the dogs obeyed immediately, including: 'Down! Heel! Come! Stay! Stop! Drop!' Finally, much to Maddie's delight, 'Shake hands!'

'Can I try that, Fred?' she called out excitedly.

'Of course,' he replied, with Bubble and Squeak only too willing to oblige.

'They're lovely dogs,' she exclaimed afterwards, 'and so well behaved.'

'Well, you're welcome to help me walk them this afternoon,' Fred suggested. 'Thought I'd take them down to the estuary for a swim, they adore the water, Squeak, especially.'

'We'd love to, wouldn't we Rowan?' Maddie replied happily. Rowan nodded in agreement.

'See you this afters then,' said Fred as he left, with the two dogs now off their leads.

A short while later Rowan attempted to curb his cousin's overindulgent harvesting. 'Maddie, you've got enough daffs there to decorate Buckingham Palace. Don't you think we should be setting off for the cemetery? The longer we stay here the more likely we are to attract unwanted attention. If your father sees us cutting all these flowers, he's bound to put two and two together.'

'Oh, yes, you're right,' she replied, instantly standing up and making ready to leave. They began to walk towards a wrought iron gate situated at the top right-hand corner of the garden terrace. It opened onto a path, which led to the chapel. As they reached it, Bella stepped out in front of them, blocking their way with her giant frame.

'Where are you going, child?' she snapped sharply, looking Maddie directly in the eye.

'We're going to the cemetery to put flowers on Clarissa's grave,' Maddie replied, her voice trembling slightly.

'Your father know, does he?' Bella demanded gruffly.

'He doesn't need to know,' Rowan interjected. 'We are going to the cemetery to put flowers on my sister's grave and that is all there is to it.' He grabbed Maddie's arm and pulling her along with him, pushed past Bella and exited the gate. They walked on hurriedly towards the cemetery without looking back. As they did so Rowan could feel Bella's stare piercing his shoulder blades. 'Well, that told her.' He said shakily when they were well out of hearing distance.

'Look,' replied Maddie. 'There's someone coming out of the chapel.'

To their relief, as they entered the church yard, they found it was Ethel Hawkins who was coming to meet them. 'Hallo, dears,' she said sweetly. 'I hope you haven't brought those flowers to decorate the chapel. I've only just finished redoing all the vases. Come every other Monday I do, and I've been doing it nigh on thirty year now. Old Reverend Hatfield reckons I'm a right treasure.'

'And so you are,' agreed Rowan. 'No, we're here to put flowers on our mothers' and Clarissa's grave.'

'Oh, that's nice,' she continued. 'I must say I think it very sad when graves are abandoned. Some of these here tombstones haven't had visitors for as long as I've been coming here at least. Don't think I've ever seen flowers on the first Lord Eastlyn's grave.'

'Oh, which one is that?' asked Maddie with interest.

'Why that big old marble lion of course,' was the reply as she pointed to the largest tombstone in the entire cemetery. Bit sad the inscription on that one really, contains him and his little wife. She wasn't much older than you Miss Maddie. My dad used to tell she were only seventeen when she died, in childbirth. Course in those days having a child was a dangerous business, not like.' She gasped and stopped mid-sentence, suddenly realising her error.

'It's all right Mrs Hawkins, we quite understand,' Rowan said kindly, trying to help the poor woman out of her embarrassment.

'Well, I best be off,' she stammered, her face now flushed, her eyes with a distinctly sorrowful expression. 'You get on and put those pretty flowers on the graves.' She turned and walked hastily away.

They tidied up the graves together. Rowan's mother and sister shared a joint headstone. Trying to control his voice and his emotions, Rowan read the inscription aloud:

In Loving Memory Of
Elizabeth Victoria Montague
Died September 23, 1995.
Aged 28 Years.

My wife, my friend, the mother dear in dreamless sleep she slumbers here May those whose love to her was given All meet and live with her in heaven.

And of Her Daughter
Clarissa Elizabeth Montague
Died December 24, 2008.
Aged 13 Years.

Goodbye to a beautiful daughter and sister She lived a short but wonderful life and was loved by all who knew her. She will be dearly missed but will live on in our hearts for generations.

Maddie laid flowers on her mother's grave and as she did so it was as if she could hear her mother speaking to her. 'I am so glad you are come, Maddie. The flowers are beautiful. But do not forget your purpose. Read the inscriptions; you will soon understand the connection between all the Montague women laid to rest here. God bless you, my darling child.'

'Come Rowan,' Maddie said in as firm and as controlled a voice as she could muster, 'Let us see what all these graves can tell us.' One by one they slowly visited every headstone, each individually set in an oblong surround made up of a low wrought iron fence. It was difficult to read some of the inscriptions, covered as they were in thick lichen and damaged by years of harsh winter rain and neglect.

Four were engraved with two names, that of a mother and her daughter. The marble lion marked the resting place of Ellen Montague and the first Lord Eastlyn. Ellen had died in 1754 at the age of seventeen, as Mrs Hawkins had said, Lord George in the same year. It took them some time to read the inscription on the tombstone.

Finally, Maddie could make sense of it. She read.

'Be ye ready for in such an hour as ye think not.
The son of man cometh.'

A little way off to the left of the lion was a granite statue of a cherub. Here the tombstone bore the name of Eleanor Georgiana Montague. The rest of the inscription, however, was so worn away and covered with lichen that it was impossible to read. There were other headstones. Harriet Montague died 1788 aged twenty-three and Agatha, her daughter, although the day and date and Agatha's age were illegible. Constance died 1829 aged twenty-six, and Verity, her daughter, died December 24, 1842 aged thirteen. Gertrude's grave was far too weathered for the two children to decipher the inscription, but they did manage to read about Rebecca, her daughter, who had also died December 24, 1907 aged thirteen.

They were so deep in thought they hardly heard the chapel bell ringing the hour. Rowan was only conscious of the sound on the twelfth stroke. 'Maddie,' he called out anxiously. 'It's noon already. We'd better be getting back, or we'll be late for lunch.'

Maddie was standing a little way off gazing steadfastly at the marble lion. 'Typical of you, Lord George,' she thought to herself, 'to have something as pretentious as a lion for a headstone. But what did you do to bring this punishment upon us? Your wife and daughter are the first in the chain of deaths so it must be something of which you are guilty. What terrible sin did you commit to bring the family such suffering and misery? What, George? What?'

Walking side by side they hurried back to the castle. 'I'm sorry to say I now wholeheartedly believe in the rumours and superstitions about Eastlyn. Even though we couldn't read what was written on all the gravestones, we've seen enough to indicate a definite connection between the circumstances surrounding our ancestor's deaths,' said Rowan gravely. 'There's a curse on the family all right, plain as the nose on my face. When you read the inscriptions on the headstones what other conclusion could anyone draw? No wonder our parents have tried to keep us away.'

'I think we can safely say we've established that fact,' replied Maddie, 'and it's a curse which affects Montague women, at least those who specifically give birth to a baby girl. The daughters then subsequently follow their mothers to the grave. But why at the age of thirteen, Rowan, why? Clarissa suffered the same fate, as will I, unless we solve this mystery,' she concluded in a voice full of fear and trepidation.

Sensing her anxiety, Rowan added, 'Well there's one other thing we know for sure. "*The Black Stag*" is key to all of it. December 24, the date Clarissa died, the date all the daughters died. It's far too great a coincidence not to be significant. We just need to discover more about the shipwreck.'

'That's the problem, Rowan. How are we going to do that? I'm feeling more confused than ever.' They had reached the castle and, on entering through the massive front entrance dominated by its three-storey Ionic portico, all discussion between them ceased.

After lunch they accompanied Fred in walking the dogs. Maddie insisted on holding at least one lead on the way to the estuary and both on the walk back. The dogs had great fun fetching sticks thrown out onto the river, dropping them at feet and then, barking eagerly wanting them to be thrown again.

It was exactly the light relief the two young cousins needed after their harrowing morning and by the time Bella brought a tray of chocolate brownies, cream scones, and a pot of tea to the library for them, they were in much better spirits. Bella's mood, however, had clearly not changed since their encounter with her on the top garden terrace before setting off for the cemetery. She hardly spoke a word as she set the tray down but gave a rare unguarded glance at Rowan. The expression displayed an undoubted hint of animosity and resentment.

'Oh dear,' said Rowan as soon as she had gone. 'I must have annoyed her this morning. Did you see that look she just gave me? Don't be surprised if I drop down dead.'

Maddie laughed as she reached for one of her absolute favourite cakes, a brownie. 'I'll be mother, shall I?' she asked, moments later, as she began to pour two cups of tea. A voice screamed in her ear. 'Stop, stop him!' Instantly Maddie shouted out the same instruction, 'STOP,' at the top of her voice. She so startled Rowan he dropped the scone he was about to bite into. It fell to the floor and broke in pieces. Buried deep in the cream was the body of a large dead wasp.

'Thank goodness you stopped me, Maddie. I'd have bitten into that. Can you imagine the sting it would have given me? But how did you know it was there, you couldn't have seen it?'

'I didn't,' she replied, 'Clarissa warned me!'

Maddie stood for some time watching Uncle Thomas's car disappear down the drive. Rowan sat in the back gazing through the rear window at his much-troubled cousin. It had seemed to them both that the more they discovered things about the family and the castle's secret past, the more confused they became. Far from helping discover the task which lay ahead for them, they had no more idea now than they'd had at the start of the Easter holiday.

Neither of them waved. Aunt Frances and Uncle Thomas had been surprised by how little conversation had taken place when the children parted company. There had been no need for words their goodbyes had been given already. Everything that could be said between them had been said, everything that could be done, disappointingly achieved. It was like putting together a jigsaw puzzle. Sections were beginning to come together but the full picture remained far from clear.

Late in the afternoon, carrying a small wicker basket and a pair of scissors Maddie went out into the garden to cut yet more flowers. A little while later armed with an array of brightly coloured daffodils and tulips she returned to the cemetery. Graves which had not been tended for centuries now received loving attention. Mothers and daughters united in death and previously long forgotten had softly whispered prayers said for them. No longer were they lying beneath bare, lichen covered gravestones, but ones now painstakingly bedecked with masses of spring flowers. Names and inscriptions were read aloud, and as Maddie made ready to leave each one, she would utter these words:

'I'm so sorry for your suffering but I hope you are able to lie at rest.'
Empty basket in hand she walked slowly back to the castle. A gentle breeze kept her company, rustling the leaves of the row of maple trees which lined the path. So deep in thought was Maddie she barely heard the sound of green foliage dancing in the soft evening wind as if dozens of murmuring voices were whispering, whispering in the air all around her. 'We are with you Maddie, have no fear,' the hushed voices seemed to say. Maddie left for school the next day.

Chapter Twenty-Seven
Finding the Doll

The school term had passed even more slowly than usual. Maddie was glad to be home. A poor summer, blighted by bad weather, had curtailed many of the events Maddie normally looked forward to. Hardly any rounders, tennis or athletic matches had taken place, rain-soaked pitches had seen to that. Even the annual summer concert had been cancelled due to severe flooding on the roads. Concern for the safety of visiting parents and guests had deemed the cancellation necessary. All Maddie's hard work practising her songs and pieces on the pianoforte had been for nothing. She felt bitterly disappointed.

'You can perform for me in the great hall when you get home,' her father said, trying to console her. After dinner on her first night home, Maddie had played and sung for Aunt Frances and her father. She excelled their expectations by some margin. 'Maddie, we really must do this more often, that was wonderful, truly wonderful,' her father remarked.

'Absolutely right,' echoed Aunt Frances, 'a talent such as Maddie's should be heard at every opportunity.' As Maddie left the great hall to rapturous applause, she imagined herself walking offstage at the Albert Hall after performing her first professional concert and went to bed happy. She did not sleep well, however. Repeatedly she was awoken from her slumber by a strange noise, as if a baby was in the castle somewhere, a baby crying. The next morning at breakfast, she asked her father whose baby it was she had heard crying in the night.

'What are you talking about?' Lord Robert replied looking puzzled. 'There are no babies here.'

'Perhaps it was one of the cats you heard,' suggested Aunt Frances helpfully. 'They do make the weirdest sounds at times. Her aunt's explanation seemed a most reasonable one and so Maddie forgot all about hearing a baby cry until the next evening.'

It was the middle of the night and very dark. The summer had continued in a similar vein to the school term and so thick black cloud blotted out both moon and stars from the sky. No light shone through Maddie's open curtains. She sat up in bed and switched on her bedside lamp. A quick glance at her watch told her it almost 1 am. She listened and sure enough there it was again, the sound of a baby or a small child crying. 'It's not a cat, Aunt Frances,' she said aloud to herself.

Climbing out of her warm bed, she slipped on her dressing gown and slippers and made her way to the bedroom door. Quietly opening it she peered outside into the long, dark corridor beyond. The castle was silent, no lights showing in any of the rooms. Everyone but her, it seemed, was asleep. She shivered in the cold night air and was about to turn round and go back to bed when the crying started again. Maddie stepped out into the passageway and closing the bedroom door behind her began to follow the sound. The noise was definitely coming from one of the upper floors of the castle. In the darkness she made her way along familiar corridors and staircases.

Without realising, she suddenly found herself outside Aunt Frances's room. 'Ought she to wake her aunt to help her discover whose baby it was that was crying?' Much as she loved the castle and knew it like the back of her hand, wandering about on her own in the middle of the night and in almost total darkness was a little unnerving, even scary to say the least.

'How embarrassing, though, if we were to find it is just one of the castle cats with a litter of kittens and I wake her up simply to discover she was right all along. No, I best be brave and go by myself,' she decided.

She continued on her way, eventually coming to the staircase which led to the fifth, the uppermost floor of the castle. This was an area she rarely visited, comprising numerous attic rooms used merely for storage. She felt along the wall for a light switch. No one lived up here, so there was no danger of waking people up if she turned on a few lights. She found the switch and flicked it on. Nothing happened. She tried several times but still no light bulbs came to her aid, the staircase remained in darkness. 'I'll come back in the morning,' she thought to herself, 'and have a good look round in the daylight, when I can see where I'm going.'

Just then the crying began again, more audible, and closer to her than ever. She could hear that it was coming from one of the upper rooms on the floor above. Undeterred by the pitch blackness which surrounded her and throwing caution to the wind, Maddie started up the stairs, holding the banister rail firmly in her right hand for support. At the top of the landing, she paused and listened again. The sound seemed to be emanating from an attic room a little way off to her left. Feeling along the wall, eyes straining in the darkness, she walked slowly down the narrow carpet which lined the middle of the floor. The sound stopped. Maddie stopped. All she could hear now was the sound of her own heart, beating loudly inside a ribcage rising and falling so rapidly she thought she might faint. The silence was oppressive, threatening. Maddie felt as if her nerves were in tatters, and she simply could not control her breathing.

'Oh, for goodness's sake, get a grip Maddie,' she whispered to herself. Taking a deep breath and drawing on her courage she moved on again, this time her hand touched a door frame. Trembling fingers fumbled to find the knob. Grasping it she began to open the door very slowly.

Without any warning there came a loud, high-pitched shriek, as a clearly terrified cat leapt from inside the room, firstly crashing into the door Maddie had been attempting to open, slamming it against her and causing her to fall backwards. She only just managed to stay on her feet. The door bounced back off Maddie's body and as it did, so the cat made good its escape. She could just make out its arched back and outstretched legs as it landed on bare, oak floorboards only a foot away from her. Maddie could hear claws scratching furiously on polished wood as it tore off down the passageway in a desperate effort to flee from whatever it was in that room which had so terrified it.

She stood for several minutes rooted to the spot. She honestly didn't know who had been most scared, her or the cat. 'Gosh, that frightened me. I nearly jumped out of my skin.' She was just congratulating herself on not waking Aunt Frances to discover the sound had come from a castle cat as anticipated and was about to head off back to the comfort of her own bed, when the crying started again. Maddie was instantly alert, hesitant feet tip-toed to the door, nervous fingers turned the door handle and she entered. 'Hallo is anybody here?' she asked in a voice sounding so strange she didn't recognise it as her own. The crying immediately stopped. No reply came from the total darkness which now surrounded her. 'Hallo,' she said again, 'can I help you? Is there anyone here who needs help?'

Out of the blackness came the whisper of a sob, barely audible. Maddie's head jerked towards the sound. It came from her left. She stepped towards it, immediately bumping into a tall, narrow object which had been standing upright directly in front of her. Whatever the object was, it toppled over, crashing to the floor, the sound of breaking glass deafening against a backdrop of total silence. Maddie quickly retraced her steps back to the door. She had made up her mind, 'Enough is enough, no more exploring tonight. I'll come back in the morning AND bring a torch just in case I still can't get the lights to work. At least I'll have the daylight, however meagre that might be!'

A very few minutes later, Maddie leapt back into her bed. She pulled the covers right up to her chin and curled herself into a little ball, desperately wanting to feel warm again. Her body felt like ice and every inch of her skin was covered in goose flesh. The crying started again. Maddie pressed her pillow to her ears. 'You'll just have to wait until morning,' she said. 'No way am I leaving my bed for a second time tonight.'

The next day her piano teacher left at eleven o'clock. There was a good two hours before lunch, plenty of time to investigate what was in the attic. First, Maddie went to see Arthur to borrow a torch. 'What do you want a torch for, Miss Maddie?' he had enquired.

'Only that I think we might have had a power cut last night. I couldn't get the lights to work. If I have a torch in my bedroom, I won't be affected should we have another one,' she replied.

'You're not afraid of the dark are you, not at your age?' he asked with a quizzical look in his eye.

'A little,' she answered, blushing slightly. 'I really don't like the dark or thunderstorms especially. I know it's silly.'

'Well, you're not the only one. Take my Ethel, for example. Sixty odd years she's been on this planet, and she's still frightened of the dark. Don't tell her I told you so! And goodness only knows how often I'll find her hiding under a table when there's a thunderstorm going on. Scared witless she is, bless her,' he said fondly.

As Maddie made her way up to the fifth floor of the castle an unexpected thought crossed her mind. 'Whatever had startled the cat to such an extent? The poor creature had been terrified. I can't see how it can have been me. I was as quiet as a mouse last night when I tried to open the door!' Had something else, something already in the room been to blame? Maddie's pulse began to quicken.

How she wished she had Rowan for company. 'Courage, Maddie, courage,' she told herself. 'Perhaps it was just a large rat the cat had been stalking which had decided to turn the tables by becoming the predator instead of the prey. Father always says, "Attack is the best method of defence", and how many times has Arthur told me that rats can be very dangerous and often confront other animals or people if they feel threatened.'

By now she had reached the door. She stood stock still in the corridor observing dim rays of light from half open doors and several windows with partially drawn curtains situated along the landing, affording tiny beams of sunlight which penetrated the gloom about her. Torch in hand she walked to the tall, arched window at the end of the passageway and drew back the curtains as far as was possible.

As she did so, other unpleasant thoughts invaded a mind already working overtime. 'I told Arthur I was afraid of the dark and thunderstorms. I could so easily have added rats to the list.' A nervous, unsteady hand gripped the doorknob. Maddie visualised a giant rat, squatting on its haunches, waiting for her to step inside, ready to attack. Slowly, very slowly she turned the handle and tentatively pushed the door open. She peered anxiously into the room. Although it was the middle of the day, there was hardly any light. She noticed two windows on the wall opposite, still with their curtains closed and moved very cautiously to draw the curtains apart.

Daylight flooded into the room, exposing an array of old furniture covered in dust sheets as well as dozens and dozens of storage boxes which littered the floor. Moving back towards the door she noticed a long mirror, set in an antique wooden frame. It was standing upright against the wall with half its glass missing. 'That's what I must have knocked over last night,' she thought to herself. 'But who had stood it up again and picked up all the broken glass?' It was obvious the floor had been swept clean, for not one single shard remained.

Maddie began to investigate the storage boxes. Some contained bits of unwanted pottery, others old oil lamps, or pewter pots, or earthenware no longer in use. It was then she noticed a battered looking trunk with a very ornate iron clasp. Kneeling on the floor beside it, she read the initials engraved on the top, AFS. Instantly she realised the trunk must have belonged to her mother. 'Abigail Faith Sinclair, my mother's maiden name,' she said aloud. Maddie was overjoyed with her find and couldn't wait to see what lay inside.

Excited fingers quickly undid the clasp. Carefully, so as not to damage anything, she lifted the lid open. Wide eyes alighted on a pile of old dresses, neatly folded, and lying one on top of the other. Some were clearly for summer use and made of brightly coloured silks and satins, others for winter use made of wool and velvet. One in particular had a beautiful white, ermine fur collar. Lifting several out she went back to the half-broken mirror and holding the dresses up against her shoulders noted they must have been worn by her mother when she was about Maddie's age now. They were the perfect length and fit.

Unexpectedly, a sudden noise startled her. She turned to look back at the trunk. The sound, a baby's cry had come from inside! Heart pounding, she returned to the trunk and kneeling down, slowly, systematically began removing garment after garment, layer by layer. It was then she found it, right at the very bottom, a doll. A small black doll carved out of wood. Picking it up Maddie carried it to the window. Now in the light she could see just how exquisite it was. The skill of the doll maker was immediately apparent. Fantastically sculptured facial features, sculpted stomach, shoulders, finely shaped legs and arms, fingers, toes, even a necklace of beads carved into the wood and looking so real Maddie had to touch them to see if they were separate to the doll itself. They were not. It was a work of art, a most beautiful African doll and Maddie instantly loved it.

'You are so beautiful,' she said observing the pretty face with its large eyes, delicate nose, and painted rosebud lips. As she gazed with admiration at the doll, she was astonished to see a single teardrop emerge from one of the sad brown eyes, a tear which began to trickle down the smooth ebony face. Maddie touched it with her finger, gently brushing it away. 'Don't cry,' she said, 'you don't need to cry anymore. I've found you now and I'm going to love you just like my mother did.'

Aunt Frances had quite a shock. She had been sitting at her writing bureau quietly composing reply letters to old acquaintances from whom she had recently received mail. Suddenly someone hammered on her door so loudly she was surprised it hadn't fallen off its hinge. 'Good gracious,' she called out at the top of her voice, 'are the roundheads come to arrest a cavalier?'

'No, no, aunt, it's only me,' Maddie replied laughing. 'I've got something really special to show you. Can I come in?'

'Yes, of course dear,' answered her aunt. Maddie raced into the room and hurried to her aunt's side. Smiling from ear to ear she laid the doll down on top of the bureau.

'Well,' she asked eagerly, 'what have you got to say about this?'

Aunt Frances picked up the doll and began to examine it. 'Very pretty,' she replied, 'of African origin I believe. Carved out of ironwood, I would guess and very skilfully done. How have you come by it?'

Maddie could barely contain her excitement. 'I found it in an old trunk in one of the attic rooms upstairs. The trunk had my mother's initials on it—AFS. Don't you see, Aunt Frances? The doll must have belonged to my mother. I'm so happy to have found it.'

Aunt Frances looked strangely sad, confused. She hesitated before speaking. 'Maddie, I was your mother's personal maid for many years, but I can honestly say I've never seen this doll before.'

For a moment Maddie looked flummoxed and then an expression of relief settled on her face. 'But, Aunt,' she said, 'how old was my mother when you became her maid?'

'Twenty-five, when she married your father,' was the reply.

'Exactly,' Maddie continued. 'I'm certain this was her favourite toy when she was about my age. I expect she'd grown out of it by the time she got married.' She took the doll to lunch and presented it to her father.

'I'm so sorry, Maddie, if this was a favourite toy of your mother's I don't remember her ever showing it to me. It's a beautiful thing though. Whoever made it had remarkable skill.'

'Look at the pretty face, Robert,' said Aunt Frances, 'who does it remind you of? Except for the darkness of the skin, I think she resembles our own Maddie, the shape of the chin and mouth; and the eyes especially.'

'Well, well, now you come to say, yes, I agree,' replied Robert laughing, 'a definite likeness. Well, I never!'

'Really, do you both really think she looks like me?' asked Maddie sounding more pleased than ever.

'Why don't you ask Bella about the doll, she might know something, after all she's been here longer than anyone else,' continued Aunt Frances.

'What a good idea,' responded Maddie, 'and she's from Africa. She might even know how my mother came by it. Incidentally, father how long has Bella been at the castle? Whenever I ask her, she simply says, "too long". You know Bella. She never gives anything away about herself.'

'Surprisingly, Maddie,' replied her father, 'I'm not altogether sure. She was here when I was born though and since that was forty years ago, I'd hazard a guess at fifty, even sixty years.'

'Too long,' repeated Aunt Frances grinning at the pair of them.

'Quite so,' echoed Robert as they all began to laugh.

'Is Bella around?' asked Maddie as she skipped across the kitchen floor to stand at Mrs Reed's side. Mrs Reed was whipping egg whites to make a lemon meringue for dessert that evening.

'No, Miss Maddie, haven't seen her at all today. Have you tried her room?'

'Yes, she's not there. I've searched the entire castle,' Maddie explained, 'can't find her anywhere.'

'Well,' replied Mrs Reed, 'like the proverbial bad penny, she'll turn up at some point. I've never known anyone able to disappear like Bella can and I've given up on sending the servants to find her even when I've had something urgent needing to be done. Waste of time!' she remarked with feeling.

'What do you think of my new doll?' asked Maddie, changing the subject, and holding the doll up for Mrs Reed to see.

'Oh, she is so beautiful. You should show her to Arthur, he'd be the first to admire the artistry that's gone in to making her. Arthur prides himself on his wood carving skills, but that Maddie,' she stressed vehemently whilst pointing her whisk at the doll, 'now that is truly a work of art.'

Maddie was not disappointed with Arthur's assessment of the doll. He went into raptures over it, 'made by a rare artist with a unique talent. This is fabulous, wonderful work Maddie. You must treasure this doll young lady. It's a masterpiece, better than anything I've seen in my lifetime. Why, even Augusta Savage would be proud to put her name to it. The quality, Maddie, the detail; it's unbelievable.'

On her return from the walled garden, where Arthur had been busy harvesting a crop of mixed summer berries, she spotted Bella coming out of the tallow room, carrying a large cardboard box full of candles.

'Bella, Bella, stop a minute,' Maddie called out as she raced towards her. 'I wanted to ask you about my new doll. Have you seen this before?' she asked breathlessly. 'I think it belonged to my mother originally. Have you ever seen her with it?'

'No,' Bella answered looking steadfastly at her young charge. 'Never seen it before, where did you get it?'

'I found it in one of my mother's old trunks, up in an attic room on the fifth floor,' she replied happily.

'Give the doll to me, child. Let me have a closer look at it.' Bella put the box of candles on the ground and took the doll in her hands. Maddie watched, delighted, as Bella turned the doll over and over in her thick, stubby fingers, scrutinising every inch of it as well as every small detail.

'What do you think of her?' Maddie asked excitedly, whilst jumping up and down on the spot and with arms flapping wildly.

'I think you is going to take off any moment,' she replied handing the doll back to Maddie with a rare smile on her face. 'But she's truly a beauty child, prettiest doll old Bella has ever seen. Pretty as a picture, just like you.'

'What should I call her Bella? You must know some African names which would suit?'

'Why don't you wait a while before deciding,' Bella suggested fondly. 'Sleep on it. A special doll like this deserves a special name. An idea will come to you in your dreams.'

'Yes, you're right,' answered Maddie. 'I'll think about it before I decide. The name just has to be perfect for her.' She skipped happily back to the kitchen, hoping to sample some of Mrs Reed's delicious lemon curd.

'You found her then I see,' said Mrs Reed who had been watching from an open window near the sink. 'Did Bella recognise the doll?'

'No,' Maddie replied, 'but she thinks it's as lovely as I do.'

'Seemed like you caught her in a good mood too, don't think I've ever seen her smile before,' Mrs Reed continued.

'Oh, she was.' Maddie glanced about the room and after the briefest of pauses added, 'is there any lemon curd left over?' She was immediately given a mixing bowl and a wooden spoon which had been sitting ready for washing next to the sink. She began to lick them clean. 'Yum, you are such a good cook.'

Now it was Mrs Reed's turn to look happy.

Chapter Twenty-Eight
The Dreams Start

The long summer days passed slowly. Her cousins were not due to visit until late August and so without company of her own age and with the weather showing little sign of improving, Maddie spent much of her time in the library. Her nose was hardly ever out of a book containing information about Africa. The doll barely left her. She even took it to bed with her. 'Aunt Frances,' she said one day whilst they were out walking, 'I'm having the most amazing dreams in my sleep all about my lovely doll. I think she was a royal princess, and do you know, she could do all sorts of things I can't, like swim in rivers, climb trees and even hunt with a bow and arrow.'

'You've been spending too much time with your head in a book about Africa just lately!' Her aunt replied soberly. 'No wonder you're dreaming about your doll.'

'There's one really old encyclopaedia in the library with the most amazing pictures of Africa in it. I'd love to go there on a safari one day,' Maddie said eagerly, 'and see all the wildlife especially.'

'Well perhaps you will. However, for today we shall have to be satisfied with what creatures the estuary has to offer.' They had reached the familiar walk above the river. Cold, clear, fast running water glittered under a sun too long missing. Summer had finally arrived. 'Let's see if we can spot any otters?' Aunt Frances suggested cheerfully.

'Oh, I do hope so,' Maddie agreed enthusiastically. 'If we see some new babies let's take it in turns to give them all names.'

'Speaking of names,' replied her aunt, 'have you decided what to call your doll yet?'

'I think so, but I wanted to run it past Bella first, her being from Africa and all. See if she feels it's a suitable choice.'

'Maddie, it's your doll, not Bella's! What does it matter what the old woman thinks?' There was a brief pause in the conversation. Maddie was surprised by the tone of her aunt's voice and by her obvious hostility towards Bella.

'You don't like Bella, do you aunt?'

Aunt Frances blushed slightly. Maddie had asked an awkward question. 'Well, it's not that I dislike her exactly,' she answered finally, 'just that she gives herself airs and graces at times, takes liberties. I expect she feels she's allowed them bearing in mind the long years of service she's given to the family.'

'She looks after me well enough,' Maddie added.

'Yes, there is that too, I suppose,' her aunt admitted, even if reluctantly.

It was bedtime. Maddie was waiting for Bella to arrive to check her lights were out. True to form Bella appeared at the allotted hour. 'What are you doing still awake, child? Time you were asleep.'

'I wanted to speak to you,' was the reply. 'I've chosen a name for my doll,' she explained, holding the doll up for Bella to see. 'I'm going to call her Adana. Princess Adana. What do you think? Will the name do?'

'It will do very well,' Bella answered in an unusually soft tone of voice. 'It's a name worthy of a royal queen and will suit your little princess perfectly. Goodnight Miss Maddie, goodnight Princess Adana. Sleep tight,' she said as she left the room with unseen tears collecting in eyes normally void of expression but now showing a depth of misery no human being should ever experience. Maddie fell happily asleep, oblivious to Bella's ancient pain and eternal grief.

The dreams of Africa, of Princess Adana continued unabated, but they began to change; so subtly at first that Maddie noticed no difference. For one thing all the early dreams had been of memories of events which had taken place during the hours of daylight. These were times when Adana had been out with friends, children of her own age with whom she played. Through her eyes Maddie had seen visions of great herds of buffalo, elephant, giraffe, zebra, or antelope roaming freely, grazing the lush savannah, or gathering to drink at communal waterholes.

In particular there had been one dream when a herd of elephants containing a number of young calves had gathered to drink at a wide river ford. The adults had enjoyed a good wallow in the mud, covering their thick hides inches deep in red slime, protection against blood sucking insects, whilst the youngsters had engaged in a water fight. Trunks were used like hose pipes to squirt each other as they cavorted about in the shallows.

Maddie loved her dreams about animals, and it seemed as if the little princess shared her passion for anything to do with wildlife. In one such dream a troop of monkeys appeared to get into a drunken state, eating over-ripe berries from a tree laden with fruit. They behaved very badly, throwing handfuls of food at one another, pulling faces, gesticulating madly, and arguing for all they were worth. No sooner had the monkeys staggered off having eaten more than their fill, than a company of parrots had arrived to consume the remaining fruit. Three had become so inebriated that they had fallen off the branches and lay in a stupor on the ground for some time.

One night she dreamt about a clan of meerkats being tricked by a very clever bird. One of the meerkats had caught a small lizard. Before it had time to eat it, the bird had cried out, mimicking the meerkats alarm call. The clan disappeared immediately back down into their burrow for safety, whilst the bird swooped in to steal the hastily discarded lizard.

There were dreams too of children playing in lakes and rivers, all of them competent swimmers, fearless, swinging out over the water on giant vines, only to drop or plunge from a great height into the cool, clear waiting watercourse below. They would often jump or dive from sheer sided rocks situated at the water's edge, laughing happily, and trying to mimic one another in the funny shapes they made with their bodies or in their chaotic movements.

Then came the first night dream and Maddie watched a crash of rhinos gather in the bush under a full moon. Surprisingly, the animals seemed very sociable, rubbing noses whilst snorting and chuffing to each other. The latter part of the dream was not so pleasant, she watched a large wasp as it laid its eggs inside a host spider, stinging it first to paralyse it temporarily. When the eggs hatched, they would eat the spider from within.

Slowly, slowly, fewer daylight dreams were to be had. Night dreams became the norm, animals hunting, merciless kills and menacing predators hiding in the darkness waiting to strike at unsuspecting prey. Now too, she found herself experiencing terrifying dreams of terrible storms, of thunder and lightning so fierce that Maddie congratulated herself on living in England. Her own experience, though frightening, had seemed far less severe by comparison with the storms witnessed by Princess Adana in Africa.

It was then that Maddie began not to take the doll to bed with her and for the first time since she had discovered it, it was left in the nursery with all her other toys for the better part of every day. She returned to her old ways, reading in the library, walking the castle grounds with Aunt Frances, riding Eclipse in the paddock with Sam, or helping Arthur in the garden. However, one particular thing began to disturb her. No matter how carefully she put the doll back in the playroom, it somehow always managed to find its way back to her bedside table when she woke each morning. As soon as she opened her eyes, she would turn to look at it. There it would be, standing upright on the table and gazing into space with its beautiful sad, brown eyes. For reasons even Maddie could not explain, she would take hold of it again, kiss it, hold it close and apologise for being afraid.

Since finding the doll there had been one other notable change in Maddie's life, which again she had somehow failed to notice. She had stopped dreaming about her mother. Her mother no longer came to her in times of worry or stress. Hence, she did not hear her voice in her dreams or in the back of her mind, talking, advising as she had always previously done, like the voice of conscience or common sense. Clarissa also no longer called out to her from the grave. Their voices were silent, only Adana spoke to her now.

Chapter Twenty-Nine
Trapped in a Storm

The final two weeks of the summer holiday had arrived, and her cousins were due at any minute. 'Uncle Harry, Aunt Mary and the boys will be here for lunch,' her father had advised over breakfast, 'and everyone else by teatime. So don't stray too far today.' Maddie nodded as she chewed on her piece of toast.

'Arthur tells me he's opened the bog garden again,' said Aunt Frances, 'the water levels are back down to normal so it's safe to go in.'

'Oh good,' replied Maddie, 'Tristan and Harry might like a game of hide and seek later. I know Rowan will be up for it. He always finds the cleverest places to hide.'

As it turned out, everyone but Rowan and Uncle Thomas arrived at the castle in time for lunch. Poor Mrs Reed struggled to serve sufficient food. Her information had been that only Aunt Mary and family would be present. The early arrival of Aunt Kate had quite thrown the kitchen into uproar. Providing lunch for twelve instead of seven, whilst preparing a celebratory dinner for fourteen was no mean feat. As always however Mrs Reed had risen to the challenge.

'Uncle Robert are you coming to watch dad and I sail the new Firefly on the estuary this afternoon?' asked an excited Edmund between mouthfuls of coronation chicken left over from the night before.

'No,' replied Fred. 'You've already volunteered to give Finn and me a driving lesson, haven't you, Uncle Robert?'

'Indeed, I have. However, should we back in time. I'll come down by all means and have a look at this new boat I've heard so much about.' Robert said smiling at his nephew.

'Ed's won every sailing competition he's entered this year Robert,' commented Aunt Kate proudly.

'He's destined to be the next Ben Ainslie, by all accounts,' boasted Uncle William, 'His sailing teacher at school tells me he's really quite the expert already.'

'I wish I could sail,' Maddie added sadly.

'You can come out with me in the safety boat,' ventured Aunt Kate trying to rescue a difficult situation.

'No thanks,' replied Maddie, 'sitting in an old motorboat, wearing an oversized life jacket is just plain boring.'

'A little ungrateful Maddie,' remarked Aunt Mary. 'Your aunt was only trying to help.' Maddie received a more than frosty look from her father before apologising in a less than genuine tone.

Lunch over, the party went their separate ways.

Uncle Harry and Edmund were to take the Firefly out on the estuary. Uncle William would join them in his single dinghy, whilst Aunts Kate and Mary were to follow in the motorised safety boat. Finn and Frederick left with Uncle Robert for their driving lesson. Tristan excused himself from the dining room to take dogs Bubble and Squeak for their afternoon walk, leaving Maddie and Harry junior to entertain themselves alone.

'Well, this is fun,' said Harry sarcastically as the two of them sat in silence.

'Do you fancy a game of hide and seek?' asked Maddie. 'The bog gardens open again after being closed for nearly a month. The water levels have been right up, all the usual pathways were completely submerged. I bet we could find some great hiding places in there. We'd have to be careful going over the steppingstones though. They're bound to be really slippery.'

'Yes, sounds like a good idea,' replied Harry enthusiastically.

Harry, a year younger than Maddie, raced along by her side. They entered the bog garden through its only entrance, a tall, narrow, intricately made wrought iron gate to which an open, metal padlock was attached. The garden was surrounded with a stone wall, six feet in height and with jagged pieces of glass embedded into its concrete coping to deter robbers from trying to climb over should they attempt to steal any of the expensive, exotic plants contained within. A winding dirt path covered in wood chippings led down into the centre of the garden. 'I'll hide first,' Harry said, 'but we'll have to synchronise our watches with only two of us playing.'

'How long should we give each other to get back to the den?' Maddie asked.

'Ten minutes should do it. What do you think?'

'Yes, ten's fine by me,' she replied eagerly.

They began by exploring the bog garden in its entirety. The thatched wooden hut at its centre would function as the den once again. As they meandered up and down the twisting, turning walkways both were on the lookout for good places to hide. 'This is a fabulous garden,' said Harry. 'I feel as if I'm in some kind of sub-tropical forest. Some of these plants are incredible, the colour and size of the foliage especially.'

'I never grow tired of crossing the watercourses,' remarked Maddie. 'I just adore going over all the steppingstones.' After an hour of exploring, the game finally began. Watches were synchronised, Maddie covered her eyes and Harry went to hide. 'Ninety-nine one hundred,' Maddie shouted. 'Coming ready or not.'

Less than four minutes later Harry shouted, 'Home.' He laughed as a disappointed Maddie returned to the hut. The triumphant cousin added to her annoyance by admitting his first hiding place had been her choice too, although of course she didn't tell him. 'I was hiding in that clump of bamboo, just over there,' he said, pointing it out. 'You came right past me and looked inside. I nearly died. I was sure you had seen me.' The game continued. Maddie hid under a massive Gunnera, not too far from the hut. She held her breath as Harry strode past, probing at the foliage with a long stick. Round two went to her.

The first drop of rain fell when the score was 4-3 to Harry. Maddie was hiding in a giant fern right at the edge of one of the water courses. The only way in and out was across a series of steppingstones which were very exposed. Anyone crossing would be easily seen. Maddie had to wait until Harry had moved well away before she could risk coming out of her hiding place. The rain grew heavier. Harry looked at his watch. There were still seven minutes left before Maddie's time was up and he was already soaked to the skin. It wasn't that he was being especially spiteful, but for reasons best known only to him he decided to play a trick on Maddie. He made his way back to the wrought iron gate, exited through it and closed the padlock shut. Without a second thought for Maddie, he sprinted back to the castle.

He had not covered fifty yards before the first flash of lightning ripped through the dark sky overhead. Seconds later came the loud rumble of thunder. Maddie was petrified. She left her hiding place immediately and raced back to the hut for shelter, shouting at the top of her voice for Harry to join her. The hut was empty and deserted. She stood in what little shelter it afforded, calling out

Harry's name, begging him to come in, explaining that she had surrendered. Horizontal rain, driven by an increasing wind tore against her. There was a second flash, forked lightning lit up the sky in a blaze of yellow, the sound of thunder rent the air, so loud it was almost deafening.

Maddie shot like a rabbit in headlights from the hut. Wild-eyed, shaking with fear, she hurtled as fast as her legs would carry her back to the exit. She was horrified to find the gate closed and, worse still the padlock fastened. Trembling fingers fumbled with the mechanism, desperately trying to undo it, to escape.

As Harry burst in through the kitchen door looking like a drowned rat, he found Finn and Frederick being helped on with raincoats by Arthur and Mrs Reed. 'Thank the Lord for that,' said Mrs Reed sounding very relieved, 'they're back.' All eyes were focused on the door waiting, expecting Maddie to appear at any moment. She did not!

'Where's Miss Maddie?' asked Arthur in alarm.

'Still in the bog garden,' Harry replied. 'She's locked in.'

'What, in this storm!' exclaimed Mrs Reed. 'The poor child will be petrified.'

'You go on, lads,' said Arthur to the boys. 'You can run a lot faster than me.'

Finn and Fred shot from the room and ran as fast as they could. When they reached the entrance to the bog garden, they could see Maddie kneeling on the ground, head bowed, sobbing uncontrollably. The iron bars of the locked gate were clasped firmly in her hands. At first, she refused to let go, too terrified to move. 'Maddie, Maddie, we've come to get you,' shouted Fred against the noise of the downpour and a now howling wind. Another great flash of lightning illuminated the ominously black sky. Maddie screamed.

'Maddie. Maddie, I need you to stand up. Climb up on our hands. Look here, see our hands, we can get you over the gate easily.' Fred insisted. 'Come on, I know what a brave girl you are. Stand up. Here, look, put your foot in my hand. Finn and I will soon have you out.'

'Come on, Maddie, do what Fred says. There's a good girl. I won't drop you I promise. We'll get you back to the castle and when the storm is over, we'll go and see my little foal together.' Maddie lifted her eyes to look in Finn's face. As they finally began to help her to her feet, she held firmly onto his hand. Not once did she let go until she was safely over the gate and back inside the castle.

'Well done, boys,' said Mrs Reed as she stoked up the fire. 'Here, Arthur, pour them all a cup of that hot chocolate I've just made. Why, child, you must be chilled to the bone,' she declared, turning her attention to a bedraggled looking Maddie, and taking hold of one of her hands. 'Oh, my dear! You're as cold as the grave. Bella's gone up to your room to get dry clothes, Maddie. She'll be back down in a minute. There you go,' she said comfortingly, as she wrapped a large, warm towel around Maddie's shaking shoulders.

By the time Bella returned with a change of clothes Harry was a blubbering wreck. However, Maddie was too cold, too shocked, to show any sign of forgiveness, try as he might to plead his case. 'Best leave her to us now, boys. You all need to get dry clothes on too. Bella and I will see to Maddie. You can apologise later, Master Harry, when she's had time to recover.'

Finn and Fred led a reluctant Harry away. 'I just want to apologise to her,' he kept repeating. Bella's harsh stare followed him to the door.

As Bella stooped to help Maddie take off her wet clothes, Maddie's arms fixed about her neck. Bella could feel how chilled Maddie's body was and as her young charge clung to her, shaking and shivering, she remembered a day in the distant past when another little girl had turned to her for comfort during a storm. Bella began to sing softly—an old Dahomey lullaby she thought she had long since forgotten.

When Uncle Thomas and Rowan arrived shortly before dinner, Maddie had already been put to bed. She was running a slight temperature after her ordeal in the bog garden. Supper, consequently, was brought up to her bedroom by Bella and served on a tray. 'Poor old Harry,' said Rowan when he came to collect it. 'He's had the worst telling-off of his life from just about everyone. No one can understand what possessed him to lock you in.'

'Habit,' Maddie replied simply. 'I've been the brunt of their cruel jokes for so long, it's become second nature to be spiteful to me.'

'Well, from what I heard Frederick and Finn say about you over dinner I can honestly say I think those days are over.'

'Why, what did they say?' She asked out of curiosity.

'They like you. They think you are smart, clever, and kind. Finn was especially complimentary. I gather you acted as his nursemaid when he broke his leg and that it was your idea to give him Warrior's foal. He's clearly very grateful.'

'That's nice,' Maddie said happily, 'now on to more important things. Tomorrow, if I'm allowed up, we are going to make a search of all the attic rooms on the fifth floor. They are currently being used for storage, so if the family bibles have been put away for safekeeping, it would not surprise me to find them there.'

Sadly, the next day, Maddie's temperature had gone up instead of down. Rowan began the search alone. Empty-handed he returned to Maddie's bedroom after lunch and dinner. 'I've only managed to search two rooms today,' he informed her. 'There's just so much stuff up there. It's taking ages.'

'I know,' she replied, 'I saw for myself when,' she was about to say, 'when she found her doll,' but at that moment the bedroom door opened and cousins Frederick, Finn, Edmund, Tristan, and Harry entered the room. Harry was carrying a package.

'I've brought this for you,' Harry stammered, 'by way of an apology. I'm really, really sorry Maddie. Can you forgive me?' Maddie took the package from him and began to unwrap it. To her delight, she discovered a brand-new chess set.

'It's no ordinary chess set,' Harry explained. 'If you open the box up, you'll see what I mean.' Maddie lifted out a knight and a bishop. 'Can you see?' he said, 'they are all hand decorated pieces representing the two opposing armies in the most famous battle ever fought on English soil. Look at the two kings, Maddie. This one is Harold, he leads the Saxon forces, and this one is William, Duke of Normandy. The set is based on the Battle of Hastings of 1066. Oh goodness, I hope girls play chess. Do they?' he added suddenly in a worried tone of voice.

'Of course, girls play chess,' Maddie answered reassuring him, 'and anyway, I'm not one of those soppy girls who like playing with dolls, dressing up, or practising wearing make-up. Give me a football or a pair of roller skates any day.'

'Good old Maddie,' said Finn wholeheartedly. 'She's one of us.'

'Absolutely,' echoed Fred, 'one of the boys.'

Several chess games later, Bella arrived with a tray of cocoa for them all and to see to Maddie's lights out. The six boys were duly handed a mug each and then escorted from the room. As Maddie lay back in her bed, she decided she would say nothing to anyone about her doll, not even Rowan.

Chapter Thirty
The Boating Accident

The next morning Maddie was fully recovered. A beautiful day had dawned without a cloud in sight. The sun was shining in a bright blue sky and a light breeze heralded the perfect weather for sailing. Over breakfast, plans were made for a picnic lunch to be served down by the boatsheds.

Much to her father's annoyance, both Rowan and Maddie declined the invitation to join the sailing party. 'We'll come down for the picnic lunch though,' Maddie explained. 'It's just that we have certain things we need to do here in the castle.' They spent another fruitless morning searching through old cupboards, boxes, and wardrobes. The bibles could not be found.

'Gosh, Maddie look at the time. We need to get down to the boatshed for lunch. Your father looked annoyed enough at breakfast, when we said we would not go sailing, without us being late for the picnic too!' Rowan said anxiously.

'Best go via the kitchen,' Maddie suggested as they made their way downstairs, 'in case Mrs Reed wants us to take anything with us.' Even before they had reached the kitchen, they could hear a commotion going on inside. They opened the door to find the whole family gathered inside. Only Aunt Mary, Uncle Harry and Cousin Harry were missing.

'Are we putting you out, Mrs Reed, if we eat in here?' asked Lord Robert. 'I'm afraid no one feels much like a picnic after what's happened. We've brought everything back up with us, but it just seems like extra work for everyone if we carry it all to the dining room.'

'Not at all,' replied Mrs Reed. 'Please sit down. I'm sure a bite to eat will make everyone feel better.'

'What's happened?' Maddie asked Aunt Frances moving to stand at her side.

'There's been an accident,' replied her aunt. 'Harry was knocked out of the Firefly. The boom swung across as they were tacking. Hit Harry on the head. He ended up in the water unconscious. If it had not been for Edmund's quick thinking he might have drowned.'

'Where is he now?' Maddie continued.

'Hospital,' she replied. 'Your father called an ambulance immediately. Aunt Mary and Uncle Harry went with him. They're going to ring when they're ready to be picked up. What a day,' she added, 'and after such a promising start. Edmund can't understand how it happened.'

Overhearing the conversation, Edmund was eager to express his thoughts on the accident. 'The conditions were almost perfect. I say "almost" because if anything the sea was too calm for my liking and the wind too light. How the boom came to swing across with such ferocity is a mystery to me. I'll never forget it,' he said. 'It hit him with such force!'

'Yes,' commented Fred, 'we heard the impact even from where we were.'

The afternoon search of the attics was abandoned. The family waited for news from the hospital which fortunately was good. No serious harm had been done and Harry was on his way home.

It was the penultimate day of the holiday and there were still three rooms needing to be searched. Uncle Thomas and Rowan would return to Bristol the next morning, so it was imperative for them to finish their task today. Immediately after breakfast they jogged upstairs together, faces set and sharing a real sense of purpose.

'Let's hope we have better luck today,' said Maddie as they entered a particularly dark and dingy attic room, packed in tight with ancient furniture, rolled up carpets, wooden crates, and discarded tea chests. They tiptoed across the floor heading for the windows on the far wall and in seconds were covered in cobwebs. Rowan drew back the curtains causing a cloud of dust to rise into the air. Dead bluebottles littered the windowsill. Both children began to sneeze, noses and throats clogged with dust. The sneezing lasted for several minutes, followed by a fit of giggles.

'Come on,' said Rowan finally composing himself, 'I suggest we start with that cupboard over here.' As they moved towards it more cobwebs snapped on their clothes and skin. Brushing the evidence of spiders from their faces they worked together to pull the huge dust cover off and immediately exposed two enormous, leather-bound books resting on the top shelf. Rowan carefully lifted one down.

'Eureka!' he exclaimed. 'We've only gone and found them Maddie. I'd almost given up. These are the family bibles.' Two excited children carried the heavy books to the window. Sitting cross-legged on the floor they carefully opened the first of the bibles between them. Dust still poured through the welcome beams of sunlight as Rowan read a hand-written date on an opening page. The ink was very faded but the writing still clear.

'Ye sixth day of January 1697, born to us this wet winter morn ten o'clock in ye forenoon, our first child, a son, George James, Praise be to God.'

'That's George himself, the first Lord of Eastlyn, the Captain of *The Black Stag*. My God Rowan,' Maddie exclaimed, 'he and I share the same birth date! How awful; and here in the margin it says, Christened third day of February.'

'Maddie am I right in saying you were born in 1997?'Rowan asked pensively. Maddie nodded. 'Exactly three hundred years to the day. How strange is that!' he concluded.

They spent the entire morning examining the bibles. By lunchtime all had been revealed, their early suppositions vindicated. They had been quite right in their assessment of the family history. Events, circumstances kept repeating through the ages. Montague wives died in childbirth but always when giving birth to a daughter. The same date, December 24, clearly written time and time again as being the day those daughters had died, but only after each one of them had reached the age of thirteen.

Two depressed children entered the dining room for lunch and clearly, neither had much of an appetite. The food they were served was pushed around the plate rather than eaten, nor did they contribute to the conversation around the dinner table. The adults put their low spirit down to an imminent return to school and the end of the summer holiday.

After lunch, they joined their other cousins to watch Tristan working with a dog trainer. Bubble and Squeak were being put through their paces on the main lawn. 'Tristan thinks mums called the trainer in to help with the dogs. Actually, he's here to teach Tristan how to handle them. It's cost a fortune.' Edmund explained in a wicked tone of voice.

'Well at least it appears to be working,' commented Finn as he watched the dogs obey numerous commands. 'I'm impressed.'

After the training lesson they all walked the dogs down to the river for one final swim in the estuary. Rowan and Maddie bringing up the rear and consequently slightly detached from the rest of the group were engaged in a serious and private conversation. 'The trouble is, Rowan I still have no idea what Clarissa meant when she said I would be the family's salvation. The bibles actually told us nothing we didn't already know.'

'Maddie, we have to hope, to pray that somehow or other we'll know what to do when the time comes. I can tell you one thing for certain, Clarissa will not let us down.'

'I believe that,' Maddie replied, linking her arm in his. 'I do have faith and I'll tell you something else, I'm not afraid.'

'That's my girl,' Rowan said, resting a comforting hand on hers. 'I've already asked Dad to make sure we arrive back at Eastlyn for Christmas as soon as he can close his business down. We mean to start the holiday at the earliest opportunity. I'm sure by then Clarissa will have shown us exactly what it is we have to do.'

After waving everyone off, Aunt Frances accompanied Maddie back to her room to help with her school packing. Bella was already placing skirts and sweaters in Maddie's trunk as they arrived. 'You can go now, Bella,' she said, 'I'll help Maddie finish off.' Not deigning to make any kind of reply, Bella gave Aunt Frances one of her frosty looks before leaving, Maddie could sense the coldness between them. You could have cut the atmosphere with a knife.

It was then that Aunt Frances spotted the doll inside one of Maddie's suitcases. 'You're not thinking of taking that doll back with you, are you?' she asked sternly.

'Well, yes, I was actually,' Maddie replied tentatively, sensing her aunt's disapproval.

'Too risky, Maddie, too risky by far. My advice is to leave her here with me. I'll look after the doll for you if it makes you feel better. How would it be if she were to get broken, lost, or worst scenario, stolen? When something has a special sentimental value, it really is best to play safe. One of the other girls might just take a fancy to her. She is very pretty after all, and I know how much it means to you to have a toy which once belonged to your mother.' The decision was made. The doll would be stored in the trunk above Aunt Frances's wardrobe for safe keeping. Maddie could collect her as soon as she was back from school.

The term passed pleasantly enough, except that Maddie could not dismiss nagging thoughts concerning Clarissa's prophecy and, even without the doll, her dreams were full of frightening visions. She remembered her aunt's words, the doctor's diagnosis that Clarissa had somehow drowned in her sleep. What lay ahead, what was she supposed to do? She wanted to be brave, but there were times when she felt utterly terrified.

However, true to her word, the instant she got home she collected the doll from her aunt's room. It was then that the dreams took a turn for the worse.

Chapter Thirty-One
The Nightmare

Steep steps plunged downwards. In the pitch black, Maddie's eyes strained to see into the depths of the tunnel. As she peered nervously into that dark void an even deeper darkness seemed to seep out towards her. She felt the darkness clawing at her face, scratching at her eyes, and somehow drawing her tiny frame closer, pulling her in, body and soul, as if it was intent on sucking her whole being down into the very bowels of the castle.

Bare feet, already feeling like ice, stepped onto the rough-hewn rock and equally cold, frozen fingers reached sideways, desperately seeking some kind of support. She knew she would find it—the thick rope of fibres so coarse to the touch that the skin of her hand would hurt and chafe within seconds of gripping it. Nevertheless, it was her lifeline and she clung to it religiously. The rope was fixed against the right-hand wall of the tunnel and held in place by large, circular rings of wrought iron which had been systematically hammered into the rock face at twenty pace intervals. Maddie had counted the steps many times before.

She knew how the nightmare was going to end. A terrible fear clutched at her breast, making her shiver violently as with pounding heart and feeling breathless she bravely began her slow descent, hoping against hope that this time it would be different.

'*Adana. Adana. Please, please save Adana!*'

Maddie's heart skipped a beat as that instantly recognisable voice called down to her in the desolate blackness. The voice was pitiful to hear. In all her life Maddie had never heard a sound so melancholy. It was as if the person crying out carried all the world's woes, sadness and suffering on their shoulders. Maddie felt tears prick her eyes as the plea echoed repeatedly as if travelling through vast, endless catacombs, piercing her heart with almost tangible pain. Then from high above her came a mighty rush of air, something ghost-like flew past her, almost knocking her over and causing her to stumble in fright. She could hear it descending, quickly and so powerfully the sound of its movement broke through the thick, perpetual night that filled the tunnel. Maddie waited, afraid and confused until the silence returned again.

The tunnel drew a terrible, soundless breath and air already heavy as if dragged down by a black, suffocating blanket, tugged at her nightgown, pulling her closer. Maddie was unable to resist the call and shuffled her feet along until they reached the edge of each step. Clutching the rope tightly she would descend to the next level, nervously afraid of whatever it was lying in wait for her in the blackness below.

Time dragged alongside her feet as she made her way down the tunnel. At fifty paces she waited for the familiar sound. There it was, a horrifying cackle followed by the familiar rumbling moan, as the great brick doors through which she had entered swung shut behind her, trapping her, encasing her in a thick, hopeless night. Now, not even the dimmest light infiltrated the black air. Maddie stood there, too petrified to move for several minutes, waiting for her eyes to adapt to the deeper darkness. As time went by a spiralling staircase dissolved out of the distance beckoning her downwards. She obeyed its command and ventured on, listening to the sound of her own feet shuffling across granite.

Maddie began to tire, muscles to cramp in the coldness but still she continued her descent, dragged downwards by the tunnel's silent inhalations: firm pulls that gripped her insides and led her on into the abyss. An eternity seemed to pass, with each movement mirroring exactly the one before. Step followed step until she had counted to two hundred. She knew the number she would eventually reach. At intervals she would peer back up the tunnel, hoping to see a light, a way of escape. She could see nothing, no indication of where she had begun her descent, no glimpse of her progress, just pure, desolate blackness in a world starved totally of light.

'Save her. Save Adana,' the voice cried out again.

As she counted two hundred and thirty, the small speck of light at the bottom of the tunnel became visible. The miniscule prick of light grew steadily as Maddie climbed down towards it. Soon it was the size of a postage stamp, then a book, until it was easily large enough for Maddie's fragile frame to fit through. She wanted to step into the light to get out of the oppressive darkness, yet somehow, she knew she had to continue on into the gloom.

A face loomed up at her from the abyss below a beautiful face, black of skin with a full mouth and wide sad eyes, the face of a young girl about her own age.

'Help the child,' a voice cried.

There was something about the voice which triggered a memory in Maddie's mind. Ought she to have known whose voice it was? She couldn't think, she couldn't remember as fear began to take over. Two hundred and fifty, the bottom had been reached, the chamber awaited, and Maddie knew a terrible evil was ready to pounce.

Grasping the final length of rope and with tremendous courage, Maddie hauled herself out of the darkness of the tunnel and into a dimly lit chamber. An eerie silence lingered like a physical presence. The air remained heavy and thick; it was almost solid. She stood for a moment, forcing the viscous air into her empty lungs, attempting to regain her energy, whilst her eyes struggled to adapt to the flickering light. There was a smell of burning wax. Her eyes focused on numerous candles, pressed into small niches carved into the rock walls. But there was another smell too. She moved forwards into the chamber and as she did, so she felt something wet and soft under foot. She looked down, she was standing on a small pile of feathers, feathers in a pool of red.

Something moved in the darkness behind her. She heard her nightdress rip and felt a rake of pain sweep across her back and shoulders as if she had been clawed by a tiger. Instinctively she raised her hand to touch her shoulder, it was sore. Removing her fingers, she saw that they were covered in her own blood. At that moment, the sharp claws of a cockerel landed at her feet as if discarded by an unseen assailant.

Worse still, the walls of the chamber were moving, no longer solid but fluid. It was as if she was surrounded not by rock but by an angry sea, a sea which crashed and wailed about her. The floor lurched upwards, causing Maddie to lose her balance altogether. She collapsed onto her knees and pressed her hands to the ground to save herself from injury. Skin, now scraped and sore with rope burns touched not rock but wood. Fingernails tore at wet planks of timber as she desperately tried to maintain her position. But to no avail, she was thrown first one way and then the other as slippery floorboards heaved up and down and all the while sluiced in wave after wave of foaming water. And then it came again, the great swell of water which hit her like a cannon ball and Maddie was falling, falling into a pure, infinite canvas of jet black.

She was sinking, sinking, she could not breathe.

It was always the same, at that very instant, Maddie would thankfully wake from her nightmare. She would find herself sitting bolt upright in her bed, with sweat pouring over her flushed skin. This morning was just like all the others. Waking from her night terror, her chest rose and fell rapidly, as her heart hammered away against her ribs. A sliver of light stung her eyes as she fell back into her bed, waiting for the adrenaline to subside. She flipped her pillow over and sank her face into the cool fabric, breathing deeply. It took some minutes for Maddie's pulse rate to return to normal. She climbed out of bed and went over to her dresser. The distinctive antique water bowl and pitcher once prized possessions of her mother, and both decorated with hand painted rose buds were waiting to be used. She poured the water eagerly and splashed her still flushed face with the deliciously cold liquid.

It was only when she turned back towards her bed that she saw it, the doll; the doll she clearly remembered putting back in the nursery the night before. The black doll with the face of an angel, which adorable as it might look, she had certainly not wanted to take to bed with her. It beggared belief that there it was sitting as it had done on so many other nights on her bedside table. Slow steps took her to it and cautiously she reached out a trembling hand to pick it up.

'I don't understand,' she said. 'How do you come to be here? I locked my door when I came to bed last night and unless I'm going mad, I know I put you back in the nursery before I came upstairs. How can something so incredibly beautiful bring such dreadful dreams and you are bringing them to me aren't you? What has happened to you, what terrible thing has befallen you?' The doll made no answer as Maddie's fingers touched the smooth ebony surface of its face and felt the wetness below its eyes. It was as if the doll was crying once more but Maddie wondered to herself, 'For whom? And why?'

'Were you really made in the image of someone named Adana? Did she drown at sea? Am I somehow meant to save her? Is this why you send me this awful nightmare? I must tell Rowan about my dreams. He'll know what they mean and, more importantly, what it is I must do to put things right.'

Chapter Thirty-Two
The General's Secret Is Revealed

Her cousins had abandoned her. She could hardly blame them. Six inches of snow had fallen overnight and all talk at breakfast had been of toboggans. Eyes kept lifting from plates of hot bacon and egg to the winter wonderland beyond the windows of the dining room. Maddie looked at her father to ask the question, 'Was she allowed to join in?' The shake of the head even before she had spoken had delivered the anticipated answer. Normally Maddie would have created a bit of a fuss, but with Rowan's imminent arrival her main priority, she was too excited, too happy to complain.

Resigned to another day by herself, freed from the risk of more spiteful practical jokes, she skipped merrily to the library. Broad beams of sunlight pouring in through the tall, Gothic stained-glass windows invited her in, an almost tangible stream of multi-coloured light leading her to the roaring fire waiting to greet her.

'Now,' she thought to herself, 'I wonder where that book is Aunt Frances mentioned, "*The Meaning of Dreams*".' The library with its vast collection of books suddenly seemed intimidating. The thousands of books she and Rowan had already searched through lined hundreds of shelves, all connected by tall, rolling mahogany ladders which stretched from floor to ceiling. 'Now, what was the name of the author?' Try as she might Maddie could not remember.

Her eyes roamed the shelves; perhaps something might jolt her memory. She was just checking out the section of books labelled psychology, when she thought she heard someone call out her name. Hoping that it might be one of the servants come to tell her that Rowan had arrived a day early, she raced to the door and stepped out into the long corridor outside. There was no one there. The corridor was empty, silent, and deserted. 'How odd,' she thought to herself. 'I could have sworn I heard my name called.'

She turned and went back into the library. It was the sunlight, or rather the lack of it that she noticed first. The windows which had earlier been so spectacularly beautiful now looked dark and gloomy and as Maddie glanced outside, she noticed that it was snowing heavily. Fascinated she walked over to the window seat and sat watching giant snowflakes tumbling from an overcast grey sky. Down and down, they fell to produce a pure, virgin, pristine landscape below. She breathed a long-contented sigh, how she loved the seasons and most of all a white Christmas.

It was then she realised how cold she had become. Her breath had turned to vapour, even with the enormous fire blazing in the hearth. She shivered and moved closer to it for warmth. As she sat waiting for the heat of the flames to penetrate the coldness about her, she spotted a large snowflake circling in the air high above her. The snowflake began to spiral down towards her. 'Maddie, can you see me?' a familiar voice asked. Maddie jumped to her feet. The voice had startled her.

'Open your eyes, Maddie. You must be able to see me.' Not only was the voice one she had heard before but the words, too, seemed familiar. As Maddie stood frozen to the spot, a white moth began to flutter about her. 'The time has come, Maddie, you must begin to see.'

Maddie watched incredulously as the moth landed on top of the General's paw. Despite the closeness of the flames, the moth remained where it was, slowly flapping its wings. It remained on the firedog for several minutes. 'Do you know me?' the voice asked again.

'Clarissa, Clarissa, is it really you?' Maddie replied, scarce able to believe the question she was asking.

'Yes, Maddie, I am come to help you, but I can only stay a little while. The General holds a secret. You must ask him now to reveal it and set you on your path. I will come again when I can.' The voice seemed to fade into the distance as the white moth took off and flew towards the window. Maddie watched astonished as it appeared to fly straight through the glass pane and was lost from sight in the flurry of snowflakes falling outside.

Maddie turned to the General and began to stroke the smooth limestone head. 'Well,' she said, 'you heard her. Clarissa wishes you to reveal your secret. Perhaps if I shake your paw, you'll help me.' Using both her hands she took a firm hold of the lifelike paw and pressed downward. Nothing happened. She tried again, this time with even more effort, still nothing. Without really knowing why, she did the same thing again but, instead of pressing down, she tried to lift the paw up. To her astonishment the paw clicked upwards and immediately a slow rumbling sound seemed to emanate from inside the fireplace. The left-hand side wall of the inglenook began to divide, starting as a mere crack at first but slowly widening into a dark aperture easily big enough for a grown man to pass through.

Maddie wondered why she had never done this to the General's paw before. She could not believe her eyes. The entrance to the legendary secret passages had been right under her nose. 'I should have returned your handshake long ago,' she said to the General patting his limestone head affectionately.

A dark passageway yawned open before her. Tentatively she stretched her head and shoulders forward to look inside. As she expected the tunnel led off in two ways. To her left there was a steep descent of rough-cut steps hewn into the rock face, steps she knew all too well! To her right there was a gentle, flat incline leading upwards which she had not seen before. Even in the dim light she could just make out the openings of narrower tunnels branching off from this main channel to other unknown destinations. It was then she noticed a small metal lever, situated at head height and projecting from the inner wall on her left. 'That must be how you open and close the entrance from inside the tunnel,' she thought to herself.

Maddie looked round sharply to see if the moth had returned, but there was no sign of it. Her heart was racing, her whole-body trembling. She had instantly recognised this place for what it was, the doorway to the pitch-black tunnel of her nightmare! If ever anyone needed a companion, a helpmate, it was Maddie now in this terrifying moment.

She stepped back from the entrance and turned about her once more, her eyes circumnavigating the library, desperately seeking the alabaster wings. It was no use, the room was empty. Maddie was alone. With hands clutched and pressed to her mouth as if to suppress the scream already forming in her throat, she hesitatingly stepped towards the entrance. Peering nervously inside she tried to decide what she should do.

A sudden draught of air blew in her face causing her to blink. She gasped, the scream almost escaped. 'I cannot do this by myself,' she thought to herself sensibly, 'I must wait for Rowan. He'll be here tomorrow, and we can explore the tunnel together. I must get a couple of torches ready. We'll never be able to see anything without any light.'

She turned back to the General and took hold of the proffered paw once more. At first it seemed as if it would not move and then, slowly, it reverted to its original position. There was a low rumble from the fireplace as the once secret door closed and sealed. Maddie was shaking. She sat down in a large high-backed armchair a little way from the fire and wondered if she would ever be happy sitting in the alcove again. Then other thoughts took over.

'So, the rumours about secret passages are true,' she said to herself. 'I wonder if they were used for smuggling. We will need to be careful tomorrow, I don't want to be responsible for Rowan falling through a trap door or anything. We will certainly have to explore during the day, that's for sure! My horrid dream always takes place at night, and I definitely don't want Rowan drowning alongside me. Gosh,' she sighed to herself, 'it will be such a relief to be able to tell someone about the nightmare.'

All day the tunnel nightmare replayed itself inside Maddie's head. She'd been having the same terrifying dream for days now and was confused about what it could mean. It was always the same; standing on the deck of a ship, washed overboard, and sinking into blackness, drowning, drowning and the echoing voices, the screaming whisper; 'Open your eyes!'

Maddie was in her bedroom high up on the third floor of the castle. She sat cross-legged on her window seat, elbows resting on her knees, supporting her chin in her hands, and gazing out into the darkness. It was a wild night with a bitterly cold east wind bullying dark clouds across a constantly changing sky. She wondered if the man in the moon was attempting to send a distress call, as moonlight in brief dazzling flashes, like some astral SOS, caught her attention. Clouds, parted swiftly by the raging gale, exposed a brilliant full moon. Radiant silver beams of light penetrated through the blackness, as if some desperate creature, trapped in that celestial body was trying to signal to her and switching a giant torch on and off in its frantic bid to communicate. Then, just as suddenly the light would vanish completely, as if the clouds, embarrassed by the moon's nakedness, had clothed her again in their thick winter mantle. Maddie could hear the wind echoing down the long corridor outside her room and shuddered involuntarily. Drawing her dressing gown about her to keep out the chill, she looked down, hoping to catch sight of the estuary and the sea beyond. But it was too dark. She sighed and accepting defeat climbed down from the window ledge and made her way back to the fire.

As always, Bella, her aged servant, had lit the fire well before bedtime, but it had done little to warm the room. She pulled a favourite, ornately carved wooden stool closer to the hearth, sat down and began to warm her hands in front of the flames. The half-drunk mug of now lukewarm chocolate remained where she had set it down. Picking it up, she drained the contents, scooped some remaining froth up in her finger and finally licked the sweet residue from her lips. In seconds, the chocolate worked its magic and Maddie's low spirits were inexplicably lifted.

Just then she caught the sound of footsteps in the passageway outside. She knew instantly who it was. The slow, shuffling noise of slippers being dragged along the floor could mean only one thing. Bella was coming to check to see if she was in bed. The doorknob began to rotate as wrinkled, arthritic, and twisted fingers worked at the will of their owner in an attempt to gain a silent entry to the room. A rusty hinge creaked, and old wood groaned noisily as the oak door opened slowly, thwarting the effort.

'Why, child, are you still awake!' The old Black woman spoke in her rasping voice and sounded surprised. Reaching out her hand, she took the now empty mug from Maddie's grasp. Peering inside, she nodded her approval of the missing contents. 'Come, child, it is long past your bedtime. You should be asleep.'

'Oh, Bella, when you go, can you take my doll with you and return her to the toy chest in the nursery? I thought I had put her back there myself, but somehow or other, she was on my pillow again when I came to bed tonight. The strange thing is that it's not the first time this has happened. I'm beginning to think she can move of her own accord!'

'Don't be silly. Dolls can't walk,' Bella snapped, sounding irritated.

'Maddie's heart skipped a beat. Arthur's words about Bella being a shapeshifter raced into her mind making her think about the doll. That too seemed to be able to move from place to place of its own volition. Could Bella have something to do with it? And the fact that the doll was an African doll! Did it have some connection to Bella?'

'Why don't you want the doll with you?' asked the old woman. 'I always thought that children like to have a special toy with them when they sleep.'

'Well, yes, they do normally,' replied Maddie. 'It's just that lately I've been having bad dreams and it occurred to me that my nightmares seem to be about the doll. I'm probably just being silly, but I would prefer it if you took her away and, in any case, I'm too old really to be taking toys to bed with me!'

'You are going crazy, child,' muttered Bella under her breath, but loud enough for Maddie to hear. 'Now into bed before you catch cold.' Maddie did as she was bid and allowed the old woman to tuck the blankets in tightly around her. Heavy eyelids slowly closed as she half watched her Negro maid, mug and doll in hand, retreat from the room and close the door behind her.

Maddie drifted off into a troubled sleep. Strange sounds penetrated her slumber and a now broken-hearted wind wailed even more loudly through the long dark corridors outside her bedchamber. Time and again the wind cried out, like a lost child crying for its mother, and Maddie hearing its despair tossed and turned in her bed, half-asleep, half-awake, but unable to fully open her eyes.

It was much later still when Bella finally went to bed herself. Exhausted from her grieving, she was asleep even before her head touched the pillow. Dreams, wonderful dreams of her homeland long ago filled the hours of darkness. She was back in her village, running barefoot in the sunshine, laughing, and playing happily with her friends and without a care in the world.

Chapter Thirty-Three
The Labyrinth

Maddie could not settle. Uncle Thomas and Rowan were due to arrive at any minute. She paced like a caged tiger up and down the great hall waiting to hear the sound of their car arriving. 'Maddie, go and get a book to read, for goodness' sake, before you wear the carpet out,' advised her father.

By the time she got back from the library Rowan was warming his hands in front of the fire, gazing up admiringly at the Christmas tree. 'Hooray, you're here,' shouted Maddie. 'Can Rowan come with me please, Uncle Thomas? I've got so much I need to show him.'

'Yes, of course,' replied Uncle Thomas. 'He can do his unpacking later.' Maddie grabbed Rowan's hand and dragged him away to the library. The others had gone out shopping for the day and Maddie was jealous of the privacy she needed for her to show Rowan all the discoveries she had made about the castle, not least the secret passageway.

As they neared the library fireplace Rowan noticed Maddie's black doll lying on the hearth rug. 'Where did you find Clarissa's doll?' he asked picking it up and looking at it closely.

'What do you mean, Clarissa's doll?' replied Maddie sounding rather offended. 'I'll have you know that doll belonged to my mother, not Clarissa.'

'Forgive me, Maddie, but I'd know that doll anywhere. Clarissa was gobsmacked when Bella gave it to her for her thirteenth birthday. Bella had never given her anything before. Clarissa always thought that Bella didn't like her, which made the gift more surprising still.' The colour drained from Maddie's face. She felt weak at the knees and sank down onto the carpet. Rowan disturbed by her sudden pallor, sat down beside her. 'Whatever is it, Maddie? You look as if you've seen a ghost. Has something I've said come as a shock?'

She turned to look at him with a face as white as a sheet. 'I should have told you about this doll before. I found it in an attic room, last summer, in an old trunk which had once belonged to my mother. That's why I assumed it was hers. Are you absolutely sure this is the same doll Bella gave to Clarissa?'

'I'd stake my life on it,' he replied soberly. 'It would be hard to mistake it Maddie, don't you think? The doll is rather unique.'

'In which case, Rowan, why did Bella deny all knowledge of it when I asked her if she had ever seen it before? This is all very mysterious, not to say worrying. I don't quite know what to think.'

Maddie began to pour her heart out. She told him about her dreams of Africa and most especially about her nightmare. She led him to the General's paw explaining how she had seen the white moth land on it and heard Clarissa's voice directing her, telling her what she needed to do to discover the secret passage.

It was Rowan who triggered the paw's mechanism. The doors slid open, making a low rumbling noise and as they did so a blast of freezing air shot from the tunnel, making them both blink. Shivering, trembling, they stood side by side peering into the darkness, hearts pounding, minds racing. Well aware of the enormity of the task which now lay before them each grasped the other's hand. A single thought filled both their minds, 'What would they find in the pitch-black tunnels waiting for them below?'

'Take one of these,' Maddie said, lifting two torches off the alcove seat. 'I left these here this morning ready for us to explore. Although it's early afternoon it'll still be pitch black in there.' Using the metal lever, she had spied when she first discovered the tunnel, she closed the door behind them. 'Follow me and hold onto this,' she instructed as she led the way and directed Rowan's hand to the guide rope. Shining their torches ahead they slowly descended the steep steps until finally they reached the dark, frightening, gloomy chamber Maddie had entered so many times in her nightmare. 'This is it, Rowan. This is where the dream and supposedly my life will end!'

Rowan recognised it immediately for what it was. 'This is a voodoo chamber,' he said aloud. 'I think we can safely guess it belongs to Bella. This must be where she carries out her witchcraft.' Shining his torch around, he could pick out all kinds of evidence to support his theory. Carved out of the rock face on every wall were small vertical niches, in which stood doll-like figures made out of wax. In the centre of the blood-stained floor a rough circle of stones had been laid containing a residue of ash and burnt embers showing that it had been used to make a fire. A large silver bowl rested on a flat boulder right next to it. Feathers and chicken claws littered the ground everywhere he looked.

Now it was Maddie's turn to shine her torch around the room. She quickly spotted a hammer and chisel lying on top of a pile of rock debris. Had Bella made a new niche recently? They examined the niches together, pulling out a small wax doll from each one. But there were other items waiting to be found. Maddie pulled out a photo of her mother from one hole, Rowan found a small miniature of his own mother in another. There were tufts of human hair too and looking closely at the dolls they could see numerous strands of varying colour embedded in the wax. 'Look at this one, Rowan, the hair's bright ginger.'

'Tristan,' he replied immediately. 'I wonder if Bella's been responsible for all the accidents our cousins have experienced just lately?' Before Maddie had time to reply, there came a slow rumbling sound from high above them. 'I think a doors just opened somewhere up the passageway,' whispered Rowan in a voice full of fear. 'Best get over to that far corner now and switch out our torches straight away!' he warned. They waited anxiously, listening to the sound of their own hearts pounding in their chests whilst at the same time trying to inhale air into lungs that didn't want to work. Maddie had to cover her mouth with her hand to stop her teeth from chattering.

In the pitch blackness they could now see the reflection of a dim flickering light. The light edged slowly closer until Bella's large shape entered the chamber. She carried one small candle with her. Unseen, hiding in the darkness they watched her approach a niche in the wall. She reached inside. The children could not decide whether she had put something in or taken something out. Then, Bella began to chant, rocking back and forth in front of her hidey hole. She spoke in a language they could not understand. Maddie did however recognise one word, the name Adana was spoken several times. Then, quite unexpectedly, Bella began to speak in English. 'I will make you very soon, little Idema, my precious, beautiful Idema. You must do your work again.'

Maddie strained her eyes to see what it was Bella was holding. It looked like her black wooden doll, but in the darkness, she could not be entirely sure. Bella turned slowly and much to Rowan's and Maddie's relief left the chamber. They waited to hear the rumbling noise again before daring to move or speak. Silence and pitch blackness thankfully returned. 'I think the coast is clear,' said Rowan, sounding breathless.

'I was terrified she was going to see us,' replied Maddie. Switching their torches back on they moved to investigate the niche Bella had visited. It was Maddie who felt inside. 'Oh, my God,' she exclaimed as she dangled the locket Aunt Frances had given her in the light of Rowan's lamp. 'Well,' she announced with indignation, 'I'm taking this back with me.'

'No, Maddie, that would never do. Bella will know someone is on to her if you do that. The locket will have to stay put, I'm afraid.' Reluctantly, Maddie could see that he was right.

Feeling inside a second time, she withdrew a wax mould of her African doll, stuffed full of long black strands of hair. 'Bella's taken this hair from the brush on my dresser,' she thought to herself. 'Look Rowan,' she said in a trembling voice, 'it's an exact copy of my doll and she called it Idema. That's her name, Idema.'

'It's a voodoo doll, Maddie. I've heard about these things before. So that's how Bella's been able to carry out her curse on the family. Now we know what we're up against at least. Come on,' he cautioned, 'best get out of here in case Bella decides to come back.' Watching for any sign of light ahead of them they gingerly made their way out of the grisly chamber and back up the tunnel. With so many steps to climb, they were breathless long before they reached the relative safety of the library. Immediately the General's paw was used to close the doorway behind them once more.

The library no longer felt like a safe haven and so they made their way to the drawing room to discuss a plan of action. The dinner gong sounded before every detail had been finalised. Well satisfied with the tough decisions made, they walked together to the dining room feeling more confident than ever before. Rowan in particular was sure they had considered every eventuality. 'If we fail now, Maddie, it won't be because of lack of thought on our part. I know we haven't missed anything! One thing's for sure, we have certainly prepared for the worst and have every reason to hope for the best,' he concluded, quoting his schoolhouse motto, courtesy of the late Disraeli.

Chapter Thirty-Four
Christmas Eve

Like Clarissa before her Maddie was summoned to the library after lunch on Christmas Eve. Her father was alone, Aunt Kate, Mary and Frances having just left him. 'Sit down, please. Maddie.' He spoke in a trembling voice. 'I have grave matters I need to discuss with you.'

'Father, I know what you are about to say to me. There really is no need to put yourself through this.' Maddie said in a firm but tender tone of voice. Her father looked shocked, miserable, and infinitely sad. 'Really father, I've known about the history of the castle, the strange deaths of the Montague wives and daughters for some time. There is nothing you can say or do which can change what will happen tonight. I am thirteen, it is December 24, and I will meet my fate.' Her father, too overcome with emotion, was unable to speak. Tears flowed like a river down his cheeks.

'Father, father,' Maddie cried out, rushing to his side, and embracing him, 'do not despair. Remember what my mother told you the day I was born. I am the chosen one. It is my destiny to deliver this family from its cruel curse.'

'Maddie, you cannot know what it is you face, the extent of the evil, the danger. We must try to protect you,' he quavered, remembering the terrible dream he had had the day before the planned exorcism. 'I am so fearful for you, my darling girl, my precious, beautiful daughter, so terrified of losing you! I could not bear it. I would not want to live without you.'

'You won't have to, father, believe me. Trust me. My mother and Clarissa were helpless and alone. They had no choice, don't you see? I have every hope and, furthermore, they will be with me.'

'I don't understand, Maddie. What do you mean they will be with you?'

'Mother and Clarissa, of course,' she replied. 'They've never left me father. They've been with me all my life. Often over the years when you have been upset or worrying about something, have you not noticed that I always know what to say to you to give you comfort or to help you? My mother comes to me, she talks to me, she loves you so much still, father. She tells me how to help you, what to say.'

Maddie smiled at him. 'It's her you've really been listening to, not me.' Lost for words and drowning in emotion, her father continued to listen in silence. 'Clarissa warned me what was to happen. She knew she was going to die. Since her death she has been helping me to understand what it is I have to do. She and mother and I believe the spirits of other ancestors will be with me tonight. I'm not afraid father, whatever it is that I must do, I shall do. Have faith.' Cupping her hands around his face, she gazed lovingly into his eyes. 'Have faith father, I need you to believe that this is possible.'

Sometime later Maddie left the library. It had been decided Aunt Kate and Mary were to sit with her through the night. She would not be left alone for a single minute and this time it would be her family who would undertake the night vigil.

Rowan went to bed at precisely 9.30 pm. He stuck to the plan religiously. He would leave pillows in his own bed to look as if he were lying there fast asleep. By 9.45 pm he would be in the back of Maddie's wardrobe as arranged and would hide there until he was sure it was safe to come out. Although Rowan had only been in the wardrobe for a quarter of an hour, already he was regretting his decision to use it as a hiding place. It was such a small, cramped space that his legs were aching and his back too, pushed up against the stone wall, felt sore.

At ten o'clock, accompanied by her Aunt Kate and Aunt Mary, Maddie had entered her bedroom. She was just getting into bed, when Bella knocked on the door and delivered the three anticipated mugs of cocoa. Maddie and Rowan had agreed that nothing would be said to her aunts about the fact that they suspected the drinks might be drugged. Maddie took her mug into the en suite bathroom and surreptitiously emptied it away. Her aunts made themselves comfortable in armchairs close to the bed, whilst commenting on how thoughtful Bella was to bring them a hot beverage. Empty mugs were presently laid to one side. Maddie climbed into bed.

'Get a good night's sleep now, dear. We'll be here to watch over you. No need to worry about a thing,' said Aunt Kate, trying to sound convincing. As arranged, Maddie closed her eyes and pretended to go to sleep.

A little while later, Rowan could hear snoring. Both aunts were fast asleep. It irritated him slightly that they had stuck to their vigil for hardly any time at all, even though both he and Maddie had guessed that Bella's cocoa was drugged. Just at that moment the wall behind him began to move. There was a soft rumbling sound as the back of the wardrobe started to open. The right-hand side was sliding across to the left and almost trapped his jacket as the two giant stone slabs crossed one behind the other.

Seconds later, pushing the clothes to her left, and inadvertently hiding Rowan even more, Bella stepped from inside. She walked calmly towards the chairs in which Aunt Kate and Mary were sleeping. From his vantage point Rowan could not see what she was doing. He heard the clink of china however as she gathered up the now empty mugs. It was then that she spoke in a hushed, but evil sounding whisper. 'Now, my little Idema, you must do your work. Bring your dreams, my precious one. Do not fail me, Idema. Remember your true mistress and avenge her.' She kissed the doll gently and then placed it carefully, silently onto Maddie's pillow.

To Rowan's relief, Bella returned to the wardrobe. Carefully closing the door behind her, she vanished back down into the dark passageway. No sooner had she gone than the doorway closed once more, the right-hand stone slab sliding groaningly across the floor and back into its original position. Rowan waited for a few minutes before struggling to his feet. Both legs had gone numb. He climbed out of the wardrobe and tip-toed over to his cousin.

'She's gone Maddie, you can stop pretending to be asleep now.' Maddie did not respond. She was fast asleep and much to Rowan's consternation very obviously dreaming. Her eyes although closed were clearly darting around under their eyelids. Rowan sat at her side, listening carefully to her breathing. It was rapid and shallow, but not the sound of someone drowning. He knew what he must do and so he waited, biding his time, until, if and when the moment came, Maddie would have to be woken.

Just before midnight, Rowan had to leave his vigil to go to the en suite bathroom. Minutes later he returned to find Maddie writhing in her bed, struggling to breathe. He grabbed her shoulders and began to shake her, noticing at once that her nightdress was soaking wet! But try as he might he could not wake her. In desperation he slapped her face hard and to his relief, Maddie woke up choking. 'Thank God, thank God, I've been able to wake you,' he said, helping to support her, his arms around her shoulders, whilst Maddie retched and vomited at the side of the bed.

The minutes passed, the clock ticked on, and the room became incredibly cold. Maddie was sitting up now by the fire, a blanket wrapped about her shoulders. Rowan had fetched a dry nightgown for Maddie to change into. It had not been touched and still lay on the floor at her feet. He could sense something was very wrong and so waited patiently for her to speak. He began to fear for her again. Why had she remained so silent? And why did her eyes have such a distant, vacant look about them? 'Maddie, speak to me, please. What has happened?' Maddie did not answer.

As they sat staring at the fire, the flames began to turn blue. The air felt icy cold. It was then that Rowan spotted the white moth hovering right inside the blaze as if impervious to its heat.

'Return to your dream Maddie. It is not over yet. You must return to your dream. I will be waiting for you. When you hear my voice again open your eyes.'

Maddie got up from the chair in which she was sitting and returned to her bed. She did not speak to Rowan and moved as if she were in a trance. She lay down slowly and closed her eyes again. Rowan did not attempt to stop her. He had recognised his sister's voice and her instruction had been quite explicit. Maddie had to return to her dream. Rowan began his vigil again.

Maddie could feel she was lying on an ice-cold stone floor. Her whole body was shivering. She could not decide whether this was due to the freezing temperature or her own fear. She lay there for a moment, eyes tightly shut, wanting to keep the spirits which she knew surrounded her at bay. Soft whispers floated in the air about her, calling to her, calling her name over and over again. Then, with immense effort, she separated her eyelids.

White, everything was white, a perfect, brilliant, dazzling, blinding white that seemed to shine from the air itself. She squinted, her eyes yet to adjust to the stark whiteness all about her. Slowly they adapted to the intense light and began to take in her surroundings. It was faultless in its serene simplicity, a featureless room without walls, doors, or windows. The floor no longer rough granite but as smooth as marble seemed to stretch on for infinity. Maddie thought it looked like heaven should; but covered in the first ever winter's snowfall.

'Am I dead?' she heard herself asking. 'Is this heaven?'

'Maddie, you must open your eyes. You must see us.' The voices echoed around her once more. She stood up and looking about her hoped upon hope that she would at least see a tiny moth, a glimpse of fragile wings, her friend returned to comfort her.

'We are all here, Maddie,' said a voice.
'Yes, Maddie, all here,' said another.
'Open your eyes. Look around you,' repeated a third voice she almost recognised.

It was strange. The voices seemed to come from all directions; but at the same time from nowhere at all. They filled the air around her but were so faint as to be barely audible, even less than a whisper. A whisper, teetering on the most remote edge of hearing, threatening to descend into silence; but clinging on desperately, dying to be heard for fear that silence would replace and erase all memory of its existence.

'What do you see?'

Maddie turned her head left and then right. Everything was the same: white. It was as if she had been encased in the centre of a massive, giant pearl which had been hollowed out to create a tranquil heaven. She stood for several minutes listening to the quiet whispers and then miraculously shapes began to form in the air around her. Eyes that had been blind began to see. Mirage-like in their shimmering whiteness, she wondered at first if they were angels. Slowly they evolved out of the mist, fluid bodies, the bodies of young women and little girls and right in the midst of them stood Clarissa. 'Thank God,' said Maddie, 'I thought you had deserted me.'

'Never,' replied Clarissa, 'we none of us will ever desert you.'

'No, Maddie, we will never abandon you,' the host replied in one voice.

Maddie could see them clearly now. She felt as if she might have been back at the museum looking at an exhibition of costumes through the ages, for although their clothing appeared all white, the marked difference in dress design and fashion set many of the young women decades apart. As she stared at their ghost-like faces her heart went out to them. They had all been taken in the bloom of youth, their lives torn from them. Saddest of all were the teenage girls, just like her on the verge of womanhood, deprived of their futures, careers, hopes, ambitions, marriage, love, and children of their own. Suddenly she realised she knew who each one was. She remembered the lichen-covered gravestones and the names indelibly printed in her mind. 'These are all my dear ancestors,' she said looking at Clarissa.

'They are, Maddie,' Clarissa replied, 'and they are come to help you.'

'Clarissa,' said one of the young women standing closest to Maddie, 'you must begin soon. The dark one knows Maddie is here. She seeks her even now.'

Clarissa nodded and turned to speak to Maddie. 'There is an evil spirit which lives within the castle, part ghost, part human. It is black of heart, filled with hatred and anger. It seeks revenge on our family Maddie. We, you, and I must defeat it.'

'You will need all your courage, Maddie,' said the woman, taking hold of her hand.

'All your courage, Maddie,' repeated Clarissa, taking hold of the other.

'I am your mother, Maddie, and I will do all I can to protect you.'

Maddie looked into the woman's face, smiled, and then lifted the soft white hand to her lips, kissing it gently. 'I am not afraid, mother,' she replied. 'Just tell me what it is I must do?'

'You must go back into your nightmare, but you must not go towards the darkness, you must follow the light. We will lead you. The Black child will call to you, will try to trick you. You must not heed her words. Clarissa is your guide, stay with her, stay with her light. Only follow the light, Maddie, only the light.' Her mother pulled her to her and holding her face in her hands, she looked into Maddie's eyes, an anxious expression on her face. 'There is one more thing, Maddie, one thing which is vital if we are to end this curse. The doll is the key. The dark spirit lives in her. Destroy it, Maddie. Destroy the doll at all costs. As soon as you return from your dream, destroy the doll immediately. Do you understand, Maddie?'

'Yes, mother, I understand. I promise I will destroy the doll.'

Without warning, suddenly Maddie found herself back in darkness. She could feel the rough stone floor under her bare feet and instinctively reached out to place a nervous hand on the coarse rope to her right. Slowly, fearfully she began her descent. The pitch blackness of the tunnel surrounded her. She felt herself pulled downwards by its silent inhalations; firm pulls that once again gripped her insides and led her deep into the bowels of the castle. A voice was calling to her.

'Save Adana! You must save Adana!'

Strange ghostlike shapes seemed to emerge out of the rock face and circle about her, floating in the heavy air. A face loomed in front of her, the mouth moving slowly, calling to her, begging her for help.

'Help me, Maddie, help me. The ship is sinking.'

Even in the lightless tunnel she could make out every feature of the face. It was Idema, the beautiful doll she had found on her birthday, the doll she now knew was a mirror image of Adana, black of skin and with huge sad eyes brimming with tears.

'Maddie, please don't let me die. Please save me.'

Maddie tried not to listen. 'I must follow the light, only the light,' she kept repeating in her head. Now she could hear Clarissa's voice calling up to her telling her to come to the light.

'You cannot save Adana by going back to the sinking ship, Maddie. She is already dead. We must go further back. Follow the light, Maddie. Do not be afraid.'

The familiar face rose up at her again from the abyss below. How could such a beautiful face be plotting her death?

'Help the child,' a voice cried. *'Go to her.'*

As she counted two hundred and thirty, the small speck of light at the bottom of the tunnel appeared once more. As always, the miniscule prick of light grew steadily as Maddie climbed down towards it. Soon it was the size of postage stamp, then a book, until it was easily large enough for Maddie's slight frame to fit through. This time she would step into it, she would trust in her mother and

Clarissa. Adana's face rose out of the blackness once more, crying out to her. Maddie ignored it and quickly stepped out of the tunnel and into the light.

'No, you will not,' screamed an angry voice from above her.

Maddie, blinded by the bright light, struggled to open her eyes. She felt as if she was suspended in thin air as if there was no ground beneath her feet. Then she began to fall, spinning, spiralling out of control. And suddenly she heard Clarissa's voice. 'Give me your hand!' Maddie stretched out her arms and felt the firm grip of two hands taking hold of hers.

'Do not let go. Do not be afraid. She cannot stop us.' Maddie knew she was listening to the voice of her mother. Without warning a dark shape emerged out of nowhere ahead of them. Maddie felt as if she were flying through a long passageway that was now about to be sealed off. She gripped the hands tightly as Bella's large Negro frame stepped in front of her, blocking her way. Maddie screamed as her body passed straight through her, as if Bella had been nothing but a mirage.

Three times the same vision loomed in front of her, each time more frightening, more threatening. She could see how Bella's face was increasingly contorted with rage and hatred, ever more and more evil as her physical shape swelled larger and larger. Maddie was petrified. She could feel herself being pulled by its energy, pulled away from Clarissa and her mother. Invisible fingers seemed to tear at her own, trying to rip them away from the hands leading her into the light.

And then just as she felt she could hang on no longer that all her resistance to the spectre's terrible power had deserted her, it was over, and Maddie found herself on her knees in long, wet grass, with Clarissa by her side.

Chapter Thirty-Five
Idema

It was raining heavily. Maddie's nightdress was soddened and clinging to her. Looking up she could just make out a filthy, ominous sky, moonless, starless but thick with thunder clouds. It was difficult in the darkness to see much else. In the distance and around a large African village, dotted with round circular huts, several small bonfires were burning. Theirs was the only light in an otherwise pitch-black canvas. 'Come we must find the doll quickly,' said Clarissa, helping Maddie to her feet.

'What's happened? Where are we?' asked Maddie in total confusion.

'We are back in Adana's village,' Clarissa replied. 'We are here to stop her being taken by the slavers. The doll is the key. If we can find her and stop Adana leaving the safety of the palace, all will be well.' Maddie looked even more confused.

'I'll explain while we look,' continued Clarissa. 'Bella gave Adana the same doll she gave us. But it's a voodoo doll, Maddie. It has special powers connected to the spirit world. Adana dropped the doll out here somewhere and when she came back looking for it, that's when she was kidnapped. If we can prevent that happening, we may be able to change the past.'

'I don't understand,' Maddie repeated as she scrabbled about in the long grass desperately seeking the doll.

'When Adana died, Bella, Nabila as she was then, put a hex on the doll, a curse to blight our family. Our ancestors have suffered for it ever since. Don't you see, if we can stop Adana dying, from being taken into slavery in the first place, we can change the past, none of this will have happened?'

'I see,' replied Maddie, 'but how do you know the doll is here?'

'Bella's dreams; she often dreams about Adana. She truly loved her, I believe. Maddie, you ought to know that I actually feel sorry for Bella. She was

241

a good woman once, a proud warrior. What happened to Adana broke her heart. That and her own suffering changed her. Ironic really, but just like the slavers themselves became hardened to what they were doing, so the same has occurred with Nabila. She has carried out this curse for so long she has become immune to the misery it causes. Hatred and revenge are all she knows.'

At that moment, a huge flash of forked lightning ripped the night sky apart. Bright electric tongues licked the ground just yards from where they were standing. Seconds later the sound of thunder rumbled loudly, ominously about them. The storm was directly overhead. Maddie had always hated being outdoors in a thunderstorm. As the thunder subsided, she could hear her teeth chattering noisily and her hands, desperately searching through the long grass, were trembling out of control. 'Are you sure the doll is here, Clarissa?' she asked in a voice full of fear.

'Yes, positive. Whilst they were locked in that terrible slave prison, Adana explained why she had left the royal palace that night, this night! She'd dropped Idema out here waiting for Nabila's army to return. I've seen this place before in Bella's dreams.'

'Here!' Maddie cried out joyfully as she picked the wooden doll up out of the mud. 'Here it is!'

'Right, now we need to get inside the palace somehow without being seen and put this back in Adana's room before she wakes up. Follow me,' said Clarissa sounding very determined.

The two girls began to make their way towards the village. There was just enough light from a dwindling fire which had been built inside one of the gateways to guide their way to an entrance. Cautiously, they edged closer and closer, anxious that a soldier on guard duty might raise the alarm if he caught sight of them approaching. They need not have worried. The two guards who should have been on the alert were oblivious to anything and everything. They lay fast asleep on the wet ground, empty beer mugs in hand and with raindrops falling into wide open mouths, snoring loudly. Maddie and Clarissa quietly crept past them.

'Quick,' said Clarissa, 'we need to put the doll back in Adana's room if possible and that won't be easy if people start to wake up. That's the palace over there,' she said, pointing out some larger huts set on a wooden platform some distance away. 'At all costs we must keep Adana away from this gate and out of any danger.' They both began to run along a wide track which led towards the main cluster of buildings. Small fires battling against extinction in the heavy rain glowed in the darkness, helping to light their way, making the path easy to follow. 'Stop!' Clarissa shouted suddenly. 'Is that her?'

Eyes straining through the rain and darkness, Maddie could just make out the figure of a child coming out of one of the doors of a long line of circular huts which made up the royal residence. The child began to head towards them. 'Yes, I think you might be right,' replied Maddie. She put the doll down on the ground, precisely in the middle of the path. 'Hurry,' she instructed, 'we need to hide!' A pile of empty beer barrels just to their left provided the ideal cover. They hid behind and waited for Adana to arrive.

Maddie wondered if Adana would actually see Idema, even though they had left her squarely in the middle of the path. She looked back. Had they achieved their purpose and left the doll as far from the gate as possible? The closer Adana came to that gate, the more she would be in danger. Maddie need not have worried. As if the gods were with them a sudden flash of lightning lit up the whole area about them and immediately Adana spotted her prize. They heard her cry out with glee and watched her race to retrieve her precious doll. Clutching it to her breast amidst a rumble of thunder, she turned quickly on her heels and like a scalded cat began to sprint back the way she had come, Maddie smiled to herself, suspecting that like her, Adana too was terrified of thunder and lightning.

There was such a sense of relief as they watched Adana return to the long line of huts. Although it was the middle of the night with thick, pitch-black cloud still blotting out all sight of the moon and stars, thanks to the flickering light of several bonfires burning directly outside the palace they could just make out the little princess's tiny frame. As she passed through a doorway and back into the safety of her own quarters, they instinctively gripped each other's hand in triumph. Adana disappeared inside, out of sight and now, out of danger. The two cousins looked at each other and smiled.

Their smile however, quickly faded. From somewhere in the darkness about them an urgent voice spoke out. It was the voice of Maddie's mother, making a desperate plea. 'She knows; the dark spirit knows what you are about! She has found you. Even now she approaches. Maddie, she is right on your back! Get out as quickly as you can. Get out NOW!'

'Do not worry, Aunt Abigail, it is done,' replied Clarissa. 'We can do no more. Time to—' Before she could finish the sentence, a mighty scream rang through the cold night air. So awful was the sound that Maddie felt the blood freeze in her veins.

Emerging from a door a little way off from where Adana had re-entered the palace, there now came a huge Amazonian warrior shrieking like a banshee. Maddie could not believe the speed at which the woman could run. She hurtled towards them, eating up the ground with every stride.

'Maddie, you must wake up now!' urged Clarissa, 'She means to kill us. Maddie, do you hear me? You must wake up! Wake up!' There was another flash of lightning. The world lit up around them and Maddie could see the woman's ugly face, contorted with hate, her wild eyes full of rage and her mouth agape. She was a terrifying spectacle. Maddie was so horrified she found herself unable to think, to act. It was as if she was frozen in time.

The woman was now just yards from them. Maddie could see her raised hands and the sharp daggers they held. She felt her body shudder as she listened to the blood curdling war-cry as the fearsome warrior prepared to aim her weapons at her foe. Maddie watched unable to move, somehow paralysed as the daggers were thrown simultaneously.

There was a sound like silk tearing as Taker of Life passed through Maddie's nightdress. Missing her torso by less than an inch it made a small hole in the cloth just below her right armpit. As she heard the knife hit the wet ground behind her with a dull thud, she turned to look at Clarissa. To her horror she saw Giver of Night hit its target. The knife seemed to pass straight through Clarissa's head. Clarissa fell to her knees, clutching her left eye. 'No! No! Clarissa. No!' Maddie cried out.

'She cannot hurt me, Maddie! I am dead already. Go. Go back! You must wake up!' Clarissa screamed in desperation. Nabila was upon Maddie, hands outstretched, like two giant claws, fingers wide open as if now intent on strangling her enemy.

Maddie was being shaken violently. Firm hands had her by the shoulders. 'Wake up! For God's sake, Maddie, wake up! Wake up! YOU MUST WAKE UP!' Maddie was instantly awake. Eyes now wide open focused on a distraught Rowan. 'Thank God!' he exclaimed. 'Is it done?'

'Not yet,' Maddie replied, her voice thick with fear and grief. Catching sight of the doll, she leapt out of bed and, clutching it in her hand raced to the fire. As she threw Idema onto the glowing embers, so the secret passageway at the back of her wardrobe began to open. Terrible screams rose up from the tunnel, the awful sound becoming louder and louder. Bella was coming!

An ice-cold blast of air streamed out from the dark opening in the wall. The icy jet swirled about the children's slender frames, blowing back their hair and causing ripples to form on their cheeks. Maddie's nightdress slapped against her frozen skin as she squeezed her eyes tight shut, trying to delay the approaching menace. 'Any moment now, and it will all be over. Bella is coming to kill me!' Blind panic began to take over and she rushed to Rowan's side for protection.

He was still kneeling by her bed as if injured, clutching his left eye. Maddie put her arms about him, and the two children huddled together, petrified by what they feared would happen next.

It was not Bella but Nabila who burst in through the now open secret door. Her huge muscular body glistening with sweat filled the entrance. For a moment she stood eyeing them, her chest heaving as if breathless from her efforts. Her face was contorted into an evil, triumphant grin. She growled deep in her throat and stepped towards them.

At that moment, the embers suddenly caught fire and Idema burst into flames. Nabila stopped dead in her tracks. The children watched in terror as the woman began to age in front of their eyes. It became Bella, old, crippled Bella and like the doll, she too was on fire. She stood in a blazing inferno and then, without warning, the flames vanished as quickly as they had come. Bella had turned to ash. All that remained was a pile of dust on the floor at the exact spot where she had been standing.

The children clung to each other as the tunnel took one final breath. It drew an even greater inhalation as if wanting to remove all the air from Maddie's room. They felt their hair and clothes pulled towards the doorway, but it was Bella's ashes that were sucked from the floor. Rising in a whirling spiral and disappearing into the tunnel as the door to the secret passage snapped shut.

For some minutes Rowan and Maddie remained sitting on the floor as they recovered from the terrible ordeal of the night. Slowly they began to regain their composure and looking about the room, Maddie noticed her Aunt Kate and Mary were still fast asleep in their chairs. Aunt Kate continued to snore loudly. Both aunts were completely oblivious to the terrifying events which had taken place. 'I feel exhausted Rowan,' Maddie croaked in an unusually husky voice, thick with emotion.

'Me too,' replied Rowan, his voice sounding strangely hushed, almost breathless.

'Are you alright?' Maddie asked, concerned that Bella had somehow injured him.

'Yes, just tired, I guess,' he replied wearily.

'Look,' Maddie continued, pointing to the fireplace. 'Look, Rowan, nothing remains of the doll, thank goodness just a few dying embers. They slid across the floor on their hands and knees to be closer to the fire, drawing comfort from its warmth. Maddie added fresh logs and instantly bright flames were rekindled, lighting the room with a soft, red, flickering glow.'

'It is over. We've done it,' Maddie said in a whisper, as if speaking too loudly might awaken the nightmare once more. She could see Rowan looked visibly relieved although his face remained pale and drawn. She wrapped her arms around him and kissed him on his forehead. 'I couldn't have done this without you, you know. Thank you, Rowan. Thank you for saving me.'

'My brave Maddie,' he replied, 'I would rather have died than fail you. I'm just so glad that we are both still alive. The danger, the curse, is over, ended, I believe. There is no need for us to worry anymore. All we require now is to get some sleep ourselves. Best leave our aunts where they are, I think,' he said in a hushed voice, nodding at the two sleeping matrons. He struggled to his feet and bent to kiss her once more before quietly leaving the room.

Chapter Thirty-Six
A Bright and Beautiful Dawn

Maddie awoke with a jump. Startled eyes opened in an instant expecting to see Rowan's anxious face at her bedside. Instead, she found herself looking into familiar brown eyes, recognising immediately that they were identical to her own. A small, round face with freckled cheeks and nose and topped with a mass of thick dark curls, grinned down broadly at her. Maddie felt she could have been looking in a mirror when she was aged four!

'Hooray, you're awake at last,' announced a smiling mouth. 'Come on Maddie, don't you remember what day it is?' Not waiting for a reply, the clearly happy and excited voice exclaimed, 'Why, it's Christmas Day and I've had the most amazing presents in my stocking! Look at this,' the little dark-haired girl continued, pulling a large, red-handled torch from her skirt pocket, and flashing the light on and off directly in front of Maddie's eyes.

Before Maddie had the time or presence of mind to complain, the bedroom door opened noisily and a tall, slim, elegant lady entered the room in haste, she was carrying a large glass of milk in one hand and an enormous red apple in the other. Even squinting, blinking in the harsh, bright light Maddie immediately recognised the woman from the white room of last night, the woman who had told her that she was her mother, her very own mother. Recognition quickly turned to admiration as she observed the wonderful head of silky black hair, the striking eyes with their long lashes and the radiant white smile she already knew and loved so well.

'Molly,' said the woman in a tone of voice clearly denoting her displeasure, 'did I or did I not tell you to leave your big sister alone? You were distinctly told not to wake her up.' The happy expression on the little girl's face changed to one of dismay and a pair of eyes the colour of coffee dropped sheepishly to the floor. There was no reply.

'Well,' continued the woman approaching the bed, 'I'm waiting for an apology. I don't like being disobeyed on any day of the year but especially not on Christmas morning.'

'Sorry, mother,' a now contrite and flushed face replied, 'but Sam's in the yard waiting for Maddie. He asked me to see how long it would be before she's ready to go for her ride.'

The woman sat down on the bed and reaching out her hand gently brushed a lock of hair from Maddie's face. 'Well, my darling, shall we put your sister out of her misery and see if we can get you ready in less than ten minutes. Here's breakfast,' she added, handing Maddie the milk and the apple. 'I'll have hot bacon butties ready for when you get back. Molly, go back to Sam and tell him she'll be down in five minutes.' A delighted Molly skipped out of the room, anxious to deliver her message and satisfied that her mission had been accomplished.

Maddie was speechless. The word "sister" had invaded her consciousness like water gushing through a burst dam. Her mind was racing, trying to make sense of what was happening here in her own bedroom and after such a night. And, what a night it had been, fraught with danger and full of daring. She could scarce believe how bravely she had acted, overcoming fears that had tested her courage and determination to the limit. The question remained unanswered, and instead she heard herself asking, 'Have you seen Rowan yet this morning?'

Her mother was quick to respond. 'Oh yes. He and Clarissa were up bright and early. You know how much they look forward to their Christmas morning ride. Sam has had Eclipse saddled up ready for you this past half hour. I should think he's fed up, of walking Rowan and Clarissa round and round the yard whilst they wait.' Two more words pierced Maddie's brain, "Clarissa" and "Eclipse!" Could it really be true, that Clarissa was alive, and that Eclipse was her horse, her very own horse and that she was actually allowed to ride by herself? As Maddie tried to take a bite of her apple her eyes filled with tears.

'Oh, darling, whatever is it? I just want you to eat something before you go. It is very cold outside, and the ground is covered in snow,' said her mother with concern.

'Nothing, nothing's the matter,' replied Maddie in a voice thick with emotion. 'Just that I don't really need any presents this year. I have everything I could ever want right here with me now.' Maddie put her arms around her mother and pulled her close. In that moment she knew that everything would be wonderful. The curse had been lifted. A great wrong had been undone and that from now on, everyone's life would be as it should be. 'A white Christmas, how fitting, how perfect,' she said finally biting into her apple, 'time I was up I think and enjoying it with my cousins.'

She raced down the main staircase, admiring the giant Christmas tree in the great hall. It was as if she was seeing it for the first time. It had been beautifully decorated. 'Better work than mine,' she thought happily to herself. Her father was standing by it, showing its brightly coloured baubles to the twin babes in his arms. She made a quick detour to kiss him and them.

'Isn't life grand, Maddie, is not God wonderful? What a Christmas present your mother has given me,' he said holding her baby brother and sister for her to see. Maddie's heart felt as if it were about to burst. She had never known such happiness.

The last morsel of her "eat on the run" breakfast was being chewed as Maddie entered the stable yard. Eclipse was tethered to a nearby rail, ready and waiting. 'Happy Christmas, Clarissa! Happy Christmas Rowan! And a happy Christmas to you too, Sam,' she shouted cheerfully as she mounted up. She noticed that Sam was holding the reins of the two horses her cousins were riding. He had walked them to the far end of the yard but on hearing her call, slowly turned the horses around and began to head back towards her. As Maddie watched their approach, she was surprised to see how small Rowan's and Clarissa's mounts were. Her own grey mare looked at least a good three hands higher. 'Surprising,' she thought to herself, 'my cousins are two years older than me I'd have expected them to be on bigger horses.'

'Merry Christmas to you too!' shouted the twins excitedly.

Maddie looked up to give them her widest grin. As her eyes settled on their happy faces, her smile vanished. Clarissa was wearing her riding hat, but underneath it, Maddie could see her hair was pure white. Rowan by contrast, had not yet put on his cap. He was holding it in one hand. A wide, rogue streak of hair the colour of virgin snow ran down the centre of the otherwise jet-black curls. But it was their eyes that shocked Maddie to the core.

The brilliant emerald eyes were no more. Instead, in their place were grey, opaque, sightless orbs, without pupils or expression.

'Here you are,' said Sam, handing Maddie the reins. 'The boys left half an hour ago. Fred was going to take them through Coxall Forest first and then join you on the estuary bridleway later. Make sure you meet him. I've told Warrior

249

that Miss Clarissa has got his Christmas mints as usual, and you know how he understands every word I say.' Maddie took the reins in silence and with heavy heart.

'Let's go, Maddie,' Rowan said eagerly.

'Yes, come on, Maddie, lead the way,' echoed Clarissa joyfully.

Maddie forced a reply from her lips, 'Okay, hold on tight now.' Eclipse moved off at a brisk walk.

'Hooray,' the twins shouted simultaneously.

Maddie's mind was racing. She knew the curse had been lifted. The three of them had succeeded in the terrible task they had been given, but at what a cost! Clarissa and Rowan blinded. She felt as if her heart would break.

Rowan interrupted her thoughts. 'You're very quiet this morning, Maddie. Come on tell us what you see.'

Maddie brushed wet tears from her cheeks and with a conscious effort to control her voice and her emotions she answered as cheerfully as possible. 'Well, it's a truly glorious day. I'd hazard a guess that it's been snowing all night but thankfully not anymore. We have a clear, bright blue sky overhead and a shining December sun directly above, trying to do her best to warm us. Everything is white, the fields, the hedgerows, the hills about us. The trees are amazing, they may have lost their leaves, but bare branches now laden with a thick dusting of snow look almost architectural.'

She paused for a moment to look about her again. 'There must have been a harsh frost this morning I can see dozens of spider webs in the hedgerows, shining like jewels in the sunlight. Honestly, they look just like diamond necklaces. In fact, my dear cousins, I would not be exaggerating if I were to say that this is the prettiest winter wonderland I've ever seen. It's as if we were riding through Narnia. It must have been quite windy last night too. There are huge drifts on the left of us, so I shall need to walk Eclipse quite slowly down this lane. The drifts have made the path too narrow for our three mounts to manage easily.' Maddie fell silent whilst she carefully shortened the reins and drew the horses in a little closer.

'Tell us more,' Clarissa called out loudly, obviously enjoying Maddie's very detailed description.

'I can see the tracks the other horses have made in the snow quite clearly. We'll miss out the forest and head straight for the bridleway along the estuary. I dare say the river will look fabulous today. It'll be a wide expanse of vivid blue, sparkling in the sunshine. Best of all, I'll be able to see our reflections on the water as we ride along above it.'

And suddenly Maddie felt comforted. She knew what she had to do. She would be their eyes. She would paint their world with colour, and she would make it bright and beautiful.

End

Epilogue

On the abolition of the slave trade in the British colonies on March 25, 1807, a certain family received £14,683 from the government (a sum which would be worth millions today) in compensation for the freeing of 764 enslaved people working their plantations in Jamaica. This number does not include those who had perished, either in transit or in situ due to the horrendous conditions in which they were kept. We will never know the exact number who died. What we can be sure of, is that not one slave received a single penny in compensation for their violent abduction and the subsequent suffering they were forced to endure.

Bury Me in a Free Land by **Frances Ellen Watkins Harper** (1825–1911)

Make me a grave where'er you will,
In a lowly plain, or a lofty hill;
Make it among earth's humblest graves,
But not in a land where men are slaves.

I could not rest if around my grave
I heard the steps of a trembling slave;
His shadow above my silent tomb
Would make it a place of fearful gloom.

I could not rest if I heard the tread
Of a coffle gang to the shambles led,
And the mother's shriek of wild despair
Rise like a curse on the trembling air.

I could not sleep if I saw the lash
Drinking her blood at each fearful gash,
And I saw her babes torn from her breast,
Like trembling doves from their parent nest.

I'd shudder and start if I heard the bay
Of bloodhounds seizing their human prey,
And I heard the captive plead in vain
As they bound afresh his galling chain.

If I saw young girls from their mother's arms
Bartered and sold for their youthful charms,
My eye would flash with a mournful flame,
My death-paled cheek grows red with shame.

I would sleep, dear friends, where bloated might
Can rob no man of his dearest right;
My rest shall be calm in any grave
Where none can call his brother a slave.

I ask no monument, proud and high,
To arrest the gaze of the passers-by.
All that my yearning spirit craves,
Is bury me not in a land of slaves.

Back Cover

This novel is a powerful, grim, historical fantasy story, based around the slave trade of the seventeenth and eighteenth centuries and its repercussions on a family whose wealth is built on it. The first part of the story introduces the present-day 10th Lord of Eastlyn, Robert Montague, and his family, who continue to endure the consequences of a voodoo hex placed upon them centuries before.

The second part describes the 1st Lord of Eastlyn, George Montague, a wealthy but cruel and callous slave trader, and the enslavement of an Amazonian warrior named Nabila. Much of the novel's strength is rooted in its foregrounding, which depicts man's inhumanity to man and the vile and heinous nature of slavery.

The final part shows the effect the curse has had on the Montague family and describes the actions and courage of young cousins who set out to free themselves from the voodoo hex. The twists and turns that take place as a result are comprehensive and will provide entertaining relief for the reader following this tale of human suffering and vindication.

Ingram Content Group UK Ltd.
Milton Keynes UK
UKHW020755210623
423798UK00007B/179